SEE NO EVIL

Novelization
by

DAN MADIGAN

Based on the motion picture screenplay
by Dan Madigan

World
Wrestling
Entertainment®
B·O·O·K·S

POCKET BOOKS
New York   London   Toronto   Sydney

POCKET BOOKS, a division of Simon & Schuster, Ltd.
Africa House, 64–78 Kingsway
London WC2B 6AH

ISBN-1-4165-2034-1
EAN-9781416520344

This Pocket Books paperback edition May 2006

10   9   8   7   6   5   4   3   2   1

Visit us on the World Wide Web
http://www.simonsays.co.uk
http://www.wwe.com

Printed and bound in Great Britain
A CIP catalogue for this book is
available from the British Library

For my wife, Karen, who believed in me
when I doubted myself.
And to my Kane, my son, my little boy,
my new lease on life.

&

For Mary French, the dearest friend
and darkest admirer,
who always said I had it in me
(had what in me, I'll never know).

Prologue

THE MONSTER AWOKE. HUNGER PAINS GNAWED AT HIS gullet. It was a dark hunger, one that couldn't be satisfied with food, and it was accompanied by a thirst that couldn't be quenched with water. The pain burned deep within the monster's belly. It was a craving that made his flesh itch and his muscles ache. The monster's head throbbed as pain traveled from his stomach to his brain. As his skull started to constrict once again, the bones of his large head felt like they were crushing his mind. His eyes bulged, and his tongue hung from the side of his mouth, a stream of hot saliva falling from his thick lips.

As the pressure increased, the pain grew and the monster began to shake with convulsions that gripped his head in agony and traveled like seismic waves across his enormous shape. The monster babbled in low, painful mutters, and then a sick whimpering escaped his mouth as his mighty hands squeezed his face, trying to push the pain out of his head. But the pain was unrelenting. It wouldn't stop until it had been fed. The monster staggered to his feet, his shape casting a mammoth shadow across the wall. It was as if an eclipse had been created by the ogre's body and darkened everything that fell in its path.

The monster stumbled down the long hallway toward the back room where the pain would be fed. Once the agony had consumed its fill, it would lie dormant for a while, granting the monster a few hours of reprieve, a few precious hours that would allow him to sit in the shadows and wait. Wait for the pain to awake, ravenous once more.

> *"We are all born mad. Some remain so."*
> —SAMUEL BECKETT

1

DUSK. THE TIME WHEN DAY SEEPS INTO NIGHT. THE changing of the guard. Not quite afternoon, not yet night. A time when the weary head home and the troubles of the day are locked outside.

The orange sun was drowning behind a landscape of abandoned factory smokestacks and old rusty machinery, remnants of a once industrious and prosperous time, now empty reminders of recession and foreclosures. Long, darkening shadows stretched across the city, past the old industrial parks and toward the road that led up to the hill where no one had ventured for some time.

Down a deserted cul-de-sac, the patrol car cruised in front of houses in long need of repair, abandoned and empty. The street sat on top of a hill where the view of the city was that of small pale lights flickering on and off in indiscriminate rhythms in the distance, like lonely stars that can't find their way. The whole neighborhood had slowly eroded away. First one family moved, then another family, then another. Gone. Vanished. What had been planned in the fifties to be a suburban prototype of tranquil community living had turned into a fiscally unsound settlement. In the seventies, when toxic waste from a dump on the other side of the hill had spread its tendrils deep into the area's water supply, dream homes had turned into nightmares as sickness and lawsuits claimed the community. Apathy had settled in these streets, and everyone who could do so had taken to the open highways. The neighborhood had silently died out.

Quiet permeated the hillside. Occasional gusts of wind blew up from the gullies below. The frightened yips of hungry coyotes were the only sounds that crept upon these dormant dwellings when the sun was up. At night it was a different story. At night the sounds came. Different sounds. Fearful. Unrighteous. Sometimes voices followed, often screams. Desperate pleas. Unanswered prayers. Salvation was never an option. Mercy was never granted. The sounds of machines, mechanical and cold, reverberated throughout the deserted streets. The shrill combination of machine sounds and man sounds flowed down the hillside and into the gullies and ravines, where they dissipated, then disappeared among the rusted wreckage of an impromptu auto graveyard that littered the underbrush and that had deftly been hidden away from curious eyes for years.

The patrol car stopped at the last house, a dilapidated building that sat quietly, ominously at the end of the street. It was a house where a child's laughter or a parent's call never echoed within its walls. Instead, fearful sounds, rich with the timbre of human suffering, emanated from the house under the protective cloak of night.

In the distance, the sun's final rays slipped behind the dark velvet curtain of night that had slowly descended upon the valley and was making its way up the hillside, creeping ever so steadily toward the large house on the hill. The long shadows stretched hungrily, ready to consume any remaining vestiges of day.

Officer Frank Williams stepped out of the patrol car, the tired look of a cynic etched upon his hard face, the same look that he had acquired his first day on the job eighteen years earlier. It was a look that had been handed down from his father and grandfather before him. Francis Xavier Williams had inherited his father's features and his family's calling. He was the third generation to wear the dress blues and would be the last in his lineage to wear the fierce gaze that went with the uniform.

Some of his fellow officers would have called him unsympathetic, but never to his face. He had a strength of will that had been etched harder and deeper with every call he received—every domestic disturbance, every liquor store homicide, every missing child. With every scene of depravity and brutality he stood tall and silent, never batting an eye, never flinching. He just sucked it in and held it deep inside. The years that Williams had been on the job had been long and harsh. Each one of them had melted a bit of his compassion.

Every day—every hour—he served his city had chipped away at his goodwill as if it were an engraver's plate submerged in an acid bath. Yet every day he stood ready, but tired, to once again answer duty's call.

Williams never let what was burning inside of him show. He couldn't. If he did, even once, he was lost. And he knew it. "Neutrality—a word despised by patriots but held dear by the enlightened" was his motto. His creed. Williams knew if he took on the burden of one case or victim personally, it was over for him. His effectiveness was in the efficient and direct manner in which he could gather and assimilate data. He couldn't let it matter that the store owner who was lying dead had four children and that now the family found themselves days from being homeless. He couldn't allow himself to care for the six-year-old girl who stared glassy-eyed at him, trying unsuccessfully to cover the dried blood on the inside of her bruised thigh with her torn dress. He needed a description of the man, the car, the weapon. He needed the facts, not the tears that came with them. Not the misery. Not the pain. Because if for one moment, one second, he did let himself get involved, if he let his stoic guard down and let human emotion slip past the hardened shell he had carefully created, it was over. If Williams let one of these things in, he knew he'd take his service revolver, his shotgun, and every round of ammunition he could carry on his back and kill every motherfucker in the city.

Williams looked over the hood of the patrol car to see himself of eighteen years ago. The eager face of rookie partner Neal Blaine caught the last shimmer of sunlight. His boyish features shined in the fading rays.

He still had an air of innocence that had not yet been touched by the harsh elements of human turmoil. He still wore the mask of sincerity tightly screwed into place. *Give him a few years of this shit. A few seasons of murder, molestation, and mayhem. A few winters of human depravity will knock some of the luster off his face. It'll sullen the optimism in his eyes. A few years until his personality inside and out will match his uniform—dark blue. Just wait, Neal, you poor bastard, just wait,* Williams sadly thought.

Blaine, anxious and ready to serve and protect, walked briskly behind the veteran officer.

Toward the dilapidated house both men went, up the long, crooked walkway that wound through a thick underbrush of weeds. Past a lawn barren of grass but plentiful in dirt and up the old stairs that sank deep under the strain of gravity.

The house was a large three-story Gothic structure. Once nobly erect, its pointed gables now sagged and bent painfully under the weight of age and weather. Grayed and stained, the house gave off an ominous air of foreboding. The architectural design of the house was foreign to the other houses on the street. It was unique in its concept and strategic in its placement. From the attic, one could see both the entire city laid bare below it and the street leading up to the front door. This house wasn't built but created, its every timber and shingle, every brick and stone, set down with a purpose not meant for living but for something else, something not right. As the two police officers reached the front door, the senior man felt all of this. The unworldly sensations that poured out of the house made the hairs on his muscular forearms tingle.

7

From behind the door, from deep inside the house somewhere, the sound of music unnervingly rang out.

Williams knocked on the rotted door. The hum of music continued.

"Well, somebody's home," Blaine commented almost apathetically.

Williams checked the address of the house in his black notebook. "This is the place." He scanned the lonely, darkening street for any signs of life other than themselves. There weren't any.

"Someone reported a disturbance from this location."

"Yeah. What type of disturbance did they say it was?" the older man asked.

"Screams."

"That would constitute a disturbance," Williams replied dryly, looking around the empty front porch. "Who reported it?"

"Some worker from the gas company was out here today looking around. Said he heard screams," Blaine answered, trying to gauge his partner's reaction.

Poker-faced, Officer Williams knocked again. The door creaked open. The music grew louder once they stepped inside the dust-covered foyer. Williams tried to place the tune. It was a sickly sweet children's rendition of something he knew. Something he couldn't put his nervous finger on. Loud banging sounds crashed along in accompaniment to the music, as if someone were keeping time by smashing pots and pans together.

"Do you hear that?" Williams whispered over his shoulder to Blaine.

"Yeah."

"You know what that sound is?"

"Very bad church music?" Blaine replied sarcastically.

"No, that's the sound of probable cause."

The melody was sweet and the lyrics comforting, but the sounds that echoed off the old walls of the house felt wrong. There was something hidden beneath the chorus of children's voices that filled the darkness of the house. Something sinister.

A suspicious look passed between the men—the unspoken dialogue understood by all police officers on the beat. They pulled out their guns.

"Call for backup!" ordered Williams.

Blaine complied without hesitation. Knowing reinforcements were on the way, he began to feel a sense of relief. Briefly, he wondered why he was even afraid. This wasn't the first time he had been out on a call, nor the first time that he faced potential danger. In fact, as far as Blaine knew, the reported screams meant nothing more than that the fellow inside had gotten careless and may have injured himself. The poor schmuck probably hurt himself walking around this dark place. He tried to tell himself that this call was going to be like the rest of the calls he had gotten all week—nothing but a big bust. *Nothing to worry about, Blaine, nothing at all.* Even so, he wondered why his testicles had started to tighten and his breathing was becoming shallow as he stood in the shadow of the big house.

Williams nodded to Blaine. They continued into the dark house.

"Police Department! Hello! Police Department!" Williams yelled, trying to make his voice heard over the music that filled the house. "Is anyone home?"

Williams laughed at himself. *Is anyone home? No, the record player is working by itself, you idiot.* Of course someone was home. For some unknown reason, that prospect put a chill in his heart.

Williams's hand crept along the wall, looking for a light switch. His fingers found it and flicked it on and off in quick succession. Nothing. The power had been cut off long ago. *There has to be power somewhere in the house. How's the turntable working?* he thought. The house continued to darken slowly as the golden rays of sunlight filtered through the moth holes that perforated the dirty curtains. Caught in those final rays of warmth, Williams watched as dust particles floated softly and aimlessly around the sheets that covered the living room furniture.

Both men followed the music—and the crackling, cracking sounds of a chipped needle running along the well-worn grooves of old vinyl. The music was beckoning them. Teasing them. Tempting them. The voices of the young singers sounded out of place, out of time. Williams thought how old the music sounded, and he imagined that the group of youngsters who were serenading them now must all be either very old or very dead. The thought of hearing the captured voices of dead children in this darkening place made him feel uneasy. It made Blaine feel uneasy too.

They were used to the loud, unmelodious pounding that was hip-hop—they were assaulted with it from every street corner they passed in their patrol car. It was as if the harsh music on the streets were a tribal warning that the enemy was approaching, urban voodoo drums sounding an alarm that "the man" was in the area. It was a musical talisman to ward off the evil of the men in blue. But this was different. The holy music that was playing for them now was something far more displeasing to their ears. It was crying for redemption. It was Christian reverence dripping from the lips of wide-eyed innocents, and it was skin-crawling creepy.

They walked out of the living room to the back of the house. Down a long hallway, toward the music and into the belly of the beast.

In 1973, as eighteen-year-old marine private Frank Williams trudged through the rice paddies of Southeast Asia, he carried an M-1 rifle tightly in his arms and the advice of his sergeant firmly in his head. *Shoot first. Then . . . shoot again* was Sergeant Lipton's sole piece of advice to his men. Lips, as every man in his squad called him, believed in one thing: survival. And *your* survival usually meant that someone else's survival would have to be forfeited. *Fuck 'em. If they're standing in front of you when you start shooting, tough shit.* In the bush nobody asked questions, in the bush nobody knew what was going on, in the bush you better be on your game, brother, 'cause you didn't have a second chance to make things right. As Private Williams marched deeper into the quagmire that was Vietnam, he had a trusted companion that marched alongside him. At first his companion was an enemy that transformed itself into an ally. His ally soon became his best friend. His best friend's name was Fear.

Fear had been the greatest government-issued side-arm Williams received after his induction. It hung closer to his heart than his dog tags. Fear was what kept his rifle clean and working properly. Fear kept his eyes sharp and his ears open. Fear whispered him to sleep at night and barked him awake in the morning. Fear helped him keep his mind sharp, his reflexes quick, and his instincts accurate. He had come to love fear more than baseball, his mom's apple pie, and America all rolled up in one big red, white, and blue joint. He would love, honor, and obey fear as they joined in an unholy matrimony of man and emotion. Without fear to carry him through, Private Frank Williams was lost. Fear kept him safe, it kept him alive, and all it asked in return was his soul. It wasn't a bad bargain for a kid fresh out of high school who pissed himself silly every time a twig snapped or a branch shook. Fear kept Private Williams alive and healthy— physically, at least—and they parted company two years later when Saigon fell by the wayside and thousands of rabid V.C. regulars painted the town commie red with civilian blood. The last time Private Williams had seen Fear, it was waving good-bye to him, blowing him kisses from an embassy rooftop, as he hugged his seat in the last chopper out of town. And under the whirling winds of the helicopter's blades he sadly left behind the only friend he had come to know and trust in Vietnam.

The helicopter blades that whirred away in Frank Williams's memory melted away into the sickly sweet chorus of children singing to the Almighty. And standing at the end of the hallway was a trusted old friend Officer Frank Williams hadn't seen in years.

Hello, Fear. You're looking good. Put on a little weight, but that comes with the territory of swallowing all those souls, huh? What is it, old buddy? I should be afraid? Beat you to it. I'm already scared shitless, but thanks for the heads-up. Come on and join me. Why are you giggling? Is there something I should know? Officer Frank Williams once again was keeping step with a trusted companion as he and his partner headed farther down the hallway and closer to the music.

The hallway was long and wide. From the outside of the house one would assume that the hallway would be half this long. Once you entered, the place seemed to take on dimensions of its own liking. Only the dying strains of sunlight from the living room meekly fingered their way down the hall, casting off one final glow of receding daylight. The farther Williams and Blaine walked into the shadows, the more the darkness smiled and greeted them into its open arms. Halfway down the hall, both men pulled out their flashlights and switched them on. Two strong shafts of light shined over moldy chairs and dust-covered end tables. A pair of yellow pools of light darted across the floor, illuminating their way closer to the sound.

Williams sniffed, and something tickled the back of his throat. It was a scent he hadn't smelled in years, something that triggered an olfactory memory that had been locked away and forgotten. It was the same scent he had known when he'd been in the bush, the same stink of depravity and inhumanity. The stench of man, only this reeked worse. Fear smelled it too and held its nose.

The music continued. The sound of the needle

being dragged across a record punctuated the musical interlude that both men walked into blindly.

The quickening heartbeats of the two men in blue pounded in anxious unison. Williams stopped at the last door in the hallway. As his hand went out to reach for the handle, he noticed the wall. An image on the wallpaper caught his attention. Pausing, he tilted his flashlight up and stared at the picture before him. He studied the image curiously, with the vague feeling that he had seen it before. Although his shadow hadn't fallen across a house of worship in over twenty years, Williams knew the image of a crucifix when he saw it. His eyes darted along the wall, and he realized that what was hanging on the walls was not traditional wallpaper. From ceiling to floor, the entire wall had been covered in scripture, thousands of pages torn from a bible, plastered haphazardly on the wall, and held there by filth and grime. He quickly slid his gun back into his holster and leaned closer to see the torn pages. He reached out to touch the crumbling parchment and felt the brown and crusty coating that covered the yellowing paper. It was dried blood. Lots of it.

Suddenly the men heard a loud scream.

Something had fallen behind the door, causing a loud metallic thud. It sounded like a careless workman dropping his tools for the day. Both officers jumped. Their hearts almost stopped beating. The thud quickly took Williams's mind away from the thousands of pages of blood-smeared gospel that surrounded them. He pressed his fingers against the door and gently, ever so gently, he pushed it open. It hadn't even occurred to Williams and his partner that neither man had taken a breath since they had started down the hallway. Now, with their lungs bursting with anxiety, the door opened slightly and a sliver of red light spilled out of the room, casting a narrow scarlet stripe down the center of Williams's face.

Williams grasped his revolver and quietly slid it out of its holster. He pushed open the door, using the barrel of his gun. The room was dim, almost black. One lone candle burned quietly on an old table in the middle of the room. A bare lightbulb dangled from the ceiling in the middle of the room. Sounds from an old Victrola spinning in the shadows leaked out from the darkness that engulfed them.

Williams moved his flashlight quickly around the room. Within the oval pools of light it cast, he caught quick glimpses of decay and deterioration. Mold, filth, and fungus clung to the walls hungrily. He could tell the room had rotted; the musty scent of mildew was strong. Years, decades of neglect had caused the house to decompose from within. Blaine coughed behind him.

A human figure quickly shuffled out of the shadows past Williams's flashlight. The dark silhouette stumbled toward a large chair that was partially illuminated from above by the blood-encrusted bulb.

"*Jesus Christ!*" Blaine cried out in an octave that made Williams's ears ring.

Williams just caught himself from jumping out of his own skin. Shaking the reverberations of his partner's scream out of his head, he pointed his flashlight toward the figure that was now lying on the floor. The figure was curled up and pressed against the wall. He saw it convulsing with sobs.

Williams walked closer to the chair. He passed his

light over the figure and saw that the subject was female. She was dressed more in dirty rags than in clothing. She buried her head deep within her arms, crossed protectively over her chest. The sobs grew louder, deeper.

"It's okay. It's okay. We're here," Williams reassured the filthy, frightened woman. She tightened herself into a ball as he knelt down in front of her chair. "Ma'am, you're safe now. Please, tell me who you are."

Williams laid his gun on the moist old carpet. He held his flashlight with his left hand and with his right he gently stroked the woman's hair. He moved his hand easily down her cheek and under her chin.

"Everything is going to be all right, miss," Williams said as he carefully started to tilt the woman's head up. His flashlight lit her from underneath and he saw the woman's face. Once he saw her clearly, Williams—a decorated war veteran and with eighteen hard years on the job—knew that everything was definitely not going to be all right.

He heard Blaine gasp behind him.

"What . . . the . . . fuck?" Williams stammered.

Then it happened.

In a blur of frenzied movement a massive shadow sprang to life from the dark corner. The shadow was huge, monstrous. The gleam of metal sparkled out from the darkness as Williams's flashlight caught a glimpse of the axe blade being aimed at his partner.

Williams fell back against the wall. He saw the monstrous shadow descend upon Blaine. The man stood, transfixed and terrified, as the shadow raised the axe high above its head.

A pinkish glow was cast around the room as blood

speckles started to burn on the hot glass of the overhead lightbulb. As weakness started to spread through his body, Williams turned his head, trying to block the scene from his sight. Instead, he saw Blaine's butchery played out as shadows on the wall.

Unable to tear his eyes away, Williams watched the shadow puppet show as the monstrous dark shape chopped Blaine all the way to the ground. The axe fell repeatedly, hard and fast, severing Blaine's head from his body. Each blow from the axe produced a sickening sound of sharp metal slicing skin and crushing bones. The noises escaping Blaine's body reminded Williams of another time in his life. They were the sounds he had heard in combat: bowels, guts, viscera spilling out of the human cavity and splashing upon the ground.

Williams grasped the handle of his revolver. The shadow raised its axe. Williams's finger crawled around the trigger.

The shadow approached.

Williams's torso jerked with a final burst of energy and he turned himself onto his side. His old buddy Fear was there to lend a well-needed hand and help him up. Williams raised his gun.

The shadow closed in.

It kept coming.

The revolver was as heavy as an anvil in Williams's hand. His strength was seeping into the carpet. Fear once again jumped in from the sidelines and gave Williams one final push of adrenaline. Knowing this might be the last action he would ever complete in this life and the last thing he would probably ever say, Officer Frank Williams pointed the gun at the approaching shadow's head and fired.

"Fuck you, cocksucker!" Williams screamed as he started to plunge headfirst into a dimming world of unconsciousness.

The bullet splattered into the shape's head. Chunks of shadow flew off from its skull as bone and blood erupted out from the darkness.

The shadow swayed.

With its axe, the thing stalked over to the officer and prepared to attack. Williams felt the sharpened steel slice into his muscle. The sound of flesh and bone crushing created a distinct resonating sound that shattered the silence engulfing the red room.

An arterial spray exploded across the room, extinguishing the candle in a crimson wave as Williams fell back, trying to clutch an arm that was no longer there. When he looked down, he saw that his arm had been sliced off in the middle of his bicep. The severed limb was still clutching the flashlight. As it shook in spasms, the flashlight's beams wildly shot around the room.

The pain transcended thresholds unimagined by Williams. Then, a life-draining numbness started to push the pain away as blood gushed out in crimson torrents.

Williams's heart beat thunderously. Each beat pumped out more blood until his life was slowly oozing from his body. Death by sanguination was mercifully moments away, if he could live through the decapitation that seemed to be seconds away. The monstrous shadow started toward Williams.

The will to live had been locked away in the back of Williams's mind long ago. It had been something that had been complacently stored away and forgotten about. Suddenly, it broke loose. Fear urged him on.

The creature slowly stalked across the room toward the bleeding police officer. It was in no rush, the dying cop was not going anywhere.

With a force that he didn't know he had, Williams fired his gun again.

The monstrous shadow fell into the darkness, like a giant rhino falling to a hunter's bullet. The body landed with a massive thud against the door, crushing the rotted wood. Seeping into the room were those last tarnished rays of sunlight that had followed Williams down the hallway. Williams watched as the massive black shadow staggered into the gloom of the hallway and stumbled away from the sounds of sirens blaring up the lonely street. A window crashed somewhere in the house. Williams collapsed onto the carpet, his head splashing into a sticky red pool as his eyes rolled back into his head. With the remaining dregs of his strength, Williams reached for his radio.

"Officer . . . down." He struggled to get the words out of his mouth.

Williams's dying arm was still convulsing on the ground. Both the limb and the flashlight twitched. Yellow streaks of light illuminated portions of the room.

Barely staying conscious while death tugged him over to the other side, he saw the girl. The young woman's face, or what was left of it, stared blindly out at Williams. Her eyes were gone. Her empty eye sockets were cavernous and dark. His flashlight cast horrific highlights on her face, and it looked like shadows were dripping from her sockets. In reality, the shadows were a gory mixture of blood and tears streaming down her cheeks.

Sirens screamed in the streets. Eventually, they gave way to the sounds of hurried voices traveling down the hallway toward the back room. Police radios crackled as the house started to fill with reinforcements. All of these sounds followed Officer Frank Williams as he started his journey to the next life, as he marched with his old faithful friend Fear leading him by his one remaining hand, toward the abyss.

The monster staggered down the alley. The red neon sign hissed and crackled and cast down a pinkish glow. Dirty rain puddles glistened brightly off the wet brick walkway. Stacks of trash bulged over Dumpsters. Aside from the monster's deep, heavy breathing, the scurrying of rats with their hungry little scampers was the only sound in the alley. The monster's head throbbed, a burning seared deep inside the thing's brain like the gnawing of a buzz saw. The giant, for all its immense size and misshapen proportions, stayed hidden within the cool black shadows that flowed narrowly down the long alley. He moved expertly and with much guile, as though living in the dark and far from the eyes of society was second nature to it. The monster's mind went back to a time when he had been in the alley—it was as if he had been there in another life, when he wasn't an evil being, when he was something else. A *human?* But that had been lifetimes ago. He remembered this place, the door, the man, his face. He remembered that the man behind the door knew magic—the man was some type of shaman, one who had a gift to take the pain away. The woman had taken the monster to see the man. The man who performed magic. The man who took the pain away. The monster remembered the woman and man whispering in hushed secrecy and nodding in his direction. But the man had many secrets and skills, and the most important of those skills was his ability to take the pain away.

Now the pain was back, worse than ever. The monster had long ago forgotten who the woman was. He knew that she was someone from his past. The past was a world that was dead to him now.

The pain was now starting to leak out, seep out of the bullet holes in the side of his head. The monster knew instinctively that if the holes weren't filled, the world would be able to look in, look deep into his head, and see all of his secrets and fears. He could *not* allow that. No matter how bad the pain, the fear of having the world see his soul was a thought that petrified the monster. He stopped in front of the gray steel door at the back of the alley. It was the only door to the building, and he vaguely recalled how big and ominous it had looked a lifetime before. Now the mighty door seemed cardboard-thin and flimsy to the wounded behemoth that stood in front of it.

2

MILES BENNELL WALKED AROUND HIS MAKESHIFT OFFICE and searched for the bottle of gin he knew no longer existed. Knowing that the bottle was not there didn't stop him from hoping that he would find something else in his little quest. His hands were on the first phase of their nightly jitters, and soon the slight trembling would work its way up his forearms and shoulders. When his limbs started to shake, he resembled a palsy victim with a tick. But it wasn't a neurological disorder that plagued Miles Bennell, it was an emptiness. The emptiness of a circulatory system without a steady flow of alcohol surging through its veins and arteries. Miles was a few quarts low, and the booze-fueled engine that kept the skinny, sickly chassis that was his body was about to seize up. He pulled open drawers, and his skinny fingers angrily groped over neglected medical supplies. Bandages lay in dirty rolls, and old blood-encrusted instruments were stacked together in a sticky mass in the center of the drawer. Miles Bennell had an affliction that was an equal opportunity tormentor—there was no bottle of gin, bourbon, scotch, whiskey, or tequila that was not in danger of being consumed. It didn't matter what breed the mongrel was, Miles Bennell would gladly sip the hair of the dog. Tonight the kennel was empty, and Miles looked toward another painful reentry into the sobriety that the morning brought. His teeth had started to chatter, as his body shuddered with the numbing dread of facing the first waves of delirium tremens that threatened to swell up and drown him if he didn't find an eighty-proof buoy to cling to and ride the storm out.

"Goddamn it!" he cursed, though there was no one around to hear him. Goddamned was right. The moment his lips had tasted the harsh, bitter sting of cheap home-brewed whiskey some forty-odd years earlier, Miles Bennell had been bitten by an elusive serpent whose venomous poison forever flowed within his weakened body. He had carried the stigma with him all through high school, hid it well in college, and almost concealed it from the world during his first three years of postgraduate study. The pressures of medical school were nothing compared to the unrelenting hunger that ate away at his insides. The only solace Miles Bennell could find was at the bottom of a bottle. Night after night he sought refuge there until his grades slipped into an academic danger zone and his body fell into a state of undernourished sickness. What had been so close—the respectability that went with the title of doctor—fell from his shaky grasp months before graduation. The exclusive admittance into a world where his affliction would be seen as nothing more than a few afternoon martinis at the country club was now passage to a world of drinking the cheapest wine out of a paper bag on a street corner.

He had flunked out of medical school, failed in all his ambitions, and ruined the dreams that his mother and her years of scrimping and saving had put into a pipe dream of maternal hope for her boy. Now his career was over before it had begun, stillborn in the last trimester of study. His mother was now dead, buried in a shroud of shame. Miles Bennell, the man with the once glowing future, sat shivering as his prospects slowly faded in a filthy back-alley office where he was nothing more than a fourth-rate street abortionist and underworld wound healer. He had been reduced to destroying the unborn and unwanted and fixing up the criminal denizens of the neighborhood. His name on the street was Doc, and no other word in the world cut him as deeply as those three letters. It was a constant reminder of what could have been, of how close he had come to becoming a doctor. A man to be respected. A man to be admired. A man. Now the gangbangers, young and old, the wise guys, the pimps and their sorry women all sought his attention when they had an injury or ailment that needed quick treatment away from the prying eyes of the medical establishment. He was nothing more than a drunk with a few Band-Aids and scalpels who dug out bullets, stitched up knife wounds, and snuffed out drug-ruined fetuses for the lowest of the low.

Miles Bennell was the physician of purgatory and banging at the gates of hell was a monster that came calling from the pit.

Miles sat and listened to the banging on the steel

door behind him. At first he thought it was coming from deep inside his head, but the resounding crash of bone bashing against metal made him quickly realize that beyond that door duty once again called. The force of the knock jolted him out of his self-poured misery, and Miles found himself walking toward the door as if enticed by the thunderous blows being rained on his door. The loud and fearful bangs—and the unknown entity that was making them—caused considerable apprehension in Miles's stomach, but somehow the fear of not opening the door was greater. Miles reached for the lock on the door and hesitated. For a moment he considered not opening the door and keeping whatever stood behind the threshold at bay. But fear of the strength of what was on the other side, fear of what he did not know made Miles's long fingers reach for the lock. He unlatched the door and stepped back . . . And the Devil walked in.

The stench that encircled the beast at his door made Miles take an involuntary step backward. The monster neither noticed nor cared. Revulsion preceded him wherever he traveled.

Miles tried to take in the thing that loomed before him. Its size bordered on inhuman. Unlike most men that are extremely tall, the thing that stood in front of Miles Bennell was proportionally massive in bone density and musculature. Miles's mind could not compute the thing as human, and not just because of the being's shape and size. There was something else, something unseen but not unfelt that made Miles prickle with the awareness that deep inside this mountain of muscle was a depravity that if unleashed would be insatiable.

Miles stared at the monstrous creature and noticed the dried blood that clung to the side of its bald head. Two bone-jagged holes had erupted in the thick skull, one over the right eye and the other in the temporal bone. The giant man said nothing. His large eyes bored into Miles's, and the faintest glimmer of recognition started to rise over the hazy horizon that was Miles Bennell's memory. He had seen this . . . *thing* before. When? Where? In what form? No amount of alcohol over any amount of time could have washed away the image of this thing that was burning in Miles's brain. He knew he had seen this hulking creature in an earlier stage of its primeval development.

And then he remembered. It had been years ago. Twenty, at least. There had been that woman. The woman who had brought her son to him, the strange-looking kid who seemed to be bigger than he was supposed to be. The pair had traveled through a labyrinth of back alleys trying to find relief for the boy—the relief that only someone like Miles could give. He remembered asking the woman why she had come to him, a man who did not even hold a medical degree. The woman didn't answer, but the roll of hundreds that she laid on the metal table did all the talking that was necessary. There was a reason the woman wouldn't take the child to the proper authorities. There was a look in her eyes that spoke of the fear that once her son was caught in the tendrils of red tape, he would never escape its crimson grasp. Miles thought that perhaps the boy had done something wrong, something terri-

26

bly wrong, and they couldn't have the authorities involved. And the woman, Miles assumed, was the boy's mother. No sane woman who did not spawn such a monstrosity could have shown this thing any type of compassion, or want the boy healed. The boy suffered from pain, headaches that caused the man-child to bang his head in a brutal, futile attempt to gain a temporary reprieve from the buzzing that roared inside his skull.

Now, years later, he recognized the behemoth in front of him as that same boy. Somehow, with the guidance of some demonic hand, the creature found himself standing in front of the would-be doctor, needing relief from the buzzing that had returned to accompany the bullet wound in his head.

The monster raised his hand and pointed to the holes that now decorated his thick skull like an enormous dour child pointing to a boo-boo. His finger seemed as thick as a barbell.

It shouldn't be alive, Miles thought. *No one could survive a shot there. Impossible.* Miles shook his head and closed his eyes, hoping that when he reopened them, the massive blood-smeared apparition would have vanished and that the next creature that was summoned from his subconscious bestiary to torment him wouldn't be as horrific as the wounded beast that stood before him now. But the monster was still there when Miles opened his eyes. *It's real . . . he's real.*

Fear and panic were in a dead heat racing up Miles's legs and trying to see which one would make his knees buckle first. Something in Miles Bennell snapped to attention. Was it regret that he never got to practice legally, was it medical curiosity, or was it the most basic of all drives, the instinct for survival? Whatever it was, the force prompted him to action. A bedside manner that he never thought possible took over. Miles poured his partially sober skills and all of his intoxicated talents into a cocktail of clinical detachment, which he quickly drank. With his nerves steadied for the first time by fear rather than liquor, Miles gestured for the monster to walk into the light that hung over the metal table.

Once the harsh glow from the bright bulb highlighted the monster's features, Miles could see where nature had taken a scary scenic route into the realm of the unreal. The man/monster that tilted his large head into the light was a medical curiosity. The bones of his skull were thicker than normal, almost subhuman in their density. Miles fumbled for a second and found a magnifying glass so he could look into the wounds.

The ogre did not want the man to read his secrets. He did not want him to see deep inside, where he kept all those dark thoughts and bad dreams. But he knew that the magic man needed to peer inside his mind. The man had to see how many of his dreams and thoughts had escaped the prison of his head and had fled into the night.

Miles wondered how the force of the bullet hadn't taken the top of the thing's head off. He looked closer, through the thin, pallid skin that clung tightly to the wide cranium. He saw the thick lines that separated the temporal, parietal, and frontal planes. He saw the sagittal and coronal sutures that fused the plates of the thing's skull together. To Miles's eyes, the sutures that tied the cranial bones together reminded him of the abandoned trenches of old battlefields he had seen in books. Deep, dark crevices kept all the horrors that raged inside the thing's skull behind a wall of dense bone. Now the dikes that held back the torrents of unspeakable depravity had sprung a leak, thanks to the well-placed but unfathomably nonlethal bullet holes. Miles knew that somewhere in the gray matter that festered beneath the surface of the thing's moonlike skull was at least one bullet that had to come out before infection set in.

The thing's stench was something that Miles would have compared to that of a dead animal's body in an old refrigerator on a humid summer's day. The type of smell that grabs the back of your throat with rancid, clutching fingers. The type that would make a statue gag.

Miles had seen the unspeakable damage a gun could render before—even before he'd set up his "practice" in this hellhole. In medical school, he had seen a woman who had been shot by her husband. A shotgun blast to the head can change the surface of a human face with the focused fervor of an abstract artist attacking a canvas. Bones, muscles, and flesh hung in wet strands, and anything resembling human form had evaporated once the trigger had been pulled and the hammer had fallen. He had seen gunshot victims, dozens of them, come through the same steel door that this "person" had also entered. The ones that weren't fatal, the ones that walked in on their own, for the most part walked out on their own; the ones that had to be carried in screaming or whimpering usually left a short time later, always quiet and still. No one had ever come to Miles with a wound as bad as this one and lived. It was a medical impossibility. It was against the laws of nature that this thing should still be breathing. Apparently, nature claimed no responsibility for the thing that sat stonelike in front of him. Whatever force kept this thing's heart beating, whatever higher being watched over this monster's life, was not a deity of benevolence. Any loving god would have mercifully ended this creature's existence long ago.

Miles tried to talk to the massive individual that sat in his "office." It was like David trying to get a friendly discourse going with Goliath before the battle.

"I'm not going to ask you how you got these," Miles said, referring to the holes that looked like a pair of dark rosebuds blossoming and dripping on the monster's white skull. It was the etiquette of his trade; you never asked a patient how he received his or her wounds. You simply engaged in a cold cash transaction. In many ways Miles Bennell was like a whore who stood on a corner whistling through parched lips at the cars that slowly cruised by. He performed a service for your body, no questions asked, and you left the money on the table before you went back out in the world. His skill level had diminished over the years, but without review committees and malpractice boards to watch over him, he had free rein to apply his "expertise." He stayed in business thanks to a local drug lord who needed his services from time to time for his faithful flock, and to the occasional walk-in who needed his attention or drugs. He was the Albert

Schweitzer, Mother Teresa, and Doctor Frankenstein of the seedy streets, all tightly bundled up in a dirty lab coat. Even though he did not have the necessary forensic evidence to prove it, Miles suspected that the bullet fired into the thing's head came from a police service revolver. Police meant trouble, but that type of trouble paled in comparison with the thing that occupied a good portion of Miles's office.

"I am going to assume that the bullet is still lodged inside." Miles himself could not believe what he'd just said. This thing should have slumped over and died the moment the bullet entered its head. "As you can see, I do not have an X-ray machine here, so there's no way of knowing where and how far in it is." Miles paused, trying to read the thing's face. It sat there emotionless, its large eyes unblinkingly impassive. "You know there is a chance, a very good chance, that this may become fatal." He thought that the comment was an understatement. He waited for the thing's reaction, for a response. The thing said nothing, gave no indication that if death was standing behind its back checking its watch that it mattered one iota to it. Miles did not know if his patient even understood what he was saying.

The monster heard the man speak. He knew the sounds. Words. Although no one ever spoke to him in that tone before, in such a smooth, calming voice, he understood the meaning. In the past, everyone who spoke to him usually babbled in pain, screamed in terror, or stammered in fear. This was the first person, since the woman, who did not try to escape from him.

The "doctor" was also the first person in a long time not to meet the monster as a prisoner in its own lair.

Miles reached for a tray of instruments that were as sterile as a sewer rat's ass. He grabbed a handful of tools and placed them in a small basin. Opening a cabinet door, he looked for a bottle of alcohol to cleanse the tools. Then it hit Miles: there were no more bottles of alcohol. They had all been used up as cheap substitutes to quell the unquenchable thirst that had been plaguing him for so many years. Without missing a beat, Miles turned on the hot water in the small sink and let it pour until a white plume of warm steam wisped up toward his face. He felt the heat of the water and washed his hands. Without bothering to look for a towel, he dried them on the inside of his sweat-stained lab coat.

Miles looked for something to numb the pain—not his patient's, but his own. But there was nothing there for either one of them. Miles's meager medical supplies and narcotics either had run out, had been stolen by crack whores whose fetuses he had aborted, or had been used by himself in some mind-altering binge. Now he had to tell the man/monster that there was nothing he could give him and that there was nothing he could do.

"I'm sorry. I can't do anything for you. I have no anesthetics, nothing to stop the pain." Miles stared directly into the monster's dull gaze, which was at a level with his own even though the monster was sitting down. "Then there's the bleeding. I have nothing to stop it. I can cause permanent damage." The last line struck Miles as being both cruel and funny. *Permanent damage. How the hell could you damage this thing more than it was?* Miles knew he had no other options. Cleaning the old instruments was a useless gesture; they could never be used. This wasn't a small twenty-two shell in some gangbanger's ass, this was a bullet lodged inside a brain. It was beyond hopeless. "I'm sorry."

The monster reached over with his long arm and pulled the instruments out of the hot water that was filling up the small sink. He dropped the hot tools onto the metal table next to Miles with a metallic bang. The monster picked up a scalpel and held it out for Miles to take. The back of Miles's throat went dry. He shrugged his shoulders.

"I don't have the facilities here. I have no nurses, no medicine . . ." The monster placed the scalpel in Miles's hand and firmly pressed the man's fingers around the warm stem. The monster's eyes rolled white, like a hungry shark's when going in for the kill at a helpless swimmer. The monster was putting himself in some type of self-induced state of alternate consciousness. Miles leaned in toward the wounded skull and did something he hadn't done in thirty years. He prayed.

It wasn't skill that Miles used to keep the monster alive. It was fear. Miles poured some of the hot water from the sink over the wounds to wash away the dried blood and to get a better look at the impossibility that lay ahead. If the hot water on the skull or in the wound itself caused pain to his pathetic patient, Miles didn't notice. The thing didn't respond. After he cleaned the wound, Miles had a better understanding of the topography of the skull. He daintily prodded the edge of the first bullet hole with the tip of the scalpel. He tried not to inflict any more pain than was necessary. The fact that this thing was upright and not flinching was a testament to the supernatural. Miles almost wished he had had a friend, a peer to share this with. *You'll never guess what I did today. I operated on a fucking monster's brain, without using the proper tools or anesthetics, and the kicker is, the big fucker didn't even have insurance.*

It must have been fate that decreed the monster's demise would not come that night. Miles tilted the thing's head back into the light so he could see the first bullet hole over the monster/man's eye. Wearing glasses with magnifying lenses attached to them, Miles prodded around the inner layer of the skull and saw that the bullet had made a clean exit. The bullet had barely pierced the uncommonly thick furrow of bone that ran across the thing's forehead. What surprised Miles the most was that the man/monster/behemoth/thing that was in front of him had an incredibly powerful ability to clot and stop his own bleeding. He could have written endless articles for medical journals about this patient, all under the heading "Science Fiction in the Field of Medicine," but no one would have believed him.

To the thing's credit, it never moved or flinched during the entire procedure. But now, for the real test of man, medicine, and monster, Miles had to seal both wounds. He wiped them down again with hot water and noticed that the bullet had definitely gone in through the frontal lobe. Further injury to the wound would cause untold harm, ranging from brain damage or coma to death. Here was a patient who had walked in off the street as if he had an annoying boil that had to be lanced, while in reality he had one of the most severe wounds the body could tolerate.

Miles pulled out a small, powerful flashlight and shined it directly into the jagged hole in the side of the thing's head. Although the bullet had exited the thing's body, it had left a trail of damage. Miles would have to take a closer look to determine how much damage the bullet had caused. He was stumped as to how to begin the process. There was nothing he could do without the proper instruments or equipment. He stood there, staring directly into the mind of madness, without a thread of hope of even stitching this thing back into one piece.

The monster's hand reached out over another tray of tools, one that was seldom used. Stopped as if controlled by some unseen puppeteer, the monster's hand dropped onto a circular bone saw. He passed the saw to the frightened pseudo-physician.

Miles started to shake. Not from the familiar effects of alcohol withdrawal. It wasn't even fear; it was something far greater than the sum of both ailments combined. Miles was about to walk into a world he never thought existed, a world of savagery and sadism. He was afraid that once he treaded on its unhallowed ground, he might never walk back safely into his comfortable world of disparity and squalor. Miles stared down at the tool, its teeth sharp and numerous and ready to devour.

"Jesus Christ, guide my hand." Miles sighed as the saw made its first pass over the skull of the immovable monster that sat there in quiet defiance. The sound of the saw's teeth filing sharply over the thin layer of skin down to the thick substrata of bone made Miles queasy. Miles never once looked up at the clock. He continued to saw away.

The clock's hands had rotated two and a half times by the time Miles was finished. Almost three hours of constant hacking, sawing, and excavating the monster's almost impenetrable skull. Finally, Miles had cut out a perfect square that measured four inches by four inches. With clamps, he gently lifted up the piece of damaged bone and severed all the connective tissue that hung on the inside. The monster stayed rock-still the whole time. Miles wondered at the incredible amount of agony this thing could endure. Not once did he scream out or howl in pain. It was as if there were nothing left to burn but an empty shell, as painful as setting fire to the shedded skin of a snake.

Miles Bennell thought back to some old medical lore that had been swept away by a tide of cheap liquor store bourbon and recalled a procedure that was by some accounts still practiced in parts of the world: the barbaric, fascinating art of trepanation, the primitive practice of drilling holes into the human skull to relieve pain or cure disease. Trepanation was started by medical practitioners hundreds of years before there was even a Hippocratic oath to break. And now, in the twenty-first century on a humid, rainy night, Miles Bennell stepped back in time and walked the path of early man. With each bone-slicing stroke of the saw over the monster's skull, Miles moved farther and deeper into man's dark, frightened past.

The bullet, which would have killed any other man

if it had entered his head, had created a path through the right front part of the frontal lobe—the part of the brain responsible for reasoning, planning, speech patterns, movement, emotions, and problem solving. *Nothing of major significance*, Miles sarcastically thought to himself. Whatever crazed thought patterns this thing possessed before would definitely be altered. *But how? How could this small amount of hot lead make this thing any more inhuman than it already is?*

After some pricking, prodding, and praying, Miles saw the full effect of the damage caused by the shell. With the dexterity of a seasoned clockmaker, he tinkered with the great gray mechanism that kept this creature. His skill, or lack of it, hardly mattered, considering the damage that had already been done by the bullet, not to mention the germs that teemed inside the wounded brain like bacteria in a petri dish.

As Miles stood back and looked at the man/monster, with a fairly neat geometric shape sawed out of its skull, he felt a funny sensation start to worm through his empty, alcohol-craving mind. It was the unknown feeling of satisfaction, the faint spark of self-approval starting to smolder proudly inside of him. This was his greatest medical accomplishment, a feat of unparalleled surgical skill that would never be duplicated. He had just finished something that only one doctor in a thousand, no, a million, could have performed. And *his* patient was the one in a billion that could have survived. Survived without the aid of plasma, anesthetics, proper medical care. Miles then realized that the job wasn't finished yet. He could not put back the skull fragment that he had cut away. The bullet had done just enough damage to the thick skull that covered the diabolic brain inside that monstrously misshapen head. He knew he couldn't leave the brain exposed. While his patient had sat silently during the entire surgery, there was a big chance he would develop some type of infection that might prove fatal. Miles paused, wondering what the hell his next step should be. With reborn medical skill and the basics of sheet-welding knowledge, he fitted and formed a stainless steel plate from the metal tray that had previously held his instruments. He then screwed the homemade plate into the thick skull of the monster.

This is as good as it is going to get, Miles thought, and hoped that the thing would die soon after this primitive procedure was finished. He just prayed that when the thing died, it would do so far away from Miles and his dirty little secret of an office.

The sun was starting to wash the dark morning sky with a pale golden hue, but the colorful start of the new day was lost on Miles and on the patient that sat in his windowless office. Miles did not realize it yet, but this was the first time in over three decades of desperate drinking that he had made it through the night without the aid of alcohol. His muscles were sore and knotted from a nighttime of cutting and sawing. His abdominals clenched in a way that caused him to almost double over in pain as he fought the fear that burned in his stomach. Miles hurt all over, but before he let himself fall into self-pity, he thought about the pain, the unimaginable and insufferable agony the man/monster had endured and would continue to endure. A sharp pang of sympathy resonated in Miles, not the same type of empathy one had for a fellow human being in trouble but the sad, helpless feeling one gets when seeing a mindless animal suffer. Remorse tinged with guilt.

The monster, the thing, the shape, the beast, the behemoth—whatever moniker Miles's mind could conjure up for the grotesquely misshapen man—stood up and walked toward the gray steel door. Without a word being said, the monster knew Miles was done. The magic man was finished.

Miles tried to say something. He wanted to impart some words of kindness or concern, but he could think of nothing. *Better let the thing walk out of the room and out of my life*, Miles thought. Then the monster stopped at the back door, and the fear that was burning in Miles's stomach all night ran like wildfire throughout his body. The thing turned to look into Miles's eyes, and a silent, dire understanding passed between them. The monster would not kill Miles for repairing his head, and in return Miles would never utter a word to anyone about the last eight hours. Without a spoken word, the oath was sworn and the pact was sealed. The devil walked out of the office and into the alley, which was still dark from the retreating night. Like obedient dogs happy to see their master, the shadows once again pounced on the monster and covered him in their black cloak of invisibility. The monster and his darkness departed, never to be seen by Miles Bennell again.

Miles stared at his hand and noticed that the nervous tremors and early-morning jitters were not there. He leaned against the sink and eased himself into the chair the monster had occupied moments earlier. Then he turned and wretched into the sink as a lifetime of poison poured out.

3

FOUR YEARS LATER

FRANK WILLIAMS WOKE UP TO THE BLARING COUNTRY music of his alarm with the feeling that the day was going to be difficult. The past few years had not been easy for him. After the incident with Blaine, it had been a while before he felt he could return to the "real world" again. Then there was the issue with his physical rehabilitation. He still wasn't used to the prosthetic arm that was now attached to his body at his elbow. However, he was still part of the force, and his new teen rehab project was somewhat of an achievement for him.

Passing a newspaper that had been thrown on the coffee table, he glanced at the headline: MAIMED COP FINDS NEW BEAT, and sighed. He continued to the bathroom, trying to forget the past, so he could get ready.

He still had nightmares.

• • •

Hannah Anders stood next to the idling bus and tried not to let the anxiety building in her intestines reach her stomach. She was becoming nauseous. She was unsure if the reason was because she was embarking on her first big assignment, and the prison board seemed to be looking at her with disapproving squints to see if she could handle the job. Maybe it was just the fumes billowing out from the bus's exhaust pipe. Whatever the cause, she moved away from the bus and decided to walk around to steady her nerves for the weekend ahead.

She tugged at the diamond ring that fit snugly on her finger and thought of Ronald. This would be the first time since he had asked her to marry him that she wouldn't see him for more than a day. *Was thirty-seven really that old to find true love?* she thought. *Why not? Why should love and romance only be exclusive to the young and beautiful? What about the rest of us, the other ninety-five percent of the world, the middle-aged and lonely? Where do we fit in on the love meter of life?* Such thoughts flooded Hannah's mind until she grew mad at herself for not concentrating on the job at hand. Ronald, and everything about him—and her indecision as to where he fit into her life—would have to be put on hold for the next three days. She couldn't allow her personal life to slip into her professional world. Not now. Not around this bunch. She had been warned, time and again. *Keep your distance and don't get too involved with this group of misfits.*

Hannah remembered a day when she was a young girl and went to the zoo with her father. Her father had held her in his arms as they both looked into the cage that housed the baby bears. They were so cute that

Hannah wanted to hug them. There was a big sign with red letters that warned people to keep their hands away from the cage. The animals bite. Five years old and safe in her father's protective grasp, she wondered how something so cuddly and precious could be so dangerous. "Keep your fingers away from the bars or they'll bite 'em off," her father had joked as he pretended to lower Hannah closer to the cage, closer to the bear cubs that stood behind the cold steel bars. It was then that Hannah first knew fear. Complete abject terror. Those cuddly little cubs with their pink tongues and wet noses grew into ravenous furry monsters in her child's mind. And she screamed. She screamed loudly, a deep, shrill cry that cut through the din of the crowded bear house, and every head turned to see if some foolish child had had a limb torn off by some hungry bear. The bear cubs, unnerved by the sudden change in the little blond girl's demeanor, started to cry in unison with her screams. Her father, red-faced with embarrassment, quickly carried Hannah out of the bear house and into the sunlight.

But the damage had been done, and Hannah was destined to spend the rest of her life never trusting the touch or embrace of another man. She had lived that way until Ronald entered her office last year asking sheepishly for directions to the nearest restroom. Since the incident in the bear house, Hannah had never gone to another zoo, never owned another teddy bear, and never looked at her father the same way again. Hannah learned at a young age that behind the facade of youth, and hidden beneath the face of huggable innocence, treachery and danger lurked. She knew that if she let her guard down for a minute and tried to reach out to these delinquents, they'd bite. And they'd bite hard.

The driver of the correctional bus looked impatiently at his watch as if his disapproving grimaces had some sort of control over the time/space continuum, and he hoped his frowns and overemphasized sighs would hurry the group he had been assigned to transport this morning. Once again, because of bureaucratic ineptitude, he would be running late.

He sat behind the wheel and watched the community liaison officer wander around the front of the bus, tugging on her diamond ring. *She's not half bad*, he thought. *A little on the older side, but still doable*. He could tell by her movement, the nervous circles she kept walking in, that she was fairly green when it came to working with juvenile offenders. And if she seemed green to him, then she was ripe for the picking for the group that was heading her way. *Youthful offenders*, he thought with a sneer. That's what the nervous woman fiddling with her ring had called them. He had seen some of the most vicious, unmerciful little monsters board this bus—some no older than thirteen. That was youth for you. *Youthful*, he mused. Youth was a term associated with innocence. With purity and playfulness and wide-eyed wonder. But these youths were seasoned criminals. He cringed at the thought of some of these little miscreants being released back into the community. He had seen them before, a thousand times, in the reflection of his rearview mirror. "Youthful offenders" was the catch-phrase moniker that the liberal-minded courts bestowed upon these kids, and echoed by the liberal-minded woman that wandered in front of his bus now.

He had known many "youthful offenders" in his years. *Youthful murderers, youthful rapists, youthful drug dealers, youthful child molesters.* And what did the bleeding heart assistant district attorneys want for these youthful offenders? Community service. A stern reprimand, a fatherly lecture. The old "there are no bad kids, just bad parents" routine spewed out again and again. He knew different. There were bad kids. There are bad kids. There will always be bad kids. He was a firm believer in the "born bad" theory. Some kids are just born bad. "Bad seed," as the Book called them. He always fantasized that if the doctors ever told him that he had the Big C and only a few weeks to live, he'd love nothing more than to load up his bus with those so-called youthful offenders and drive it headfirst over a bridge and right to the bottom of some river. One long, yellow metal coffin for forty little monsters. But their punishment wasn't his concern; all he had to do was drive these "poor misunderstood souls" downtown to the Blackwell Hotel and his part in this rehabilitative farce was over. Then he could kick back and head to Rafferty's for a couple of cold ones for lunch and worry about how Monday always seemed to come too soon.

The program at the Blackwell Hotel was the brainchild of Frank Willams. It was due to his hard work that Hannah was part of this project to help this first group of youthful offenders have a second chance. Project:

Renewal offered a two-fold chance at redemption. The state agreed that prison crowding on both the adult and juvenile levels was already a problem that couldn't be dealt with as things now stood, so when the prison board heard Williams's ideas, eyebrows were raised in sincere interest rather than the usual skepticism. And facts were facts: Most of the older buildings downtown were slowly rotting from neglect and abandonment, and most of the younger inmates in County and Juvey were slowly rotting away from neglect and abandonment. It seemed, on paper at least, to be a perfect fit.

Because of Williams's project it seemed to Hannah that she had a lot more to be grateful for recently. Ronald, her boyfriend, was now an important part of her life. And, working with the new program, Hannah would no longer be floating aimlessly from one cause to another, trying to find the right one. Though she'd never met the woman, she had heard that Margaret Gayne, the Blackwell Hotel representative, had done so much for the community in the past. Hannah had been told that the woman knew what it was like to lose a child and didn't want to see any other children lost to the streets. When the work to begin Project: Renewal was initiated, Margaret demurred any publicity or attention, saying that her work was best done behind the scenes, like a confident filmmaker directing her cast from afar. Project: Renewal was on its way to becoming the first step in an urban rehabilitation and restoration project in the city.

Hannah dreamed of the project having such resounding positive effects that the idea behind it could be applied at the national level. If that happened, maybe she would be put in a position of power that she never would have achieved working as a lonely civil servant. But she had to take one step at a time. "Don't put the cart before the horse," her father would say. "Yeah, don't shove your five-year-old daughter's head into a bear cage either," she bitterly remarked to herself. She checked her watch as the minute hand slowly made its last round toward noon. With each successive movement, her thoughts of Ronald, Margaret, national prominence, and hungry little bears ticked away.

The door behind the county jail opened and the first group of "recruits" started to shuffle out behind a portly corrections officer. The first in line were the four young females who had been transferred earlier that morning from Juvenile Hall. Each of the girls had been selected based on personal interviews and an extensive background check. Each had an extensive criminal record. They came from different walks of life, but somehow, they found themselves heading in the same direction on that sunny Friday morning. The committee members had been assured that violent offenders wouldn't be used in the program. As Mr. Emery, the elder statesman of the board, said, "You sure as hell don't want to put a power tool in a psychopath's hands." And of course he was right. Hannah knew that some of the kids who had been interviewed over the past six months would like nothing better than to get their hands on a sharp object and embed it into the nearest corrections officer's throat. Such a complete lack of compassion or concern for oneself or others was a mentality that Hannah would never come to understand. She had always thought of herself as a giving person. In contrast, these kids were takers, and she knew she couldn't let them manipulate her, or she would be done before the project started.

The girls all carried their personal belongings in small duffel bags. These four had been picked because they were thought to be hard workers who would get the most out of the program. Hannah held steadfast to the theory that an idle mind is the devil's playground. If she could occupy these kids' minds with something other than stealing, fighting, and drugs, they wouldn't have to face Ol' Scratch in the next life.

The corrections officer stopped in front of Hannah and handed her a clipboard with the girls' release papers on it. She picked up the pen that seemed to weigh ten pounds and stared down at the blank space where her signature was supposed to go. The straight blank line looked as serious as a flat line on an EKG. *This may be the most important thing I ever sign my name to*, she thought as she wrote her name in her very legible script. When she finished, she couldn't help feeling a quick sting of regret. It was either buyer's remorse or Faustian foreboding, but either way she had just signed her professional life away, and the next three days would see how far it would continue.

The four girls marched quietly onto the bus, never making eye contact with Hannah or the corrections officer. They took their seats on the bus and waited for their male counterparts to join them. The girls were still used to the rules on the inside, where the easiest way to stay out of trouble was to avoid making eye contact with anyone, con or cop. On the inside, if you wanted to find trouble, it was always there for the taking. Who needed any more aggravation than she already had? The smart thing to do was to avoid unnecessary altercations if at all possible. But people on the inside weren't always known for their smarts. The girls were as different as four winds; the only thing they had in common was their age: eighteen. Eighteen was the maximum age for the program, and it marked the end of adolescence. Each girl knew that if she got popped a year from now, she could be looking at real jail.

The girls knew each other on the inside, some more intimately than others. Christine Zarate was a pretty girl who tried her best to play down her looks. Her strong features looked more Italian than Hispanic. She was doing time for aggravated assault, a crime she was guilty of. She never spoke of it, unlike other girls who liked to brag. The more severe the crime they had committed, the higher their status. Christine kept quiet while she was on the inside. She thought talk was cheap.

Kira Vanning followed Christine and sat down next to her in the last seat on the bus. Kira's pale features were offset by her deep brown eyes and long black hair. She had a nervous cuteness about her. Around her wrists, colorful tattoos covered the soft white scars left by deep razor slashes. She couldn't remember all the crimes she had committed, but it didn't matter. They had nailed her for possession and intent to sell narcotics, and that was good enough to give her two years on the inside for a second offense.

Zoë Warner was the third girl to enter. She sat in a

seat away from everyone else. Zoë was a blonde who, unlike Christine, wanted people to look at her. She liked attention; she didn't want to blend in with the crowd. She knew she could get what she wanted, on the inside or on the outside, with her looks and body. They were her commodities, and she knew how to use them. She was a thief, a sneak, and a shoplifter. She would steal your shadow if you let her and smile while she was doing it. She stole from the girls who weren't affiliated with the gangs on the inside and took advantage of the younger ones who came into Juvey frightened out of their minds. No one trusted her and no one wanted to be around her. Neither Christine nor Kira wanted anything to do with her. The odd thing about Zoë was that she was a trust fund baby and didn't have to steal. She could have bought anything she wanted. To her, though, nothing tasted sweeter than fruit from another's vine. After her fourth arrest and her parents' complete embarrassment, a slight slap on the wrist wasn't going to suffice. With her own mother's prompting, she'd had the book thrown at her square between the eyes. Her mother's idea of tough love rewarded her wayward daughter with a year on the inside of Juvey and a finishing school education in larceny.

The fourth girl on the bus was an enigma to the others. Melissa Boudreaux was an average girl, slight in build but large in reputation. Melissa was the worst type of offender: a bright-eyed optimist and perpetual do-gooder. She was an angry PETA extremist with a misguided anarchist's fervor. Melissa has been on a quest her whole short life, a quest to find a cause. Any cause. The earth, the ozone, the rain forest, the indigenous people of some faraway land that no one can pronounce. Melissa was a protesting, peace-marching, rabble-rousing poster child of social contradictions. She saw injustice on every level, she felt pain for every plight. Her heart was a pincushion, bleeding nonstop from the needles of intolerance. Melissa wouldn't eat meat, wouldn't drink milk. She got all her daily nutrients from her own self-importance. She was uncompromising, unyielding in her faith in a belief system that she thought granted her all the answers to the world's problems. Unfortunately, the powers that be repeatedly refused to take her into advice. She was smarter than everyone else, more compassionate, more socially minded. An advocate for the people who didn't know they need one. And what made matters worse was that when given the option of doing community service, she *demanded* to do jail time for the crimes she had committed. In some misguided notion of martyrdom, Melissa saw time served on the inside as a badge of honor to show her radical accomplices. To the other girls on the inside she was an idiot. She found a seat in the middle of the bus and sat alone.

Hannah walked onto the bus after all the girls had been seated and smiled at them, but no one returned the gesture. She looked down and saw an unopened condom on the floor of the bus. Bending down to pick up the condom, she held it up for the girls to see.

"Does this belong to someone here?" she asked the girls but looked at Zoë.

"Why are you looking at me?" Zoë protested angrily, all the while laughing inside, knowing all too well that she had dropped the condom to see Hannah's reaction.

"Busted!" Christine yelled in a rare jovial moment. Christine knew nothing would happen to Zoë but didn't mind giving the blond thief shit anyway.

"Remember, we have to be able to trust you guys," Hannah said, trying not to come on too strong too soon with them. "Is that understood?"

All the girls nodded in a half-assed response except Melissa, who stared out the window listening to a small radio with headphones.

"Melissa?" called Hannah.

Melissa either didn't hear Hannah or didn't care to comment, so Hannah barked her name louder. "Melissa!"

Melissa took her headphones off and gave Hannah a quizzical look. "Ma'am?"

"Nothing, dear, just please pay attention," Hannah replied.

"She's the last person you'll have to worry about." Zoë looked over Melissa's head and smirked as she informed Hannah of her opinion. The statement was not lost on the girls. It was meant to be a stab at Melissa, a plain-looking girl who tried to think past false eyelashes.

Kira really didn't know Melissa, but she didn't appreciate Zoë's remark about the girl. Kira had been on the receiving end of such barbs herself and didn't like them.

"Bitch," Kira whispered to Zoë.

Zoë fell back in mock indignation. "Oh, my God. Did you hear that? The mute spoke up."

A sense of anger swelled in Christine as Zoë directed her untrustworthy tongue at Kira.

"Watch your ass, girl," Christine warned Zoë.

"You mean the same way you watch Kira's ass? You fucking dyke," Zoë replied, feeling braver with Hannah around.

They were all aware of the rumor that the two girls were an item on the inside. Zoë didn't care one way or the other. She'd swing in any direction that would be in her best interest.

"Ladies, please," Hannah said forcefully. The girls became quiet. Zoë was pleased that she had at least mentioned their "relationship." Zoë was a classic shit-stirrer. Now that she had begun to cause trouble, she could back off just enough. She didn't want to go head-to-head with Christine. She simply enjoyed rattling her cage.

Hannah placed her pocketbook down and walked off the bus to wait for the others.

Zoë looked around and saw that Kira and Christine were quietly sitting together in their seat. Melissa was staring into space again, with her headphones in her ears. Hannah was outside waiting for the others to show up.

Without drawing attention to herself, Zoë reached over her seat and let her long arm fall on the back of the seat where Hannah had laid her purse. Quietly, she let her fingers open the bag, reached in, and snatched Hannah's cell phone. Zoë pulled back her arm, which retracted like a serpent recoiling from danger. She looked up, saw the bus driver watching her in the mirror, and shot him a smile, enhanced with her pink tongue wetting her lips. The driver nervously looked away and said nothing. Zoë slid the phone into her back pocket, leaned back, and closed her eyes.

Outside, Hannah didn't have to wait long for the

males in the project to arrive. The back door of the county jail opened again and, escorted by Williams, out came four young men, not much more than boys really, but boys playing in a man's world. Hannah tried to make contact with the kids by extending a warm smile. Once again, the young men reciprocated with averted eyes and a silent but quick march toward the bus. The first in the line was a hard-looking black man named Tye Sims. Behind Tye, Russell Wolf followed, a tall surfer beached for a year for receiving stolen property. Richie Bernson, whose life of violent crime was enhanced by forays into computer fraud, walked sullenly onto the bus. The last on was a vicious-looking teenager with a naturally cruel streak that stood out like his muscular forearms. His name was Michael Montross, but his title was criminal.

Surreptitiously, Michael passed a bag of weed to Russell, who hid it in his pants for later consumption. To distract the others from his transaction, and because trouble was expected of him, Michael deliberately bumped into Tye. The outburst prompted Williams to act quickly. He separated the two with the threat of kicking them out of the Project: Renewal program. The group continued their trek to board the bus.

Williams nodded to the driver and then turned to Hannah. "They're all ours," he said.

Hannah thought she heard the slightest bit of malice in his voice.

As Hannah watched the boys climb on the bus, she greeted Williams. Each of the kids sat alone except Christine and Kira, who sat together in the back. Hannah knew that fraternization between the kids was frowned upon, but she thought it best to say nothing for the time being.

"Well, this is going to be a new start for all of us. Let's make the best of it," she said.

Hannah's optimism was met with eight looks of selfish indifference. She stood awkwardly in front of the kids, the way a novice flight attendant would face a plane load of drunken shiners, wondering what she should say next. Before she could say anything else, the bus lurched forward. Hannah grabbed the overhead rail to stop herself from toppling over. Some of the kids let out loud snorts as she tried to get her footing. She took her seat in the front and shot daggers at the bus driver, hoping that this project would not be her undoing.

Kira held Christine's hand so tightly that Christine thought she might snap her bones. Christine didn't have to ask what was wrong. She saw what had put the fear in her friend's eyes. Michael came in the form of a five-foot eleven-inch wiry boy, tightly wrapped into a package of hate and ruthlessness. Though he wasn't physically large, his demeanor was menacing. Michael's and Kira's eyes locked in a stare-down that meant trouble for one of them. Michael shot Kira a smile that was half sneer, half smirk, all intimidating. He sat down in one of the front seats, glanced back at Kira in the rear of the bus, and blew her a malicious kiss. Kira's skin crawled as if the little kiss were laced with rat poison. Christine silently watched the whole scenario play out and knew that the combination of Kira and Michael together in one area meant trouble.

The bus rumbled noisily through the depressed streets. Kira rested her head against Christine's shoulder and let out a sigh that was heartbreaking even for the hardened Christine.

"Don't worry, he's not going to hurt you. I won't let him," Christine said with an assurance that she hoped she could back up.

"How the fuck did he get on this project? *How?* I thought it was supposed to be for nonviolent offenders," Kira thought out loud. Christine didn't say anything. She knew you could con your way into anything if you were good enough and the person you were dealing with was gullible enough. Half of the kids on the bus had committed some type of violent act and were getting their time knocked down before sentencing so it didn't show up on their records. Even Christine had committed what some would have called felonious assault. She wasn't surprised that someone like Michael Montross slipped through cracks that were a mile wide in the judicial system. But even so, Michael was different from other hard cases she knew. He didn't mind the pain that came with combat. On the contrary, from the little she knew of him she had come to understand that the pain was what he sought. Pain—both giving it and receiving it. That was how people like Michael functioned. The pain became so commonplace, so ingrained inside of them that if they didn't deal with it, they were lost. Christine knew this about Michael because she was the same way. She didn't want to think about it, but she speculated that beneath the tattoos and muscles he had, he and she were very similar. And that thought made her sick to her stomach.

4

LANGLEY BLACKWELL WAS A DEVIANT. IT DIDN'T MAT-
ter how much money Langley had acquired through
business dealings, shady or not, his tastes still ran the
gamut from fetishistic to criminally suspect to morally
reprehensible, and no amount of money or power or
influence could whitewash the dark stain that was his
soul. He had come from money, so many people said
that his ways were already established at birth. His
blue-blooded lineage was a natural conduit to the colorful depravity that he would unleash upon the world.
His people were robber barons, and he picked up the
mantle as the entrepreneurial vice-lord at a young and
impressionable age.

Langley was a man who liked to dabble. His long,
boney fingers found themselves in various financial
undertakings and many frilly undergarments in his day.
Whether it was an oil well about to burst in Oklahoma
or a thirteen-year-old girl's cherry about to pop in a
Saginaw whorehouse, Langley Blackwell found himself

in the midst of many intriguing scenarios, often bene-
ficial to him but mostly detrimental to others.

Money and sex were his gods, and in the 1920s no
better duo of deities were honored with as much relish
and loyalty as these two. Langley prayed to both with
feverish devotion and a zealot's passion. Langley, the
disciple of the dollar and debauchery, built the most
ostentatious altar to his gods to show them how deep
and demented his faith in them had grown: a twenty-
one-story monument to the dark desires that swirled
and festered in the back of Langley Blackwell's mind
and a magnificent home for the two gods that guided
his hand in all facets of his life. What better place to
serve and worship his gods than in a temple designed
and constructed using the most debased desires of man
as a blueprint?

It came to Langley one night as he lay in his massive oblong bed. The black satin semen-stained sheets
were draped over a whimpering young girl lying at the
foot of the bed. Her twin sister lay in a semi-comatose
state next to him as he stared up at the reflection of
her bruised and naked prepubescent body in the mirror on the ceiling. Her blank eyes played over again
and again the scenes of her participation in Langley's
lecherous stunts, which would haunt her for years to
come. It was a guiding vision that came to Langley
Blackwell that night as he lay among the two budding
siblings he had just defiled, degraded, and deflowered,
a vision of pure indulgence. Like a burning bush
glowing brightly on a mountaintop, it shone its malevolent radiance upon him.

What fun was it to have one house, one room, one

bed to confine his amorous appetites when he could have a hundred such beds to rollick and revel in? His army of accountants and his legion of lawyers had been telling Langley to diverse his holdings for some time. Oil was good, banking was solid, but land was the bedrock of business. If you owned the land, you owned the people. People had to live somewhere, why not own where they lived? But Langley didn't want to own the dirt acres of poor farmers or the shacks of railroad workers; he wanted to own the land of his peers. The rich. The spoiled. The depraved. He knew that most of the people who attended his sexual soirées were as wanton as he was. He knew it, and he counted on it.

Now Langley found himself in a two-sided predicament. He was forty-four, and there were no more sexual conquests that excited him or financial dealings that intrigued him. He had gone on as far as he could, praying to his gods, before he found himself empty. He had all the money he needed—or thought he needed—and he had taken all the women, girls, and young boys that had come before him. Now he found himself in a state of being that he never thought he'd ever find himself in, one of complete satiation. Money no longer enthralled him, and sex, in its various forms, even forceful, brutal, and barbaric, no longer enticed him. He had surpassed his quota, and now nothing but the bleak horizon of redundancy loomed ahead of him.

But his gods did not abandon him in his time of need. They showed him the light and saved him from his despair. Like a faithful Noah, he went about building an ark to bring the like-minded within its walls: a

hotel to put his name on, with a veneer of respectability that masked the true nature of its purpose. Each
floor, each room he salivated over. He marveled at all
the things that would go on there, all the things he
could partake in, as willful participant or wishful
viewer. As host, he would be both entitled and obliged
to take a keen personal interest in all activities of a
carnal nature. Langley was so excited that night, the
night the gods blessed him with the foresight of his
sexual salvation, that he hurriedly went about planning to build his temple. He grabbed the twins'
mother from the settee where she sat counting out her
procurer's fee and ushered the naked, bleeding, crying
family out of his bedroom and into the hallway, into
the hands of his troubled servants.

The hotel would be his Taj Mahal, his St. Peter's, a
basilica of immorality that all would enter to bow down
and pray to him. But nothing fueled Langley's long
dormant desires more than the thought of knowing
that many of the guests would be unsuspecting sacri-
fices to be watched over and leered at behind two-way
mirrors and forever caught on celluloid in the newest
entertainment medium of the day: the motion picture.
That pleased him the most, visualizing the newly mar-
ried bride on her wedding night not realizing that her
every intimate movement would be watched over and
over again for his own selfish enjoyment. The combi-
nations of people, partners, and practices he imagined
took his breath away. There would be no limit to the
pleasures that awaited him on completion of the great
altar. His eyes were the mirrors in every room, his camera his memory. That night, that precious and pious

night, after a martini-fueled, cocaine-filled session of forced buggery on the catatonic twins, the seeds of the Blackwell Hotel took hold in Langley Blackwell's heart and soon sprouted into a full harvest of deceit and decadence. Langley Blackwell's true calling was set before him.

Now the once majestic Blackwell Hotel stood silent, high above the desolate neighborhood, twenty-one floors of intimidating abandonment. The hotel loomed like a derelict sentinel surrounded by boarded-up storefronts and vacant lots that lay in quiet ruin. The winds of depression had blown into this town, sweeping away any semblance of community. The once prosperous avenue that Langley Blackwell once proudly boasted held his greatest achievement was nothing but an urban wasteland. Gone were the neon lights, the red-letter marquees, the glittering signs of its heyday, now sadly replaced by torn and frayed hand-bills and spray-painted signs showing the devolution and decay of society.

The corrections bus quickly drove along the deserted streets toward downtown, its passengers anxiously waiting to get off, its driver impatiently waiting to expel the dangerous riders that were seated behind him. But what made it more unsettling for the driver was that the kids sat there quietly and calmly. He knew that was trouble for sure. The only barriers between the driver and the brooding delinquents were a put-upon corrections officer and a flimsy sheet of thin-wired fencing that ran behind the driver's seat to the front door of the bus. The driver kept looking back in his mirror at his cargo for any signs of trouble, any signs of potential danger brewing, and any chance to get another glimpse of Zoë's ass again.

As the corrections bus took a wide corner farther into this depressed section of town, the eight juveniles sat staring out at the streets before them.

A sad parade of homeless people passed before their eyes. Drug addicts shuffled along in a narcotic daze. Garishly clothed transvestites lurked on the corner like a pack of gaudy she-wolves waiting for the afternoon sun to sneak behind the tall buildings so they could bare their fangs.

The kids on the bus sat silently and studied what might be their future.

"This blows. Community service, my ass. They're getting a bunch of free labor out of us, that's all. I thought slavery went the way of Lincoln," Tye complained loudly. The first words spoken on the bus since it started its journey garnered an involuntary reaction from Michael, who looked over at Tye in contempt. It was a Pavlovian response that usually started in violence and finished in bloodshed.

"It's for a good cause. They're going to renovate the hotel into a homeless shelter," a tentative Melissa quietly responded.

"Who cares? Homeless shelter," Tye said, shaking his head.

"Maybe you should try thinking about someone else for once in your life," Melissa blurted out without thinking how someone most definitely and dangerously higher up on her valued food chain would react to her response.

"What? What did you say?" Tye asked, trying to bore a hole in the back of Melissa's head with his eyes. "Maybe you should think about wrapping your lips around my—"

"Why don't you keep your fuckin' mouth shut?" Michael stood up to cut off Tye's salacious comment.

"Come on over here and shut it, motherfucker."

Michael's quick fuse had been lit. He headed toward Tye. Both boys squared off like hungry prizefighters before the bell. Michael's outburst had nothing to do with protecting Melissa's honor. As far as he was concerned, she was a dumb cunt, but she was a white dumb cunt, and no black prick would bad-mouth a white dumb cunt in front of him.

"I'll shut it for good, bitch! You ain't so tough without your posse behind you," Michael proclaimed loudly enough for everyone on the bus to hear.

The other kids shouted out an encouraging chorus of "oohs" and "aahs." The prospect of bloodshed was imminent, and to these kids, who had been locked up for several long months, any activity, even violent or destructive, was a happy alternative to the mind-numbing boredom of Juvenile Hall.

"I don't need a posse to pound you into the ground," Tye said.

Hannah stood up and tried to say something, but she had no words to counter the rage that burned between the boys. She silently watched as the collision was about to happen and realized that she had no control over the wreckage that it would cause.

A loud metallic bang shook throughout the bus as Williams smashed the club, which was a standard part of the officer's uniform, against the grating at the front of the bus. He diverted the other kids' attention away from the would-be combatants and toward his menacingly thick nightstick.

"If you children can't play nice, I'm going to have to come back there and give you a time-out. Now sit down and shut the fuck up, all of you," demanded Williams.

Russell stood up and gave a perfunctory nod to the officer as he tried to calm Michael down. "Take it easy, man."

"Fuck off!" was Russell's payment for his intervention.

Michael and Tye glared at each other. The two had an uneasy history between them, and history was destined to repeat itself soon. They slowly sat back in their seats, their eyes never leaving each other's. Each was waiting for the opportunity to strike first. They both knew it and anticipated it.

Russell moved and sat in front of Melissa. He had read the layout of the bus as soon as he stepped foot on it. Zoë was a bitch, and if he didn't have anything she needed or wanted, he wouldn't get any play off of her. He'd heard the rumors that Christine and Kira were an item, and so that left Melissa. Russell's taste in girls ran to the tanned, tight-bodied types he had gotten used to hanging out with on the beach. But Russell had not been on the beach for some time now, and Melissa, with her plain, nondescript features and white skin, looked like a Playmate of the Year to him.

"Hey," Russell said to Melissa as he tossed his long, sandy hair away from his eyes for the maximum show of coolness.

Melissa just looked at him, not knowing what to expect after the upsetting run-in with Tye.

"So, you're like the dog pound liberator, huh?" he said, trying to ease any nervousness out of her. "That's pretty cool."

Melissa held back a smile. No matter what the others thought of her, she wasn't dumb. She knew what Russell had on his mind—he couldn't get anything going with Zoë or the two dykes, so she was all that was left. She was always the leftover dish, the one no one looked at first. But now she didn't mind. She could string Russell along, play with him for a while the way she had been played with many times before. Besides, she thought he was cute, and she had urges too. It had been a while since she had been with anyone. On the inside she felt snubbed and hurt when the others didn't make a pass at her, but now she had the full attention of a halfway decent-looking guy, and she was going to play it the best she could.

"So, why did you do it?" he asked.

"Do what?"

"Save all them dogs from getting gassed?"

"They needed to be liberated. Nobody has the right to decide what living creature lives or dies," she answered in true activist form.

"I could use some liberation over here," Tye snarled quietly as he looked at Melissa.

Russell gave Tye the "look," the signal, the unwritten code between men that he was making his play for

Melissa and not to fuck it up for him. Tye didn't know Russell well, but he didn't want to be a complete asshole so he backed off of Melissa. Instead, he sat back in his seat and thought about the best way of taking Michael out.

"You got balls, you know, for doing what you did," Russell said, getting his game on with Melissa.

Melissa finally smiled and let Russell think that his line of bullshit was working. If things worked out, she hoped to have Russell alone to herself tonight before Zoë decided to steal him away just out of spite.

The monster looked out the window toward the sun. He still marveled at and feared the bright golden orb that burned bright in the pale blue sky. The monster hated the sun, yet respected its power. Because with sunlight came the power of detection. In sunlight, one could see. Fear was burned away when the sun rose to its regal perch in the sky, and the wet, blood-soaked terror that night brought was dried away. No one was afraid in the daylight; the monster knew that. That was why he did what he did when the moon had gathered enough courage and chased the sun into hiding again. In the night, the monster's world came to life, the sounds echoed louder, the shadows moved on command, and the screams tasted sweeter. Nighttime would be here soon enough. When it came he would venture out in the humid evening and walk again in the darkness that had adopted him as one of its own.

• • •

In the back of the bus, Christine gazed out the window. With bloodshed averted between Tye and Michael, two people she couldn't stand, her attention quickly faltered and her mind began to wander to life outside of the bus.

Kira had more interest in the would-be fight. She would have loved to have seen Tye beat the shit out of Michael. She would have loved to see Tye kill Michael. That was it. She wanted to see Michael Montross dead, his lifeless body at her feet so she could spit on him the way he had done to her so many times. The nights he had her on the streets selling his drugs and her body, with her seeing nothing of the profits from either transaction. She wanted him dead, as painfully as possible. Even if Tye did kill Michael, Kira would swear on a stack of Bibles that it was in self-defense. She'd lie on the stand and she'd lie in front of God. She had done a lot worse on the street to stay alive, and God was nowhere to be seen then. Kira knew she couldn't spend three minutes locked up with Michael, let alone three days. *The moment we're alone he's going to kill me*, she thought.

Michael Montross thought he was doing time because of Kira's testimony. Actually, the real reason Michael Montross was doing time was because he was a violent psychopath who would rather put his fist through your head than look at you. It wasn't Kira's testimony that put him in jail; it was Michael's own uncontrollable nature. Kira just happened to reaffirm what everyone else knew but couldn't prove in court. And that pissed Kira off also. She'd put her neck on the line, literally. Instead of setting her free, they dug up an old beef and tossed her in Juvey. Some reward for getting a snitch jacket. But most of all, Kira was mad at herself for believing that those assholes in corrections actually gave two shits about her. As far as she was concerned they could all go to hell, every single one of them, especially that bleeding-heart do-gooder who was sitting ten rows in front of her. *The hell with everyone*, she thought . . . then she felt Christine's hand around hers and she amended quickly: *to hell with everyone . . . except Christine*. Kira knew the moment Michael walked on the bus that her control was going to break. It didn't matter to her what the others thought. It didn't matter if she let Hannah Anders down. It only mattered if she let herself down. She wasn't going to wind up with her throat crushed between two tattooed forearms, which was Michael's specialty.

As Kira moved closer to Christine, her hand fell on her friend's knee. Christine didn't mind; intimacy was something that had been shared between the two girls for some time now, and Christine had come to welcome Kira's warm touch. It didn't matter that the first time Kira approached Christine, she was coldly rebuffed and called "a freakin' dyke" to her face. Both girls had kept their distance after that. Christine wanted to be alone, and Kira found a cute little petty thief to hang with who didn't mind her advances as long as she was rewarded with cigarettes and candy bars. Everything on the inside has a price, and the most expensive price tag is on companionship. Love never comes into the equation; companionship had nothing to do with love. It is a bargain struck up between two lonely and scared parties, a deal that mutually benefits each. Some girls join gangs that are culturally and racially exclusive. You had to form such an alliance early in order to avoid being targeted by the others. Christine did not join a gang because she did not want to be recruited into something she had no control over. Even though she was Hispanic and could have had easy membership in either one of the two Hispanic gangs that were housed inside Juvey, Christine preferred to be alone. Her snubbing of the outstretched hand of sisterhood did not sit well with some of the leaders of these gangs. But Kira, Melissa, and Zoë, who weren't Hispanic or black (the two dominant controlling groups inside the female juvenile corrections center), found themselves alone in a system created by adults for the benefit of kids that was neither protective nor rehabilitative.

Christine, being an attractive girl, was naturally a prize on the inside, the highest, in fact, for Esmeralda, the leader of Las Locas. Ezzme had a large scar that ran down the side of her face from her temple to her chin that was the parting gift from her boyfriend. Ezzme, like Michael, had a naturally cruel and possessive streak, and what she wanted to possess was Christine. It was more Christine's beauty that she wanted, something Ezzme had once and that was taken away from her by a tattooed cholo doing a double life bid. Ezzme didn't want merely to own Christine, or Christine's body, she wanted to be what Christine was. Unmarred, unscarred, and unblemished. Perhaps if

Ezzme had known that Christine's scars ran deeper and uglier on the inside, the two would have become friends instead of rivals. Instead of hunter and hunted. But Ezzme neither cared nor wanted to know about what was on the inside of Christine unless it was her own fingers or tongue. And she let it be known through the grapevine that Christine was going to be hers in body and soul. Christine would be able to do little to stop it.

Ezzme always had at least seven to ten girls at her beck and call, whereas Christine had only herself for protection. The odds were not in Christine's favor. Every day in the cafeteria and every night when lights went out, Christine's stomach knotted, her muscles clenched as she waited for the onslaught that was to befall her. Going to the guards or the head of corrections would have gained her only a condescending grin, and people outside the system were always openly skeptical: "Well, they're only girls. What harm could girls do?" Plenty, and Christine knew it. She had parceled out enough punishment in her short life, and now it looked like she was going to get some thrown back at her. So she waited and plotted. She got herself a long, thin piece of sturdy wire from the springs in her mattress and sharpened one of the edges, then carefully wrapped it around her wrist like a bracelet and covered it with a wrist wrap. She might be jumped, she might go down, but she was going to either blind Ezzme or give her a nice matching scar on the other side of her face. The worst part was the waiting, and Ezzme knew it. She would look over at Christine from her dinner table across the hall and smile at her. A cruel smile that was both delicious and deadly. Sometimes Ezzme would roll her tongue slowly around her lips and blow kisses in Christine's direction. Ezzme knew that the pressure of the wait would put a strain on Christine, a strain that would cause her to break and mess up. Then, when she was vulnerable and ready, Ezzme would make her move. So they both waited, Ezzme for her conquest and Christine for her attack.

The time came one night when Christine awoke from a nightmare. She couldn't remember what it was, only that something dark and big and . . . *evil* was after her. Something horrifying, something that made Ezzme's threats a welcome proposition. Something that made Christine bolt up covered in sweat. She woke up groggy and afraid, as if she had just swum through a violent current of subconscious fear and almost drowned before she could pull herself up to a welcomed world of harsh reality.

Half asleep, Christine walked to the bathroom with a full bladder. She tried to put away the lingering pieces of her puzzling dream. Life was hard enough when she was awake, trying to stay in one piece. She didn't want those few precious hours of sleep to be lost to fear also. So she tried to drive the unclear images and the sounds, that skin-crawling buzzing, and the cold metallic rustling from her mind. As she sat on the toilet, Ezzme and two of her *cholas* walked into the bathroom. Christine was trapped. Her sharpened bracelet was under her pillow. She quickly got up, pressed her back against the wall, and waited for the beating. Waited for worse.

71

Ezzme took her time crossing the bathroom floor. She wanted every step in Christine's direction to pang sharply with fear in Christine's stomach. Ezzme's lips curled into her cold, delicious smile. Her face brushed against Christine's cheek and her breath, hot and viscous, whispered into Christine's ear.

"I can make it easy on you. I can make it bad for you." Ezzme pressed a homemade razor against Christine's throat, painful but not deep enough to draw blood or leave a mark that would draw suspicious looks from the guards.

"Get on your knees," Ezzme commanded. Her two cohorts stood on both sides of Christine. There was no escape. And Christine had thought of the other times she had found herself in the same predicament on the outside. She felt her knees begin to buckle, her eyes start to burn with tears. Not tears of fear but tears of anger for not putting up a fight, tears of frustration for being caught with her guard down and her weapon under her pillow. Ezzme laughed as she pulled sharply at the back of Christine's hair.

"It ain't that bad, bitch. I'm clean." Ezzme's girls laughed as Ezzme's hand pushed down on Christine's shoulders.

"Leave her alone." Christine heard the words as the cold bathroom floor touched her bare knees. She looked up past Ezzme to see Kira standing in the doorway of the bathroom. Ezzme and her two girls stood and stared at Kira, stunned that someone would dare interrupt the little party they had planned so long.

"What the fuck, bitch! She ain't yours. Wait your turn or get your ass kicked," barked Ezzme.

Kira didn't say anything. She lunged quickly. From behind her came the mop handle she had stolen from the supply closet the moment she had seen Ezzme and the other girls go into the bathroom after Christine. Kira didn't waste time with threatening talk or useless banter. She had been around enough to know that valuable ass-kicking time was wasted on posturing. She caught the first girl, Ezzme's second, square across the temple. The sound of wood and bone connecting echoed in the bathroom. Christine punched Ezzme in the crotch. Ezzme bent over, her face close to Christine's. Christine punched her hard in the throat. Kira started smashing the other girl across the head and shoulders with the wooden mop handle. By now, the whole dorm had woken up and girls rushed into the bathroom to watch and cheer on the battle. Guards quickly followed, and before a mini-riot could break out, several of them had Christine, Kira, Ezzme, and the other two pinned against the wall.

The rule on the inside was silence. It didn't matter who started it or why, all five girls would have had to adhere to that rule when they went up in front of the head of corrections the next morning. After a good night's sleep in a solitary cell, Christine was ready to face Ezzme. But fate sometimes acts in a way that no one can comprehend or predict. On her way to her cell in solitary, Ezzme lashed out at one of the corrections officers with the homemade razor she had previously pressed against Christine's throat, only this time she didn't hold back, and her accuracy, whether intentional or not, was pinpoint. The crude, sharp razor cut deep into the guard's carotid artery. The dying guard sprayed Ezzme and the other guards with a thin crimson geyser before she hit the ground. Christine heard all the gory details the next morning from the other girls. She had slept through the night not knowing that her rival lay in intensive care after the other guards had to use deadly force to subdue her. In fact, the vengeful guards used force again and again, and Ezzme's future looked like it would be one of unending slumber, with the constant beep of the heart monitor to keep her company. With Ezzme in a vegetative state and her spot in the hierarchy in the gang being quickly filled by someone who thought it would be wise to stay away from *las gringas locas*, Christine and Kira, Christine had a reprieve.

Christine never thanked Kira for her timely intervention. She never spoke to her and never looked in her direction. The feeling of obligation hung over her head like a guillotine, and she was afraid of the blade of payback falling down on her at the wrong time. She didn't want to be in Kira's debt. She didn't want to go from Ezzme to Kira. Christine thought that when you're down on your knees, every bully looks the same. At the same time, Christine was surprised that Kira never reached out to her, never approached her. As far as Kira was concerned, it was just something that happened, a reflex on her part. She didn't know where the reflex came from or if it would ever come back.

Kira didn't like Christine. She found her attractive, but she didn't like her. If Christine never wanted to thank her, then that was fine. Life goes on. But Kira would lie in bed at night and wonder why she acted the way she did. Why she reached out to help someone she really didn't know or care about. Kira was not a foolish girl. She didn't like violence, especially if she was on the receiving end. Helping Christine was the most foolish thing she had done, next to hooking up with Michael. It bugged her that she didn't know why she had gone to Christine's defense. Why should Kira care if Christine got taken and used by Ezzme? It happened to everyone in this stinking world. No one came to her aid when Michael abused her on the outside, and no one came to her rescue when Ezzme and her gang raped her on the inside, so why did it bother Kira so much that Christine was going to get what everyone else got? Kira would look over at Christine's cot, on the other side of the dorm room, and think, *Is she grateful? Does she appreciate that I put my ass on the line for her? Why doesn't she say something to me? Why doesn't she talk to me? Why can't I find one friend in this lousy fucking world?* And with those thoughts clouding her tired mind, Kira would fall off into a restless and lonely sleep.

Three weeks later, Christine found herself on work detail with Kira. She had not said a word to her since the Ezzme incident, but now she found herself in an awkward position. Both girls went about their work quietly, filling the buckets and rinsing out the mops. Kira kneeled down and tested the water with her hand. When Christine bent down to add soap to the hot water, she found herself staring into Kira's eyes. They stared at each other, neither one knowing what reaction was called for in the situation. Christine smiled first. It was a soft smile that lit up her face, and Kira felt a warm feeling come over her. Christine leaned over and pressed her forehead against Kira's. It was a gesture of friendship and a sign of solidarity. With the small smile still on her lips, she said "thanks" softly. Kira knew what Christine was referring to and that it wasn't easy for someone like Christine to be beholden to anyone. It was from that moment on that the two scared girls bonded and became good friends.

Lesbianism was something frowned upon by the authorities, but it was common when girls were in lockup. Both Kira and Christine knew that in Juvey, and prison, you were either gay or bi. It didn't matter what your personal preference or your natural inclination was, if someone more powerful wanted you, then that was going to be your inclination. Even though some of the relationships were based on domination and power, others were created out of loneliness. It was easier for two girls to hook up on the inside than for two men. There wasn't the stigma that was attached to what was considered emasculation in the men's lockdown. When you got had in men's lockdown you *was had*, and that was something you never shook no matter what joint you ended up in. Someone would always be there that served time with you somewhere else, and it didn't take long for it to slip out that you were a prison bitch and your tenure of torture started all over again. With girls and women it didn't matter. No one cared if you went dyke on the inside; it was expected and accepted. A bunch of curious, sexually blossoming young girls stuck together in such a dire situation would naturally find a way to experiment and explore themselves and others. Society had given girls a free pass to the Sapphic side. It was chic to be a lipstick lesbian today. Career-minded celebrities found it made good copy to be shown lip-locked with another pretty girl. Kira didn't know it was popular in some circles to "sway that way." She didn't turn to women to impress or emulate people. She did it because she preferred a woman's softness to the gruff harshness she had received from men. Christine didn't really care for girls, but she liked men less. With Kira it was different. Not only did Kira put her ass on the line for her, Christine knew deep down that Kira really cared for her. Really loved her with her own whacked sense of passion. It bothered Christine that she and Kira might never be together on the outside. Neither one cared what society thought, but they both knew that the two of them together couldn't last in a world without concrete and bars. Their love was born out of desperation. Its continued existence didn't seem likely once they were free.

Their relationship had started six months before, and now Christine found herself heading into an uncertain future after a boring weekend of work. The only thing she knew was that she couldn't go back to Juvey. She couldn't anyway, since she and the others on the bus were already eighteen. She knew that next time she fucked up, they would send her to the place where all the big bad girls go, and Christine didn't want any part of that sorority. She wanted the weekend to be over with already, to be gone so she could finish her sentence early. The only regret she had was that she knew Kira would get into more trouble and would find herself once again a guest of the state but with accommodations not geared to adolescents. Christine had grown quite close to Kira, closer than she had ever been to any person except her sister, and she didn't want to leave her. She didn't want to stay around and watch her friend self-destruct either. Christine knew she'd be wasting her breath trying to talk Kira onto the straight and narrow. Kira was heading down the crooked path of recidivism, and both girls knew and accepted it. So when Kira held Christine's hand tight, Christine squeezed right back. Their long fingers intertwined, their bond both tightening and coming to an end.

Kira cuddled closer to Christine. They were both used to watching each other's back. They were always there for each other.

"How you doin'?" Christine asked.

Kira didn't answer. Her mind was somewhere else. Worlds away.

"Hey. Earth to Kira. Come in." Christine tried to get Kira's attention by squeezing her hand tighter. Kira looked at her.

"Sorry." Kira smiled sadly at Christine. Kira's body started to shake. Christine moved closer to her friend, hoping her warmth would ease Kira's nervousness. "I can't believe he's here. What the fuck were they thinking letting that psychopath come with us?" Kira quietly said between shudders.

Christine looked at the back of Michael's bald head, his thick, muscular neck covered in some race-baiting tattoos. Christine thought nothing would be better than driving a homemade shiv into the neck of this prick who had mentally tortured Kira and physically abused her on the streets. To Michael, Kira was nothing more than a punching bag on which to take out his frustration.

"I gotta get out of here," Kira quietly whispered.

"What?" Christine replied, wondering what Kira was talking about.

"I have to split or he's gonna kill me," Kira said.

Christine rubbed the back of Kira's hand with her fingers. "I told you nothing is going to happen to you. I won't let it."

"Why stick around? You promised. You said once we got on the outside we'd split together. Remember? Let's just split tonight. Why wait?"

Christine remembered. She had said a lot of things to a lot of people in her life, never meaning most of it. She remembered the whispers she and Kira shared as they lay next to each other when the lights went out. The intimacy was the best thing she had experienced in a long time. For once she had someone to share her secrets and dreams, someone who wanted nothing but to keep her safe and happy through the night. Their friendship was a commodity that both girls never had on the outside, and it had taken a year on the inside for them to find someone who actually cared. Something that both knew they would never find once their debt to society was paid and they were on their own once again. The cold prospect of loneliness frightened both of them. But as scared as Christine was of being alone, she was not going to end up in jail for anyone ever again. Not even for Kira.

"You said—"

"I know what I said." Christine cut Kira off before she could get highly emotional, as Christine knew she could. "Monday morning they take us back to Juvey. We have this chance to knock a month off of our sentences. Why do you want to fuck that up? You think that Michael is going to fuck up his chance of getting out early?"

"Yeah. And come time when both of us are back on the streets, how much you gonna bet I don't see the next morning?" Kira countered.

In the back of Christine's mind that dark reality set in. Her friend's chances of making it after Michael caught up with her didn't look good. Even if they escaped now, how far could they go before the law caught up with them? Besides, Michael wasn't the type to forgive and forget; he was the type to punish and remember. And if Christine and Kira took off, where would they go? What would they do? Christine knew that it would be a matter of days before the two of them would be on the street. It was the only life they knew, the only way they knew to stay alive in a world they never asked to be thrown into. And if they found another city to go to, another street to steal and hustle from, how long would it be before Michael or one of his thugs showed up looking for retribution? Christine didn't want to live in fear anymore. She remembered the anguish she had endured while waiting for Ezzme to make her move on her. She didn't want to have to endure it all over again waiting for Michael to make his.

Christine's mind was racing a million miles a minute, then all at once it came to a screeching halt. Why did she have to wait for Michael to strike? He wasn't after her. He wanted Kira. Christine knew that if she wasn't around when the shit went down, she wouldn't have to worry. She didn't plan on being with Kira anyway once they were out. It wasn't Christine's fault after all, so it wasn't her neck in the noose. She could just slip away come Monday morning and be on her own way. That was the law of the streets. Stay alive. At any or all costs. There were no friends on the street, just accomplices, people you used before they used you. Sooner or later everyone you hang with on the outside is going to turn on you. It was the nature of the beast, and that beast didn't change its colors for love or loyalty. Christine thought of a thousand reasons why she should dump Kira, but when she turned and looked into Kira's eyes, one by one each reason for abandoning her friend melted away in the warmth of Kira's sad smile. Christine felt a sickness rising in her stomach. It was the bitter taste of betrayal, and she knew she could never leave Kira. Not now. Not when her life was in danger. She didn't know how she would do it, but she would protect Kira with her last breath.

"It'll be all right. I promise." Christine tightly squeezed Kira's hand between hers.

And Kira believed her; she had to. Resting her head on Christine's shoulder, she closed her eyes and tried to dream about a world she would never know.

The sounds came flooding back. The music that it had listened to so long ago started to drift back into the monster's brain. He remembered the melody, the words. He didn't understand what the words meant, but he knew what they sounded like. He hummed the tune to himself, his thick lips and giant teeth making the tune sound like a truck motor that was about to falter and die. His large fingers worked briskly as he hummed. The music filled his skull, like a cavernous concert hall he had all to himself. As the music grew louder, he started to sway in time to the symphony playing inside his mind. The music was good. The music kept the pain away, the hungry pain that attacked the monster when he slumbered and kept him from dreaming. The monster could dream when the music played. When the music rang between his ears, the pain did not come, most of the time.

The monster's face started to stretch into a grotesque smile, resembling something you'd see carved in stone on the side of a medieval church. He liked the music. It blocked out all memories of the past: the cage, the books, the sin. He wanted to keep the music playing in his head forever, but the music started to soften and change into something else. Voices. Singing. Hundreds, thousands of voices singing out in one high-pitched scream that ate away into the monster's mind. The pain snuck in, hidden behind the wall of screams, and the monster was once again helpless. He tried to stand, but the room started to spin around him. He grabbed the wall for support, his fingers digging deep into the plaster, crushing it to dust. The voices screamed and shrieked in a rising crescendo. The monster shook his head, but the voices grew stronger. The buzz of the swarm of flies that constantly traveled with him did nothing to block the irritating sound. He smashed his thick skull against a large beam in the wall. He did it again and again. The wood splintered as the monster's head repeatedly crushed down upon it. Finally the voices stopped. They receded once again to the back of the monster's mind. The monster squatted down and sighed. His thick fingers began to pull the splinters out of his face.

Tyson Sims looked back at the two girls sitting close together at the back of the bus. In his eyes, they were both fine. He had heard through the grapevine that they were "together," but that wouldn't stop him from making a move on either one of them. *Hell*, he thought, *I wouldn't mind doing both of them together*. His time on the inside had been focused on what he had to do to regain his top spot when he got out. Now that he was out of Juvey, at least temporarily, the urges that he kept in check on the inside were starting to swell up.

Tye was a tough character with the harsh look of the street about him. He was eighteen years old, with seven previous arrests to his credit. He had been the warlord of the Twelfth Street Assassins, the youngest to attain that lofty position. He had been the king of all he saw. All six city blocks, his entire concrete domain, awaited his return. Tye's mind quickly went from the two girls sitting in the backseat to scores that had to be settled. Usurpers tried to overtake his throne while this urban king was in exile. Former trusted comrades became conspirators. Friend turned to foe. The sweet wine of leadership turned into a bitter vinegar. Treachery would not stand in his second reign. Heads would roll on his triumphant return, but he knew that a countercoup needed funding, and his coffers had run dry while he was away. This was a minor setback for such a skilled leader. For the past year he had waited and plotted. Planned and schemed. With this program shortening his Juvey stay by at least a month, he was closer to being back on the streets. Closer to the day that his shadow would once again fall over his kingdom, his domain, his turf. And then the sidewalks would run crimson with the blood of every traitorous member who wore TSA colors. But he could wait a little while longer. He had a plan, or rather, Richie had a plan. A plan that was brought to Tye's attention on the bus. It was insane, totally out of left field, and there was a chance in a million that it would ever see the light of day. Yet with all that going against it, Tye agreed to hear the white boy out. Tye knew this scheme for wealth was the longest of long shots, but something about Richie's scared voice and nervous manner made Tye believe that Richie was sold on the idea. Tye knew Richie was a smart one. He knew many smart ones on the inside and the outside, but White Boy Richie was the type of smart you didn't find on the street. He wasn't all that book smart, but he knew other things. Things that no one thought about or understood. Someone like Richie didn't think like everyone else, and that was good. Tye needed to see how other people thought. He wanted to know what went on in other people's minds. How can you conquer others if you don't know what, or how, they're thinking?

And if it did turn out to be true, if Richie's scheme did yield something worthwhile, why shouldn't Tye take it all? After all that was what a smart leader did. Richie looked back at Tye and tried to wink, but the gesture just made it look as if he had a dust speck stuck in his eye and couldn't get it out. Tye's dark eyes revealed nothing of the conspiratorial nature that lurked behind them.

The bus stopped in front of the Blackwell Hotel. Christine looked up, straining to see the front of the hotel. The large vertical neon sign spelling out HOTEL was sagging, and the red T that was supposed to be the middle letter of the word was missing. Kira pronounced the remaining letters, HOEL, as "hole."

"Great place to spend a weekend, huh?" Kira whispered to Christine. Christine didn't reply as she studied the tall, silent building. Without her realizing it, the soft, pale hairs on Christine's arms started to stand on their ends.

Hannah stood up and tried to gather the kids' attention. Her action was reinforced by Williams's club banging off the grate. The kids shut up and stared unimpressed at Hannah. Williams began to speak.

"This is it. The Blackwell Hotel. Your home and place of work for the next three days. Now, I've talked to you all individually about this program and what your participation means. You were all picked after I went over each of your case files and interviewed you. A lot is riding on the success of this program for you guys. We're not here to have fun. We are here to work, but nothing that is going to be too backbreaking. We took each one of you on your word that your full cooperation would be given. That means for the next three days there will be no drinking, no drugs, no

smoking, no incidents like what happened earlier."
Williams's attention was equally tuned to Michael and
Tye. "And no fraternizing." The last word made Hannah blush at the implications that it held. The subtle
change in her complexion did not go unnoticed by her
astute captive audience.

Michael reared back his head and brayed, "That
means no dyking out back there," as he turned to look
at Kira and Christine with twinkling menace in his ice-
cold blue eyes. Everyone else looked at the two girls
who sat together in the last seat. Kira hated when people looked at her, and now eight pairs of accusatory
eyes were staring.

What could have been an uncomfortable moment
was quickly averted when Hannah cut Michael off by
saying, "That means between anyone."

Christine appreciated the effort that Hannah gave
to defuse the insult, but it was too late, so it didn't
really matter. Everyone thought they knew what the
two girls were: two street hustlers and thieves. What
they didn't know was that the girls were frightened
and battle scarred, holding on to each other while trying not to be pulled down into a world that would
wash their futures down the sewer drain like the rest
of the trash that littered the streets.

Hannah continued trying to smooth the ruffled
feelings that Michael's outburst may have caused.

"We are all on the honor system here. Each one of
you gave your word that you would not leave the premises while you are here. This is the last stop before you
all get released, so it would be foolish for any of you to
try to esca—" Hannah tried to stop herself before she

said the word "escape." She covered herself by continuing with "leave without permission," but it was too late. Escape was what she meant and it was a buzz word for these kids. To them, the word meant one thing: they were going to a place that was nothing more than another prison, with a lot more empty rooms. No matter how it looked, prison was prison.

As if on cue, the bus driver opened the door. Hannah walked out first and felt the heat of the afternoon air on her face. It was a welcome sensation after the humid interior of the bus.

Hannah assessed the front of the hotel. The street was deserted, and the entire section of town seemed to be more dead than alive. Hannah kept her eyes open for a sign of life. Stepping out of the deep shadows of the faded, torn awning, Margaret Gayne greeted Hannah's and Williams's arrival with a perky smile.

Margaret was an attractive older woman. Despite her years, she held her head up high and she had the ability to look directly at people without looking down on them. She stood like royalty but walked among the commoners. She was a woman who had seen her share of debutante balls (when those things were all the fashion) but she had also seen the other side of the coin, which was dirty and scarred. She had cleaned her share of shit out of nursing homes and pediatric wards. For some reason, her presence made Hannah feel more comfortable.

"Well, they're here," Hannah said between pursed lips.

"Good. This hotel needs them, and they need this hotel. Don't fret, Hannah. This is going to be fine.

I don't want to see any more children's names on the police blotters or obituary. This will be a success, I promise."

With that reassurance Hannah felt that she could handle death row inmates for the weekend.

"Let's see the little dears," Margaret said in a motherly tone that did not seem out of place even when talking about a group of kids who had a combined twenty-seven years behind bars.

Russell, Richie, and Tye got off the bus first, followed by Zoë and Melissa. Christine walked in front of Kira, shielding her from Michael. He still sat in his seat and smiled as the girls quickly snuck by.

"Mother Hen ain't gonna be around all the time, Kira," he hissed.

Christine stopped to stare at the muscular boy who was like a time bomb, fully equipped with a fuse that was already burning down rapidly. She wanted to tell Michael to go fuck himself. Instead, she turned to the bus driver, who was straining to get a better look at her rear, and said, "Take a picture, asshole. It'll last longer." The girls hurried across the street to the front of the hotel where the others had already lined up. Michael took his time getting off the bus and sauntered arrogantly toward the group.

Margaret watched as Michael took his time getting in line. She knew the type. She had seen them before. He was one of those kids who were old before their time, dead before they realized they had a life in front of them. She sensed he was trouble. She had radar for these things. She knew the ones who were good trying to play bad. She knew the ones who were bad pretending to be good. Then there were the bad ones who were running headfirst into evil.

Williams handed a clipboard to Hannah and watched as she signed the acceptance of their charges. He looked over at the two ladies and shook his head in wonder. *How the hell did the board approve of letting this group of miscreants stay in the care of these two women for three seconds, let alone three days?*

"Let's go inside and I'll show you around," Margaret told the group. There was a momentary pause until Melissa broke rank and walked in. Kira's eyes bounced around the neighborhood to see if there were any potential places to run, but every storefront and building loomed hollow and empty. She walked right behind Christine, knocking her friend's shadow to the side.

The monster stirred in his lair. He found himself trying to sleep more often, but sleep rarely came now. He tried to think about the music, but the tune wouldn't come to him. He staggered around in a state of physical exhaustion and mental fatigue, his mind not his own. His thoughts were someone else's. His dreams were foreign to him. The strange dreams were vivid, painful. He dreamed of strangers, and strangers frightened the monster. . . .

The buzzing in his head woke him from a state of semiconsciousness. He listened, his hearing more acute since his dreams had been taken from him. Something was stirring in his house. Someone was in the monster's home. He shook his head, trying to clear out the lingering remnants of bad dreams. Strangers, intruders, people. These were words that the monster knew, and they upset him. He scratched the dented plate that was affixed to his head, his thick fingers running across the metal, and briefly wondered where the piece of steel had come from. *Was I born with the plate? Did someone put it there? A friend? A foe?* The monster had no recollection of his skull as it had been before the plate, the dying cop who had put the bullet through it, or the nervous doctor who had removed it. The monster's only thoughts were of the *now*. He had no past, no future. He lived only for the moment. The moment at hand brought strangers into his home.

He could not allow that.

The lobby of the old hotel was once an Art Deco marvel, but it had since spoiled away into a sad relic of a bygone era. In the corners, antique velvet couches and chairs sat in rot. Filth and mildew tinged the red fabric. Large rips crisscrossed along the upholstery and leaked stuffing. Ornate mirror frames hung on the walls, fractured portraits of the past with missing glass. Shattered chandeliers dangled from the ceiling limp and lifeless, the sparkle of gaiety having long since burned out. The once prominent black marble front desk was now a series of cracked and broken stones. Faded wallpaper, aged to a jaundiced yellow, sagged like the flesh on the arm of an old fat woman. Litter that was older than any of the delinquents was strewn all over the floor. Stinks and stenches wafted around the room, as if trying to conceal something more distasteful in their repugnant smells. There was something sinister hiding in the odor of decay. No one could identify that something, but everyone noticed it.

Kira felt a chill shoot straight up her back. Even though the sun was out, it seemed that its rays decided to linger outside the front door and not venture past the foyer and into the lobby. Daylight seemed to be off limits to this place. The building seemed to be strictly nocturnal in nature. An unsettling air of dread hung heavily within the halls of the hotel. Kira tried to formulate what that meant to her, but she stopped when Michael's cold breath grazed the back of her neck.

"Romantic, isn't it, baby?" Michael said loud enough for everyone to hear. Michael had also heard the stories that Kira and Christina had hooked up on the inside but wasn't sure if he really believed them. Christine had a tough reputation, and Michael knew that Christine and Kira were tight, tighter than the usual inside tryst. His nasty little barbs were directed at her as well as Kira. Each snide comment was a challenge, each dig a threat to Christine.

Hannah tried to gather the group's attention with a slight cough that seemed foolishly out of place. Margaret spoke up.

"All right, all right. Let me introduce myself properly. My name is Margaret Gayne, and I'm involved with the renovation of historical landmarks for the city. A little history of this place before we get to work: The city took over ownership of this lovely but neglected building over three years ago. There was some question about proper ownership of this property for some time after it closed down. There was a terrible fire here some years ago and the owner, Langley Blackwell, his wife, and several guests died in the blaze. Tragic, it was."

Margaret was trying to see empathy on any of the kids' faces. But no one even responded with a raised eyebrow. *And why would they?* she thought. *These kids have seen things in their lives that no one should see. Murders, rapes, attacks. Why would the fiery fate of people they never knew concern them at all?* She quickly tried to lay down the guidelines for the weekend.

"We toyed with the idea of reopening the hotel, but what this part of town really needs is a shelter for the homeless," Margaret continued.

"Which is where you guys come in," Williams interrupted.

"What? Homeless?" Kira's sarcasm dripped.

Margaret tried to regain control of the group. "No, volunteers."

"We didn't volunteer." Michael had her; it was over. He knew it. Worse, Margaret knew it. In the battle of wills, the first volley had been shot and the enemy retreated without a fight. But Michael's victory was short-lived. He turned around to look at the other kids with a triumphant grin, but his objection was met by groans from the others in the group and a pointed look from Williams.

Tye voiced the group's annoyance. "Damn, can't you ever shut up, man?"

"Eat me," Michael answered back.

"Good comeback," Richie taunted in a low voice.

"Fuck you," Michael snapped.

Margaret watched the exchange with an almost

horrified expression. Seeing her discomfort, Hannah interfered.

"You all know that the trade-off for your work this weekend is a month off of your sentences. That's not a bad deal."

Michael, still defiant, gestured vulgarly in response to her little speech.

Hannah and Margaret were in a daze. They wanted to say something, but both were afraid to react.

When Michael turned back to gloat in Hannah's direction, he was dealt a blistering slap that nearly stretched the features of his face like a cartoon character out of a Tex Avery short. He stumbled back and fell hard on his ass, his head ringing. The kids froze as the bully fell before them. All eyes in the room lifted and stared at the owner of the hand that had sent Michael sprawling on his keister.

Officer Williams looked down at the fallen tormentor. If looks could kill, Michael and all the other kids would already have been dead. His prosthetic hand hung close to his body.

"Let me tell you something. Listen carefully because I'm only going to say it once. Hannah and I are here because we believe in second chances. Don't prove us wrong. For the next three days, when one of us says something, you'd better listen. In any and all ways possible, which means when we say 'jump,' you say 'how fucking high?' You will work when we tell you to work and if any of you open your goddamn mouths like that again, I will personally pull your fucking tongues out and strangle you with them."

The kids, who were standing in a single line facing

the two women, stared at their pair of weekend baby-sitters with disgust and indifference. Every youngster knew what was what. It only took one word. One look. The kids knew that if the women showed fear, they would win the battle and probably the upcoming war of wills. It wouldn't be long until they all found themselves goofing off somewhere, smoking and screwing, doing whatever they wanted to do for the weekend. Everyone was calculating how long it would be before both women snapped; they were sure that the younger one would go first. She would melt like butter under heat. But the old broad they thought would take longer. Maybe an hour, two at the most, before a glare from either Tye or Michael changed her way of thinking.

Michael stood in front of Hannah. His cold eyes moved up and down her body in lecherous unison. His mind raced with nasty thoughts, and Hannah knew that those thoughts were of her. She instinctively started to tug on her diamond engagement ring. *Oh God, why isn't Ronald here with me now?* her heart pleaded, but her brain knew that Ronald would have been eaten for supper by the wolf that was leering at her now.

Hannah felt her breath go away. Where was the polite young gentleman she had met two weeks earlier? she thought. Then she realized that his earlier demeanor was a con. It was all a sham—the sincerity, the looks of earnest repentance. She had been played. She had wanted so badly to believe that she could make a difference, but she now knew that she was wrong. She had been duped by all of them, and she could see now that they all saw through her. They always had. She felt herself start to get queasy again.

Margaret was aghast at Williams's speech, but after an awkward moment, she resumed her welcoming.

"Officer Williams, Miss Anders, and I will be in charge. We have a full list of things that have to be done. The city has deemed the first five floors safe and ready for use, although no one is permitted past the second floor. The doors leading up to the third floor have been sealed. The elevator, which only recently has been reactivated, goes to the second floor as well. We have separate rooms for the boys and girls. Girls will sleep on the first floor and boys on the second. Miss Anders, I'm sure, has already explained to you all what is expected from all of you. We are on the honor system here."

Christine laughed to herself over that. It was the second time today that the term "honor system" was thrown around. *Honor,* she thought. *What honor? The only honor on the street is making it to another lousy day. What honor is it when you have to trick just to get enough money to eat? Where's the honor when a cop shakes you down for half your nightly take and decides to make up for the rest with a freebie in the back of the cruiser? Honor?* Christine didn't want honor; she didn't need it. It came with a price tag that was much too expensive. She turned her attention back to Margaret, who was concluding their little pep talk.

"I know that if we all try hard and try to get along that we can get through this weekend and all be better people for it."

"You are not guests in this hotel. You are here to work, and work you will," Williams continued as he looked each one of the kids up and down. "You *children . . .* do not impress me.

"Miss Anders?" Williams quickly changed gears, kindly directing the conversation to her.

Hannah jumped out of her stupor and walked over to Williams. "We can divide them up into work groups now. I will escort these . . . kids . . . to their rooms so they can put away their belongings later."

"No, that's okay, Officer Williams. I'll show them to their rooms," Margaret offered.

"Good," Williams said, "right after we search them."

A jolt of uneasiness passed through more than one of the kids who were carrying contraband. Everyone knew that the penalty for bringing the stuff in the building was immediate expulsion from the program.

"Officer Williams," Margaret interceded, "these youngsters gave us their word that they would follow the rules and obey them. I can't see that searching them now would do any good except unduly embarrass them."

Williams had heard liberal gibberish for years. He figured that sooner or later he would be immune to the inane banter of foolish bleeding hearts, but it never ceased to amaze the seasoned cop how completely out-to-lunch some people were. Had this woman not just witnessed a would-be mutiny not less than five minutes ago? *And who was the adolescent's rage aimed at? Her and the other do-gooder. Now comes the babying,* he thought. All of a sudden, the little shits that tried to walk over her were now victims of the system. This was going to be a long weekend, one that Williams did not want to spend in the godforsaken hotel with a bunch of juvenile delinquents he would rather see tossed back in the joint. He knew the type that Margaret was, and he didn't want to butt heads with her, especially in front of the kids. He respected and liked Margaret personally, but could not understand how she could always try to find good in everyone.

"Miss Gayne, we are required to search them," he said in such a condescending way that he garnered a modicum of respect from some of the kids. The kids knew Williams was a hard-ass and Ms. Gayne was a soft touch. But now they respected Williams more, even though he was the enemy. They knew that he was an enemy to be reckoned with. "But the instant that I find out that one rule has been broken . . . anyone smoking, using drugs, a phone, or trying to escape . . . then it's back to Juvey for all of you." He finished the sentence with such sincerity that Christine thought the guy would end up closing the whole project down before dinner.

After the search, Margaret took the kids to their rooms. When she returned, she turned to speak to the corrections officer. Williams's game face was on for the weekend, but Margaret stood in front of the stoic ex-policeman and smiled at him. Her smile was infectious, and Williams caught himself grinning back at her.

"You must think I'm an old fool, Frank," she said.

"What makes you think that?" he sheepishly asked.

"Come on, don't be coy with me. I know what you're thinking. Why is this foolish old lady wasting her time and money on a bunch of kids that aren't worth a damn?"

Williams said nothing, but his silence spoke volumes.

"Listen, Frank, I'm old. I have spent the better part of my life with my head in the clouds, not knowing how the other half lived. More like ninety percent. If I can save one child from a life of crime, then I guess I did something right after all is said and done."

Williams knew that on some level, the old lady was right, but that wasn't the way of the world. He knew that most, if not all, of this crew would end up back in jail within six months of their release. Margaret wanted to save their souls; all they wanted to do was save their skin.

"I'm not saying you're wrong. What you're doing for them is great. What you're doing for me is even greater, but I hope that neither of us gets too disappointed," he answered in complete candor.

"I lost a child to the streets. I don't know who to blame. Either there is no blame to go around or there is too much. Do I blame myself, society, the streets? It doesn't matter anymore. My child is gone and nothing can bring my baby back to me. These kids aren't that far gone. I know what you're thinking. They just turned on us and they just showed their true colors, but I don't believe that. That is how they cope and survive, to attack and to take advantage of the situation. It's good business sense. I don't want to give up on these kids, and I don't want to give up on you. It took a lot of prodding to get you to agree to this weekend. If they can have a second chance at life, why can't you?"

Williams thought about that. He thought about all those months he'd spent brooding in his room alone. Hating the world and everyone in it, he found comfort in being alone and away from everyone, saving them from his bitter moods. It had taken a long time for him to come back into the real world and to develop Project: Renewal. When Margaret Gayne had called him several months prior to the start of the program, he knew that she spoke with sincerity from the moment he'd first heard her voice. Her voice held echoes of a woman who felt lost and wanted to do something about it. She explained to Williams that she and Hannah had started this project, and they needed someone to help oversee the kids. Margaret remembered the newspaper accounts of Williams's story years earlier. She always clipped stories of social importance. New school openings, homeless shelter funding, police and community interaction stories—anything that would prompt Margaret Gayne to a call of civic duty was neatly clipped and cut and placed in a shoe box for future reference. The stories about Frank Williams and the incident (Margaret could never bring herself to use words like *attack*, *murder*, or *killing*) had always stayed in the back of her mind. Margaret thought about Williams, about his young partner, and the horrible things that had happened to them. She knew that Williams survived the incident and that he too needed another chance. It was up to her to see that he got it.

"All right, Margaret. We're all here for the weekend. I can't promise what Monday morning will bring, but for the next three days, I'm yours."

"Good. Now let's get our little darlings ready for the world that awaits them," Margaret said with so much conviction in her frail voice that Frank Williams believed in something he hadn't in years: *redemption*.

Williams made his way back to the lobby and out to the foyer. When he got there, he paused to look up and down the street, just as Kira did earlier. He did not see a living soul around. It wasn't even four o'clock yet, and the streets already resembled a ghost town. Williams knew that when the sun went down, when the light was blotted out of the sky by the harsh cityscape that jutted up out of the ground as nothing more than long, dark oblong boxes, another society came to life on the streets. A society of addicts, hookers, thieves, and worse. They prowled under a moon that hung over the city like a blind man's eye. These people did all sorts of things to others, to themselves, just to live, just to stay alive. Williams knew that pushed far enough, you would do anything to survive. *But was it worth it? Was life worth fighting for that much?* Because in the end, no matter how you played the game, you ended up six feet under.

He had already come to the cold, soul-wracking realization that the world had two types of people: the dead and the dying. He had been straddling the line between the two for years now. Sometimes he didn't know which side he was on, which one he *wanted* to be on. The dead didn't want him, and the dying found his company offensive. He spent his time alone, not out of choice but out of necessity. Whatever Frank Williams had was contagious; it stuck to you like glue. It was complete and total apathy. But now he had another chance with this program. He had another shot at doing it the right way. He viewed it as a slight chance to make amends. Neil, his career, a psychotic killer, and his arm were all gone but he was still there. It had taken a gray-haired old lady to get Frank Williams off his knees and back on his feet. The next battle Frank

Williams engaged in would be fought standing and not lying on his back, bleeding to death.

Williams took keys out of his jacket, closed the metal door to the foyer, and ran a chain between the two doors. He placed a lock between the links and with a quick turn, he cut off the outside world. He had sealed them in, all nice and tight. *One big happy family for the weekend.* He handed Margaret the keys and watched as she slid them into her jacket pocket and walked back to the main lobby. Williams followed her, and he walked straight toward a destiny he never saw coming.

5

MARGARET HAD DIVIDED UP THE JOBS FOR THE KIDS AS evenly as she could. She gave the boys clean-up detail on the first floor, mostly the back rooms. There were a total of ten rooms at the back of the first floor that had been servants' quarters. Hannah and Margaret had both agreed that if half of those rooms were cleaned out and ready for painting before dinner, they would be going at a good pace. The girls would gather up the trash in the foyer and lobby and then start on patching, priming, and painting the rooms the boys had cleaned out. No one expected the kids to do any serious repair work. First off, no one believed that any of these kids had the necessary skill. Second, and more important, no one—Officer Williams most of all—liked the idea of any of these youngsters having anything in their hands more formidable than a paintbrush or push broom.

After the kids had finished their chores and before they went to dinner, they would go to their rooms to place the few belongings they had brought with them on the bare mattresses. Sheets, a towel, soap, and toiletries would be distributed before lights out.

Russell and Michael were assigned to sweep the back rooms, with the exception of the kitchen. The kitchen had been cleaned, or what passed as cleaned, by some day laborers on the construction crew.

Russell hated that he'd been paired up with Michael, but he tried to make the best of the situation by not letting the psycho get behind him. Michael didn't really want to work with him either, but he hated Tye more than he did Russell, so it was okay as far as he was concerned. Richie was so far off his radar that he didn't show up in Michael's world at all. Russell thought it would be best to avoid eye contact with Michael, especially since the one-armed cop dropped him flat on his ass with one shot. Normally, anyone else that didn't fight back would be considered "punk'd out," but Russell was wise enough to know that Michael was no punk. He was biding his time and going to get his revenge soon. Everyone knew it, Kira and Williams most of all. Michael was a viper waiting to strike. The next several hours would be an interesting chess match between the treacherous black knight and the crippled king. Russell figured that checkmate would come before midnight, but at this point in the match it was anyone's game. Michael was tricky as well as tough. Smart too. The streets had educated him early, and he was an apt pupil in the art of brutality. As good a student as Michael was in the laws of the jungle, Williams was a tenured badass and had a slight edge over the young hothead. Russell didn't know it, but if it came down to it, there would never be a one-on-one match between the two. Williams would simply kill Michael; the tired cop did not want to tangle with the kid any more than he had to.

Michael grabbed a mop and bucket as Russell took a broom and started sweeping up. Michael was quiet after his run-in with Williams. Too quiet for Russell. A saying ran through Russell's mind. He couldn't remember it completely, but it had something to do with the quiet before the storm. As Russell watched, Michael silently mopped up the floor with measured strokes. He thought he saw gray storm clouds gathering in Michael's eyes.

Michael took the mop and swept a wide swath of wet trash into an empty storage room. He gently, quietly closed the door behind him. He waited to catch his breath; he had a fear of hyperventilating and he didn't want to do it now. He shoved the mop into a toilet that was cemented with filth and crud. The mop stuck in the old bowl. Angrily, he kicked out at the pipes behind the toilet in frustration. In one quick strike he broke the piping. His eyes began to water from the dirt in the air.

Dust started to fall onto his head from the ceiling as he heard footsteps on the floor above him. The heavy footsteps made the ceiling groan. Michael grabbed a long piece of pipe that he had kicked free from the toilet and starting swinging wildly at the ceiling above him.

"Hey! What the fuck? I'm working here!" he screamed as he smashed the pipe into the plaster, causing more dust and dirt to fall onto his head. The dust clung to the tears that smeared his face.

The footsteps stopped directly above him. Michael could feel an uneasiness start to swell up inside him. A fly swooped down from a hole in the ceiling and circled Michael's head, then took off as if it were on a reconnaissance mission. Michael looked up at the ceiling and waited. The footsteps hurried away until their sound was gone. Michael's breathing started to become heavy with anger.

Then a complete loss of control came over him. His body started to shake as if he had just been plunged into a bath of ice water. As much as his temperature seemed to drop on the outside, he was an inferno on the inside. Michael fumed as he thought of one thing: *Get that one-armed motherfucker!* He caught his breath and wiped away the dust that was stinging his eyes. He fixed his gaze on the hole above him. Whenever Michael felt himself becoming too frantic, he shut off everything else around him and just focused. It was a trick that he had developed at a young age.

Slowly, everything else started to become dark and hazy. Nothing else existed outside of his narrowed point of view. Sounds from outside the room became distant echoes. A slight humming started in the back of his mind, and he glared with a killer's intent at the large crack that marred the old drywall in front of him. He locked his eyes on the crack, the chalky white scar that gave way to flimsy wooden slats that looked like old ribs, and stared into the darkness between them. The cold darkness was where his mind now traveled. He thought back to the time when he was a different person. A better person. He saw himself at nine years old. He was on the track, trying some stretches. The other kids were running in place, doing calisthenics, warming up in ways Michael never knew how. He just mimicked the routine of some of the older boys, not knowing exactly what they were doing as they went through their pre-meet ritual.

Michael didn't really want to be in the race. It had been his mother's idea to put the boy into the event. His family had just moved up from Atlanta. Since they were new in the area, she thought it best for her son to try to fit in as soon as possible. To try to find friends, to find a place for himself before others found one for him. When she took Michael down to the park to see what type of after-school facilities it had to offer, her eyes fell on a sign-up sheet for children, ages nine through twelve, to compete in the park's annual summer Olympics. The Olympics were a series of events that the park employees were hosting so that kids could have a little fun before the summer ended and they had to return to school. The events were not meant to be strenuous or athletically challenging. They were a few races, some obstacle courses, and a relay to build the budding team spirit that coaches would be looking for in the new crop of kids going into middle school.

Michael's mother thought that this was just the thing her boy needed. She prayed it would would turn out to be a positive influence in his already troubled life. God knew he wasn't getting anything positive from his father. The only thing of quality that Michael inherited from his father's side was the cool blue eyes that sparkled brightly when the sun hit them. His mother loved to look into her son's pale eyes and imagine a life that wasn't tainted by the white trash gene pool his father had given his offspring. She always second-guessed herself and constantly wondered why she had ever hooked up with a man as foul as Johnny Montross. She knew right away why she had done it: Michael's father made her feel dirty, but dirty in a way that excited her. When she was younger, she had allowed herself to fall into a trap that she thought was love. Sex with Johnny had been hot, hard, and exhilarating. Until the time came when it became ugly and painful.

Johnny Montross was the bad boy that every schoolgirl dreamed about meeting. He was the one kid who looked like he was born to have a cigarette dangle from his sensuous lips. She remembered his pompadour that was as black as the leather jacket he wore and how tight and firm his body looked in a white T-shirt. If only he had stayed in that glorious state, the frozen image of the Southern-bred greaser. But Johnny's slicked black hair had receded to a stretch of scarred flesh, and the once muscular body now made size fifty-two pants tug at his waist. Not only had his body changed for the worse, but the man on the inside had deteriorated as well. In fact, the decay inside was far greater. Johnny Montross was bad all the way to his core and beyond. He was bad like his father and his father before him, and all the way back to those gray-coated rebels his family always toasted and cheered about.

Olivia Montross wanted better for her boy. Anything was a step up from the vile bloodline that coursed through her son's veins. The move from Atlanta was a good one for her. Here, they could make a new start, forget the past and all the bad baggage that had shackled itself to them. If her husband hadn't come along, things would probably have been better. She prayed that Johnny would find the move out west to his liking and not want to move back home. Back into the trailer with the other confederate-minded kin of his. Johnny had trouble finding work, although he rarely looked. Olivia was doing all right with her secretary's job—she could support herself and her son. It was going to be a challenge, but one she was willing to take, for Michael's sake. The farther she got him away from the Montross clan, the better chance he had of becoming a better human being. The only problem now was his father, an unrepentant obstacle of domestic abuse and racial intolerance that blamed the world and everyone with a skin color darker than his for his woes.

Olivia Montross watched from the stands as her lanky son stretched his legs in awkward positions. She didn't see Johnny around, which made her heart feel a little lighter. She loved her son so much. She had never known that she could love anyone so deeply. Olivia knew that there was no stronger love on earth than that of a mother for her child. At times, though, she felt that her love, her passion for her boy, was a bit strange—she was in love with everything her son was and everything that Johnny was not. Michael possessed the spark that had once been his father's. She prayed that the new city, school, and chance at life would help her son's confidence and stammer. It was bad enough being the new kid around, but being the new kid that stuttered and became nervous when others couldn't understand his deep Southern accent could be too much for any youngster to cope with.

Michael was signed up for the hundred-yard dash. He had never been in a race that had any type of official settings around it. He, like all kids growing up in the rural South, would run around the woods and forest until the tiredness in his young bones made his body sit down to rest under the coolness of a shady tree. But now he had to run quickly with a specific destination, something he had never done before. He had a finish in sight, a goal, which was something he didn't have back home. Back east he'd satisfied himself by running in circles until his head spun, his stomach lurched, and he'd have to dive onto the wet grass to cool off.

Michael had a nervous tick, a natural side effect for those with a speech impediment. It made him look like he was going into a seizure when all he had to do was answer with a simple yes or no. When the park counselor came up to him, he answered only with a respectful nod that didn't require too much effort. He was given his number, which his mother proudly pinned on the back of his shirt before she kissed him gently on his forehead. Her lips stayed on her son's flesh a second too long, and the consuming passion she had for him made her just want to hold him tightly and carry him away to a place where no one named Montross would ever be allowed. She forced herself to let him go and ran to the bleachers to get a good spot to watch. Her son followed the other boys to the starting line. At nine, he was the youngest in the race. One boy was ten, two were eleven, and the remaining three boys were twelve. Each boy seemed larger than Michael was, and he seemed to get lost in the lineup.

Olivia sat in the bleachers trying to blend in with the other parents. Her sunglasses were pressed tightly against her face against the extra foundation she had applied in hopes that it would help conceal the bruises around her eyes. He sole focus was on her son and his future.

When the man with the starter gun yelled, "Positions," Michael just followed what the other boys were doing, placing his fingers on the white line in front of him and squatting down. When the gun went off, the loud bang startled Michael. The others had already started the mad rush, flying down the long stretch of track. Michael regained himself and took off in pursuit. The kids in front of him seemed to speed farther and farther away from him, and he felt all alone, lagging behind them. He felt sure that every eye was on him, the little kid who couldn't keep up. He was the tall, funny-looking new kid who couldn't speak right. Michael felt the stare of every person sitting in the stands burning into the back of his neck, and he knew that the snickers were starting to form in everyone's mouth. *Hey, mumble mouth! Hey, retard, way to go.* He was waiting to hear those taunts again, the same painful chorus sung by a different choir. He couldn't bear to sit through that again. Not here, not in the new town, not when he had a chance to make everything right. Everything was supposed to be different, better even, in the new town.

His nervousness turned to energy, and untapped adrenaline pulsed through Michael's body. His legs, the lanky limbs that usually stumbled beneath his torso, suddenly started to churn like pistons. With each step he took he gained some of the ground that he needed to win, and he flew into the crowd of boys that were in front of him. He burst past the main group of boys with such speed that a few had to step aside in order not to be run over. Michael advanced to third place and was getting closer to the boy who held the second position. He could see the thin, long strand of crepe paper that was the finish line. Michael could almost taste his victory. His lungs started to burn, but in a good way, a way that made him feel like they were burning away his old life, the life that had clung to his insides like old, chipped paint. With each step banged against the dirt track, he ran farther away from Atlanta—away from his troubled past and into a brighter future.

His legs started to cramp, but he ignored the pain and passed the boy in front of him. The lone boy who was now ahead of Michael was a tall twelve-year-old, and he had a good lead on Michael. Michael used what was left of his reserve tank and caught up to him with about twenty yards to go. For a few seconds, the two were neck and neck, running side by side until Michael gained half a step. For an instant, Michael was in the lead. He was on his way to becoming a winner. For the first time in his life, he didn't mind the stares from the crowd because they wouldn't be laughing at him—they would be cheering for the champion. But fate would not be denied, and the older boy surged forward and passed Michael, just as they neared the finish line. When the boy's body broke the finish tape, Michael was so close behind him that the tape stuck to his sweating body. Michael kept running for a few paces, then stopped to watch the other boys finish up behind him. Each boy crossing the finish line shot Michael a look of "good race." Michael raised his head up in acknowledgment and felt his lungs start to fill with the warm afternoon air. He felt good. He had come in second place—the closest he had ever come to accomplishing anything on his own. He had run a good race, a damn good race, and he knew it. Now, no matter what happened after this, he knew that the jeers and taunts would be a little easier for him to swallow. He had come from last place in the race and ended up winning the second place ribbon, the only one he had ever owned. To him, it was the only validation of his worth as a human being.

He walked to the stands to find his mother and noticed a man lurking in the shadows of the bleachers. He recognized his father as the older man started walking toward him. Michael felt a bond starting to build, a feeling that he never had with his dad before. He hoped that the connection between him and his father would grow. He knew his dad had watched the race hidden away from the public so that if Michael had lost, he wouldn't have to see the pity on the faces of the other parents. Michael felt pride swelling up in his throat as his dad walked closer to him. *I didn't lose*, Michael thought to himself. *I didn't lose. He'll be proud of me now.*

"H . . . he . . . hey . . . D . . . D . . . Dad," the boy stuttered. "Did . . . did . . . you s . . . se . . . see me?"

Michael stopped in front of his father and smiled expectantly for the first time since the family had moved. He looked into his dad's eyes with a renewed confidence. Johnny Montross looked down at his son, the bearer of his family name, and hit him with a resounding backhanded slap across the face. The sound of the blow was so loud that every person in the park turned to see where the noise had come from.

The sting that seared into Michael's face was like a blacksmith's iron that burned straight to his heart. His eyes opened wide as the world around him stood still. It seemed as if the birds had stopped flying, the clouds had stopped moving, and the sun hung solidly in the air like a burning gold ball. Along with his father's beer breath and sweat reek, Michael sensed his father's rage.

"You lost to a nigger! A nigger! A son of mine losing to a fucking nigger! Ain't that a hoot? Boy, oh boy, I'm glad your grandpa is not alive to see this!" Johnny Montross bellowed out so loud that even the hard-of-hearing grandparents that had come to cheer on their grandkids looked over in complete disbelief at the open display of racism and abuse that Michael was subjected to.

Michael turned his head to see the boy who beat him. For the first time Michael noticed that the boy was different. That the boy was black hadn't meant a thing to Michael before the race had started; he was just some older kid who was a fast runner. After the race—after his father's reaction—Michael saw it differently. Now he didn't see his second place as a victory. The fact that Michael had lost was bad enough, but then he saw that it was worse than he had originally thought. He had lost to a *nigger*.

The slap was the beginning of the end for Michael.

It seared away any of the youthful innocence that was left in him. The slap stopped Michael's childhood and knocked him into his father's world, a world he was forever doomed to remain in.

Now he was filled with hate. He hated the boy who had beaten him. He hated his father. He hated his mother. He hated everyone that would ever come into his life. Most of all, though, Michael Montross hated himself.

His father looked down at his son in disgust and walked away. This would be one of the last times that Michael would see his father. At his father's wake, Michael spit on his face as the man lay in the open casket with his hands folded over his bloated belly.

As Michael's mother ran down from the stands to her son, her tears spilled down her eyes. The wet mascara that streaked her face made it look like the black lenses of her sunglasses were melting. She ran up and hugged her son and watched with a murderous rage as her husband walked away into the crowd of people that stepped away from the abusive big-mouthed bigot. When Olivia hugged Michael against her body, she could feel that the warmth that had previously radiated from her sweet little boy was gone. His body had turned cold. She leaned back to look into her son's face and saw the mark of Johnny's hand still glowing over most of his face. Michael stared straight into her eyes coldly. From that moment on, she knew that he was no longer her son; he was a complete stranger. She didn't recognize the boy who stood in front of her as the son she knew and loved. Suddenly, she recognized the malevolent look that gleamed in his eyes. She had seen it countless times before, when Michael's father would leer down at her when he was drunk enough to rape her before he passed out.

Michael had just become his father. The slap was the catalyst of the complete transformation of her son into the man she hated most in this world. Olivia tried to shake Michael, to push away any part of Johnny Montross that might be lingering in the boy, but it was to no avail. Johnny's soul had crept into her son, and nothing short of an exorcism could save her boy from following in the footsteps of the man who would end her life four years later.

As Michael looked at his mother coolly, he knew he had been marked. Tattooed with the Montross stain, like a branded calf into the herd of hate mongers. Even when the crimson color faded from his cheek, the Montross bigotry would continue to glow from the boy's face.

"Get your hands off me," were the first words that the new Michael spoke to her. Clear and precise, without a hint of stammer or unsteadiness in his voice. As well as ripping the soul out of his body, Johnny had slapped the stutter out of the boy. Michael walked away from his mother and the crowd that looked on with ashamed glances. He went into the woods behind the park to be alone.

Olivia watched as her son walked away. She wished there had been a cop around, someone to arrest her husband for murdering her son's character. She wished someone could help her find out who the imposter masquerading as her son was. From then on, she lost the passion she had for her son; the boy no longer existed.

• • •

Michael's head started to pound. His eyes had been fixated on the cracked wallboard for so long that a throbbing behind his eyes was starting to build and beat like war drums.

With a start, he realized that he wasn't at the park anymore. He wasn't running any more races. There would be no second-place ribbons for him now. He was stuck in this run-down hotel with nothing but a broken broom handle to protect him.

He felt the Montross stain start to glow on the side of his face again. For the second time in his life, he had been slapped and had done nothing about it. The shame he had always lived with and had been so careful to keep under control was inching out of its hiding place.

Christine pushed a long-handled broom on the second floor of the building. She didn't see anyone around, but she heard Zoë and Melissa bitching at each other outside in the hallway. Their voices slowly died away as they moved off. The sun had shifted in the sky, and the angle of its rays slanted in through the dirty windows. Christine looked at the skin on her arms. It seemed to glow in the late afternoon light. She thought about how vibrantly her sister's skin had shined after she had given her a bath. The way her sister's hair had smelled after she washed it and how it had felt in her hands when she combed it straight.

She pushed the thoughts of her sister out of her mind; there was no need for memories now. That was the past and she couldn't live in the past. She couldn't live with things that had happened already. She couldn't live with things she had no control over. She couldn't live with the dead.

She maneuvered the pile of trash until it filled a corner at the end of the hall and knocked the brush against the wall to shake a few pieces of paper from the worn hairs of the broom. She heard a muffled banging in the room across from her and stopped sweeping. Glancing in the hallway, she saw that the door to one of the rooms was partially open, so she walked closer to it to look inside. Her eyes made their way around the double-occupancy room and saw nothing but a series of strangely shaped shadows stuffed together. Christine entered the room, and before she was a foot inside, a long, slender arm reached out and gently wrapped itself around her mouth. Christine stiffened but quickly realized that if it had been Michael's, her neck would already have been snapped by now. She recognized Kira's touch as the girl stepped out of the shadows that converged in the corner of the room closest to the door.

"What the fuck? You scared the shit out of me," Christine said. She was angrier than she thought she would be.

"Sorry. Shhhhh. Don't be so loud. He might hear you," Kira said, looking over her shoulder.

Kira gently nudged the door and it closed with a soft click. She walked across the room and pulled aside the moth-eaten curtains, streaked with twenty years of grime. She opened the window with some effort and motioned Christine to come over and look. When she did, she saw the top of the tall glass skylight that covered most of the courtyard on the south side of the building. The courtyard looked like it was nothing but one big refuse heap. Trash from vagrants, junkies, and the homeless had been tossed over the tall wall that enclosed the courtyard, making it one big garbage dump.

"Nice view. This what you wanted me to see?" Christine asked as if she already knew what Kira's answer would be.

"This is the best way to get out of here," Kira replied.

"You think you're going to get out of here? Where? Through there? Hey, stupid. That's just the atrium they talked about. Even if you make it down there, you're still in the hotel," Christine replied, and she could feel some of her friend's energy start to drain from her.

"Shit," Kira mumbled. She walked over to the queen-size mattress that was pressed against the wall and fell back on it. Christine looked down at her and wondered where the fearless Kira that jumped up late one night six months ago and put a hell of beat down on three hard-ass *cholas* had gone. Her friend looked scared and small, like a sad kewpie doll sitting alone on an arcade shelf waiting for someone to win her and take her home. Christine sat next to Kira and pressed her back against the wall. Kira pulled out a pack of cigarettes and slipped one in her mouth. Her fingers fumbled for a lighter in her back pocket and she lit up. She took a long drag, then handed the smoke to her friend.

"Where did you get these?" Christine asked, taking in a lungful of gray smoke.

"Zoë lifted them off the bus driver today," Kira answered, tapping the button on Christine's jeans.

"And where did you get them?" Christine repeated the question.

"I lifted them off Zoë," Kira said with the innocence of a choirboy. Both girls were silent for a moment, then fell into snorting laughter.

When their laughter died into sweet smiles, Kira turned to face Christine, confidence renewed.

"I can't believe he's here. What the fuck were they thinking? How dumb is that Anders to fall for his bullshit?"

"She fell for all our bullshit," Christine countered, and Kira knew she was right.

They had all said what was expected of them when they were interviewed for this program. No one believed anything they said about being rehabilitated. Tell them what they want to hear, fill their heads with enough lies so they can't tell what the truth is anymore. Kids were natural liars, and they had honed their dishonesty on the inside. When several hundred troubled girls were housed together with no privacy, no private showers or bathroom, under the eyes of leering guards checking them out head to toe, a world is created in which lies and deception are the only two things that can keep a girl safe from unwanted stares.

"He's crazy. Like, fucking crazy. He's gonna kill me." Kira rose up on her knees and looked deep into Christine's eyes. "I don't want you around me anymore."

Stunned, the cigarette almost fell from Christine's mouth. Her heart skipped a beat.

"Why?" came out meekly from Christine's lips.

"I don't want you getting mixed up in this. I don't want you getting hurt. If he comes after me and you're there, he'll get you too. I know him; he's like that. And if he thinks you're protecting me, he'll get to you first.

119

If he knows I care for you, he'll hurt me by hurting you. I've seen him in action. He's no good."

Christine felt guilty. Earlier in the day she had self-ishly thought of ways of distancing herself from Kira before the shit hit the fan. Now Kira was here thinking not of herself, but of Christine's safety.

"I couldn't live with myself if something happened to you."

"Hey. Don't count me out so soon," Christine said. "Come on, let's get back to work."

They shared a sad smile that seemed to last forever.

The girls stood. Both took one last deep drag from the cigarette and held it down in their lungs. It was a silly game they used to play on the inside, each trying to outdo the other with the length of time they kept the smoky carcinogens in their lungs before exhaling. Kira crossed her eyes and tried to make Christine laugh. In response, Christine stuck out her tongue and touched the tip of her nose, and both of them broke out in laughter. Suddenly, Christine stopped laughing abruptly. Kira stiffened and slowly turned around. She felt a rush of reprieve wash over her when she saw that it wasn't Michael. Officer Williams stood in the open doorway. The relief quickly drained out of her when she realized that Williams had opened the door silently and had watched them break one of the rules. She regretted that Christine would get into trouble and that it was her fault.

Williams came over to Kira and placed his hand out, palm up. Kira looked at it blankly, then dropped the pack of cigarettes into it. He lifted the pack to his mouth and slid one of the cigarettes out between his lips. When he handed the pack back to her, he leaned into the girl with his cigarette leading the way.

He waited and looked at Kira expectantly.

She stood still with a blank stare on her face.

Christine nodded pointedly to the lighter that was in Kira's hand. As if she had just been shaken awake, Kira flicked the lighter open and watched as the orange flame shot up. Williams leaned in a bit closer to light his cigarette. He moved back and took a drag and walked toward the door. He looked back at the girls.

"Try not to burn the place down . . . again." He strolled out into the hallway and left them alone.

They looked at each other and laughed. For an enemy, he was better than most.

Tye approached Richie and led him into one of the empty rooms away from everyone else. He glanced around to make sure no prying eyes or ears were close by.

"Okay. What is it? What's this big surprise that's going to make me rich?" Tye demanded.

Richie tried to shush Tye, but he was angrily reminded that no one was around. Tye was getting impatient. His tolerance level was naturally low, and after his little run-in with Michael, he was ready for blood. Anyone's blood. Richie's would serve his purpose nicely if he didn't have something good to sell Tye on.

"Do you remember all that stuff about the hotel? The guy that built this place?" Richie asked.

"Yeah, so what?"

"The guy was loaded," Richie said, trying to whet Tye's appetite.

"And?"

"There've been lots of stories and rumors that he had a safe full of money hidden somewhere in this hotel," Richie said, trying to see how much of the story Tye was believing.

"A safe? Full of money? And where did you hear this?" Tye asked doubtfully.

"I got it off the Internet."

Tye rolled his eyes. *These great big plans for wealth are nothing but a computer geek's wet dream*, he thought.

"Gotta go," Tye said as he started to brush off Richie.

"No, wait! Listen, listen. I did a lot of research on this. When I found out they were sending us here for the weekend, I snuck onto a computer to see what I could find out about this place. I Googled the Blackwell Hotel and found out that it was on a bunch of these urban myths sites," Richie explained quickly.

"Go on."

"All these sites said the same thing. That people who used to work at this hotel knew for a fact that Blackwell had a hidden safe where he kept stacks of money."

"If these people knew that, why the fuck didn't they take the money?" Tye wanted to know.

"No one ever found it. And after the fire, people went to look for it and came up empty." Some of the conviction was starting to leave Richie's voice.

"Man, that's bullshit. No one ever found it. No shit, no one ever found it, 'cause there was nothing to find. I can't believe you wasted my motherfucking time on some lame-ass fairy-tale bullshit!" Tye angrily shot out. "What's next? Gonna buy some magic beans, dumb-ass?"

"Hold on. I downloaded the blueprints to this place. This gives us the layout of the building." Richie pulled out a computer printout and waved it in front of Tye.

"Your treasure map." The sarcasm dripped. "Man, if you found it, that means a million other people have come across the same fucking thing. What makes you so damn special?"

"A million other people aren't spending the weekend in this hotel, which has been off limits for years," Richie countered with such certainty that Tye was taken aback.

Maybe there's something to White Boy Richie's bullshit after all, Tye thought. He had nothing to do all weekend but clean, and that didn't sit too well with him.

"Okay. Suppose, and I mean a big motherfucking suppose, we find this safe. Then what?"

"Can you crack a safe?" Richie asked.

"I can open one as quick as I can open your momma's legs."

"My mother's a slut, so that's gotta be pretty fast," Richie replied.

Tye liked his comeback. Tye thought about his options. He didn't believe the story, but it was something to pass the time.

"Okay." Tye nodded. "Let's go huntin'."

"Not a word to anyone," Richie said.

"Not a fucking syllable," Tye confirmed as he watched a fly loop around Richie's head in a lazy circle.

As the boys left the room, they never noticed that within the darkness of the shadows in the corner of the room, something big was stirring. The flies started to swarm and fly back into the shadows, back to their master, who sat patiently in the darkness and plotted.

Christine washed the paintbrushes that she had used during the day in the deep metal sink in the large kitchen. The place was huge, and Christine had never seen a kitchen this big. The entire room seemed to be covered in cold stainless steel and rows of movable tables. Several large stoves were against the walls. The kitchen was cleaner than the rest of the hotel because day workers had already gone over most of it. The back door leading out was bolted shut, and the only ways into the kitchen were the swinging doors and the disused service elevator that served as a large dumb-waiter.

The sink was against the far wall and over it was a window that looked out into the atrium. Christine watched as the other kids walked out of the atrium, with Michael leading the way. She hated him. She would like nothing better than to see Michael gone. Dead wouldn't be bad, but gone was good enough.

The whole world is a miserable place to live in, she thought. Aside from Kira, she'd only had one person to share her sorrow with. Her little sister, Cecilla, who had died a long time ago, had been the sweetest thing in her life. Cissie had been the world to Christine. A different world, one of innocence, but that one ray of purity in her troubled life was gone. Christine didn't want to think about her little sister; it hurt her too much. When Cissie's face flashed in Christine's mind, it caused her heart to ache. She would go into a dark, brooding mood for days, a sullenness that made her sick. It was only when Kira, the screwy, troubled loner, had come into her life that some of the pain and loneliness subsided. It never went away, it just slowly sank beneath the surface, always there waiting to re-emerge once the memories started to come back.

"Cissie," Christine whispered silently, "I miss you, baby." She jammed the paintbrushes against the back of the sink and watched as the globs of white paint flowed off the bent bristles.

Williams walked in and saw Christine bent over the sink. He thought he saw the young girl talking to herself and didn't want to embarrass her, so he decided to make some noise as he approached.

Christine turned to see him walking toward her.

"I'm working," Christine said defensively.

"I didn't say anything." Williams held his hands up to show that he was not about to attack.

Williams watched Christine nervously scrub the brushes, knowing that his presence was upsetting her. He didn't want the girl to feel uneasy.

"I'm glad you were cleared for this project," he said.

"Are you now?" she replied sarcastically.

Williams knew the girl was hurting, so he cut her some slack. She was a tough kid, tougher than she had to be in a world she didn't want to be in, but she was still a kid. Williams saw a fragile vulnerability in her.

"I read your file," he said carefully, selecting how he would approach the subject of her crimes. "I know your story. Why you attacked your stepfather. What happened to your sister . . . You got a shitty deal."

"Shitty deal?" She turned to look at him, and hate burned in her deep brown eyes. "My baby sister was . . ." She stopped talking, the words stuck in her mouth. She didn't want to have to relive what happened to Cissie by recounting the terrible things that had been done to the little girl. The image of her stepfather, the man her *puta* of a mother brought into their home, burned in her memory. The pig that would sneak peeks at the girls while they were in the shower or walk in on them when they were changing for bed. Christine would never forget the day she came home from school and found him passed out on the couch. Her sister was crying, huddled in the closet in their bedroom. Christine stared at Cissie. What she saw were Cissie's eyes, reddened from crying, and bruises on her neck and shoulder. Then she saw the blood. There were red streaks that stained her sister's torn panties. At once, a black rage exploded in Christine's mind. Her world came crashing down when she saw the innocence in her sister's eyes flicker once and then die. Her little sister looked at her with a look of shame branded into her. Cissie's eyes accused Christine of neglect for not being there to protect her. They burned her with guilt as the tears welled up and she watched her sister as she cried.

Christine suddenly remembered her grandfather and the box of things he had brought with him from the old country. For some reason, the box—an old wooden cigar box with a picture of a lady painted on it—and all it held came back to Christine. The gold watch, the cigarette case, the lighter with the broken lid, and the straight-edge razor. Christine remembered the old man pretending to shave for her with the razor when she was a little girl. He had shown her how he'd cleaned the whiskers from his face when he was a young man back in Mexico. She remembered gently running her fingertip along the edge of the razor when he wasn't looking. She remembered the sharp pain and the thin red line that opened up on her flesh and how the blood quickly poured down her hand. She also remembered her grandfather's warning never to touch the blade again. The blade, the razor that sliced so deep and so quickly without any pressure, was off limits to her. Knowing this didn't stop her. The razor was in the box, and Christine knew where the box was.

As she held the razor in her hand, the ivory handle felt hot. She walked toward her stepfather, who still slumbered in his drunken stupor, a smug look plastered on his fat face. The blade shined in the afternoon sun, and the blood that spurted out was deep red. The scream that accompanied it was the music of retribution to Christine's ears.

Williams looked at Christine as she brushed her long black hair away from her face. She was a pretty girl, and she was blossoming into a beautiful woman. She would be one of those Latin beauties who had an Old World sadness in her large round eyes.

"For what it's worth, I think you did the right thing," he said.

Christine thought about what he'd said. *For what it's worth.* What was it worth to Christine? Her sister was gone; shame and guilt had forced her to run away. Her fear had led to panic, her naïveté caused her to trust the wrong person, and simple bad judgment had her step into the van that she never walked out of alive. Was it worth it for Christine? No. It wasn't. Nothing would bring her sister back, not prayers to the Virgin Mary that went unanswered, not hours of self-mutilation, not stealing or doing drugs. Not even cutting the swine that defiled Cissie had been worth it. Nothing filled the void that was in her soul like an all-consuming black hole that sucked every ounce of light out of her life and into a dark place deep inside of her. Not even the prospect of freedom was worth losing her sister.

Christine shook her head to get rid of the memories, and her long hair flew around. She watched as the memories seemed to pour down the drain with the last streaks of white paint from the brushes. Her past was over. Her sister was gone, and Christine could not afford to look back.

"You want to talk about shitty deals. Whose bright idea was it to stick Michael in the same project with Kira?" she said, coming back to the now.

"Whattaya mean?"

"What do I mean? I mean that Kira used to work for that fucking psycho on the streets. She did everything for that piece of shit and he repaid her by beating her ass. Those fucking scars she has are because of him!" she angrily stated as she shut off the water.

"I didn't know," he said, and that was the truth. He never would have allowed Michael in the program if he knew his past history with Kira. Although he didn't have the final say, Williams would have been adamant about keeping Montross out of the group.

"You didn't know? I should fucking hope not. But

what are you going to do about it? Kira testified against him. That is why he got sent up. If the cocksucker had been eighteen when they sentenced him, he'd be doing hard time, not a soft bid in Juvey. And definitely not in this fucking joke of a program."

Christine was right. Williams knew it. If Michael had been three months older when the presiding judge handed down the sentence, he'd be doing at least five years' hard time in prison. He got in right under the legal wire and received nothing more than a year at a youth facility for his crimes.

Now Williams had to watch Kira's back as well as his own all weekend.

"I'll deal with it," he reassured her. He didn't know how he'd do it—he just knew that he had to. It was the same hollow answer that Christine gave to Kira when she said she would protect her from Michael. Lip service, with nothing to back it up.

"Yeah, you go deal with it," she said as she gathered up all the brushes and started drying them with an old rag.

Williams turned and left the girl to finish her chores. He didn't want to upset her. He didn't know why he had approached her in the first place. He wasn't even mad at her—not for exploding at him, not for breaking the rules and smoking with her girlfriend, not for anything. Williams admired her from the moment he'd read her file. From the first time he saw that she did what he always dreamed of doing, he'd admired the girl. She took the law into her own hands. She wasn't a crazed vigilante or fanatic. She did what she had to do; she did the right thing. Christine made sure that her mother's new husband would not be putting his pecker where it didn't belong anymore. *Christine has more guts than most men*, he thought, *myself included. Not many sixteen-year-old girls could castrate a man and flush the offending member down the toilet.* He left the kitchen and headed back toward the lobby.

As Christine heard Williams exit the kitchen, she stared out the atrium-facing window. A darker portion of the far wall caught her eye. Thinking that it might be a way out of their prison, she vowed to find out if it was a viable option to use as an escape.

The monster watched the two boys talking quietly among the shadows. He saw their mouths move and heard their voices, but the words meant nothing to him. Money? Safe? What were these things? Were they things that the monster owned and had forgotten about? Were these strangers going to try to take them away from him? As the monster moved back into the darkness that wrapped itself warmly around him, the constant cloud of buzzing that circled his head grew louder. He had to protect his home. These strangers didn't belong here. This was the only place the monster knew as home. Wherever else he had dwelled before had long since been erased from his mind. His home, his refuge, was threatened. The monster became angry. The anger started to grow. Soon it would explode volcanically and would destroy everyone in the radius of his rage. He knew he had to wait. He had to bide his time and wait for the opportunity to strike. When he did . . . it would be bad for them.

6

DINNER WAS SERVED IN A THIN CARDBOARD BOX THAT
held a sandwich made of dry bread and a piece of meat
sliced so thin that it was almost transparent and a
smear of something that passed as a condiment. To go
with the gourmet fare, a generic bag of chips and a
piece of fruit more bruised than ripe were also in the
box. Each kid received his or her meal with a canned
soft drink. They weren't required to eat together, so
they headed their separate ways.

Richie and Tye walked into the massive atrium that
was located behind the back lobby. The first was
dreaming of wealth, the latter plotting treachery. Both
were lost in their own thoughts but noticed their surroundings.

The atrium was built as a living entity, attached to the
hotel only for the added stability that the building lent.
On its own, it would have stood high and proud, a

three-story structure with ornately curled steel for bones and beveled glass for the skin, which parceled out the rays of the sun so that the wilting heat of the day stayed out and nourishing radiance filtered into the living world growing inside. The walls on the inside of the atrium were once covered with rich vines that hung down like green leafy curtains, plush with flowers of all shapes and hues. Deep reds and vibrant purples mingled and danced among bright blotches of yellow and burnt orange. The scene resembled the delicate dabs of an impressionist's brush, the entire palette created out of a harmonious balance of petals and leaves.

A world had been created, an Eden within the heart of the city, made of concrete and stone. The primeval forest captured and cultivated was created for guests to retreat into and reflect upon. Now, after two decades of neglect, the atrium sat defeated and tired, its bones rusted and bent and its glass dirty. The life that once teemed and flourished inside it was nothing more than decay and rot. The once fertile womb that had been a paradise lay barren and broken. Guests no longer roamed through its beauty. Now strangers with hunger in their bellies and mistrust in their minds entered into its midst.

In the back of the atrium was a shattered glass doorway that opened up into the large pool area that had once been the favorite spot at the Blackwell for guests who liked to show a little flesh or take in a little skin. A high brick wall ran along the area, and dead vines now clung to the crumbling stone as if they were dried, brittle veins that once pulsated with life. The parts of the wall that were damaged were covered over with large boards, and a rusty halo of concertina wire ran along the top of the fence. It had been put up not too long after the fire, a sharp, painful barrier to keep trespassers out and visitors in. Along the inside of the brick wall, trash had accumulated so high in some places it almost reached the top of the wall.

The back of the Blackwell had been used as a dumping ground for years. Everyone in the area had seen fit to throw whatever trash the city did not pick up over the walls. Store managers with surplus to get rid of had stock boys come down and toss it onto the Blackwell land. Gas station owners who didn't want the hassle of recycling the old oil that had drained from the wrecks they picked up off the streets would back their trucks up to the wall and throw gallons of it over the wall, where it watered the ground with a thick, black viscous rain. Owners of third-hand furniture stores going out of business and not wanting to haul away the ratty sofas and trashed coffee tables chose to get rid of everything there instead of leaving them in their storefronts and letting some poor family pick over their leavings.

After several hot and humid summers the stench had grown so stifling that people who lived blocks away complained. It was then that the city decided to decorate the top of the wall with tangles of circular barbed wire, but the damage from the outside had already been done. Whole sections of the brick wall were layered with trash that had slowly decomposed into one massive mound of fetid refuse. No longer were individual pieces of garbage distinguishable. Everything grew as one all-encompassing and festering life-form that was part of the back area ecosystem.

In the middle of the walled area was a large, once ornate oval pool, now strewn with rubbish. A layer of murky stagnant water soured in the deepest part of the pool. This black water seemed to refuse to dry up like the rest of the pool had done long ago. Broken wooden lounge chairs were lined up poolside, while faded and torn cabanas sagged behind them.

Tye and Richie sat down on patio furniture close to a large fountain in the corner of the atrium. Almost all the water had evaporated; enough remained to maintain a smelly marshland filled with hatching mosquito eggs.

"You think if we find this thing, you can get it open?" Richie asked Tye again for about the fortieth time.

"Man, what the fuck have I been telling you? I can do it. I already said that it'll open easier than your momma's legs," Tye replied, examining his sandwich.

"But if you can't?" Richie whined louder.

"If I can't, then we come back with a motherfucking jackhammer and crack that bitch wide open. As long as we find it and know where it is, we'll be okay. Let me worry about poppin' that cherry. You best be worryin' that this black metal bitch be here in the first place. If I spend all night searching for something that never was, you gonna wish *you* never was."

"I told you, I did a lot of research. The fucking guy that built this place was into a load of weird shit," Richie countered, trying to gauge the sincerity of Tye's threats.

"What type of weird shit? I know a lot of fuckers

134

into kinky shit. Don't mean that their cribs are stuffed full of cash."

"This guy was whacked, man, I'm telling you. He had a bunch of different guys design this place, had all types of hidden passages and rooms built. He had lots of money, and not all of it was found after he died," Richie said with confidence.

"So? What makes you think all that cash is here? I know a couple of heavy-hitter dealers. Man, they got millions stashed in private banks down in the islands. How do you know this guy didn't have his money stashed somewhere else?"

"The last ten years of his life he never left this place. He became a recluse . . ."

"A what? What the fuck's a recluse?"

"It's like a nut that never goes out. But he had money. He had tons of cash and never left the penthouse floor in this place. He died trying to get out when the fire started. I'm telling you I did a lot of homework on this guy."

"How do you know he had the money here, though?" Tye asked as he started nibbling around the edge of his sandwich.

"He used to throw these wild, rad parties. Tons of women and drugs and shit like that," Richie said.

"Yeah, he had good taste—don't mean nothing," Tye answered as he took another bite.

"You think transactions like those were done by check?" Richie studied Tye's face for a response. "You wouldn't leave a paper trail, would you, no matter who you are. He must have paid all the women and the dealers straight up. The night the fire happened here, there was a big party going down. I read that a bunch of hookers were here that night. You know he must have paid their pimp a ton of money beforehand. I'm telling you this guy had to have a stash of cash handy for all his needs. Dig it?"

Tye laughed to himself. He found it amusing when white boys wanted to sound black, like they were down with the brown. It was as if it made them feel like they had some street cred to them. *Live in my skin for a day, motherfucker, and see how it is. Every white boy wants to be black, but no one wants to be a nigger,* Tye thought. "Okay. I can dig it. But if this thing is here, how come no one found it yet? If you know about it, then everyone's gonna know about it."

"This place was shut down after the fire. You heard the old lady. Nobody's been here," Richie assured him.

But the answer didn't sit well with Tye. *What if someone found the safe after all?* You wouldn't tell anyone. Why would you? What if one of the fire marshals or city inspectors came searching around after the fire, maybe he found it and he's sitting right now on some beach with a drink in his hand and a piece of ass on his lap? That was the risk that he took. No one would say a word if someone tossed a bundle of cold cash in your hands. So if someone else had found the safe that was supposed to exist, then the only way that Tye would find out was when he came upon the broken empty metal box. It was a goddamn urban myth, and Tye didn't believe in urban myths or neighborhood legends. He believed in the truth. The hard, harsh truth of the streets. As the truth stood now, he would be done serving his time in a few months and he'd be back on the outside without the funds he needed to reclaim leadership of his old gang. He needed for the safe to exist. He wished for its untapped bounty to bankroll his climb back up the ladder that led to the top of his world. He knew that the slimmest of slim chances of finding a safe as fabled as Atlantis was a better bet than his being able to win over any of his former allies without the cash to buy their loyalty.

Richie and Tye silenced their conversation as Michael walked into the atrium. Both fixed their eyes on the muscular teen and waited for the next unpredictable thing he would do. Michael walked up to Richie, took his can of soda, and brought it to his lips. Just before he drank from it he turned to them and sneered.

"Bitch. You didn't stick your tongue in it, did you?" Michael asked, holding back on the venom he usually laced with such comments. He had said it not to provoke a response from Tye, but because it was expected from someone like him.

The insult didn't register with Tye at all. He knew Michael was just trying to bait him into a verbal joust that would eventually get heated and probably turn into a physical confrontation. Tye needed his mind to be focused on the job he had ahead of him, not the lunatic standing beside him. Richie tried to protest the theft of his soda, but it was too late, since Michael had already taken a big swig of it.

Michael let out a big burp and handed the soda back to its rightful owner.

"Only kiddin,' man," Michael said, wiping his hand across his mouth.

"Keep it," Richie offered.

Michael sat down next to Richie. Richie felt uneasy with someone who he knew could inflict great damage to him, unprovoked.

A few minutes later, Russell and Melissa walked in. They saw the three boys at the fountain's edge and went to sit at an old, rusted wrought-iron bench that had turned a colorful mix of amber and brown. As Russell pulled back an iron seat to offer it to Melissa, its legs scraped against the slate floor. She sat facing the three boys. Russell sat next to her. Behind them, Zoe entered and settled herself at an empty table. She pushed her food away with disgust.

When Kira and Christine walked in, Kira stopped at the threshold when she saw Michael sitting with the others. Michael tilted his head with a slight nod indicating civility or, rather, the pretense that it was being offered. He knew he couldn't do anything to her while the others were around. He wouldn't risk being foolish at this point. He would wait to get her but she wanted to see if she could gauge the level of severity he would come after her with. The more coolly cordial he was, the worse it would be for her. She was aware that if he pretended that he didn't hold any grudges against her, she was as good as dead. Christine gently nudged Kira toward the table where Russell and Melissa were sitting.

When everyone was seated, they exchanged the same look of complete misery at being stuck in the same place. An uneasy truce sprang up among them; the incidents on the bus among Michael, Melissa, and

Tye were forgotten temporarily. Whatever problem Michael had with Kira was put on the back burner, still simmering. The heat would be turned up and focused on two new enemies that had to be dealt with, and quickly. The first was the one-armed cop and the second a more formidable opponent, boredom. No greater enemy threatened the kids' time at the hotel than boredom. Its mind-numbing grasp was slowly starting to smother them. Soon they would all suffocate under it. They knew something had to be done.

"This sucks," Russell commented for everyone. "This is better than spending the time in Juvey *how?*"

"Supposed to build character," Zoë answered wryly.

"All it's building is calluses on my hands," Richie complained.

"Poor baby," Tye chided. "Maybe now you realize your hands can be used for something else than fingering the keyboard on your computer . . . or your mother."

"His hand is good for this, I bet," Michael said, doing the universal jerk-off gesture. Everyone smiled at Richie's discomfort.

"And what about the prick with one hand?" Tye said. Almost as if he'd been slapped again, Michael's cheek started to sting.

"Must be hard to jerk off with your left hand if you're a righty," Russell said.

"I thought you would have killed that motherfucker dead today after he bitch-slapped you silly," Tye said to Michael.

Everyone waited for Michael's anger to explode, but

he knew the rules of neutrality and let the comment pass without reaction.

"But I never knew you was smart," Tye continued. "A dumb motherfucker would have been right back up in that white cocksucker's face poundin' the daylights out of him and on their way to a second-degree assault bid now. But a smart motherfucker . . . a smart, mean motherfucker would wait, wait till no one was around. . . . Then he'd get that guy good."

Michael lowered his head and smiled. He lifted the soda can in Tye's direction and saluted. "To all the mean, smart motherfuckers in the world."

Michael's casual reaction proved Tye's theory. Kira knew him well—Michael was one mean, smart motherfucker. No façade could hide the viper that was coiled tight and waiting to strike.

"I don't know how much more of this cleaning shit I can do," Russell complained.

"I say we burn the fucking place down again. That will clean it out," Zoë said as her eyes explored the atrium. Most of the kids nodded in support of Zoë's arsonistic approach to their problem.

"The first Friday fucking night on the outside and we're stuck in this place," Michael said. The rest of the kids were all surprised that they agreed with his complaint.

Everyone had their own ideas of how they would spend the night: Tye and Richie would go on a treasure hunt that they hoped would bear riches. Russell hoped to find a place to be alone with Melissa. He wanted to work off some of the frustration from the last six months of captivity, while Melissa was wondering what it would be like if Russell helped her work out some of the frustration that was growing in her own loins. Kira wished to be somewhere far away from Michael. Michael wished to kill everyone in the hotel before the night was through.

"This place gives me the creeps," Melissa said. "Feels like someone's always watching me."

The same sense of eeriness was felt by everyone else, but no one wanted to back up Melissa's unnerving observation. Somehow they all knew something was not right in this place. They had all been on the inside. Sooner or later, no matter how naïve you are, you pick up on certain things from your time there. Each place has a feel, a vibe to it, and the Blackwell Hotel had one hell of an uneasy one.

"Fucking place is full of goddamn flies, too," Zoë added as she sniffed her sandwich before dropping it back into the box without tasting it.

That was something else that creeped the kids out—the flies. They seemed to show up at different times and places in the hotel, always accompanied by a smell that nobody could quite place. Christine hated the flies most of all. She hated filth and vermin. Anything that was unclean made Christine uneasy. The entire hotel was not just littered with trash and garbage, it was also filthy. She sensed that it was unclean in another way, a deeper way that she didn't know how to explain. To her, the entire building was evil. She felt that the very essence of the hotel was evil—it wasn't just a building designed to house guests and cater to their whims. There was something more diabolical about the purpose and nature of the place, and although she couldn't convey her feelings to anyone else, she was completely in tune with why the hotel existed in the first place. She had read the hotel's secrets the first time she had walked within its walls. She had imagined all the things that had happened in the rooms above. The same things that happened on the streets she walked on had happened here. They might have happened with clean sheets and room service here, but the nature of the Blackwell was as devious as any cold, hard street she had lived on, maybe even more so.

Melissa dropped her sandwich with utter disgust. "Fucking imbeciles. I told them I was a vegan. Look what they give me." She pushed her boxed meal away angrily.

"Vegan? What the fuck is that?" Tye asked.

"Girl don't like meat," Michael answered.

"I will not eat any living thing," Melissa stated proudly.

"That's too bad, there are a few living things around here I wouldn't mind eating," Tye said as he smiled over at Kira and Christine. Neither girl took offense at his remark, and they caught themselves smiling back at him.

Tye could be charming and disarming with his humor, and this was the time to make sure that everyone was on the same page. Without knowing it, the group needed unity. Although each kid had his or her own agenda and couldn't care less what the others were up to, they needed to bond. They needed to stand strong for now and face the miserable weekend that was shaping up in front of them.

"What the fuck is that cop's problem anyway?" Russell asked.

"Besides being a flaming asshole?" Michael countered sarcastically.

"I mean, if I lost my arm, there is no way in hell that I'm not going to be living high on disability somewhere out on a sunny beach. Why get stuck here with us for the weekend? Man, I can think of a million other places I'd rather be than here," Russell finished.

Christine thought about Williams. She realized that he was tough enough. She knew a lot of hard cases on the streets and on the inside, and she could tell that he was one of the hardest men she'd come across, but there was something else about him. There was something besides the cold, uncaring exterior that she was familiar with on cops, guards, and corrections officers. He had a hurt to him, an ache that ran inside of him deeply. It wasn't just the fact that he'd lost an arm; it went deeper than that. Something inside of him had been hacked away, severed and torn out.

Christine knew that the missing arm was only the flesh wound that was the counterpart to the damage that was inside of him. He could have tossed her and Kira back to Juvey if he'd wanted to for smoking, but he hadn't. He didn't try to win the girls' trust or friendship; he didn't want that. What he did was telling the girls that there are rules and then there are Williams's Rules, which were the only ones that mattered. One of the major ones was: Don't fuck up. She knew he didn't care about smoking, drinking, or any other petty shit that the kids were already doing behind his back. The one thing that he didn't want was the kids to think they could get away with trying to run the show. Christine could tell that Williams was the type of guy who knew what was going on. The kids had their own world to live in and everyone else had theirs, and Williams's world was neither. He was the type of guy who didn't give two shits about the trivial stuff in life. By the looks of him, he had seen some pretty rough stuff in his day, so copping a few smokes or fucking around didn't mean much to him, as long as you didn't think you could get the better of him. She wasn't going to try. She just wanted to get this weekend and everything to do with it over and out of her life.

"Man, I cannot spend my first Friday night on the outside trapped in this fucking place. . . . No way. We have to do something," Russell said.

The kids all thought about it, about what there was to do and where to do it.

Melissa looked out into the pool area and wondered what it had been like years ago, what kind of sounds there were, and what people who sat and bathed in the sun's basking glow were like. She wondered what type of bathing suits the women wore, which songs played over the radios that had been scattered around the poolside. What the cool blue waters felt like after diving in when you were hot and tired from the sun's rays. *It must have been a magnificent place at one time. Now this place is a dump, a sad and run-down dump that was trying to get its last hurrah.* As she looked around at the fused trash that formed a barricade along the inside of the wall, she saw something moving among the long shadows. Melissa stood up and walked closer to the shattered glass door to get a better look. The cool, smelly shadows allowed a dog to walk out. Instantly, Melissa's heart was touched as she watched the poor, frightened creature walk gingerly around the lip of the large oval pool. She grabbed her box of dinner and headed out to the pool area. The dog carefully made his way around the edge of the pool, looking over to see if anything worth eating had fallen into the empty area. Melissa stood across from the dog, a gray and brown mongrel whose ribs showed through a thin layer of matted and dirty fur. The dog sat and stared at Melissa with suspicious eyes. Melissa smiled at the poor animal and started to talk to it in calming tones.

"Hey, boy. Hey. You must be hungry. You hungry, fella? Here you go, boy," Melissa cooed as she opened up her uneaten meal and unwrapped her sandwich.

Melissa started to walk around the pool toward the dog, whose naturally distrustful instincts were temporarily overrun by its instinct for survival as it sniffed the air where Melissa was waving her sandwich. The dog's eyes widened and its stomach growled as Melissa neared the ravenous animal. The girl was a few yards away from the dog when the other kids came out to watch her. Christine, who never really cared for Melissa, thought this was the most unselfish act she had seen in a long time. Russell figured that if a hungry dog got Melissa all worked up, he was going to have his way with her with a string of sad abuse stories that he had had to endure as a child. He was already inventing the lie of an evil stepmother. He continued to formulate as Melissa got close to the dog.

Melissa bent down. Her sandwich was inches from the mongrel's face. The dog sniffed and decided that the offering was worth the risk when a crashing metallic bang sounded out in front of him. An explosion of warm soda soaked both the dog and Melissa. Everyone turned to see that Michael had just tossed his can of soda, with pinpoint accuracy, inches in front of the dog. When the can exploded, the dog took off in a whimpering run into the long shadows of trash that clung to the brick wall.

At once everyone turned on Michael with a defiant chorus of obscenities.

"You stupid motherfucker!"

"Ignorant cocksucker!"

"Fucking jerk-off!"

"Shithead white trash racist cracker!"

"Goddamn fucking asshole!"

"Piece of garbage!"

Michael stepped back and was actually surprised at the outburst of hostility thrown at him.

"Whoa, whoa, whoa! Hold on! Hold the fuck on, right now. What the fuck is wrong with you people? Did you ever hear of rabies? That dog probably had fucking rabies. You want to get bit and get infected, go right ahead and be my guest," Michael said defensively.

He knew he'd fucked up. He didn't even know why he had thrown the can of soda in the first place. He had felt the same pity as Melissa had for the poor dog when he'd seen it, which was one of the reasons Michael didn't want the creature around. Anything that could cloud Michael's judgment or his well-practiced mean streak couldn't be allowed to be around. He didn't want to hurt the dog, but he knew he couldn't help the creature either. He was afraid of actually showing concern and affection for the dog. To show the others that he had compassion for anything, even a poor stray, was a sign of weakness, and he couldn't afford to show weakness to anyone. Not Tye, not Christine, and especially not Kira. He had felt remorse, something he rarely felt anymore, as soon as the can had left his fingers. It was an unfamiliar feeling to him, one he didn't want to feel again, so he quickly hardened himself to defend his cruel act.

The group walked away from Michael and back into the atrium. Melissa gently tossed her sandwich to where the dog had fled and headed back to the atrium herself. She walked past Michael without even giving him a second look, but the feeling of loathing she had for him raged so strongly that his skin felt like it was burning her as she brushed by.

Kira turned to Christine and gave her a look that said, "See, I told you. He's fucking crazy."

The other kids hadn't felt like eating in the first place, and their appetites were not any better after Michael's cruel outburst against the dog. Michael walked into the atrium and felt everyone's eyes boring into him. He didn't want to be in this position. He had relished the role of playing the villain, but he had stepped over that line and now was considered a punk for scaring the dog away. They didn't have to say it, but that was what they were thinking. Michael normally didn't care what people thought of him, but he didn't want the others to distance themselves from him too soon, not before he had a chance to get his revenge. Not before he had a chance to get at Tye, the cop, and Kira. He needed to do damage control, and he needed to do it quickly so that the wall of resistance that was between him and the others wouldn't be too insurmountable later.

"Hey, I fucked up. What can I say? I thought she was gonna get bit," Michael said to the group. When he heard his voice, he realized how contrite he sounded without trying to force it. The others realized that Michael, in his own fucked-up, twisted way, was trying to apologize for his deed. Without coming out and asking for absolution, this was the closest thing to an apology he had ever given. The kids knew that they would never hear anything like this from him again.

Michael looked around. Carefully, he made his next move. He pulled out a baggie of pot from his trousers and let it dangle out before him. "How about a little piece offering? Whattaya say we smoke some of this shit up later on?"

Surprise went through the others as Michael made his offer. No one thought he would be the one wanting to try to form any bonds of unity after his attempt to intimidate Miss Anders had backfired earlier in the day. Yet there he was holding a bag of weed that could get him tossed out of the hotel and back into Juvey, and probably county, if the one-armed cop caught him.

"Motherfucker. Where'dja get that?" Tye said as he watched the baggie's plastic glow with the afternoon rays that streamed in from the broken glass panels above them.

"I have my ways." Michael beamed proudly. And he did. If you were smart and connected enough, you could smuggle, sneak, and hide almost anything on the inside. Weapons, drugs, money, anything of value could be bartered and traded on the inside. What most people didn't know was that Juvenile Hall was actually a finishing school for the Big House. Every larcenous trick and sneaky secret they learned in Juvey would come in handy when they went to prison and faced hard time. What Michael was most happy about was that the one-armed cop hadn't searched them as thoroughly as he'd wanted to at the beginning of the day. That reprieve had given Michael ample time to find a place to stash the stuff and pull it out now. Sneaking it in and out of Juvey wasn't a problem; it was trying to keep it hidden from Williams that was difficult. With the help of that fool, Miss Gayne, Michael had succeed in smuggling in contraband that would have gotten them all thrown out for good.

"I say after lights out we throw a little party for ourselves," Michael tempted the others as he waved the baggie of pot over them.

"Yeah, but where? We get caught, we're fucked royally," Russell reminded everyone.

"Up there," Michael said as he nodded toward the top of the hotel. "The penthouse."

"You all heard what's-her-face. The guy that owned this place was one really wild fucker. I bet that there's some wild shit still up there," Michael coerced.

"Maybe there's a bar up there," Zoë chimed in, getting excited at the possibility of some excitement coming her way.

"Sounds cool. I wouldn't mind going up there and seeing how the other half used to live," Russell said as he looked over at Melissa, who had a nice shade of curious red blooming in her cheeks.

Tye glanced at Richie. Both boys knew they wouldn't

be part of Michael's party, but neither wanted to say so just yet. They didn't want any suspicion cast their way, so they both nodded in agreement with the rest of the group.

"Then it's settled. After lights out, we'll hook up and head there." Michael was careful not to make it sound like a command, more like a request asked in earnest.

Kira shot Christine a disinterested look. "I want to get out of these clothes and take a shower."

She walked out of the atrium, and the others watched her go until she was lost in the darkness of the back foyer.

Michael shoved the pot back in his trousers and left the atrium, a sense of smug satisfaction coming over him. The dog incident was behind him, and the others would now go along with him when he ventured upstairs. All he needed was to get Kira to join them. Somehow he had to figure out how to get her up there with the others. He knew she feared him too much to take him up on his invitation. She would see through any offer of clemency he pretended to grant her. He wanted her upstairs, far away from everyone's eyes, so that when she fell to the ground—with some assistance from him—her death would look like an accident. He was mad at himself for coming on too strong when he'd first seen her today on the bus sitting next to that spic she had hooked up with. He had planned on being cooler when he saw her again, but his temper and attitude had conspired against him and gotten the better of him. Instead of lulling Kira into a false sense of security, then getting her when her guard was down, he had reacted foolishly and in haste. He had said things and acted in such an aggressive manner that she had put her defenses up. Now it would be almost impossible to convince her that he meant no harm to her. He wondered why he acted the way he did at times. Why today, the day he needed to be cooler than he had ever been, he had acted so stupid when he'd seen Kira. The one thing Michael never thought about, the one emotion he never encountered, came and slapped him across the face just as sharply as Williams's backhander. He would never recognize it for what it was: jealousy. Michael was jealous of Christine. He was jealous that Kira had found protection. And it bothered Michael to think that the girl had ratted him out. And now, the one person who had been closest to him in the last ten years was being safeguarded by someone else. A girl to boot. This didn't sit well with Michael's already beleaguered ego.

"Fuck her," he said to himself as he thought about what the evening had in store for him.

Christine started off, ignoring the rest of the group. She looked for the dark streak in the wall she had glimpsed from the kitchen window earlier. As she had hoped, it turned out to be a crack in the wall. Almost nonchalantly, she leaned closer to determine how big it was.

Kira was in one of the rooms assigned to the girls. It was outdated and musty, but still cleaner than Juvey, and bigger than she had imagined. The girls shared two connecting suites, with the doors between the rooms removed. Privacy wasn't total, but it was a hell of a lot better than where they'd just come from. Zoë and

Melissa took the room with the two single beds. The other room had a twin-size bed pushed into it, leaving only a few inches between it and the queen-size bed that was already occupying the small space. The mattresses were fairly new, probably brought in from Goodwill sometime in the prior week. The sheets were clean and didn't have the smell of sweat and dirt that couldn't be washed out that they were used to on the inside.

Kira went into the bathroom, which had been cleaned up somewhat for their arrival. It was the biggest bathroom she had ever been in. The black marble sink, although cracked in certain places, was still beautiful and cool to the touch, even under the fine layer of dust that had settled back over it after it was cleaned. The tile floor had an intricate mosaic design that matched the one on the wall. The room had a shower/tub combination in the corner next to the toilet. Kira kneeled next to the tub and ran her finger along the bottom of it. A little grit stuck to her fingertip, but the tub was in better condition than she had hoped for. When she turned on the tarnished spigot, the faucet sputtered and the sound of water pulsing through newly replaced pipes rattled upward. A stream of dirty brown water shot out and splattered against the bottom of the tub. Kira ran the water until it turned clear and then scrubbed down the tub with some dirty clothes. It took her fifteen minutes, but she cleaned the large tub as best she could and washed away all the filth that might have been hiding in it. She thought she could use a bit of relaxation, and a hot bath beckoned.

Kira noticed that the light switches had dimmers on them, so she turned the knob until the room darkened and the three lightbulbs over the sink softly died down so that only the slightest speck of light glowed weakly from within. The atmosphere of the room softened as the lighting dimmed.

Kira took off her sneakers and socks. Her T-shirt and pants followed before she stepped out of her panties. Her young body was battle-scarred and covered in tattoos, a colorful tribute to her harsh existence. Religious symbols decorated her skin; her back was etched in bright defiant imagery. The crosses and angels that flowed over her back looked haphazardly placed, but like the tattoos that covered her wrists, they served to hide the scars that were burned and branded into her soft flesh. For every wound she received in the battle to stay alive she awarded herself a colorful medal of honor to conceal it. The campaigns she had survived had made her a hardened veteran of the streets by the time she was sixteen.

She looked at her pale, naked body in the mirror, thinking that the lack of light made her look scared and anemic. She was hairless from the head down, and like most girls, she hated her body. She thought she looked too tomboyish and unattractive, but it didn't matter what she thought. Chrstine said that she loved the way Kira was, and would whisper words of love to her when they were alone after lights out. She stood staring at her reflection until her image was blurred out of focus and there was nothing more than an unfamiliar specter looking back at herself. Kira ran her fingers over the tempting soapy water that lay still beneath her. She couldn't remember the last time she had had a bath. She could not conjure up a memory of having such an extravagant way of washing herself. On the inside, you had your daily showers and you tended to make those as quick as possible unless you were the property of one of the girl gangs and your job was to wash down and clean up the members. Showering with twenty or thirty other girls in close quarters was rough, no matter what you preferred. Too many people is just too many people. And those few seconds you had your eyes closed to wash the shampoo from your hair was just enough time for someone to grab a quick feel off of you. Many girls not affiliated with any of the gangs would shower together just so someone could stand watch for the rest when it came time to clear the soap from their hair and eyes. When she was on the inside, Kira felt dirty even when she was getting clean.

Kira slipped her foot into the hot water and let the sensation of heat travel up her body. She placed the other in and slowly moved herself under the shower head, letting the backs of her thighs and rear slowly get used to the steaming temperature of the water. She took a bar of soap and washed her body, starting at her feet and working her way up calves, thighs, between her legs, and over her belly as if she could wash the day away. Kira scrubbed her torso under her arms and behind her neck with a soapy cloth with such force that it almost felt like she was trying to scrape off the tattoos that decorated her.

Sweat beaded up on her forehead, so she poured water over her face. She felt her scalp tingle as her hair clung to her head. She ran the cloth over her face and scrubbed her features until they glowed pink and fresh. When she was done, when she felt that she had removed a level of strata that had covered her with sin and she had washed down to another layer of herself that was unsoiled, she leaned against the wall of the tub and let the hot water guide her down a river of stillness. Her eyes closed and her mind drifted off to a faraway place. She felt like she was in a womb of warm water that shielded her from accusatory stares and cruel eyes.

Kira quickly found herself traveling into that world that lay between the land of waking and the realm of sleep, those funny little seconds when her brain didn't know if it was thinking or dreaming, and strange and fanciful thoughts, vivid yet ethereal, were projected to the parts of her mind not quite blanketed by unconsciousness.

In that peaceful dreamy state, she dreamt about a lake, a park. A place where the grass was green and smelled fresh from the morning dew that was clinging to its blades. There was a blanket, white and wide, that she lay upon. Looking up, she admired the vast, clean blueness above her and watched as frosty, thick clouds moved slowly across the sky. She imagined the clouds growing and stretching into whatever shapes they wished. They created a menagerie of snowlike creatures that lived and played in a world of soft azure. A feeling of happiness and tranquility came over her, two feelings that she had never known when she was awake, but here, on the borderline between wishes and dreams, she felt safe.

Slowly, the colorful sky with the harmless clouds hanging above them started to change. Winds rippled across the horizon, and the playful creatures that the puffy white clouds had created started to stretch and blend as gales swept down from the north. The clouds morphed into obscene gray shapes that filled the air above her. The sound of rain forming in the bellies of the clouds started to grow and resonated loudly throughout the land. The grayness merged into a darkness that burned across the sky like black smoke billowing out of a forest of hot smokestacks. Fear started to swallow Kira. She turned and found that the white sheet she had been lying upon was now an old mattress, bobbing up and down, in an endless, angry sea. Waves threatened to crash over her as their skeletal white crests pointed down at her with malice and menace. The sounds of the ocean bottom tearing asunder and swallowing the sea whole roared in Kira's mind as she fell out of that world and emerged into reality, where she was shivering in a bathtub with pruned fingers. Her lips were tinged blue, and there was a deep droning in her ears. She did not know how long she had been asleep, if one could call it that. She knew she hadn't been awake. She must have been out for a while because the warmth that had enveloped her when she had first slid into the hot water had all but vanished.

The hum in her ears grew and raced around her head until her eyes caught the source of the commotion. A fly landed on the tiled wall next to her. She looked at the filthy thing, its body fat and ripe with disease, and slapped her palm against the wall, flattening the insect before it could fly off and torment her any more. She wiped the slimy remains on the outside of the tub and sat in the cool water, wondering what time of night it was.

She sat gazing at the tiles that surrounded her and the bloody streak that was all that was left of the fly. She stared deeply into the wall.

The wall stared back.

Kira's brain needed a minute to recalibrate. What she was seeing wasn't real. It couldn't be. Through a long crack in the tiles, an eye stared out at her. Kira shook her head, closed her eyes, and leaned closer to the wall. When she opened her eyes to look again, it was still there. It looked large and sickly and white, like a giant shell-less egg that was peppered with black specs where a pupil should have been. The thing rolled up and down in the narrow crack, scrutinizing every inch of Kira's body and vulnerability. Even in the murkiness of the dim bathroom, the eye seemed to glow and radiate with an unnatural luster.

Kira backed out of the tub and slid ass-first on the tiled floor. She fumbled for a towel and tried to cover herself, to hide from the unknown eye that studied her with a microscope's intensity. Her feet slipped as she went to turn around and the towel dropped. She made a desperate attempt to grab it before it fell to the floor. Kira had always been shy, but she had learned that she couldn't afford to be timid when she was doing time or living on the street. People are going to see you naked, stripped down and baring it all to the world. Modesty went with humility if you wanted to eat. Exposing her flesh was something she didn't want to do, but it was something she had to do at times. The stares and glares she received from the pervs and creeps were a little more tolerable with something in your stomach. But the thing that looked out at her was different; the pale, large orb wasn't just staring at Kira, it was looking right into her. Straight down where she hid all her secrets and memories. The eye peered deep into her, to places she'd never known existed. A chill started to grow in her belly and coolly worked its way outward until her body started to shake. As she turned to leave, she suddenly stopped. The fear of the eye lurking behind the wall was replaced with the terror of death when she saw Michael walking into the bathroom.

Michael's eyes widened, and he smiled at Kira's nakedness.

"Nice tits," he said as he continued his stroll into the room and backed her against the sink.

She tried to cover herself with the towel, but the now-wet material wouldn't contour to her modesty. She stood in front of him awkwardly, trying to move it up and down her body. She didn't know why she was ashamed to be seen naked by Michael. Of all people, he knew her body better than anyone else. Many of the scars and gouges that had been carved into her body had come compliments of him. Now he was here to put the finishing touches on her.

"What are you doing here?" was the only thing she could muster out of her mouth. She knew the answer already and didn't really want to hear his response. She only hoped that he would be done as quickly as possible, as swiftly as she knew he could.

With an alley cat's sadistic glee, he teased the trapped girl who stood cowering and shivering before him.

"What am I doing here? I'm enjoying the show. You always did like performing for me when we were alone," he taunted. It made her think of all the times she had been debased and humiliated for his pleasure. She couldn't have known it, but Michael's pleasures had been much like Langley Blackwell's.

Kira felt the blood starting to drain out of her legs. Soon they would be rubbery and unable to hold her up, but she didn't want to go down without any type of a fight. In a last irrational move of desperation, she called out angrily.

"Fuck you!" She punctuated her remark by reaching out and slapping Michael across the face.

Her slap wasn't as hard as his father's or as sharp as Williams's, but the feeble attempt at defiance stung worse than the two blows together. Instead of throwing gasoline on the fire that was already burning brightly inside of him, her slap knocked some of the rage back into check. He laughed, but the sound came out as a stilted giggle. The tension that swelled through his veins started to subside a bit. He was playing with her, and he didn't want the game to end before it got interesting.

Kira sensed his plan and knew that if he had wanted to kill her, she would already have been lying on the floor with her neck twisted around or her head submerged under the water in the tub. He was going to do it at his own pace; to him, the chase was better than the catch. Kira knew that when it came to giving chase, Michael Montross was in for the long haul.

"Get out!" Kira screamed. It sounded more like a threat than a plea. The high tone of her voice surprised even her. *If he is not going to kill me, then he could get the hell out*, she fumed.

"Shut your goddamned mouth," he spit out. He had his hand around her neck before she could even see the blur that was his arm shooting up toward her. His fingers tightened and her soft Adam's apple started to get pressed to the back of her throat. He applied just enough pressure to let the smallest amount of air into her lungs with the greatest measure of fear.

When Kira's hands flew up to pull his grip away from her neck, Michael ignored the feeble fist that caught him on the tip of the jaw. His face neared Kira's, and she felt like her bladder would burst any second. A bright light flashed in Kira's eyes. For an instant, she thought it was the fabled white light people saw when their lives finally came to an end. It took her a second longer to realize that someone had turned the dimmer knob all the way up.

"Let her go!!" Christine's shout rang in Kira's ears as she and Michael turned to see her standing in the doorway with a box cutter in her hand.

Michael raised his arm a fraction of an inch, just enough to have Kira on her tiptoes as his hand covered her thin neck. He locked eyes with Christine and read her fear instantly. He knew she wasn't ready for a fist-fight because if she were, she would have struck him by now. He didn't want to provoke the girl any more than he had to. To have to attack her now would be to act out of haste. His plans for full-scale payback would have to be altered. At this late stage of the game, Michael didn't want to go back to the revenge drawing board.

He loosened his grip and Kira slid down, catching herself on the sink. Air rushed into her lungs, and it sounded like she was drowning on land. Michael's mouth stretched into a smile that seemed to cover the width of his face. He opened his hands and strolled with fingers spread apart and his palms facing toward Christine. She stepped back and let him pass, the box cutter tightly in her fist, ready to slice him if need be.

"I'll be seeing you," Michael hummed out quietly, as he walked to the door that led to the hallway without turning his head or looking back. Then he was gone.

Christine ran over to Kira, who was already trying to steady herself. Kira fell into Christine's arms and she hugged her petrified friend. Kira buried her face deep into Christine's neck and sobbed painfully. Each wave of tears seemed to be summoned up from a deep well somewhere at the bottom of Kira's soul. The tears poured freely and angrily down Christine's chest. Christine was mad. More than mad, she was enraged, and her fury was divided between the lunatic Michael and herself. When Christine found herself at Ezzme's mercy six months ago in a lonely bathroom, Kira hadn't waited by the door to see what would happen. She sprang into action and fought like a wildcat, throwing caution to the wind that could have turned into a hurricane of an ass-kicking for her. Now Christine burned with guilt because when she had seen Michael strangling the person she cared for most in the world, she just froze. Instead of ripping that box cutter across his neck when his back was turned, she tipped her hand to him and he knew that she was afraid of him. Her bravado was a farce, and she knew Michael left not because he was intimidated by Christine. He stopped the torment so he could pick it up at a later time.

Kira cried until it seemed that she was empty. Christine wrapped a dry towel around her and led her to the bed, where she laid her down under the sheets and covered her. The rush of fear and adrenaline left Kira as fast as it came, and her body was sapped empty of all energy. A troubling sleep overcame her quickly, and thoughts of Michael, Christine, and the large glowing eye were pushed back into her mind. Images of other things started to take shape as growing, hulking shadows blotted out the landscape of her dreams.

Christine watched her friend fall into an exhausted slumber. Slowly she realized what her worst fear was. She couldn't protect Kira; she would be useless in trying to defend her from the psycho's onslaught. Christine hated herself for being weak and scared. She sat at the foot of the bed and plotted Kira's escape route in her head.

And in the bathroom, the large white eye reappeared in an unseen hole near the mirror and looked out into the bedroom at the two girls on the clean-sheeted mattress. One was tossing and turning in her sleep and the other was dutifully sitting by her side. The undetected orb glistened with curiosity, blinked once, and vanished into the darkness that permeated the building.

The monster made his way back to his lair at a hurried pace. For all of his immense bulk, he maneuvered deftly and quietly throughout the old hotel. The building, with its many floors and vacant and lifeless rooms, had been the monster's domain since he had first entered the building, years before. There had been others who lived within the walls of the hotel when he first arrived—vagabonds and vagrants who had taken up residence in the place that had once housed the influential and rich. The monster soon rid its new kingdom of all interlopers. After that, he alone reigned as lord and master over the Blackwell. Others had come over the years and ventured into the unholy and unhallowed halls that the monster roamed, and all met the same fate: they never were seen again. Lately, the monster had become worried. More and more unwanted guests were encroaching upon his kingdom. During the day hostile armies banged, sawed, and worked feverishly on the lower tiers of the monster's castle, readying themselves for combat.

The monster studied their strategy from within the shadows and realized that the invading horde was trying to destroy the castle from within: tearing down the walls, ripping up the floors, sweeping away the layers of crumbling skin that the monster knew. These armies painted their encampment in dull primer and white paint. They brought ladders and tools as their weapons, coming when the sun awoke from its dreams and leaving when the moon crossed the sky to chase its sleep. They had sent scouts to spy on the monster's stronghold, to see where the breech in its protection was and to rush in to try to dethrone the monster. But the monster was intelligent, and fear had made him smarter than he had been in the past. He let the scouts with their hammers and levels and tape measures come up and walk unimpeded through the halls. The monster followed their every step, trying to envision what kind of sinister attack plan they were formulating. But he knew he couldn't let them venture into the heart of his kingdom, into the master chamber of his castle. The monster barricaded and bolted the top tiers in such a manner that the most ardent and militant of the advance party soon gave up in sweaty frustration after hours of trying to break through and retreated back down to the main body below.

But soon the armies that came in the day would try to move upward and take the monster's kingdom, and the monster would slowly lose territory, floor by floor, room by room, until it was banished to the top, where it would make its final stand. He had prepared for this ultimate conflict; he would not lose his kingdom without a fight, without a war on such a scale that the enemies' offspring would regale their children for eons to come with distorted tales of their ancestor's heroics.

Now a new enemy had joined in the fray, a group that did not run and retreat once the bravery-inducing sun fled the sky. This dispirited band dared stay within the walls of the monster's castle when the night came, when the heat of the day dwindled away and the safety of the sun was beyond their reach. This group was different, and the monster knew that they fought among themselves. There were no bonds of unity to worry about, just individual strands of resistance that it could conquer without much damage to itself.

The monster speculated that this was a mercenary force sent to drive him out, a different band of warriors who would use tactics that were new to him. He was ready and anxious to do battle. They had one among them that was a valued prize, a shaman of their tribe, one who covered herself with the deeds of their victories in symbols and shapes the monster vaguely knew.

He recognized them, although he could not understand the significance of the drawings. There were images of cruelty and piety mixed over her flesh, a testament to their struggles. She was a living totem; within her skin, the power of her tribe lived. He would possess that power; he needed the pulse that beat within her bosom. He needed to drink from the red knowledge that flowed in her veins. He needed her vision, her gift of sight. To own her sacred pelt to wear as his mantle was his destiny. To wear a crown of her bones was his desire. Yes, the time for a call to arms was at hand, and the monster mentally prepared what he had to do as he crawled up the elevator shaft like an enormous spider spinning out a web of steel chains that wrapped around its mighty torso. Swiftly, he ascended back into the protective darkness that was his lair and ravenously prepared for victory.

Later that evening, Christine and Kira made it to the hallway outside the kitchen. No one had noticed them sliding in the shadows; they'd been using the darkness to cover their way. Both girls stopped at the doors that led into the kitchen. As Kira turned to look at Christine, a deep sorrow burned inside of her when she held her friend's hand.

"Come with me," Kira said in a final attempt to win Christine over. She knew what the answer would be.

Christine softly shook her head and pressed a wad of cash into Kira's palm. Kira looked at the gift with surprise.

"It's all I have. If I had more, you know I'd give it to

you," Christine began. "The windows in the kitchen face out toward the atrium. They have no bars on them. There's an opening in the wall. It has to lead somewhere. That dog that Melissa tried to feed before must have come from somewhere."

Knowing that if she succeeded with her escape, this would probably be the last time Kira would see her friend, she pulled Christine into her arms and hugged her.

"Be safe," Kira whispered into Christine's ear. Christine just nodded; she couldn't say anything. She was holding her emotions back, and anything could send them flooding out. She squeezed Kira tightly and felt the warmth of her body and knew that she would miss it.

"*Vaya con Dios*," Christine gently said as her lips brushed against Kira's cheek. Kira peeled herself away and quietly slipped past the creaky swinging doors that led into the kitchen and to freedom. Christine waited in the hallway to make sure no one would come upon Kira's escape. She waited and listened to the last sounds of the only friend she ever had fade away into the darkness of the kitchen.

In the atrium, the hungry dog reappeared from behind the shadows. The poor creature sniffed around and found the spot where Melissa had tossed her unwanted sandwich earlier that day. It devoured the food with a ravenous gulp as its saliva dripped down to the ground.

7

THE MONSTER PACED FURIOUSLY AROUND HIS LAIR, cutting a wide path through the swarm of flies that kept him company with their constant buzzing. The monster readied itself for the inevitable; attack was imminent. He held on to the chains that for so long had been his closest allies in repelling back invaders. His thick fingers felt the sturdy links, each one crusted with dried blood. He felt the hooks that he carefully and lovingly sharpened each night before falling into a fitful sleep, and their sharpness filled him with a reassuring warmth. He wore the chains now like bandoliers. Dangling from his hands, the long lengths swung in a slowly building rhythm. Soon he would slash out and tear through the flesh of the advancing armies with the metallic extensions of his limbs that were anchored deeply in the twisted maze that was his soul.

He thought about his plan of attack. He focused and formed strategies. His large white eyes rolled back into his skull. Sometime during his planning, his mind began to wander, and fragments of a past life flashed before him. His memories were a shattered mosaic of images, replayed until they were almost faded ghosts that stalked the rocky and treacherous landscape of the monster's subconscious.

He saw the cage, chicken wire mingled with the bars. He saw the filth that surrounded it. He saw the boy and heard the whimpers and the cries. A youngster, no older than ten, was sitting in his own filth, smeared in feces, urine, and blood. He watched as his fragmented recollection flickered against the inside of his skull. He knew the boy; he had felt what the boy had felt. The boy's sobs were loud and painful, much like those of the tattooed girl whom he had spied on in the bathing chamber earlier. The boy held his head between his knees and mumbled something, a plea for forgiveness or an attempt at absolution. The monster could smell the child reeking in a funk of dried sweat caused by fear. He could hear horror in the boy's voice. Somehow, he could sense what the boy was feeling; a shadow had fallen over the cage. Someone looked down at the boy, someone far more versed in evil than the monster could ever wish to be. The figure was blurred, its shape coming in and out of focus in the monster's mind. The monster watched helplessly as the unrecognizable figure moved closer to the cage. The figure held something out in front of it. The monster remembered what it was. It was something he had seen before, something that sang out in a high, shrill sound to tell the figure that it was ready to cleanse and burn away sin. The person approached the sniffling boy. The monster recognized the metal teapot glowing brightly with the heat of salvation boiling from within.

The monster wanted to warn the boy, to rush to the child's side and protect him, but he was frozen to the spot on which he stood and watched in horror as the boy in his mind was trapped. The figure stood above the small makeshift cage and looked down at the naked boy. The figure spoke quietly to him. To the monster's ears, it was nothing more than muffled mumblings. When the figure raised the teapot, a hot flume of steam escaped into the air above the cage. The monster tried to scream for the child, but it was too late. Boiling water rained down on the helpless child and his screams ripped into the monster's brain. The boy bellowed out an inhuman shriek as the monster watched the boy's body bubble and burn.

The monster cried for the boy, his tears burning his face as the teapot's water seared the child's cheeks. The boy whimpered once and fell into the wet puddle of warm mud that he was sitting in. The monster shook his massive head as if he were trying to shake images of the boy, the teapot, and the unseen figure out of his mind.

The monster staggered to the wall, and the pain in his brain came back in a sharp wave of unmerciful little rips in his skull. The monster started to bang his head against the wall: bang the pain away, bang the boy away, and bang the past away. His head hit the wall with such force that large chunks of plaster and wood caved in. Each time he pounded his head into the wall, he did it faster and harder. The monster rammed with a jackhammer's velocity and pounded the battered wall until there was nothing left but a few strands of wallpaper dangling from the massive hole his head had created. The flies had scattered and watched the curious ritual their master underwent. When he was finished, the monster sank to his knees. The scared, naked boy had gone into hiding and the unseen figure was banished to the dark side of his mind. The pain was temporarily beaten back behind a wall of forgetfulness.

The monster's breathing was heavy and he labored to get it under control. He stood up and looked around at the indescribable squalor that was the only home he remembered. He looked down at his massive forearms and hands and noticed that blisters had formed and were starting to bubble over his flesh. The burning pain of salvation had followed him from his past life into the present, once again. He stood ready to bring heaven's fiery retribution to all those who dared to enter his kingdom.

Richie had swiped a flashlight and held it out in front of him as Tye followed closely behind him. Both boys moved through the seventh floor with as much stealth as they could. The fire that killed Langley Blackwell and the other guests years before had damaged the floor. The severity of the damage wasn't as bad as some of the other floors above. After all these years, Richie found it odd that the smell of smoke still lingered and permeated the hallways. The walls had been blackened, but not burned. End tables and chairs had been singed and the carpet still had a thick layer of black soot underneath all the trash that had accumulated over the past twenty years.

"The fire must have stopped here," Richie said, casting the flashlight around the charred corridor.

"What makes you say that?" Tye asked.

"The damage ain't that bad."

"Bad enough to kill some people."

"Yeah, I guess that's pretty bad."

They walked down the main hallway, where the elevators were, and turned the corner to the hallway in the south wing of the hotel. Several of the doors leading into the rooms on the right side were gone or destroyed, so moonlight shot in from the suites, illuminating the hallway before them.

Richie checked his computer printout of the floor plans and determined that they were nowhere near where the safe would have been.

"It ain't here," he told Tye.

"What makes you say that? Here's as good a place as any other to start looking."

"No, the safe is probably on the top floor. The penthouse," Richie mumbled, second-guessing himself.

"What the fuck, bitch? You said the safe was probably on the floors where the fire broke out. We're on the first floor, where that motherfuckin' fire started, and now you're telling me it ain't here. What gives?"

Tye's anger was something Richie didn't want to stir. "Nothing, I just got to thinking, that's all."

"That's a first," quipped Tye as he looked around the charred hallway.

"If you had all this cash on hand and you kept it in a safe, you'd keep it handy, right? Blackwell lived in

171

the penthouse. He wouldn't keep something as valuable as a safe full of cash on a floor he didn't live on."

"True. But if this guy had all these secret passages and hidden rooms you keep talking about, he could hide the motherfucker anywhere. No one would know it was here," Tye said.

Richie didn't agree with Tye's reasoning, but he didn't see any harm in searching the seventh floor for a while, until Tye got bored and Richie could lead him to the penthouse to search for their pot of gold up there.

They walked through the shafts of moonlight and banged on the walls. Neither knew what sound they were listening for, it just seemed like the thing to do when searching for something. They looked into several of the rooms and were surprised that some were much narrower than others. Then Richie figured out that the rooms that weren't as wide as the others were always side by side. He assumed that some of the secret passages must have been built there, between the adjoining smaller rooms.

Tye wanted to test Richie's theory, so they entered one of the narrow rooms and Tye entered the closet. His fingers searched around the back of the closet. He could feel that the back wall had a little give to it. He pushed harder and some of the old paneling pushed back and he peered into the darkness behind the wall.

"Goddamn. You're right, motherfucker. There is a room back here." The excitement in Tye's voice was infectious.

Richie was excited that his assumption was correct, and he jumped in the closet with Tye to look into the secret room. Richie cast the flashlight into the blackness that waited for them, but nothing of value was to be found. The room, small and windowless, had nothing in it. Richie shined the light over the ceiling of the small room and saw a trapdoor.

"That's how he must have gotten from floor to floor without being seen."

Tye tried to enlarge the opening in the back of the closet, but the panel would not give. Something was blocking it. The closet wall would move no farther, and they stood staring into the secret room through the twelve-inch opening and contemplated their next move.

"Shit. We know the motherfucker ain't in here, but it's gotta be someplace," Tye said.

The discovery of the small secret room made Tye more confident that the mystical safe actually did exist. The funny thing was that some nerdy white boy, whose biggest crime was hacking into the school computers and fucking with everyone's grades, would be the one to find the thing. But that was okay with Tye. He'd let Richie have his few moments of glory when they found the safe. Tye had it all planned. There was no way Tye could open a safe and he knew it, but Richie didn't. He knew that the white boy believed that every street nigger knew how to crack a safe, hot-wire a car, make a homemade silencer, all that bullshit that movies and television portray urban blacks as doing. Tye couldn't do any of those things, but it didn't matter.

Once the safe was discovered Tye would make some futile gesture at trying to open it and finally give up in disgust. He'd warn Richie not to worry, he'd come back with some tools and dynamite and blow that fucker sky-high. All Tye had to do was get Richie out of the equation. He would promise to bring Richie back when they were done with their community service time. Tye had no intention of bringing Richie or anyone else back to get the safe. He didn't want to have to do any harm to Richie, but he wasn't against spilling blood if it greased the wheels of industry. He didn't need any more shit hanging over his head, so instead of Richie getting a baseball bat to the back of the head eight or nine times, he'd just bury Richie in a pile of jive bullshit so deep he wouldn't be able to climb out. After Richie was out of the picture, and before he realized that he'd been double-crossed, Tye would come back with the necessary tools to do the job. It didn't take brains to use a jackhammer. Although Tye had never used one before, he would make damn sure he knew where he would be able to steal one. If that didn't work, Tye knew some badass street niggers who were into all types of bad shit that went "boom." He'd blow that fucker open or die trying. He preferred the former. It made less of a mess.

"Let's try another room," Richie said as he hurried out of the closet with the flashlight, leaving Tye alone in the dark closet.

It was in that split second of being alone, totally alone in the dark closet with the blackness of the secret room inches away from him, that Tye felt his stomach clench with fear. It was a fear he couldn't place. He had been shot at and stabbed before. Staring down at a pistol or a switchblade, Tye had always kept his cool. He knew fools always got hurt worse in street situations when they lost their heads. He was no coward. Pain, violence, and an untimely death were all things that he knew were headed his way in the not-too-distant future, so fear of dying never bothered him, either. But now something did. Something worse than death. And it seemed to linger next to him in the darkness of that small closet. He felt as if he were standing up in a coffin and at any moment someone was going to toss the first handful of dirt on him. He felt it, and he knew that the hotel was a bad place. The man who had built it was bad. The people who had come to it were bad, and the acts they did to one another were bad. The things that went on within its walls were the worst of all. Suddenly, the closet seemed to close in on him and the blackness weighed heavily on his shoulders, as if the shadows trapped inside with him were trying to pull him down. He felt his legs shake.

Richie came back into the room looking for him. He shined the flashlight into the closet to see Tye sweating. Tye's back was pressed against the wall, and he was almost slumped down to the floor.

"You okay?" Richie asked.

"Yeah. I'm cool. I'm cool," Tye said, catching his breath.

"Well, come on then." With that Richie was gone again, and with him the flashlight, and Tye was once again plunged back into the darkness of the casketlike closet. Tye gathered enough strength to jump up and march out of the closet. He fled from the room and went down the long hallway where welcome moonlight guided the way.

• • •

Williams entered the large ballroom that had once played host to some of the hottest swing bands of the day. Now, its silence was so deafening that the shadows seemed to roar with loneliness. The rows of empty tables sat mutely facing a bandstand that would never again ring out with the sounds of Dorsey, Ellington, or Callaway. Williams sat at the long bar whose only customers in the last twenty years had been rats and roaches. He leaned back and looked at the broken mirror that traveled down the length of the bar. His cracked and shattered reflection seemed to stare out at him in a million infinities. The bottles that lined the bar were either bone dry or lying in pieces. The rummies had made sure that anything worth drinking was drunk up decades ago. Now a soft blanket of cobwebs held all the bottles within its gray, misty grasp, undisturbed and empty.

Williams reached over the bar and found a shot glass. He rubbed his handkerchief around the inside and dry-washed the glass like a seasoned barkeep. He pulled a flask from his jacket, poured himself a shot, and eased back in the torn leather bar stool. Toasting his broken reflections in the mirror, he drank.

He thought about Blaine. He remembered the day his partner had died and tried to fight back the memories, but he was not strong enough to put up a good fight. Suddenly, he found himself lying on that bloody rug, staring up at the monstrous shadow that seemed to walk in slow motion toward him. The only thing he could make out clearly was the reddish glow of the axe blade dripping hungrily with Blaine's blood as it made its way toward him. He remembered that deep within the darkness that cloaked the enormous killer, two large eyes bore down on him with an inhumane desire. He could hear and feel his heart beat in a fast staccato rhythm like frantic jungle drums. He remembered the smells, the stench of the killer and the reek of the blood that poured from Blaine's body, which had already been split and sliced open to the bone. He remembered lifting the gun and firing . . . and firing . . . and firing . . . Out of what seemed like a million shots, only one had struck the large shadow that killed his partner and almost succeeded in killing him.

Anyone else would have fallen dead on the spot. Anything else would have stopped moving, but the thing in the shadows wasn't anyone else. The thing wasn't human, and it wasn't playing by human rules. Oh, it had a human name and a human history, one that Williams tried to piece together later, but he knew that the killer was not human. It was something more than a human being but something less than a man. It was a throwback to a time when light was afraid to show itself upon the earth. It was a relic from an era when monsters walked the land with impunity, and legends of their misdeeds and murderous ways were told to children to keep them from wandering away from their parents. The killer was from the land of blackness, home to where Grendel roamed and the boogeyman reigned, where big bad wolves ran in packs and hungry giants lived on top of beanstalks. He was from a land that no man ever ventured into or dared to invade. He was from the dark side of the mind.

After the attack, the authorities were able to find out who had once lived in that house. The suspect, the alleged killer, was thought to have gone by a name that was both insidious and innocuous: Goodnight. A surname that rang out with a pleasant feeling and dreadful finality. As best they could figure out, Goodnight had killed, tortured, mutilated, and ravaged within the walls of that house for some time. The name was the only thing the sole living, eyeless victim had ever uttered after she had been taken out of that hellhole. It was the only word she ever spoke again.

The original owners of the house were long gone, thought to be numbered among the bones that were littered around the house or that decorated the crudely constructed ossuary in the basement. The official body count at the murder site was seven, but everyone knew there were more—many more. Bits and pieces of bodies were found scattered all over the shrub-covered hillside. The coyotes had been hungry, helpful accomplices, making identification almost impossible. Only a few complete skulls were found, and those were the ones inside the premises that had been used as some type of macabre decoration or barbaric drinking vessel. The severed heads that weren't completely devoid of flesh and muscle were never reported to the public at large, but they all had the same physical trait: the eyes had been removed. Some slowly and methodically, with skill and precision, and others just ripped out with inhuman force and sadistic brutality. An altar of atrocity, a shrine of depravity, was found on the top floor of the house. It was described by the forensic expert who had uncovered it as "the singularly most horrifically beautiful and unsettling thing I've ever seen."

A four-foot-high statue of Saint Lucy stood on a

thick, blood-covered workbench. Williams had learned that she was a Christian saint who was martyred for her belief, her eyes plucked out of her head by the tyrannical Diocletian. The statue stood forlorn and alone. Trails of dried, bloody tears ran from her empty eye sockets down her soft, cracked ceramic face. Her white mantle was densely speckled a sanguineous reddish brown. The bloody hue had built up over the years until the entire statue seemed to glow with a crimson patina. She was surrounded by dozens of doll heads that had been severed at the neck, their plastic faces burned until their features sagged in mock reverence. Their eye sockets were empty or worse. Some of them had human eyes shoved and stitched into the mutilated crevices. Around the Saint Lucy statue were tall glass bottles with over sixty pairs of human eyes floating in a clear liquid, all staring out blankly at the lifeless statue. Hundreds of white candles illuminated the shrine. Bones, teeth, and hair mixed with the melted wax that covered the workbench like ghoulish frosting on a cannibal's birthday cake. The entire morbid scene looked like a horrific homage to Fatima designed by the evil architectural firm of Gein and Dahmer.

Whoever kneeled and worshiped at that altar did not pray to a god known to any sane man.

Williams had heard all the stories. He had tracked many of the leads himself, once he had been able to move again, but by that time most of the trails were dead ends. Once, he thought he had something. He brought in a skid-row doctor who he knew performed two-bit coat hanger jobs for the working girls and who would patch up some of the local bangers for a nominal fee, away from the scrutiny of the legal medical profession. Rumors had circulated that an interesting customer came calling one night to see the good old doctor. It happened to be the same night Williams's career had come to an abrupt halt and Blaine's life came to a brutal end.

The guy's name was Bennell, and Williams had known of him for some time. His story was that he had a gift for medicine but a bigger thirst for the bottle. All alcoholics are the same: they can survive only a short time without booze. It is only a matter of time before they, like sharks out of water, start thrashing and gagging, fighting not to suffocate. All Williams had to do was sit and wait. He had all the time in the world since he was off the force. He tracked the drunkard down to his place of business, a shithole of a dive in some back alley that seemed more appropriate for some third world slum, and sweated him out. After thirteen hours the guy still hadn't cracked. To Williams's dismay and surprise, the feeble fellow just sat there denying everything that Williams kept throwing at him. Every question about a wounded, massive man with bullet holes, every inquiry about strange visitors with injuries that would have gone unreported was met with denial.

"There was no man who came to see me. There was no man!" The bleary-eyed sod kept repeating the words like some time-worn mantra that had been rehearsed until he believed it himself. The truth was that Bennell was right: there was no man who had come to see him. Whatever living being had crossed his threshold that night was not a man, not a recognizable member of the human race.

Williams watched as Bennell squirmed and shivered. The drunk's body took turns shaking with chills and sweating with hot flashes. Williams watched intently as every nervous tick and sick tremor shot through the other man like an electrical shock.

Bennell was a slave to the bottle. For the thirteen hours of dry dock that was his interrogation, Miles Bennell was the obediently silent servant to another lord, one whose dark might made all the powers of Bacchus seem pale and harmless by comparison.

Someone—no, something—had stirred such a deep fear in Bennell that he was able to call upon an untapped will he never knew he possessed. No matter how badly his body ached, his mind craved, or his soul begged for alcohol, Bennell denied everything. Even when Williams poured out and emptied not one but two bottles of Jack Daniel's in front of him, one drop at a time, he did not crack. During the entire ordeal, Bennell's nervous eyes kept darting back toward the door, as if anticipating an unwelcome guest at the first mention of a wrong word.

Williams knew Bennell was holding back, but in the end, as the thirteenth hour passed, Williams was no further along than when he had started. It always struck Williams as funny that Bennell didn't crack and tell him any lie he wanted to hear in order to stop the torturous interrogation. But Bennell didn't lie; he just didn't tell the truth, which made all the difference in the world for anyone who would believe the tale of a disgraced would-be doctor cutting through the skull of a monster to retrieve a couple of bullets.

Williams left Bennell and ended his search because

there weren't any more leads to track. The bodies in the morgue, the pieces of bone sitting in the medical examiner's drawers, the line of cars stripped and destroyed hidden at the bottom of the ravine, all pointed to the same suspect: unknown assailant.

But one thing had always gnawed at Williams, a dark thought that haunted him for years. After going over the murder site as soon as he was capable months after the attack and after studying every report on the crime scene, Williams came to the scary conclusion that Goodnight, the name the killer was baptized with by the boys downtown, had not acted alone. When he brought this theory to his supervisors, he was met with a transparent barrier of bureaucratic stonewalling. Williams could see through the fence. He knew that others had come to the same conclusion but were afraid to voice their opinion. There were things about the case that even Williams didn't know about, details and leads that were quickly covered up by the higher-ups. It was months before Williams had been able to get out of a hospital bed, let alone be ambulatory, so by the time he was able to review the murder scene, all of the clues had been long gone. The house had been stripped bare by the authorities; the area around the premises had been gone over with a fine-tooth comb. Nothing remained.

The last time Williams had seen the house was when he had gone there one afternoon by taxi. He stood on the hillside that led down to the ravine where the victims' cars had been thrown like discarded toys by some bored, gigantic child, and looked up at the three-story structure that loomed on the hilltop. The house looked down at the city below. The windows on the top floor seemed to peer into every corner of every neighborhood and read every secret that was hidden in the shadows. The house sat like a beacon, high on the hill so that it could be seen from almost everywhere in the city. The thousands of people who had looked up at the house, never giving it a second glance, had no idea what types of evil lived there.

That day on the hillside, the sun had started its slow descent behind the mountain range in the far distance. The house's shadow started to grow and flowed toward Williams like a hungry cancer trying to devour him in its dark maw. Just before the shadow enveloped him, he stepped to the side, back into the few remaining rays of sunlight, and looked up at the house. A chilling sensation shot through his body and down through the artificial arm that was attached at his elbow, to the hand and fingertips that let him perform certain daily tasks. The house seemed to be smiling at him. A cold, sinister smile, the kind of look that an unrepentant killer shoots you the moment before the switch is thrown at his execution.

Even though he knew that the house was only a building, made of nothing more than brick, stone, wood, and timber, to him it felt like it had been built out of fear and terror. Blood, flesh, bones, and skin were the mortar and cement that bound it together. Williams hurried away from the house, away from its smirking windows, and ran back to the taxi that waited for him. He left the top of the hill, left the house and the street, and never looked back.

He knew deep down that the killer did not work alone. He couldn't have; someone would have seen a thing of that size roaming around and reported it. A rumor would have been spread, a lead would have been followed up on, but nothing came to light. Someone had to have been covering his tracks. How did this thing live day to day? How did victims find their way up the hill, to that house and to their unpleasant demise? These questions nagged at Williams, but he had never found the answers. Who would work in concert with such an ungodly force of nature? Why would anyone be in league with such a depraved individual unless there was something the accomplice got out of it in return? Williams knew that every criminal union was a symbiotic relationship, one partner feeding off the inadequacies of the other; Burke and Hare, Lucas and Toole, Leopold and Loeb. For every pairing of soulless twisted minds, one always played off the other. Who could gain anything working with Goodnight? What could anyone gain from being in cahoots with one of the most vile killers in the annals of law enforcement? Williams shuddered at the notion that not only did the massive killer still exist and walk the streets, but someone else walked the streets with him, keeping up with the killer's bloody pace.

Williams tried to push the morbid thoughts away as he sipped the liquor and let the warm, stinging sensation work its way to the back of his tongue. The taste of dust and dirt was slowly melting away from the back of his throat when he heard Hannah enter the dance hall behind him.

He turned to greet her and realized how attractive she really was, if you looked. She was a fine figure of a woman, just hippy enough around the waist and full-bodied enough to want to hold and not let go of her on a cold night. He watched her as she walked toward him. He imagined what she would have looked like at the height of the hotel's popularity, thirty years prior. He saw her parading through the same large entrance in a silky black, form-fitting dress, her hair curled in a Veronica Lake style and her painted lips glistening crimson under the ballroom lights. He envisioned her sauntering through the pale wall of cigarette smoke, past the tables of big-money men and their expensive women. Every step she took toward him was in soulful syncopation with the haunting wail of Chet Baker's trumpet that heralded her appearance from the bandstand. In another lifetime, Hannah Anders would have been his woman; in another lifetime, Frank Williams would have been another man.

Hannah sat next to Williams and looked at the empty shot glass in front of him on the dusty bar.

"Any more in there?" She gestured to the flask.

Williams reached over the bar, grabbed another shot glass, and wiped it with his handkerchief. He placed it in front of Hannah when she had sat next to him. He filled both their glasses and toasted the end of the day.

The liquor made Hannah's overly stressed system slowly unwind as she leaned back into the leather chair.

"What a day, huh?" she asked.

"I've had worse," Williams said, unconsciously tapping his prosthetic hand against the bar.

"I really blew it today. I froze. When he challenged me, I didn't know what to do. I've never been in that situation before in my life . . ."

"Forget it." Williams wanted to cut her off before she took the weight of the world on her shoulders. "You did nothing wrong. You were out of your element, that's all. These kids have seen it all—and then some. They live by rules of intimidation and the con. It was only natural for Michael to make his move. If he didn't do it, one of the others would have. And don't think they still won't."

"Do you think there'll be any more trouble?" she asked in an almost meek tone.

"Count on it. Trouble follows these kids. That's all that they're used to. I don't think they would know how to react in a situation where trouble was hanging over their heads. That Montross is one to watch. He'll try to get back at me. I know the type. Worse, I think he has it in for Kira. We both better watch her back," Williams said, hearing more concern in his voice for Kira than he expected.

"Why does he want to hurt her?"

"I could give you a million different answers or I can give you one simple reason: he's a product of the streets. That's all he is and that's all he knows. I think he and Kira must have had some type of thing going on the outside. Something more than the usual pimp/whore, supplier/dealer relationship. I've watched him all afternoon. He's trying to play it cool, but you can sense that he's going to blow any second."

"I have to be honest, I never even saw that in the interview process," Hannah confessed.

"You wouldn't. These kids know how to play the system better than anyone who runs it. They say what you want to hear. They act the way you think they should behave. They're smart. They saw this program for what it was, an easy way out. And they jumped at the chance."

"And what do you see this program as?" she countered.

"I don't know yet. Hopefully a second chance for me as well as them. But the night is still young. Let's drink to a peaceful evening," he replied as he refilled their glasses.

Williams noticed Hannah twirling her engagement ring around on her finger. It was still on her right hand.

"I don't want to sound like I'm an expert on these things, but shouldn't that thing be on the left hand?" Williams asked casually, pointing his shot glass toward her ring.

"I guess I'm just test-driving it for now. I haven't given an official answer just yet."

"He's a decent guy, right?"

Hannah smiled warmly. Williams knew the answer before she nodded her agreement. In a way he felt a twinge of jealousy toward a man who he would probably never meet.

"He treats you good?"

Her smile widened even more. Williams thought about her body, the way her shape flowed from her breasts to her legs in sensuous curves and the way her sweet scent covered every inch of her soft flesh.

"Has all his own teeth, doesn't he?"

She let out a funny giggle. He pictured her naked, her pale skin smooth and warm to the touch, her mouth and lips moist and dripping with her taste.

"Then why wait? Trust me, if you have the chance to be with someone you love, jump at it. Don't let him wait too long," Williams advised, and banged his shot glass down with a hard thunk that was more an attempt to knock out the tempting image of Hannah Anders than to make his point. He was casting the naked image of his colleague into the back of his mind, to remain with the nameless killers that stalked and vacant houses that laughed at him behind his back.

Tye and Richie walked down the hallway of the eighth floor. They hadn't found anything on the seventh, although their search hadn't been that thorough. They had decided to go to the next floor because the atmosphere on the lower floor was stifling and unsettling. Hoping to find better conditions one flight up, they found the accommodations for treasure hunting even worse. The shadows from behind them crept up as they moved farther into the dark heart of the hotel, causing both of them to second-guess their venture.

Richie flashed his light and saw a door labeled SERVICE HALL at the end of the hallway. Both boys hurried to it. Richie tried to open the door but couldn't. Tye tapped Richie on the shoulder and told him to stand back. He pulled out a hairpin and twisted it straight. He bent down and jimmied the straightened hairpin into the lock. One. Two. Three. Click. The door opened.

Richie beamed in awe at Tye's larcenous skills, and Tye just played it cool, knowing it had been a one in a hundred chance that got the door to open. Although he couldn't boost a car or crack a safe, Tye had a few street skills up his sleeve. One of them was that he could open a door or window if he wanted to get to the other side.

"Nice going," Richie said. "I told you we'd make a good team."

Tye thought about Richie's statement. The irony was that Richie had no idea that Tye planned on being a team of one if and when the safe was found. They walked into the hallway and met complete and total blackness. Richie flashed the light into the hall and the beam fought through the thickness of shadows.

"Man, you smell that?" Tye asked as a musky odor seeped out from behind the door he had just jimmied.

"I bet no one's been up here since the fire," Richie replied as he started to cover his mouth.

It wasn't the lingering odor of burnt carpets and singed wallpaper that they were smelling now. It was something akin to decay, something that Tye remembered from the time he'd found a dead cat in the alley behind the tenement he'd lived in. The cat had been shoved against some trashcans. Its neck was broken and its tongue hung out, dry and stiff. Tye had prodded the cat with a stick and lifted up the animal's head. He had peeled it off the ground with a pulling tear, for it had stuck to the cement of the alley. Tye remembered the smell, the maggots that spread across the poor creature's face, and the sound of the cat's head as it landed back on the dirty ground after he'd dropped it.

For some reason, he remembered all of those things vividly as he walked deeper into the corridor with Richie's light leading their way. They walked for a while before they realized that they had covered a lot of ground and had nothing to show for it yet. The hallway seemed empty of anything except trash.

Seconds before Tye was about to suggest that they change directions, Richie's light fell on a pile of cardboard pieces torn and ripped into various lengths. Tye kicked over the pieces and saw the various slogans that were written on them, including, "WILL WORK FOR FOOD," "HOMELESS VET," "ANYTHING HELPS, GOD BLESS," and other messages scrawled over the signs to elicit sympathy and guilty generosity. Next to the signs they saw a pile of clothing, torn and tattered into nothing more than a mound of filthy rags, and a pile of hypodermic needles, crack pipes, and old pint bottles of booze, many still half full.

Tye kicked through everything, mixing the three piles together with his foot.

"Why the fuck would some bum leave all this stuff here?" Richie asked as the first nervous strains started to play in his voice.

"I don't know. Maybe someone found the safe. They got rich and don't need this shit anymore. And that leaves us holding our dicks in the dark," Tye answered, sifting through the debris with his sneaker.

Tye kicked away a large portion of the clothing and revealed a corpse lying underneath. Richie froze on the spot as Tye took a step back. For an instant, Tye didn't know if the guy was going to get up or not, but after the smell came up from under the dirty shroud of clothes that covered the body, Tye knew that the guy would never get up again. The corpse was that of a fifty-year-old man. Drugs and drink had aged him to a haggard and hard-looking seventy.

"Holy shit!" Richie stammered as he started to back away.

"Stand still, motherfucker!" Tye barked at Richie. "And point that light on him."

Richie complied with Tye's order and placed the beam of light on the body. The light jittered over the corpse. The man's head was tilted to the side, half hidden by shadows.

"Look at him. Is he dead?" Richie asked, already knowing the man was but hoping he wasn't.

"Man, if this motherfucker ain't dead, he's in for a lousy weekend. Yeah, this guy is long gone. Probably died from the fire," Tye said with some certainty.

"No way, man. No way. That fire was thirty years ago. This guy would be nothing but bones. You know that. He's fresh! What the fuck!" Richie faltered as he started to bounce the light around.

"Okay! Okay! Damn it, motherfucker. Keep that light still. You're startin' to freak me out."

Tye was trying to get a better look at the corpse. He had seen dead people before. It was something that you were exposed to growing up on the streets, but it was something Tye never got used to. The one thing Tye knew for sure was that sometimes dead men *did* tell tales, especially if there was anything of value on their person when they went to meet their maker. Tye fought back a surge of revulsion and pressed his hand against the dead man's clothing. The mixture of humidity and stink made the whole room reek of rotten fruit as Tye's fingers gingerly crept over the old army jacket the corpse wore. Just as curiosity prompted him to prod the dead cat when he was younger, curiosity once again nudged his better judgment aside.

"What the fuck you doin', man?" Richie freaked.

"You never know, man. This dude may have some cash on him. Why let it go to waste up here with him? He ain't gonna need it," Tye answered.

The boy's instinct for easy money overtook his revulsion and the little regard he had for human dignity. When Tye tugged at something inside the man's jacket, the corpse's head rolled over into the light and came face-to-face with him.

The man's eyes were gone. In their place were two deep, dark holes that were encrusted with a thick layer of dried blood that looked black in the bright light. Tye's heart stopped as he was looking at the dead man, who glared back at him with an accusatory sightless stare. Out of the corner of his right socket, a large cockroach crawled out, sniffing the smelly air as if it were wondering who had disturbed its home.

"No way, man. No way! I'm not here. I can't be here!" Richie sobbed as utter panic flooded his body. He spun around, and the beam from the flashlight ricocheting over the wall and floor as he turned to run away.

"What the fuck! Richie! Stop! Richie!" Tye screamed out after him. He got up and tripped over something. In the back of his mind he imagined the dead man sticking out his leg and tripping him.

Tye saw Richie running down the hall in a frenzy, the flashlight careening around the hallway and creating an erratic, strobe-like effect. Richie ran out of the service hall and heard the thick door slam behind him as he left. The hall was once again plunged into an impenetrable blackness that enveloped Tye in its heavy, humid stench. Tye clung to the floor, trying to breathe. The wide space of the hallway seemed to be closing in on him, making him feel that he was drowning in the balmy blackness. His mind whirled out of control and a million thoughts flashed by as if someone were flicking his fingers over a deck of cards imprinted with his memories. He thought about the cat, the dead cat that he'd played with as a child. He pictured that same creature slinking toward him in the dark, its head snapped to one side and purring with a sick meow, wanting to have its dirty head scratched.

With his imagination running wild, Tye began to shake when he thought he felt the pile of clothes he had fallen on start to move. He knew the dead man was getting up. Tye's mind imploded with terror as the image of the dead man burst into his brain. The eyeless corpse was furious that someone would upset its sightless slumber. Tye's skin crawled at the thought of the dead man wanting revenge. The man would want payback, and he would take it from Tye. *What do I have that this asshole wants?* His eyes. Tye's body started to tremble. The dead cat and the eyeless corpse were closing in on him. He needed to leave; he had to get out now or he knew he would never be able to leave that long, humid tomb. He started to crawl among the trash that was strewn all over the floor, past papers and cardboard signs. He creeped over broken bottles that ripped into his forearms and through needles that jabbed his fingers with sharp little pricks. He scuttled harder and faster, trying to get farther away from the corpse and the feline that were advancing in the dark. He picked up momentum as he scurried along the floor. He moved like a soldier on maneuvers, trying to struggle under barbed wire at a fast clip.

Finally he got up onto his knees, took in a deep gulp of the rancid air and dashed down the hall. He ran in complete darkness, as if his eyes were closed or worse—gone. He banged into the walls but kept going. When he began to stumble, he made himself straighten out and continue. He never missed a beat until he came to the door that they had first entered. He rammed his shoulder into it, expecting it not to budge. He felt relief as it opened and he tumbled into the main hallway that seemed to be glowing with outside light from the moon and the brightness of the city. The warm summer air that greeted his face felt cool compared to the hot gloom that permeated the hallway. He staggered and fell against the wall and slid down, shaking. He looked into the doorway he had just escaped from. He thought he'd see the corpse walking out of the shadows any second with the dead cat in his arms patting the thing's head. He kicked the door shut and tried to breathe.

Richie, he thought, *that motherfucker. I'm gonna kill him.*

Richie ran in a complete panic. He had no idea where he was or where he was going. He gripped the flashlight so tightly that his knuckles turned white. He followed the frantic light down the main hallway. He knew that he was lost; the route he'd taken on his departure from the service hallway was not the one they had used to get up there. He kept running and turning corners, seeing places he did not recognize. He was like a petrified lab rat in a maze, running from an unknown predator.

He scurried past a service elevator and never noticed that the doors were starting to open. Flying out of the elevator was a chain with a sharp hook on the end. It sliced into Richie's shin with the same expertise a cowboy uses when he lassoes a steer. Richie let out a scream and fell. The flashlight dropped to the ground.

He looked down at the sharp hook that was embedded in his lower leg, but his mind couldn't comprehend what it was. Before he could try to pull the hook out, the chain was yanked quickly, causing the hook to dig deeper into Richie's muscle and pulling him closer to the open elevator. The flashlight rolled around in front of him, its light shining away from him. Richie found himself being dragged into the dark elevator. His screams turned into one long, painful wail that could be heard all the way at the other end of the hallway. He hoped that Tye would use them as a homing device.

The louder Richie screamed, the faster Tye ran toward him. When he'd heard the screams coming from the hallway that he had recently exited, he'd had no choice but to follow them. Tye thought about beating the shit out of Richie for leaving him alone, but when he heard the deep screams growing louder he figured that someone had already beaten him to the punch. As Tye raced around the same labyrinth of hallways that Richie had just run through, Richie's screams showed him the way like a big shrill sign. When Tye turned the corner, he saw a massive figure holding a chain like he'd never seen before stepping out of the service elevator. Tye stopped. Instinctively he stepped back into the shadows and watched as the behemoth lifted the chain and held Richie up as if he were a proud fisherman admiring his catch for the day.

Tye had never seen anyone so massive before, on the outside or in lockup. He knew lots of big men, huge men, even muscle heads and gym rats. Guys that were juiced to the max on 'roids and growth hormones. On the streets, size meant respect. The vast bulk of this individual alone would have commanded the respect, awe, and fear of legions.

As Richie dangled upside down from the chain, he glimpsed Tye standing in the corner. Even from his point of view he could read Tye's horror. Their eyes locked. Tye plead quietly for Richie not to say anything. Richie's mouth opened. Whether to scream, yell out a warning, or cry for help, Tye would never know. Just as the sound began to escape from his mouth, the massive figure jumped back into the elevator and Richie's head bounced off the door so hard that his cry was shoved back down his throat as he went limp.

The doors closed and the service elevator ascended. Tye stood in the shadows. He was starting to shake from his head down to his feet. He couldn't control himself—every muscle and bone in his body felt as if it were being pulled in opposite directions by a fear he never imagined.

• • •

Inside the monster's penthouse lair, glass jars of various shapes and sizes, filled with a thick gelatinous substance and stuffed with human eyes, sat on a low table. Dozens of lifeless orbs looked out of the yellowy viscous fluid at the lair that was forever to be their new home. The sight was unsettling.

Kira made her way through the kitchen to the sink where Christine had told her the window led out to the atrium. She climbed up on the steel counter and kneeled down, trying to get better leverage to push open the window. Although it wasn't locked, a thick coat of paint had sealed the window shut for a while. She searched for something to open the window with. A knife. A steel spatula. Anything she could shove between the window and the sill. She found a spatula and began to pry open the window. Frustration started to set in, but she didn't let it stop her. She was too close to getting out to have a tiny obstacle like a stubborn window stop her from getting away from Michael. As Kira pressed harder, her knees dug into the cold steel counter. When the window wouldn't budge, she pushed again with all her strength and lost her balance. She reached out for something to break her fall, but there was nothing to grab on to. She landed on the floor with a painful thud.

"Fuck," she muttered under her breath.

Kira stopped for a moment. It hadn't occurred to her that she wouldn't wake up to see Christine in the morning. She had grown accustomed to waking up and looking over and watching Christine sleep peacefully in the cot next to hers. When they were in Juvey, the girl occupying that cot had been easily bribed to move her spot for two cartons of forbidden cigarettes. It was a costly proposition, but one that both girls thought was well worth it. They both contributed a carton each, and the hassle they'd had to obtain them was a testament to their mutual affection. But now there would be no one to wake up to, no one to watch over in the showers, or to hang with and talk with, to share secrets with, to be one with. There would be no one for her now.

Suddenly, it hit Kira like a barroom sucker punch; she had no idea where she would wake up tomorrow morning at all. Where did she plan on going? How did she plan on getting there? The money that Christine gave her and the money she saved and stole wouldn't be enough to get her a room for the night or even a bus ticket out of town. In a few hours the sun would be up and she would find herself once again on the same streets doing the same thing. It would be a matter of time before she was picked up again or killed. She thought about forgetting about escaping. She thought of going back to Christine and finishing up the weekend and trying to start some sort of life once they were free, but the dark specter of Michael stood in the way of her plans for happiness. He would never let her be happy, never leave her alone. And the chances that he would let her see her first morning of freedom were almost nonexistent. Her options were to stay, try to fight him and get badly hurt, and probably see Christine hurt in the process, or she could just split now. She'd have to leave the girl she'd come to know as her only true friend and hit the streets to what she knew would be certain misery for her. She chose to run.

Kira stood there, knowing that any second Williams could barge in and it would be the end of the line for her. But it wasn't Williams who came bursting through the swinging kitchen doors. Christine opened the door just enough to stick her head through the opening. There was a strong sense of urgency etched on her face.

When Christine saw that Kira was fine, she just shook her head.

"Jesus Christ, girl, you want to wake the dead? Be quiet!" Christine whispered.

Then she looked at her and tried not to laugh. Kira looked funny standing among the kitchen's filth with an expression that said she had no idea what was going on. She gave an innocent puppy dog frown and laughed with Christine. Once they'd stopped laughing, Kira picked up a saucepan and turned back to the window. Christine didn't want to watch her go so she went back to the hallway to see if anyone else had heard the commotion.

Kira resumed her attempts at escape as her friend watched out for her. She stopped as a fly buzzed out of the darkness and flew around her head. The girl swatted the fly away and felt a hot gust of air down her back, as if some type of animal was breathing behind her. A stink so foul came from the blackness of the dumbwaiter that it made her back up.

Damn, she thought to herself, *something smells like it died in there*. She imagined a dead rat or some dead stray dog rotting away inside the dumbwaiter, something vile and putrid to cause that stench.

Williams watched Hannah as she looked at her engagement ring.

Neither one heard Margaret until she was right behind them. When she spoke they were both startled.

"Someone is using the elevators," she said with so much concern you would have thought the place was on fire.

Williams expected as much. They were kids. They were horny, curious, and foolish, a combination destined for trouble.

"I'll get them," he said as he stood up from his seat.

"No. I'll get them," Hannah said, putting her hand on his good arm. He liked the way she felt. He knew why she wanted to go. She had to save face; she couldn't let the kids think they had gotten the better of her that afternoon. She would confront the kids and bring them back down. Williams knew it was the right thing to do: the kids had to respect her as much as they feared him. She headed off and left the big ballroom and went toward the elevators. Williams and Margaret watched her go.

"Don't you think you should go with her?" Margaret worried.

"No, she wants to do this alone," he answered.

"Will she be safe?"

And Williams thought about that. *Would she be safe?* She had no one to fear, really, except Michael. Williams knew that although Michael was a thug, he wasn't stupid. If anything happened to Hannah, both Michael and Williams understood that Michael's life would end in the Blackwell Hotel with Frank Williams standing over the young man's lifeless body holding a smoking gun in his one good hand.

With each step that Hannah took down the empty hallway, her heels left a chilling click in their wake. The elevator doors opened almost immediately after she pushed the call button. As she entered the lift, Hannah noticed how the light glinted off the diamond that was still on her right hand.

Hannah thought about what Williams had just said. He was right, there was no reason why she shouldn't marry Ronald. She loved him, she thought that she might love him more than she had ever loved anyone before. Why did she have the slightest bit of hesitation about fully committing to him? She had already given him her body and heart. What was left, her soul? Part of that was still left in the zoo, inside the bear house where she was still clinging to her father's chest fearing and hating the man she had loved and trusted. Was it that she was afraid to fully trust Ronald with all of her secrets and wishes the way she had trusted her father? Hannah got mad at herself for letting it bother her again. It was so long ago, a silly prank that fathers tease their kids with. One of a hundred little teases parents play with their kids, like, "I've got your nose," "Don't let the bedbugs bite"—it was done all the time. Then why did Hannah still hold a coolness toward her father? Why did she hold back a little every time she saw him again? It wasn't the bears that turned into monsters in front of her eyes, it wasn't the fact that he teased her, it was simply that she could not trust him if she was vulnerable again. She had never trusted anyone else since then. Ronald was the first man she had met since that day that she felt she could trust and love completely. She was a grown woman now, a big girl, and big girls aren't supposed to be afraid of monsters. Making her decision to accept Ron's proposal, she slipped the ring off her finger and placed it on her other hand.

The elevator doors opened slightly on the second floor. Though Hannah had repeatedly pushed the "2" button as if it would make the elevator do what she wanted, the doors closed solidly in front of her. As if it were being controlled by someone somewhere else, the elevator rose to the eighth floor. When the doors opened again, they revealed a dark, empty hallway that was not nearly as inviting as it had been in the height of the hotel's popularity. The odor that was emanating from the hallway was enough for her to start gagging.

A lone fly entered the elevator as Hannah pressed the Door Close button, willing the thing to return to a lower floor. A few of the fly's friends followed into the small room. Hannah swatted them away with disgusted impatience.

When she glanced up to see why the elevator was still not moving, she looked straight into the eyes of the devil.

"Oh, God . . . please," she begged in a whisper.

Unfortunately, her prayers were not answered in the way she had expected. The beast in front of her reached out and slammed her against the back wall of the elevator. When he let go, her body slumped to the floor. He placed his massive weight on top of her so that he could have a better angle for his next task. Bending slightly, the brute bent down and pierced her skin with his sharp fingernails. He plucked her eyes out of their sockets so that he could return them to the rest of the bits of his soul that he had recovered from his other victims.

He left her on the ground with her body contorted and her arm sticking out of the elevator. Hannah lay in a puddle of her own blood, mixed together with her captor's drool. The doors to the lift tried to close, but they were impeded by her delicate limb.

The glimmer from her diamond ring was now obsured by the red curtain that had ended her life.

8

THE MONSTER SAT IN SILENCE AS THE GIRL WITH THE
olive skin and dark hair walked by him. She stopped in
front of where he hid. She sniffed, and the monster
could sense she felt something was not right. She
looked into his secret spot, but her eyes weren't strong
enough to penetrate the darkness that had long since
become his ally and kept prying eyes at bay. It was the
eyes of the interlopers the monster feared most, for he
knew that once the ungodly cast their gaze at you, they
ate away at your soul with every glance. With every
hungry blink and ravenous stare, they ripped chunks of
the monster's essence away. He could feel himself
being devoured alive every time an outsider looked at
him. It was why every person he'd met shivered and
screamed every time they saw him. Their insatiable
appetites could not fathom the immense bounty of the
monster's purity. The monster knew that his pureness
and grace were too much for the wicked to comprehend. They could not have his soul; they could not

consume the righteous fire that burned in his heart and mind. Their eyes would not steal away what the monster had tried to keep holy for so long. The words came back to him. Someone had spoken them eons ago, but now the words started to take shape inside the monster's head. Slowly they grew and he could read them. They glowed like a sacred fire: "If these eyes offend thee . . . pluck them out."

The olive-skinned girl hurried away from the monster's hiding spot and left the other girl alone. The one with the holy paintings adorned over her body—the one the monster wanted to possess—was still in the kitchen. He already had one from their tribe, their leader, the one that gave orders. Her pelt would be hung up with the others and soon he would dwindle their numbers down until there were none. With their leader gone, there would be no unity in the tribe and he would be able to attack with impunity.

He caressed the chains that were wrapped snuggly around his thick frame with his fingers. The sharpness of the hooks felt comforting in his calloused palm. His eyes focused on the girl with the holy paintings on her body. She was carrying a large metal pot. She positioned the heavy pot so she could destroy the window, break the glass, and flee the monster's domain. But it was too late for escape. She should never have come here in the first place. She would tell others so that more of them would come with their weapons and their troops. They would try to breech the monster's castle.

No, the one with the holy paintings on her body could not leave; her time had come. He would lead his attack against the unholy hordes that tried to take his kingdom from him with her head on a pole and her flesh wrapped around his torso. The blasphemers and the unrighteous would not prevail in the monster's house. He might be a beast, but he was still one of God's creatures. He would do God's bidding, as he had always done in the past. He opened the doors to the dumbwaiter, pushed his large bulk out silently, and crept toward the girl.

Kira glanced around the room for something that she could break the window with. She figured one good swipe would take out most of the glass in the window. She could pick out the rest in seconds flat. She estimated that in three minutes tops, she would be outside the atrium and finding the opening in the wall that the dog had used. Three minutes until she was free.

She squatted down and planted her feet firmly on the countertop next to the sink. She turned to get the best swing possible and readied herself to shatter the window and flee. She blew at an annoying fly that started to circle her head, and just before she swung, the fetid odor of decay and rot filled her nose and made her gag.

She flung the pot toward the window. In the same instant, a razor-sharp hook ripped into her shoulder. The curved blade was so sharp that the pain took seconds to register in Kira's brain as she was being yanked off the countertop and onto the floor. It was when her body slammed into the floor and her head cracked on the hard cement that all the synapses and pain receptors in Kira's body kicked into overdrive. The agony that electrified her body was beyond excruciating. She tried to scream, but the pain was so intense, her throat constricted and she choked on her own blood-curdling shriek.

The monster yanked the chain and the hook embedded itself deeper into Kira's flesh. The motion jarred her scream loose, and she let out a wail that sounded like last call in hell.

"Aaaarrrrrrrrrhhhhhhhhhhhhhhhhh!" escaped Kira's twisted mouth so loudly that it made the monster's ears ring and the plate in his head vibrate.

Christine's heart stopped when she heard Kira's scream resounding throughout the hallway. She froze, looking at the kitchen doors at the end of the long hall. Her mind went blank, trying not to picture what Michael was doing to Kira.

Williams dropped the shot glass from his good hand the second he heard Kira's scream. He had heard screams before, wails of sorrow, yells for help, but he had never heard anything like this. Not in the jungle, not in the streets, not even in his nightmares. He was up and out of his seat racing out of the old ballroom before he knew what he was doing. He was going on pure reflex and stored-up adrenaline. He charged toward the kitchen, with Margaret trying her best to keep up behind him.

• • •

Christine's feet started moving without her knowledge. She saw herself racing toward the kitchen door, but the door seemed to pull farther away, as in a dream. The faster she ran, the farther the kitchen moved away from her. She felt as if she were running in slow motion. Kira had stopped screaming, but the echo of her pain still reverberated off the walls. Christine started to pick up speed but threw on the brakes when Williams came flying down the other hallway and nearly knocked her over. Williams's eyes gave Christine a quick once-over, and he knew that she wasn't the one in peril.

"Kira." Christine trembled.

Without being told anything else, Williams ran toward the kitchen with Christine and Margaret.

The monster savagely pulled the chain closer to him the way a mighty fisherman pulls in a fighting marlin. Kira's arms and hands wildly flayed about, her fingers grabbing on to a frying pan lying on the floor. The monster jerked her up and she swung the frying pan at his face. He blocked the pan with his fist, which never even moved when the cast iron smashed into his hand.

"Help me, please! Somebody, help me!" Kira bellowed.

The kitchen was still dark and she couldn't even see what her massive assailant looked like. She only knew he was the biggest thing she had ever come across and that his stench was something that could only come from dying flesh. The monster grabbed her body; his powerful hands pressed into her flesh and pulled her toward the dumbwaiter. As he entered the dumbwaiter,

Kira gripped the wooden frame with her fingertips. The monster hoisted the chain, and the hooked blade tore so deep into Kira's back that it sliced into her clavicle, severing the bone. Her fingernails were ripped from her fingers and left embedded in the wooden frame surrounding the dumbwaiter.

The monster started his ascent, the mighty chains wrapped around his body. His prized possession was dangling at the end of his chain.

Williams and Christine burst into the kitchen in a dead heat, with Margaret pulling in close behind. They all stopped for a second to let their eyes adjust to the darkness of the room.

Christine heard a painful gurgle and turned to see Kira's body being lifted up into the dumbwaiter. She ran toward her friend. Williams followed.

Christine was six feet away when Kira's entire body shot up. Her head splattered against the wooden frame so hard that the bone practically cracked and the wood splintered. Kira's eyes rolled over, and blood spurted from her mouth like projectile vomit. In an instant, she was sucked into the dumbwaiter and was gone. They all listened in mute shock as Kira's body banged off the walls of the long shaft that led up into the unknown regions of the Blackwell.

Michael put on his best game face and smiled at Russell as they went to find Melissa and Zoë. He didn't want the anger of the day to ruin his night. He wanted to blow off some steam; he needed to. He was still sore at himself for coming on too strong and scaring Kira away too quickly. Since it was only Friday night, he'd have all weekend to get at her. And the cop—he had all the time in the world for him, as long as it happened within the next two days.

He liked what he saw in Zoë. He didn't usually like her type, but he liked her looks and understood what she was all about. Girls like Zoë were easy to read, almost transparent in their needs and wants. Zoë was too bored being a spoiled little rich girl and saw Michael as her chance to go slumming over the weekend. Michael knew and didn't mind at all. If Zoë wanted to spoil herself with the working class, then fine by him. He would enjoy spoiling her. Zoë had a cocktease's walk with a ballbuster's attitude. She would shake her ass and give you shit at the same time, but she didn't know if she wanted to fuck or fight.

Michael thought that she was just as screwed up as every other girl he had come upon out on the streets. He knew plenty that were just as hard up as she was. She had an absentee father, a mother who liked her liquor cabinet's upkeep more than her daughter's welfare, and a slew of overly friendly "uncles" that her mother paraded in and out of their million-dollar home. She also had every material thing she could ever want at her fingertips. So why did she steal? Simple. Because she could. Michael understood the logic behind it, or rather, the lack of logic. Zoë was a thief. She liked to steal, she enjoyed taking things that weren't hers. Zoë relished the fact that her thefts would cause someone else frustration, anger, and unhappiness. The reason she stole was to make strangers miserable. Because Zoë was unhappy. She tried to disguise it with a "who gives a shit" attitude, but deep down she was in a constant state of misery and self-loathing. Misery loves company, and if someone out there was suffering a little by Zoë's quick, thin fingers, then it made life all that more bearable for her.

Michael tapped the lead pipe in quick soft succession against the old banister, a crude Morse code that signaled their arrival. He'd been keeping the pipe as a talisman of sorts since he'd found it. Out of the shadows, Zoë and Melissa slinked out. They met the boys with nervous giggles. The anticipation of getting caught was a potent aphrodisiac, and Melissa could feel a warm wetness starting between her legs as Russell came smiling toward her.

"Shall we get this party started?" Zoë asked, trying to take the reigns of the group.

"Why not?" Michael asked as he looked Zoë up and down, noticing how much cleaner and prettier she looked now than she had earlier in the day.

"Where to, then?" she asked as she smiled at Michael's eager reevaluation of her body.

Michael's eyes tilted upward.

"To the penthouse, to places where dreams come true."

Michael led the way, with Zoë close behind him, closer than she had to be. After Russell stepped back and bowed to let Melissa pass him, his long, sinewy arms wrapped around her waist and pulled her against him. She could feel the bulge grow in his pants. She felt the excitement that was sparked between them and she hungered for the moment they could be alone.

Williams checked for a signal on his cell phone but could not get one. He punched the up button on the elevator and watched as it descended from the eighth floor.

"I thought this thing only went to the fifth floor," he said in a questioning tone.

Margaret didn't respond, as she had no answer to give him. Christine just paced and worried.

"Goddamn it! I can't get any fucking reception on this piece of shit!" Williams said, shaking his phone in frustration. The elevator made it down past seven.

"Listen, I want you to get everyone out of their rooms and out of here," Williams told Margaret.

"No one is in their rooms," Christine informed him.

"What?" He stopped to look at the girl. The elevator was at the sixth floor.

"Some of them went up to party in the penthouse," Christine told him.

"Goddamn it! Who?" he demanded.

"Zoë, Melissa, Russell, and Michael," the girl said, fearing what his response would be.

"Fucking figures," was all he said. The elevator was at five.

"Oh, dear. Oh, dear," Margaret repeated. The elevator was past four and coming down faster.

"Margaret, I want you to find Richie and Tye and get them out of here, now!" Williams said. He handed her his cell phone.

"When you get outside, call 911 immediately. You'll have better reception once you're out of this place," he said as the elevator reached the ground floor.

The doors opened up and Williams stepped in. When he turned to look at Margaret, he saw that she was standing stoically with confusion in her eyes. She was staring at the phone in her hand as if it were a foreign object.

"Where are you going?" Christine asked.

"To find Kira. Wherever the hell she is," he replied as he punched the button for the penthouse. The doors started to close and he saw Margaret mumbling something to herself. Before they shut, Christine jumped in the elevator with him.

"What the fuck do you think you're doing?" he yelled at her.

"I'm going with you!" Christine answered, emphatically indicating that taking no for an answer wasn't even an option.

"Fuckin' great," Williams sighed as they went up.

It wasn't until the doors closed all the way that Williams realized that the elevator was dim. One lone light was flickering in a valiant attempt to illuminate the elevator. Williams banged the wall with his good hand. The bulb seemed to get a boost of energy, and the lighting was boosted from dim to semi-visible.

"Where should we start?" Christine wondered.

That's a good fucking question, he thought. *Where would one look to find someone in this place?* Margaret had said that the dumbwaiter in the kitchen went to every floor in the building, including the penthouse. Although it wasn't supposed to go past five, the elevator was stopped at the eighth floor. Williams made a quick calculation in his head, and figured that Kira was somewhere between the eighth floor and the penthouse. That meant thirteen floors would have to be searched quickly to find the girl before any more harm came to her. It was an impossible task for one man to do. *A man with one arm and a nervous teenager. She was as good as dead,* he thought. *What the hell could have happened to her? Who could have taken her like that . . .*

Then it hit him. It hit him like a donkey kicking him in the guts. There was only one person, one thing, that would do something like that.

He was here.

Williams's body became electrified at the possibility. His missing fingers and hand started to tingle with phantom pains of anticipation. Williams looked at Christine; her face showed fear. She was chewing on her lower lips, but her eyes had a sheen of determination starting to glow within the dark brown irises. The elevator seemed to be going up considerably slower than when it had come down. Time seemed to stand still once they both stepped on. It was then that Williams noticed a red splotch on Christine's shirt. Blood. Fresh and wet.

"What happened to you?" he asked.

"Huh?" she answered, not paying attention to him.

"Did you hurt yourself?" He nodded at the blood-stain on her shirt.

Christine looked down at her shirt and saw the blood. She did a quick check in her mind and realized the blood wasn't hers. *Probably Kira's,* she thought.

Kira had spit up a lot of blood. That image made her heart sink.

"No. That's not even . . ." Christine stopped as the bloodstain started to expand.

Williams and Christine stared at her shirt as more specks started to appear on the material. The blood wasn't flowing from Christine; it was falling on her. They both looked up. The lone light buzzed and crackled. Smeared across the broken glass and ceiling was blood and matted hair.

"Hannah," Williams said quietly without even knowing he was talking. He knew it was Hannah's hair and blood. Something bad had happened to her, something very bad, and he hadn't been there to protect her. A sickness started to swell in him as he thought of the massive killer having his way with her somewhere in the hotel. He reached behind his jacket and pulled out his service revolver. He clicked off the safety.

They were passing the sixth floor. He smashed the button to the eighth floor. He felt the gun in his hand. The familiar heaviness was reassuring. He had practiced shooting the murderous shadow over and over for the last four years. He'd killed the unseen monster a million times. Tonight it would be a million and one. Tonight it would be for real. Tonight it would end.

They stopped at eight. The doors opened up to the dark hallway that had greeted Hannah. Williams held his gun out and walked out of the elevator, Christine right behind him. The doors closed and they started a search that they prayed wouldn't end with more people they knew being carried out in body bags.

• • •

Tye found himself totally disoriented as he tried to retrace his steps. Nothing looked familiar to him. The hallway seemed like one continuous burned-out maze that seemed to go nowhere. He tried to count the room numbers to gauge how far away he was from a stairwell, but someone had removed all the numbers. When he did happen upon a stairwell, he could neither budge the door open, break it down, nor pick the lock. It seemed that someone had eradicated all his previous steps and had blocked off any route he may have used to escape.

He tried to fit all the pieces of the puzzle that the night had thrown at him together. *One: Richie's gone. Two: Richie's gone because some massive crazy-looking motherfucker harpooned him like a mackerel. Three: There is no way back down to get the fuck out of here. Four: That crazy motherfucker is still around here somewhere. Five: No one knows we came up here. Six: There's a good chance that motherfucker won't stop with just Richie.* Tye didn't have to fit in the rest of the pieces to see what the picture looked like: it looked damn bleak.

He had to remain calm. He knew that if he was able to come up here, there had to be a way down. Even if their original way was blocked off, there had to be some other way to get off the floor. He had to keep his cool. *Gotta get out of here, gotta get out of here!* his brain yelled out.

In frustration, he punched the wall. His fist broke through the fire-damaged plaster and crushed into a crunchy mass behind the wall. He tried to pull his hand out, but it was stuck. Something started to cover his

216

flesh. Tye became frantic and ripped his hand out of the wall. It was covered with cockroaches. He freaked and smashed his hand against the wall to rake the bugs off his skin. He started to run. He ran through the hallway until he couldn't breathe anymore.

He didn't know where he was running to, he just knew it led back to where he started: nowhere. He ran until his lungs burned and his muscles ached. When he stopped, he bent over and gulped in the humid summer night air. He didn't want to end up dead, not yet, and definitely not by that big psycho's hand. He caught his breath and calmed his mind.

Finding a way out was his goal, so he started checking the rooms for an exit again. Inside one of them, he walked to the window and pulled off the flimsy boards to look out. He saw the neighborhood eight floors below him. It was deserted. Not a soul was on the streets. Only a few of the streetlamps worked, but as he looked down both sides of the street he could tell by their sporadic glow that nothing was open and nobody was coming. Two blocks over he could see cars riding down the avenues. He could even make out people on the sidewalk. He thought that maybe he could try to call to them, signal to somebody for help. But who would hear him? Who would see him? Then he wondered if he saw someone screaming for help eight stories up in a deserted hotel, would he help? The answer was no, and Tye felt the sting of cosmic retribution for being such an asshole his whole life.

The highway was just half a mile away. Cars sped by in both directions and they looked like nothing more than pairs of red and white eyes zooming off away from each other, getting lost in the night. Beneath him was life; up there with him was death. He had to get down. He didn't care about the safe anymore; the money didn't matter to him now. What good were riches if you weren't alive to spend them?

He looked up and down the side of the building, hoping to find a fire escape, but it was dismantled from the twelfth floor down. No one could make it down unless he had wings. He thought about lowering himself down from ledge to ledge, but he knew that was an impossibility, something you only see in action movies when some overpaid, overhyped white star is outgunned and outnumbered but still manages to kill all the bad guys, get the hot chick, and say a couple of funny lines. If this was a movie, then it was a horror film. Tye had seen enough of those to know how the black brother usually ends up: dead before the third act. Angrily, he banged the ledge with his fist. He let out a scream as a sharp pain tore into his knuckles. He looked down and saw that all along the ledge, pieces of sharp glass and rusty old nails were strewn. The row of sharp deterrents extended all the way down the ledge and around the corner. He looked down and could see that the ledge below and the ledge below that one had the same setup. Somebody didn't want anyone out on the ledges. Even if Tye wanted to chance jumping down to the next ledge, the option had already been taken from him.

"Motherfucker," he spat out in anger as he shook the blood off his hand.

The moon seemed to be right over him. It was full and appeared to take up most of the sky. He could make out the craters on the surface, which usually registered to the human eye as nothing more than faint gray circles. The lunar image reminded him of the thing's head that took Richie. Big and barren, holes and craters all over its sickly skin. That thing might as well have been from the moon or from some other planet, because it would be hard to classify it as an inhabitant of earth.

Tye wished he had a weapon. *A pistol would be nice. A machine gun would do better, and a flamethrower would be just right.* He looked around for something that could be used as a weapon—a club or a pipe, anything that could cause damage—but he found nothing. Even when he tried to break a table leg off to use it as a cudgel, it splintered into slivers from years of exposure and shoddy workmanship. Langley Blackwell may have spared no expense in building his hotel and designing it to be a confusing maze to everyone except himself, but when it came to furnishing it, the bastard cheaped out.

Tye thought about staying put, finding a place to hide to spend the night. He could easily barricade himself in a room or a closet and wait for the morning sun. By then, the others would have realized that he and Richie were gone and go looking for them. Hopefully they would assume they were upstairs and hadn't split the premises altogether, so they wouldn't start searching other places in vain. Tye thought that was a good idea. He would hole up somewhere in a corner room and block the door. He would have to make sure he had an escape route in case Jumbo the Killer Moon Man tried coming for him. He knew he couldn't have himself trapped with his back against the wall and no place to run.

The thought of monster movies entered his head again, and he remembered watching an old movie that had scared the shit out of him. He didn't remember the name, but a bunch of dead folks were coming back to life and eating people. Tye was young when he had seen the movie, but the black-and-white images of those pasty-faced, slow-motion ghouls had never left him. He remembered that the hero was a black dude, which was probably the main reason why the movie stuck in his head and why he kept thinking about having some kind of escape route in case all them hungry dead white folks busted down the door. Tye knew the brother was right, but then he thought about the end of the movie and remembered that the black guy gets killed in the climax. *Dumb fucking nigga gets his head blown off anyway. Stupid fucking movie.* He needed to find a spot to hide in quickly. He needed to have a place to run to if he was discovered. He needed for the sun to rise and he needed to be the fuck out of this goddamn building. He left the room and went back into the burned hallway and tried to find somewhere to wait for the welcoming rays of the morning sun.

Tye was ten steps into his new plan of attack when he heard someone coming up behind him. He held his breath. He knew no one else would be up here at this time of night. No one else was as stupid as he and Richie were, so that left only one person who could be heading his way. The big-ass pasty-faced ghoul.

"Fuck," he whispered to himself as he hurried down the hallway. The sound was coming closer. He needed a place to hide quickly. All of the doors to the rooms in that section of the hallway were either burned through or off their hinges. The footsteps were just about to turn the corner. Tye didn't want to be out in the open, and he definitely didn't want to be stuck in a room that had no door to barricade. *Fuck the escape route now*, he thought. He ran up the hallway and saw a room with a door that seemed to be in one piece and sturdy. He turned the handle, but the door would not open.

"Cocksucker," he seethed. He pulled out his bent hairpin and started to jimmy the lock. The footsteps were closing in, and he couldn't hear the lock click open. The footsteps were right behind him. The door wasn't opening. He moved the bent hairpin around the keyhole; he was trying to latch on to the locking mechanism. He could hear voices now behind him, but he blocked everything out of his head. The only sound he needed to hear was the sound of the lock clicking open. Sweat burned his eyes, his hands shook, the voices behind him became a dull murmur as he focused all his concentration on the lock. Opening the lock. He could feel someone's breath on his back. Someone was behind him. The lock clicked open. He heard it open like a giant explosion going off in his head, but it was too late. Tye knew that right behind him someone stood. He slowly turned to face a death he wasn't ready for. He froze when he saw who was there.

Standing behind him was Williams and Christine. The cop had a gun out pointed at him, and the girl was saying something. It took a second for her words to become clear, to knock out the silence of concentration.

"What the fuck, asshole? Didn't you hear us callin' you?" she asked him angrily.

Tye shook his head no, then he realized that the sounds he heard and the voices that were talking to him were not that of the killer but came from Christine and the one-armed cop. He was never happier to see any two people in his life.

Tye jumped up and almost hugged the both of them. Williams pushed by him and entered the room. Tye and Christine followed.

"Man, I'm fucking glad to see you. This massive dude got Richie," Tye gushed out.

"What?" Williams and Christine said simultaneously.

"This fucking dude, man, was huge. I mean big. Godzilla-fucking big. Bald and all fucked-up looking," Tye said.

Williams's knees felt as if they were going to give out. Whatever off-the-wall, million-to-one theory he'd had about the massive killer, everything became cemented in hard cold fact as Tye described a walking nightmare from Williams's past. Williams's eyes stared into space as he started to relive the horror again.

Christine saw that Williams had started to go to a place far, far away.

"What's wrong?" she asked Williams.

"What's wrong? Take your fucking pick!" Tye barked at her.

"Shut up, I'm not talking to you," she snapped back at him.

"This can't be happening," Williams mumbled in disbelief. He could feel his heart starting to pump faster.

"What can't be happening?" Christine asked without trying to sound too nervous.

Williams's mind flashed back. It moved as if his brain were on superspeed rewind and millions of faces and images zipped by in a second and stopped back at that day in the house on the hill. He could see his arm lying next to him, his fingers clenched around the flashlight and the beam of light falling on the young girl sobbing in the corner. As if his mind were stuck on slo-mo, the girl lifted her face and Williams once again felt that surge of nausea hit him as he looked into her eyeless face.

"Who is this guy?" Christine demanded. She sensed that Williams knew more than he was willing to say.

Williams didn't know how to answer. How could he give a synopsis of man's total depravity in thirty seconds? He couldn't even recall what was fact and what was fiction anymore, his dreams had blended so deeply into his memories of events. Entrenched somewhere between reality and fable lay the truth.

"He's a nightmare," was all he could say to answer. It was enough for Christine.

"We have to find them. We have to find Kira and Richie," she said.

"Fuck that! I ain't goin' searchin' for someone that's already dead," Tye answered as he moved farther away from them.

Christine didn't want to think that Kira was already dead. She had to believe that she would find her, hurt and banged-up, but alive.

"Why did he take them? What is he after?" Christine wondered, not asking Williams directly, just throwing the questions out there.

Why did he take them? Williams thought. And he knew. He knew what horrors the sick mind that sat damaged in that big skull-like head was plotting. Williams knew of only two people that had ever escaped once they had crossed the killer's path, and neither one had made it out whole. The first was the girl who still sat eyeless in a mental ward somewhere, silently rocking back and forth, forever reliving the unspeakable things that had been done to her as her fractured mind played them over again and again in an endless loop of excruciating pain and terror. The other survivor was himself, who was just as blind to the world as the poor girl who was locked away for the rest of her tortured life.

He knew damn well why Goodnight had taken Kira and Richie. He'd taken them to prove to an unbelieving world once again that pure and unadulterated evil does exist and that an ineffectual God does nothing to stop it. If there was a chance that Kira and Richie were alive, it was slim. If there was any hope left that they were not yet harmed, it was fading quickly. He knew he had to find the kids now. He knew that he had to kill the uncatchable phantom that had haunted him for years. He knew he had to set things right for himself, Blaine, the girl in the institution, and the countless others that Goodnight had attacked.

"Listen, we don't have much time. Where are the others?" Williams asked, referring to Michael and the other kids.

"I don't know. I didn't know anyone else was up here except Richie and me," Tye confessed.

"Do you think Margaret has called the police?" Christine wanted to know.

"Yeah, if she went outside and got reception, back-up should be here any minute." Williams was hoping that Margaret didn't end up the way he knew Hannah had.

"Then let's just wait here till the cops show up," Tye suggested.

"We don't have the time to sit here and wait. Trust me, every second we aren't looking for them is another second that something bad can happen," Williams said. As soon as he spoke, he saw the look in Christine's face and realized he shouldn't have said anything. It was too late to take it back, but if she couldn't figure out what was in store for her friend, then she was a fool.

"He won't hurt her," Williams lied, trying to boost Christine's confidence. Then something flashed in his mind's eye. The eyeless girl he discovered in the house years ago had religious tattoos. *Was it a symbol? Did those markings mean those girls had some chance of reprieve from death? Was facing a lifetime of blackness their prize instead?* Answers came flooding into Williams's brain. The tattoos were religious symbols; the killer's house had a shrine to Saint Lucy in it. Of course, religious implications were involved. The killer must have some type of special affinity with his victims who had such symbols on their body. Maybe it didn't mean he wouldn't kill them, it just meant that he had something else in store for them before death mercifully took them from this life.

"Does Kira have any tattoos?" he asked Christine.

"Yeah, a cross on her arm. A bigger one on her back.

Some angels," she answered, thinking about her friend's body and fearing the growing prospect of never seeing it alive again. She wondered why he was asking about Kira's tattoos now.

Once he'd heard Christine's answer, Williams knew he was right. Kira had some time before whatever was going to happen to her did. Unless Richie had a tattoo of the Sistine Chapel's ceiling under his shirt, he feared that the youngster's life was already over.

Williams knew that men follow a routine, something they are comfortable with. A sense of familiarity that helps him cope through the day. Criminals are the same way; their deeds follow certain repetitive patterns. The reason they get caught is that they can't break those patterns. He was banking on the killer having the same routine, going through the same ritual. That ritual had kept the eyeless girl alive for hours before Williams and Blaine had literally stumbled upon her. Williams had pieced together enough of the killer's past rituals to know that there was a cleaning process before he got down to business. What he had to do now was interrupt that process before it got started. He had to find Kira.

He pulled out a stun gun from his jacket and handed it to Christine. The girl looked at it with an odd frown.

"I'm going after them, alone. You two find a way to get downstairs and get the hell out of here," he told them.

"That's a great idea," Tye said, seconding Williams's motion.

"No. I am not leaving. I'm going with you to find her," Christine said with such fierce conviction that

Williams wasn't even going to try to talk her out of it.

"What? Do you want to die, bitch?" Tye asked her.

Christine didn't answer. Williams nodded his acceptance to the girl.

Tye didn't want to try to find a way out by himself. Being alone in the hotel frightened him a lot more than looking for trouble with Christine and Williams. And Tye thought they had an edge. The fucker might be big, but Williams had a gun. Tye had known lots of big men who had fallen hard to little bullets. But if Tye knew what Williams had already experienced firsthand, he would not have placed so much faith in firepower. He shrugged and quietly agreed to go with them, knowing that in the long run, he would regret the decision.

Christine looked at Williams. She was ready to go.

The sense of grudging respect Williams had had for Christine earlier had now grown into full, glowing admiration. He knew she was a warrior. The chances that they were going to get killed were good, but at that precise moment in Francis Xavier Williams's life, after fighting side by side with some of the bravest men in the jungle and with some of the toughest men on the streets, there was no one he'd rather go down swinging with than the eighteen-year-old Mexican girl who stood in front of him.

"Let's go," he said.

With that, they all went hunting for a monster.

Michael was leading Russell, Melissa, and Zoë up the back stairwell toward the top of the hotel. Both he and Russell had the flashlights that they had taken from the supply closet earlier. The strong beams of light bounced around the walls, showing that the back stairwell was not built for aesthetic purposes. It was rather plain and did not have the overly ornate style of the front stairs and foyer. This place was meant to be functional, not fanciful. Michael kept his long piece of pipe in front of him as he cleared the stairs of any debris that was in their way. He stopped to shine his light over the railing to see how much ground they had covered since they'd started their little journey. The shaft of light went straight down over the descending stairs, and the shadows seemed to slink eerily away from the yellow light.

"I think we're on the eighth floor," Russell said, looking over the railing and watching the steps they had just climbed slink back into darkness once the flashlight passed over them.

"We're on nine," Michael corrected him. He spit over the railing and watched his saliva fall down until it couldn't be seen anymore. It splattered somewhere on one of the floors below in the darkness.

"Gross." Zoë sneered at him.

Michael smiled and nodded for Zoë to come closer to him. She stood back and swayed, a glint of mischief twinkling in her eyes. He nodded to her to come closer again. When she did, he placed his hands around her hips and nudged her forward. Zoë held out her hand and Michael gave her the flashlight. She pointed the light to the next floor and they went up together, while Melissa and Russell followed hand in hand.

"Why do you think Kira and Christine didn't want to come up?" Melissa asked with such perfectly timed naïveté that Zoë could have kissed her. It was the perfect opening she needed; Zoë knew the time was right to start priming the deep well of Michael's aggression. Melissa was so wrapped up in her own self-important world of do-gooding that she hadn't sensed the friction that was between Michael and Kira.

"Christine wants to stay down below so she can make out with Kira," Zoë said with just the right pinch of malice in her voice to get the hairs on Michael's neck to stand up and take notice. She could feel the hand that was around her hip involuntarily tighten as she said it. She knew that she could play this game for a while before he got too out of control. She decided the best plan of attack was hitting his ego, which was already on the ropes since it was almost kayoed by the cop earlier that day. Zoë planned on knocking it out for a ten count before the night was over.

"Those two really go at it. I've seen them a couple of times. I have to admit, it's kinda hot to watch them. Christine really knows how to turn Kira on," Zoë instigated. She sensed Michael tense up again at the thought of his ex being enthralled with another person, let alone a female. They kept walking up into the darkness, their flashlights the only guide to stop them from stumbling and tripping over themselves. Michael started to bang the lead pipe in front of him, like a blind man tapping his cane.

"You've seen them?" Melissa asked, with curiosity making her voice higher than normal.

"Yeah, back in Juvey. I'd watch them sneak out after lights-out. Sometimes Christine would slip into Kira's bed or they'd sneak out into the shower room. Man, you should see them go at it," Zoë said, measuring the weight of each word. She knew that Michael was slowly cracking from the pressure of having Kira around. She didn't want to overdo it too soon, so she decided to stop her barbs for the time being. Michael had enough mental pictures in his head to get him mad enough. *Later*, Zoë thought, *later. I'll get him so crazy mad that he'll jump down the stairs to get to Kira*.

"Fuck, that's cool. Keep talking. What did you see them do?" Russell asked, clearly enjoying Zoë's little embellishment. She had seen the girls kiss and be affectionate with each other, but she was just speculating about the other stuff. Being honest didn't matter to her; it was the effect of the story that she was trying to get across. She knew Russell found her tale hot and erotic, but what she wanted was to have Michael find it burning and irritating, like a deep emotional itch he couldn't scratch.

"You talk too much," Michael interrupted in a dull tone that made everyone know that he didn't want to hear any more about Christine and Kira.

Zoë's little head games with Michael came to an appropriate halt when Hannah's cell phone rang in her pocket. Since stealing it, she had already made more than a dozen phone calls and had distributed her "new" number. The sharp ring echoed off the enclosed stairwell.

"What the fuck is that?" Russell said as the ringing phone broke his daydream about Melissa's body next to his.

Zoë reached into her pocket and pulled out the phone and started talking away, ignoring the others.

Michael took the flashlight from her hand and proceeded to march to the top.

"Where the hell did you get that?" Russell asked Zoë.

"She stole it from Hannah on the bus today," Melissa answered him.

"Fuck, you can't leave that girl alone for a second," he said in awe.

Without breaking away from her conversation, Zoë turned to Russell and sweetly lifted her middle finger. When they had reached the next level, Melissa said that she was too tired to go on. Russell agreed; he didn't want all of her energies wasted walking up stairs when they could be used on him. Throughout their trek between the ninth and tenth floors, Zoë serenaded them with a one-sided conversation as she blabbed into the stolen cell with a litany of *no way*s, a few *as if*s and several *that's so stupid*s.

After a brief rest on the tenth floor, Michael shined his light toward his three companions and asked if they could continue. Russell thought so, Melissa agreed, and Zoë ignored the question and kept on talking on the phone. When they reached the sixteenth floor, Michael grabbed the handle of the door and pushed. The door gave with a little struggle, the wood having swelled in the frame with the passage of time.

The place wasn't as bad as some of the other floors. The higher up the floors went, the more elaborate they became. The kids walked down the long hallway that was still lined with some old paintings on the walls, a thick layer of darkness and dust obscuring the subject matter. A few small tables and chairs were placed strategically down the hallway to break up the distance between the doors leading to the suites. Michael flashed his light down the hallway and it shone on a partially open door. When they got to the suite, Michael noticed that there was some moonlight coming in from several picture windows. The suite had a big sitting room with a bar and several couches and wide doorways that led to the other rooms and bedrooms. He shut off the flashlight and entered. Russell was behind him with Melissa. Zoë said a quick goodbye to whomever she was wasting Hannah's cell phone minutes with and followed the others.

"A bar!" Zoë exclaimed as she pushed past Melissa and walked to an old wooden bar with a liquor cabinet behind it.

Zoë searched the bar for something to drink and had the same results that Williams had had in the ballroom. Melissa found several candles that were brittle but still usable. Russell lit them and placed them around the room and along the bar to get the best use of the light.

"Shit. There's not a drop to drink in this fucking dump," Zoë said as she brushed dirt from her hands. She took an old bar towel and wiped away some of the dirt from the mirror that was behind the old bar. She took out some lip gloss and applied it slowly around her lips. Her eyes stared back at Michael, who was watching her. He was tapping the metal pipe in rhythm against his thigh. She was so intent on getting Michael's ire up and ego down that she didn't notice the hulking figure that stood on the other side of the mirror. Even if she looked into the mirror intently, it wasn't likely that she would have noticed the difference in it. Langley Blackwell had made sure that the two-way mirrors he installed throughout the hotel were of the best quality.

"Don't forget why we came up here in the first place," Michael reminded the group as he pulled out his bag of pot. Since he had taken it out and shown it to the others earlier that day, he had snuck away and rolled the five thick joints that filled the baggie now. "Let's all pray to the sacred herb."

"Spark that shit up," Zoë said, pulling herself away from her reflection.

Michael pulled out a joint and lit it up, passing it to Zoë before he took a hit. She inhaled deeply and filled her lungs with the smoke. It was cheap shit, not the stuff she was used to on the outside, but it would have to do for now. She handed the joint back to Michael, the smoke still deep inside her.

"So, you and Kira used to be a thing, huh?" she taunted casually, knowing full well what Michael and Kira's back story was.

He just shrugged, his face impassive. The gesture was meant to convey the message "the past is the past," but his eyes told another story. They burned with the threat "the future is going to be painful."

"You could do better," Zoë said as she coolly exhaled and blew the smoke in Michael's face.

The monster observed the strange pre-combat ritual with captive fascination. *What weird ways*, he thought as he watched the interlopers smoke some type of powerful potion that would ready them for battle. His face was pressed against the glass of the two-way mirror. His fetid breath bounced off the glass and came back toward him, but he didn't notice the stench. His massive hand was lying on the glass and his thick fingers traced the face of the girl who applied glowing ointment to her lips. *Some type of medicine maybe*, the monster speculated. He counted their numbers slowly to himself, *One . . . two . . . three . . .* He knew there was another person in the room, but numbers were sometimes problematic for him. The act of counting was an abstract way of thinking, a way that was foreign and painful to him. He counted again to himself, *One . . . two . . . three . . .* The last number was stuck somewhere in the monster's mind. He concentrated. Numbers and words and funny symbols flashed through his mind. *Five*, the monster proudly thought. *There are five of them.* And he watched the four kids pass the strange smoky potion back and forth.

Melissa took a hit and let it out with a harsh cough. She passed the joint to Russell, who sucked in a mouthful and held it deep in his chest. He beckoned her closer to him. When she was close enough, he leaned in and pressed his lips against hers to let the smoke float into her mouth. She held him tightly and let his tongue slide in to taste the sweet, smoky insides of her mouth.

She was watching Russell through the mirror as he started to nuzzle the back of her neck when she saw something move behind the mirror. Her attention left Russell's mouth and went to the glass mirror they stood in front of. She thought, no, she *knew* she had seen something move behind the glass, beyond their reflection. It was like staring down into the ocean's depths and barely making out the shape of some sort of massive predator lurking in the depths out of view.

"I keep seeing things," Melissa said as Russell nibbled on her ear.

"I told you this shit was gold," Michael proudly boasted, holding up the baggie.

"You ain't smoked enough to hallucinate yet," Russell said, holding Melissa to him.

"No, I'm serious," she said. She pulled away from Russell and started running her fingers over the mirror.

The monster held his breath as the girl approached the mirror. *Does she know?* he wondered. *Does she have the power to look through the glass at me? Are her eyes ready to tear in and devour my soul?* He watched the girl get closer to the glass. His nose was a few inches away from her touch, separated by only the mirror's thickness. Her eyes were widening and becoming glassy. She was getting ready for combat. He knew that he had to strike soon, but he didn't want to attack when their numbers were so plentiful, in case one of them escaped to warn the others. After all, there were five of them.

Russell came up and grabbed Melissa from behind. He whispered some enticing encouragement in her ear and she let out a schoolgirl's giggle. Russell led her out of the room and away from Michael and Zoë for some privacy.

"You go, girl," Zoë yelled out to her.

Melissa stopped and turned to Zoë to answer.

"You wanna come? I know you like to watch," Melissa teased. Russell pulled Melissa out of the room as Zoë laughed at the intriguing proposition. Michael watched the couple leave with his mouth open in shock.

The monster was pleased that they had divided their forces. Now it would be much easier to get rid of them. *Soon,* he thought. *They will all be gone. Dead, like the others that have tried to come and take my home away from me. Dead like the ones that are now sightless—the ones that tried to eat my soul.*

He looked down at the girl with the holy images painted on her body. Her mouth was gagged and her hands were tied. She bled a lot, but the monster did not want her to die just yet. She had to stay alive until the war was won. He needed the powers that were etched onto her skin. He would use these powers against the others who dared to intrude upon his domain. The monster had stitched the wound in her back with some thin wire. He had stitched her the same way he had stitched himself after suffering various wounds from the different battles he'd fought defending his realm. The girl screamed when he pierced her torn flesh with the needle and pressed the two flayed flaps together and quickly sewed up the massive deep wound that ran down her back. She would live a little while longer. That was all he wanted, all he needed. He picked her up with one hand and dragged her out from the secret room behind the mirror. *There are others to get to before these*, the monster decided. The two people on the seventh floor were starting to work their way up and the monster wanted to make sure they didn't have a chance to get back down. He would watch their progress and attack them when he knew they would have no chance of escape.

The monster contemplated his captive. This one did not put up as much of a fight as he had anticipated. Three of the intruders were either dead or his captive. Not one had put up anything amounting to a struggle. The monster figured that they all would be easy to overpower and kill. He would make an early night of it and go back to his lair to prepare their hides. He would quarter and cut their flesh, remove their eyes and reclaim the pieces of his soul that he'd had to surrender to claim all of his enemies' pelts. He would have a victory celebration and dine on fresh meat instead of the old carrion he had stored away, putrefying in the heat. When he had eaten his fill, he would reward himself with the girl with the holy images painted on her body.

He would clean her, wash away the sins she had brought in from the outside world. He would have his way with her. She had to be purified, made holy before their union could take place. Most of all, her sight had to be taken away from her. Her eyes could not look down at his *thing* as he entered and defiled the body she had come to blaspheme with pagan and strange drawings. He thought that the night would be a pleasurable one. A thousand little voices sang out in a chorus of hungry agreement, and he hummed along with the tune that was in his head.

• • •

Kira tried to focus, but the very act hurt her eyes. She was no longer bound and gagged. She was pressed against some grating and had just regained consciousness after passing out from pain. She was in a cage, a makeshift jail, made up of random pieces of metal, wire, and reed bars that were bent and shaped into an inescapable pen that was four feet high. A crude wire door with a lock kept her inside.

It wasn't a nightmare; this was real. She found herself in some type of demented reality that she had no idea how she had entered. The pain, the searing pain that burned in her back, quickly brought her back to the unreal world. Her flesh was sliced open, her muscles were torn, and her bones were severed, but she knew she had to maintain focus. Her eyes cleared. She rubbed them hard and tried to put the image that was in front of her into perspective. Kira was not alone in the cage.

The corpse of a woman sat silently in the corner of the cage. She had been homeless for years after bad luck had forced her onto the streets. Destiny had guided her to the hotel for sanctuary, and fate had taken over from there. The woman's tongue was bloated and black. It stretched her swollen lips into a sardonic grin, revealing a handful of dark yellow teeth that pointed in different directions. Her skin was ashen. Distended veins covered her arms and old sores were scabbed over the length of her exposed limbs. Her eyes were gone, but it seemed as if the two empty cavities stared at Kira. Bits of tendon hung out like frayed string and flies walked in and out of the sockets.

Kira pushed away. Her back was already pressed hard against the cage. She screamed, and a rat that had been feasting on the corpse ran away through the bars.

"Help me! Somebody help me!" she cried. Kira looked through the bars for the first time and realized again that she wasn't having a nightmare. She was already in hell.

The place, which was once a large suite before the walls had been smashed away, was in bloody disarray. Covering parts of the floor were bits of old carpet that were soaked and caked with old and new blood. The rest of the floor was cement littered with bits of unrecognizable flesh. An army of cockroaches dined on whatever morsels lay scattered about. Chains, axes, and knives of all shapes, sizes, and sharpnesses hung from the walls, turning the room into a medieval torture chamber that reeked with the smell of rotting flesh.

Several lights had been strung across the ceiling, and bare bulbs dangled down. Covered and crusted in blood, they cast the entire room in a crimson glow like macabre Christmas decorations. Somewhere, a crude source of electricity was generating enough power to illuminate the insanity of this place. There was a massive hole in the ceiling, and leaning up against the wall and up into the next floor was the giant "T" from the neon "Hotel" sign. It had been pried off, and metal struts and steel pipes that had anchored it to the building stuck out every which way so that the thing resembled a giant glass and metal crucifix. Across from the "T," Hannah lay in the middle of the floor. Her neck was broken and her head was turned almost completely around so that it looked like she was coming and going at the same time. Kira looked at Hannah's face and saw that her eyes were gone too. Fresh blood dripped from the hollow sockets, and her head rested in a warm, red pool. Roaches had just started to wade across it, and they moved hungrily to the soft, fleshy parts of the exposed sockets. An oppressive air of humidity and stink filled the entire place.

Kira's body temperature dropped and she started to shake. Shock was starting to set in. She trembled and rocked uncontrollably. Her eyes rattled inside their sockets. From the corner of her eye, she saw Richie. Kira closed her eyes and hugged herself tightly to try to push the shakes back down. The sight of the glass containers filled with preserved eyes scattered throughout the room was making her more nauseous than she could bear. When she had regained some control over her body, she looked back to see Richie tied spread-eagled to the far wall. His head was encased in a rusty metal contraption that looked like it had come out of the Inquisition. Blood dripped from an ugly wound in his lower leg into a large bowl underneath him. He was unconscious, and he was losing life a drop at a time.

"Richie," Kira whispered, not wanting to be as loud as she had been seconds before. She suspected that she had better talk in a quiet voice from now on. Richie didn't respond.

"Richie," she quietly said again.

A large shadow fell over Kira; a slight chill ran down her spine even though she was stuck in the hot, muggy cage. She looked up to see who had cast the shadow that she was now trapped within.

Her eyes traveled up the enormous body and she looked at the face of the monster that had captured her and brought her to his filthy den. The red glow of the room made it look like the monster had just emerged from the lower depths of Hades. Kira saw that he stood over seven feet tall. His body was thickly corded with muscles that stretched his pallid skin to the point where it looked like it would burst. Veins wrapped around his forearms and pulsated like live snakes beneath the flesh. His head was large and skull-like, with a rusty metal plate awkwardly screwed into the bone. A halo of flies buzzed around his head and crawled over his face, but the monster paid no attention to them. Kira fell back and tried to push herself away from the creature that looked down at her.

The monster squatted down and peered into the cage. He watched Kira, who was trying to hide behind the body of the dead woman. He studied the young girl, captivated by the tattoos that were etched on her wrists and arms. He smelled her fear, an odor that was mixed with urine, blood, and sweat. A low moan came from across the room and broke the monster's concentration. He turned to see Richie starting to gain consciousness. The monster stood up and walked over to the awakening boy.

Richie blinked several times before his eyes could fully absorb the behemoth that stared at him. When his eyes widened in panic, the monster stepped back. The monster could feel the boy's gaze starting to chew into him. He thought that Richie was trying to sneak little nibbles of his soul while he was strapped helplessly to the wall. The monster looked into Richie's eyes; he thought he was peering into the boy's soul. It was black and filled with sticky things, all unclean and unholy. The boy was a sinner. *Just like all the others, a sinner and transgressor against God's will.* The monster's god, an intangible and supreme being that blessed him with the gift of prophecy and sight, would be served once again.

The monster rubbed his thick thumbnails under Richie's eyes. Slowly he ran his fingers, with cracked crusty cuticles, around them. The monster pressed in and drove his jagged nails into Richie's eyes. The boy screeched inhumanely.

Kira screamed in reaction to the gruesome sight. The rats in the corners squeaked. The flies buzzed. The bloody chains on the walls rattled and the whole place seemed to come alive with the sounds of insanity bouncing off the walls.

Zoë took another hit from the joint that Michael had lit. They had already shared two others. She sucked in and once again filled her lungs with the cheap pot. She held her breath, and a ringing started to echo in her ears. She thought she heard Kira's voice, far away and in pain. She exhaled.

"Did you hear that?" she asked, blowing the smoke away.

"No, I didn't hear anything. We're all alone up here," Michael answered. He pulled the joint out of her hand to indicate that the two of them had all the privacy they needed.

Zoë listened again. She could have sworn it was

Kira's voice she had heard somewhere off in the distance. She relaxed with the sweet smell of pot around her and forgot about it.

"Remember how I said you could get better than Kira?" Zoë asked seductively. She was stretching out on the couch and letting her long limbs dangle suggestively over the edges.

"Uh-huh?" Michael eagerly responded as he looked her over with a predatory glance. He anticipated Zoë doing all types of nasty things for the right price.

"I didn't mean this much better," she said, letting him know that his chances to score with her were nil. She let out a loud bray at her own joke and threw her head back in an uncontrolled fit of giggles. She was in cocktease mode, level four. Zoë pulled out the cell phone from her pocket and dialed. She moved away from Michael and sat at the edge of the couch.

"Hey, bitch. What up? Keep this number, girl, I'll be using this phone all night. Yeah, free minutes," she chuckled to whomever she was talking to on the other end.

Michael got up and walked to the doorway to the next room.

"I'm going for a walk," he announced.

Zoë ignored him and continued chatting away. Michael was furious. He felt his blood starting to heat up again, and his temples started to pound. All he could think about was Kira with Christine. He walked out of the room with murderous thoughts forming in his mind.

• • •

The monster cut the dead boy down. He held the boy's eyes in his big hand and gently rolled them around in his palm. He could feel his body starting to mend. The holes in his soul that the boy had tried to devour with his eyes were starting to fill in again with the monster's essence. He lifted up the lid of one of the glass jars and dropped the eyes into the rancid liquid. They landed with two plops, and he sealed it shut. The monster watched as the eyes sank into and merged with the other dead orbs that floated in the glass jar. Bits of tendon hung from the eyes and drifted up like willowy pink tails. The monster realized that if the eyes ever got out, he would be lost. Parts of his soul were still trapped in the dilated corneas, and he would be at the mercy of others if they were to come into possession of his most precious prizes. He placed the jar back with the others and felt better. He had plenty of time to do away with the boy later, but now he had to deal with the girl in the cage. He had to possess her powers before she died; he needed to keep her alive before he got to the others.

The monster watched the girl in the cage as she tried to hide herself behind the dead body that was trapped in there with her. He couldn't remember when the other woman had attempted to come into his home, but she must have, or she wouldn't have ended up dead and eyeless in his cage.

The girl trembled and the monster thought back to the boy, the young boy who he remembered in a similar cage a long time ago. He couldn't recall how the boy ended up in the cage. It seemed that he was born into it, for the monster could never remember a time that the boy was outside of the wire and bars that entrapped him. Why had the boy in the monster's memory been imprisoned? What crime could a child that young have committed that warranted such punishment? The loneliness. The shame. The beatings. The scalding water. The monster thought the child in his mind to be innocent of all the sins ascribed to him. *No one that little and weak was a danger to anyone, so why was the child tortured and tormented? For whose sins did the boy pay?* The monster could hear the voice, the same voice that the child had heard. It was a cold and distant sound, fully lacking in pity or compassion, that resonated with righteous indignation. The monster did not understand the words the voice spoke, but it knew the tone they were spoken in was one of severity. He could sense that some of the words were bad. Some of those words still rang in the monster's mind: sin, flesh, women, sex, slut, whore, defile. These words had no true meaning to him. He knew sin was bad, sin was a word that had been seared into his mind and could never be taken out. All outsiders had sin on them. Sin was dirty. It carried germs, and germs make you sick. When you are sick, you die, and when you die, the worms eat you. Yes, the monster knew sin and knew that he had to destroy it. The other words were just as bad, even if he didn't know what they meant. The voice had told him so. The voice had taught the child the same lesson and reinforced it with the boiling water that had washed the sin away from the boy's body and the monster's soul.

Now, looking down at the girl with the holy images painted on her body, the monster started to have the same feeling it once had for the boy. He unlocked the cage and looked in. The girl kept the corpse in front of her, as if it would, or could, protect her. The monster gestured for the girl to come to him. The girl hid her eyes and shook. The monster reached in, grabbed her foot, and dragged her out. She tried to hold on to the bars and wires of the cage, but the monster had designed them so that little barbs covered everything she could grasp. The monster had learned that he would have to do that from the cage the little boy had been trapped in. He remembered how the little boy's fingers bled and tore when he tried to keep himself from being pulled out of the cage to receive the special treatment.

The girl came out. When the monster lifted her up and looked into her eyes, she turned her head. She did not want to stare at the monster. She did not want to try to eat away at his soul. The monster thought that it was smart on her part, but maybe she would try to look at him when he wasn't aware. She would probably try to rip pieces of his soul off and hide them away so she could feast on them later. He would have to watch this one; she was sneaky.

Now it was time to cleanse her. She was covered with sin and he couldn't allow such disease carriers to stay alive too long in his home. He brought her into the room of cleansing. He did not know that outsiders called this place a bathroom; he had no need for such frivolous words. All he knew was that the holy water flowed from the gold fountain that helped clean the tainted of mind and soul.

He turned the handle, and there was a rattle deep

inside the wall. The old tiles shook as water started gushing up through the pipes. As he pushed the girl into the stall, water sputtered out and a brown wet clump of muck shot out, hitting her on the head. The cold liquid started streaming out. The monster had wished that the fountain would pour out hot water to burn her sins off, but the hot water had stopped flowing some time ago. Now he was faced with the task of scrubbing away the evil that this girl bore on her skin himself.

Kira knew what she was in for; she saw it in his eyes. He was going to rape her, kill her, and maybe something worse. What could be worse was something that she didn't want to think about. The water was cold and her teeth started to chatter. She knew not to look at him, not to give him any provocation to kill her yet. There was a chance, a very slim chance, that if she did the right things at the right times she might get out of this alive, at least physically alive. She knew that behind every predator lurked an urge that was bestial. She knew she had what those urges craved, but she had to make sure that she didn't come on too strong or forceful. She didn't want to give her captor too much cause to doubt her sincerity. The water was freezing and her skin was turning cold.

He grabbed the girl by the neck and bent her over. He pulled at her shirt and yanked it up so that he could look at her body. The images that covered her white skin sparked something in his memory again. There was a large "T" etched on her back, along with the two small winged creatures that floated above it and flowers he had never seen nor smelled. Everything that was drawn on the softness of her skin reminded him of something, but he did not know what it was. A sense of familiarity and a feeling of foreboding came to the monster as he looked at her.

His fingers ran along the large "T" painted on her back. He remembered that it was a symbol, something to do with salvation, and then he realized it wasn't a "T" after all. It was a cross. And the cross was redemption. He thought about the boy. The boy had undergone such cleansings. How had the boy suffered back and forth between the burning waters of salvation and the freezing current of redemption? *Did the young boy ever become clean?* He wished he could remember who the young boy was. *Was he a friend? A sibling?* The monster had never known either, so the boy remained a mystery—a stranger who lived and shared his dreams and memories, an unknown tenant who resided in his mind.

His fingers spread across the girl's body as the water beat down on her. Then the voices in his head started to clamor. The sounds of the mob grew louder, and his concentration was being torn into millions of little pieces. The voices all rang out and grew until they were an ear-piercing shrill. The monster walked away from the girl. As she slumped down under the water, he listened for the sounds again. They became louder. He looked to see that one of his bells was shaking uncontrollably. The monster tried to think quickly. *The bell sounds when someone is near.* The monster grabbed the girl by her hair and pulled her toward the cage. He tossed her in. She was shivering and wet.

He watched as the bell kept ringing and ringing and he remembered where it led. *Someone must be near.* He would have time to finish cleaning her later. Now he had to find out who dared disturb his most sacred of ceremonies. He locked the door with the key and went to find the cause of the ringing bell.

9

RUSSELL HAD TAKEN MELISSA TO A ROOM AWAY FROM
Michael and Zoë. Even if Zoë was inclined to watch,
or even if she enjoyed joining in when others were
getting it on, he didn't want to be in the same room
with Michael if he was getting down with a girl. That
thought didn't sit well with him. Michael was too
unpredictable to have hanging around when everyone
was high and horny. Russell wanted his thoughts
focused on Melissa, and the feeling was mutual—she
wanted all of Russell's attention lavished on her. They
found a room at the end of the hallway that was
cleaner than some of the others on the floor. Melissa
pulled the dusty comforter off the bed, and they lay
on the faded white sheets.

It had been a long time since Melissa had been with
someone, and the boys she was used to were just that:
boys. Russell was a man, or bordering on manhood,
but he was manly in all the places that counted. His
muscles were long and lean, and his stomach was hard

and flat. His whole body seemed to have been honed by surfing, swimming, and endless hours on the beach. She didn't want it to be over too quickly. She didn't want a repeat of her junior prom, when the boy she was dating, a chess club computer nerd, had gotten so excited at the prospect of getting to second base that he struck out in the batter's box and had nothing left in his bat when he went to the plate. Melissa remembered how frustrated she had been lying in the back of his mother's car with her dress up, her legs open, and Prince Charming's pecker limply pointing south.

For some reason, she knew Russell wasn't going to end up like that. She could tell by the way he walked and moved that he was used to sex. He was made for it. She wanted to be with him.

Russell was on top of her, his hands moving with assurance over her stomach and up her shirt. Her tongue buried itself in his mouth and his fingers felt the edge of her bra strap. Like an expert he unclasped the bra and she let it be pulled away without any protest. She started to lift up her shirt for him as his fingers cupped her breasts underneath the tiny bra that was still hooked on her arms and massaged her tits. They weren't too big, but just big enough for his hands to fit snuggly around. Melissa felt her body tingle as his mouth worked all over her breasts. She was getting moist and hot.

He placed a hand between her legs and started stroking her through her jeans. Melissa arched her back as Russell's fingers started to take down her zipper. She looked over to the large wall mirror across the bedroom; she could see their reflection moving together, gyrating as their bodies intertwined. She imagined what it would look like when Russell took her, how she would be helpless in his arms, at his command to please him. It excited her, picturing Russell behind her as she was bent over, exposed and vulnerable, her body his to take any way he wanted.

She began to moan. Her body vibrated and began to perspire. A tasty glow of sweat started to shine on her body, and Russell's hands feverishly groped her soft flesh. His fingers were working their way through her zipper so that he could feel the softness of her pubic hair. He already felt her moisture dampening her panties. Melissa knew that at any second, her pants would be off. She turned her head to the mirror on the opposite wall so that she could watch, as well as feel, everything that Russell was doing to her body.

As the two teens rolled on the bed, they didn't realize that wrapped tightly around the coils of the box spring was a thin wire. The wire had previously been attached to a bell in the chambermaid's quarters, but now led to another destination: into the monster's lair. The monster had constructed a simple but highly effective warning device. All of the rooms in the hotel between the eighth floor and the penthouse now had some type of contraption that alerted the monster when intruders were present. The bells that had been in the chambermaid's room and the bellhop's station were now all nailed onto the wall inside the monster's home. The wires connected to them from various strategic locations so that they could signal when troubled approached.

This time, the trouble was approaching from two

horny teenagers. The harder they rocked back and forth on the bed, the tighter the wire pulled and the louder the bell rang in the monster's domain. The system was ingenious but uncomplicated. As Russell and Melissa moved and moaned, groped and groaned and shook the mattress like two wanton butterflies trapped in soft, silky cocoons, they had no idea that a hungry spider was closing in on them.

Williams was in front of Christine and Tye as the three of them walked cautiously down the hallway. Williams had his gun out, and Christine held the stun gun out almost defiantly. Tye looked like he was ready to bolt. They had come to another section of the eighth floor where the fire had raged and ravaged a good section of the hallway. Everything was black with soot. The chairs and tables that weren't cinders, the doors, the floor, and the walls were all coated in the same burnt black. Major parts of the ceiling were scorched through, and they could see the doors on the floor above them.

"Shit. Looks like the fire started here," Tye said, looking around the place and not being able to discern where one burnt thing started and another finished.

He was right. The fire started in Room 837 over thirty years before. It was an accident that occurred when one of Langley Blackwell's dirty little secrets got out of hand. The room, with its two-way mirror and hidden passage, was Langley's hiding spot. It was from here that he watched the drugged girl on the bed being taken by the two men he had paid to perform for his pleasure. The young girl was fresh from her wedding reception, being held in the banquet hall below. An hour earlier she had been the blushing bride. Now she found herself the star of one of Langley's private movies. Langley watched, with the woman that most people thought was his common-law wife, from the safety of the dark little room as the two men ripped the wedding gown off and started to abuse the unconscious girl in all sorts of ways, the ways that Langley had instructed. She was defiled and violated on her wedding night, a virgin until Langley decided otherwise.

Langley's confidante, Valentina del Rio, was something of a lounge singer who sang torch songs in the Blackwell nightclub. She had, at one time, been a very attractive woman. Langley kept her hopped up on drugs and well lubed with liquor, and she had fallen hard for him. She had left her husband and kids to be Langley's sexual pet. She would do whatever he wanted, to him and whomever else he wanted it done to. For ten years she had lived in a mind-numbing haze of narcotics, alcohol, and sexual abuse. For ten years she had been obeying him, always pleasing whatever dark whim Langley desired.

She watched the men take turns with the girl and saw Langley get excited. He played with a gold lighter, rubbing it and flicking it on and off every time another painful position was tried on the girl. Valentina kept her head down, not wanting to see what was taking place in the other room. Langley lifted her chin with the lighter and told her to watch and enjoy the show. She tried to fight back her revulsion at watching the two men rape and brutalize the girl. She did not hear the girl's muffled moans, only the whirring sound of the movie projector recording every despicable act for perverse posterity.

Then, as one of the men moved away from the bride, Valentina saw who was being raped and sodomized in the other room. The bride's face cleared away the blurry haze of her memory. Only when Valentina saw her daughter's face, the sweet little girl that she had abandoned ten years earlier, did her lucidity return. She could see Langley smiling in the darkness, the bulb from the projector highlighting his features as he pleasured himself to her daughter's debasement. Something inside her snapped. It broke through the wall of drugs that had sealed her off from the world and turned her from a docile slave to a homicidal maniac in a matter of seconds.

She saw that Langley had just finished pleasuring himself and she saw him for what he was: pure evil. He was nothing but a malevolent cancer that ate away at the fabric of society, vile and wretched to the core and well beyond that.

He'd had her daughter raped and abused in front of her, on the girl's wedding night. The girl she had not seen or spoken to in over ten years had just been debased, just so he could see Valentina's reaction. Valentina finally realized that she was nothing more than Langley's whore. Langley had had his fill of Valentina, there was only one thing he wanted or needed from her anymore. This violent indignity was the last thing he wanted from her. He wanted to cherish the look of terror and shock on her face for the rest of his life.

Without thinking, she grabbed the bottle of cognac

that Langley kept by the projector and bashed it over his head at the same instant that he was lighting his cigarette for his postcoital puff. The alcohol spilled over the open flame and in a fiery instant, Langley's head became engulfed in a blaze of bright orange retribution. He screamed as he flew around the small room that was bursting into flame. Valentina tried to get out of the hidden room. She tried to get to her daughter to stop what was happening to her child, but confusion reigned as the fire spread quickly. She watched as Langley fell on the floor in spasms.

Smoke filled the room as Valentina struggled to get out. The doors were closed and only Langley knew where the button was to open them up. The fire's tendrils quickly spread from behind the two-way mirror into the bedroom. The two rapists left the young girl unconscious on the bed as the fire started to burn its way toward her and ran, naked, into the hallway.

Valentina banged on the glass, trying to wake her daughter, but the fire moved with such stealth and deadly intent that the bed was ablaze before she could break it. Valentina drowned in the black smoke. The last image she had was of her baby being incinerated in an inferno. Then she fell on the floor next to the roasting Langley.

The flames washed over both of them and left nothing but blackened bones. Still hungry, the fire spread out ravenously and devoured the room and the hallway in its fiery maw. Before the hellstorm could be satiated, it had ravaged four floors and consumed twenty-three lives. It was a miracle that the entire place did not go up like one dry cinder, not a miracle performed by

God but one granted by the dark deities that Langley so eagerly served and one that he now faced eye to eye in hell.

The fire, the outrage, and the aftermath that caused the Blackwell to shut down, sending its owner to his overdue just rewards, was started in the room Christine was looking into. The sins that were burned into the walls by the fire went unseen but not unfelt as the young girl began to shiver.

"Something bad must have happened here. I can feel it," Christine said as she looked around the room, unaware of the unspeakable acts that had been performed there about three decades earlier. Williams felt it too, something he couldn't put his finger on, but he had been around long enough to know that certain places have an unknown quality to them. Some places are just bad, and the essence of evil still lingered in Room 837. No fire could totally burn away the specter of depravity that still lurked in those corners or behind the mirrors.

Williams closed the door. The sound broke the spell that Room 837 was starting to weave around Christine. Before the door had closed, she had seen the image of a woman in a wedding dress standing at an altar with flames wrapped around her body. Christine did not know where the vision had come from, but it vanished as soon as the burnt door clicked shut.

"There has to be a way up," Williams said, looking around the hallway.

"How? If we can't get through the stairwell, and we

can't find the elevators, how the hell are we going to get down?" Tye asked.

"We're not going down, remember. We're headin' up," Williams corrected him.

"Oh yeah, how could I forget? I'd rather find a quicker way to die than to escape," Tye complained sarcastically.

Williams looked up at the ceiling and saw that they could make it up through the burned-out ceiling to the next floor with a little effort. Maybe they would have better luck on the ninth.

"Come on. We can make it up to the next floor through that hole up there," Williams said, nodding at a large opening in the ceiling above them caused by the fire.

He turned to look at Christine, who was readying herself for the battle that she knew was ahead. She smiled at him, and a renewed confidence started to grow in him. The sense of purpose that had been hacked off four years earlier began to spread through his body and he felt that redemption was at hand no matter what the night brought.

He could see her deep brown eyes sparkle in the darkness. Then he saw them widen with confusion and almost fall out of her head with horror as a hook embedded itself deeply under his chin. Williams never saw the chain fly out from the hole in the ceiling. He hardly felt it pierce his skin until it was yanked and the sharpened point ripped up into his throat and caught under his jawbone. His body clenched in one tight spasm as a billion flashes of agonizing white light burned his eyes. His body rose as he was pulled up into the dark hole above them, as if he were being reeled in by an experienced fisherman. Williams couldn't hear Christine's and Tye's screams. A deafening pounding was in his ears as the last rational thoughts in his mind collided with high-velocity impact in a frenzy of confusion.

This cannot be happening. The pain is not real. This is a dream. A nightmare. It can't end this way, his mind repeated as he was lifted up and out of sight of the kids below.

The darkness of the ninth floor was diminishing as Williams saw the familiar silhouette start to emerge from the shadows. He knew that what had begun years ago would soon finish. He was suspended in midair as the monster's mighty arm held him high to get a better look at the intruder he had caught.

Williams tried to move, but the power in his body was gone. The pain was insufferable.

The monster looked at Williams. He studied the dying man's face. Something about this one looked different, familiar. The monster had seen this face before. *But where?* His large eyes bored into the intruder he held up. *Who is this?* the monster's troubled mind began to question.

Williams saw Goodnight face-to-face for the first time. In a thousand dreams he had seen the killer appearing in a thousand different guises, but none were as horrific as the one Williams was staring at now. He knew that within seconds, he would be dead. His only thoughts now were of Christine. He'd let her down. Now she was going to die as well. His fingers started to curl in pain and he realized that his pistol was still in his hand, his grip on it frozen. When he tilted the gun up, the strain on his wrist felt like it was going to snap.

The monster recalled who Williams was, what he was. *He is the one, the one that caused all the bad dreams.* He was the one who harmed the monster, the one who put the nightmares back into his head after they had been banished by time. The one who hurt him. The bad one. He had come back to finish the job and destroy him. The monster's eyes started to quiver with fear.

Williams squeezed the trigger. It took the last ounce of life he had. The first bullet flew up past the monster's head. The second ricocheted off the metal plate.

The monster panicked. He quickly dropped Williams. The man slid from the sharpened hook and fell through the hole toward the eighth floor, toward Christine and Tye. He was dead before his body fell at the girl's feet.

Christine screamed as she saw Williams's corpse land in front of her. Tye was running in place, ready to take off. He was as jittery as a track star hopped up on speed, waiting for the starter's pistol to fire.

Christine heard the mighty footsteps above her take off and disappear somewhere on the ninth floor. She looked down at Williams but tried not to look at his face. She could tell he was dead. The amount of blood that covered him made it seem as if he were a portrait painted in scarlet. She reached down and felt his hand.

"What the fuck are you doing?" Tye moaned.

Christine's fingers wrapped around Williams's gun. The barrel was still warm from being fired. She pried his fingers off the handle and took the gun.

"Sorry," she whispered.

Tye was already backpedaling as Christine looked at him. She knew it would be up to her to save Kira now. Save the others if there was a chance. If they were still alive. She hoped that what Williams said about Kira being kept alive for an extra few hours for that monster's ritual was true and not something he said just to make her feel better. There would be no more feeling better for her now, not now or ever.

She felt the gun in her hand. It felt heavy. It felt good. It felt like Williams was still there with her. She took off and raced to catch up with Tye. She never looked back at the dead cop.

The monster ran down the hallway, away from the man with one arm, away from the one who made his head hurt. He ran so quickly that the flies that circled his massive head in faithful accompaniment trailed behind as one long line of buzzing confusion. Fear was coursing through the monster's mighty body—these were not ordinary interlopers: these intruders were different. They were bringing back the ghosts from the monster's past to haunt him. *How is it possible?* the monster worried. His damaged brain could barely comprehend the fact that his old foes were trying to come after him. *Who is next?* the monster wondered. *How many of the fallen ones will rise up against me?* There were too many victims for the monster to remember all of them.

All the screams and pleas, cries and begging had melded into one long screeching wail in his memory long ago. They were a cacophony of fear that never ceased or eased. Every voice of the freshly killed added another voice to the choir that sang out in pain in the monster's troubled mind. The man with one arm had come back. The monster did not understand how. The man had been in his dreams ever since the day he had breached the monster's first domain, the house on the hill. It was there that the monster had struck out at the man and his young valet who had dared to sneak into his lair.

But the man had been like no other he had faced before. He lay mortally wounded, hacked to ribbons, yet he fought off the monster with some type of power that made the monster's head hurt. The pain was like none he'd felt before, and it sent him fleeing from his own home. The monster remembered the anguish of the wound and the shame of retreat as he left the only place he had ever known security. He'd had to travel into the city that he was forbidden to enter and travel back to the dark place that lingered in his memory. He'd had to go back to the shaman in the alley who could take the pain away.

The sickly medicine man had taken the pain away, but he had replaced one pain with another, one that never left the monster's head. But now the pain was back tenfold, and the same terror that the monster experienced that day had returned.

They are coming to get me. They will find a way in. There will be no place left for me to hide, to run to. The world will see me for what I am, a monster, and they will eat away at me with their eyes until there is nothing left.

The monster paced in a small circle, fidgeting with a problem that he had no idea how to solve. He was so unnerved at seeing the one-armed man he feared that he forgot to take his treacherous eyes. The monster did not want those cold, lifeless eyes. He was afraid to have them staring at him from his glass bottles.

Those eyes know too much. Let them rot in the man's head. Let the bugs feast on them until there is nothing left but a hollow nothingness and there is no flesh left on his bones. He knew he had one thing to do. He had to destroy all of them now. He needed the power that the girl with the holy pictures had. He needed it to fight off the others. He needed it now. The intruders would have to die before the sun came up, before they could get out, before they could reveal him to the world.

The swarm of flies finally caught up with their hurried host. They circled his head and buzzed melodiously, putting his anxious mind at ease. The flies sang the same song that always played in his mind. They communicated in sympathetic cords and helped clear away the fright so that the monster could breathe easily again. The monster would repay the black-winged bugs that covered his face like a diseased cloud. They would feast along with him as he dined on the tasty souls and skins of the ones who dared to challenge his right as the master of his kingdom.

The monster watched the two outsiders on the bed together. It fascinated him to see all of the bizarre behavior that the intruders had brought from the outside world. In a strange way, it pleased him to see the young couple on top of each other. He felt a warmth coming over him. He knew what they were doing was wrong. He thought he had seen it before. His mind fought to bring the memories back. He had seen a weird configuration of naked bodies like this someplace else. He recalled seeing outsiders all tangled up in books that had pictures. He remembered the funny shapes their bodies made when they were stuck together and the expressions on their faces that seemed that they were in pain from playing such a strenuous game.

What he remembered most of all were the soft ones, the girls. He had always wondered why they didn't have a thing that dangled between their legs like the others. Something about their shapes made the monster uneasy. At the same time, he was curious. He remembered studying the book with the pictures at night, and the sensations that he'd felt thinking about how he would have liked to be playing the games that the outsiders played. He had a desire to play the games with the soft ones, the girls.

Then he remembered the voice. It came screaming out at him for looking at the book with pictures. He remembered the sharp pain of the strap across his back, the blurry figure that stood over him, the voice cursing him. All of his memories came back to him and pushed away all the thoughts of the soft ones with no clothes on. The monster recalled crying and he saw the young boy again in his mind's eye. The boy's back was crimson with welts just as his had been. He remembered the pain that the boy felt; the monster felt the same pain. He remembered the boy being dragged into the cage and being left there. There was also that word that the voice had repeated so many times. It was shouted so loud that the boy had broken.

264

He'd shattered into a thousand pieces, like a fragile mirror bursting and scattering all over the dirty floor of the cage. The monster remembered looking down at the pieces of broken glass, the ones that had been the boy, and seeing only thousands of sharp and jagged reflections of his own hideous face staring back at him. The whole time, the word kept ringing in his head.

The word was *sin*. And it was bad.

And now the two outsiders on the bed were committing sin. They were doing it in the monster's house. Doing sin where the monster lived. The monster could not allow that to happen.

Russell began leaving a trail of hickeys on Melissa's neck, and her body quivered with each sucking sensation on her flesh. Her eyes flittered rapidly, anticipating what was coming. She looked at their reflection and got turned on even more. She saw their flesh exposed and pressing into each other.

She saw something move behind the mirror.

Melissa raised her head and looked deep into the mirror, beyond their images. She looked for something else. She didn't see it again. It had been fleeting, as fleeting as the image she thought she had sensed behind the mirror in the other room when they had been with Michael and Zoë. Something was there, something was hiding behind their reflection. It felt like those sunny days when you are outside and the shadow of a cloud quickly darkens everything for a moment but then vanishes before you can gather your wits. She felt it. An instinct or a premonition. Melissa knew deep down inside that they were not alone.

"Russell, something's wrong," she whispered in his ear.

"What?" His thoughts were solely on getting her zipper down and her pants off.

"Russell, wait. Something's wrong!" Melissa repeated emphatically.

Russell could feel her body starting to tense up. He thought he had the solution when he pulled out a condom from his back pocket. He smiled at her, thinking he had just assuaged all of her concerns.

"Not to worry. I brought a raincoat, in case of showers," he said, holding the rubber out in front of her.

"No, you idiot!" Melissa shook with a feeling that made her go cold. She pushed him off her. Russell looked down at her and saw that she wasn't joking. She was scared.

"Russell, someone's watching us," she said in a hushed voice.

Russell looked around. They were alone in the room. Only the shadows were spying on them.

"Don't look. Don't let them know we know," she whispered to him as she started to zip up her pants.

"Don't let who know what? What the hell are you talking about?" Russell asked as he realized that his first taste of trim in over six months was about to get up and leave him alone with a raging hard-on.

"Someone is watching us. In the mirror," she told him in a voice so low that she was practically mouthing the words. Russell looked over to the large mirror on the wall. What he saw was his own look of disappointment.

"Do you know what's wrong with that mirror? There isn't a reflection of me and you getting it on. That's what's wrong with it," he said, getting off the bed. He pulled up his pants as he walked toward the mirror. He stood in front of it and looked at himself, his smug face rolling his eyes. He looked at Melissa sitting on the edge of the bed, her hands gripping her knees. Then he noticed it. A slight movement. A shape. A shadow. Whatever it was, it was big, and it was there. Russell took three steps back before he realized he was moving away from the mirror. Then it happened.

The mirror exploded. Melissa screamed. Sharp shards flew out and ripped across Russell's face as two large hands reached for his head. Russell dodged the hands and fell to the side. He grabbed Melissa, who was sitting in shock, as she saw the massive creature that seemed to be from another dimension escape its world and break into theirs. Russell pulled Melissa up and dragged her out of the room. He slammed the door behind them before the massive figure totally broke through its glass wall.

Russell flew down the hallway. Melissa was practically off her feet as Russell pulled her along. He had no idea what had just happened, but pure instinct had taken over because he knew that someone that he did not want to tangle with was coming after them. He heard the door to the room they just fled from burst open. The footsteps that were thundering after them sounded like those of a charging rhino. Russell knew he couldn't look back. He couldn't turn around to see what was after them. He didn't want to get a good look at the thing that was hunting them.

Russell heard Melissa scream. He assumed that she must have seen the thing that was pursuing them. He turned the corner. The long hallway they entered was filled with moonlight that came in through the large window at the end of it. The light allowed him to see that the hallway went in two different directions. He knew that they couldn't make it to the end of the hallway before whatever was after them turned the corner in pursuit. He quickly figured that they had about a four-second lead on the big thing that was rumbling after them.

Stopping at the door, Russell grabbed a handle and opened it. He threw Melissa in so hard and fast that she flew across the room. He jumped and closed the door quietly behind him, and locked it. He grabbed Melissa and squeezed his hand over her mouth to keep her silent. He listened as the mighty footsteps turned the corner and ran down the hallway. The footsteps stopped.

Russell could feel Melissa's body start to shake. His hand closed tighter around her mouth. His eyes met her petrified gaze and they spoke in an unspoken language. *Be still, be silent, or be dead.* They could hear breathing, labored and angry, outside the door. Russell looked down and saw the handle of the door slowly starting to move.

When Melissa started crying, the sound of her sobs was blocked by Russell's hand.

The door shook once in the frame. The handle stopped turning. A silence crept in from under the doorjamb. Russell held his breath. His heart stopped. He waited for the door to break in. He didn't want to think about what would happen if it did. He heard the footsteps behind the door move away. They hurried in urgency down the hallway and finally were gone.

Russell sighed. He released his hand from Melissa's mouth and saw that his fingers had made deep bruising impressions over the lower part of her face. She couldn't speak. She trembled and Russell hugged her.

"Don't talk. Don't say anything," he whispered into her ear. Her head buried itself into his shoulder. He looked around and he could see that they were in a storage room. The room had one window with broken panes. From the night sky that came in, he could see that the place was filled with supplies that had not been used in decades.

Russell assessed the situation quickly. Whoever was after them didn't want them here, and may be back. Russell pried himself away from Melissa and looked around the storage room for something to protect themselves with. Nothing he saw would be formidable enough to go against whatever they had just escaped. Russell never got a good look at what was after them but he didn't want to stop and have a portrait burned into his memory. All he knew was that he didn't want to see it up close and personal again. He looked out the window and saw the top of the glass atrium below them.

"We have to get out of here," he told Melissa as he started looking around the room.

"How?" she replied in a meek, frightened voice.

"The atrium is a few floors below. It's kinda tall, but if we can get to the top of it and climb down on the metal beams, we can make it to the ground and get the hell out of here," he said almost matter-of-factly.

"Are you insane? How the hell do you think we're going to get down there from here?"

"We're going to find something long enough to lower us out the window and out of this fucking place," he answered, looking through the shelves for something that might fit the bill.

Russell found a piece of rope. It was too short and nothing more than twine. *No good.* He found several extension cords. *No good.* He pictured himself getting unplugged and falling to his death. He rummaged through the items on the shelves, past old boxes of detergent. He tossed aside cartons of liquid soap, but there was nothing. He had started to panic when he saw it sitting crumbled in the corner. It was an old fire hose that sat in the dark like a tired coiled snake, too weary to strike out. He grabbed the hose and could feel that it was old, but it still had some strength within its strands. The weight of it felt solid in his hands; it felt reliable. He turned to look at Melissa and she shot him a look as if to say he had just asked her the stupidest question in the history of mankind.

"You can't be serious?" she asked him.

"Damn straight I am. This is our only chance to get out of here."

"Why can't we just wait here until help comes?" she asked in a soft, desperate tone that made her words sound more like a plea than a suggestion.

He didn't bother to answer and she knew why. Whatever was outside that door more than likely would be back. Russell opened the window and looked down. He saw the same guerrilla traps that Tye had encountered on the ledge. Russell used the metal head of the hose to bend the nails down and bust out the broken pieces of glass, making a smooth path where the hose could travel freely. He uncoiled the hose but couldn't tell if there was enough length to get them to the top of the atrium. There was enough to get at least several floors down, and if worst came to worst—and he couldn't see things getting any worse than they were right now—they could try to break a window and get to another floor, away from whatever wanted to harm them.

"Listen. I'm going to tie this around you and lower you out," he said to Melissa.

"Fuck you. Are you retarded or what? I am not going out that window."

"Melissa, we have one chance, one, to get out of here. If that guy comes back and finds us, I don't have to tell you what's gonna happen. Don't worry. I'll tie this thing so tight that it won't come undone. I'll lower you slowly. When you get to the top of the atrium, keep it on and I'll guide you to a window to the third floor. Then get the hell out of here," Russell explained to her.

"What about you?" she asked him.

"I'm gonna wait here until you come back with help," he said, giving her a brave smile.

It was a crazy idea, something that Melissa would never even have entertained in her wildest animal rescue days. But the last few minutes of her life had become completely insane. She wondered how in such a short time she had gone from almost going down on Russell to rappelling down the side of the hotel. It didn't matter how quickly things had progressed. She had seen what was after them. She had turned her head to look at the thing that wanted them and she had seen something in the massive thing's eyes. It was a dark look, a look of deviant desire. Melissa could just imagine what that thing thought about when he looked at her. It made her sick. She'd rather chance climbing down the side of the building than face the insatiable wants that she knew the big bald thing had burning inside it.

Russell wrapped the end of the hose around her waist and pulled it tight. He wrapped it around the leg of the shelves and pulled it even tighter. He tried to pull it apart with all his strength to make sure the knot stayed in place. It fit snugly around her body.

He guided her to the open window and helped her sit on the window frame.

"It isn't tight enough. It's going to untie," she said nervously.

"No, it won't. I promise. It will become tighter when you hang on it," Russell reassured her.

"I'll get stuck on the glass roof," she said.

"Then kick it out. The beams between the glass panels of the atrium will be strong enough to hold you. They're made of steel. Just keep on the beams."

She knew she had no other options now. Her hands brushed away Russell's hair from his eyes. He leaned in and kissed her. It wasn't a kiss of passion or sexual desire. It was a kiss for luck, and it was the sincerest thing they had shared in their all too brief courtship.

She leaned back. She felt like she was going to plummet to the ground. Her breath became rapid and her fingers tightly gripped the coarse fire hose, but she didn't fall to her death. Slowly, she started to descend. And the hose did tighten around her waist. It was so tight that she thought she was going to have trouble breathing. She looked up to see Russell looking down at her, his face straining as he tried to control her descent.

"Russell, I'm scared," she called up to him.

"Shhhhh," he whispered down to her.

Melissa didn't want to look down. She just stared ahead and watched the bricks pass her by as she made her way to the roof of the atrium below. Slowly, the hose began to tighten even more around her body, making it feel as though her ribs were going to cave in. She tried to fight back the fear inside of her. She tried to forget the insanity of the recent past and concentrate on getting out and finding help for Russell and the others instead. She peeked down to see the ceiling of the atrium appearing larger and nearer. She realized that there was more than enough hose for her to safely reach the top and find access down. Her feet were within inches of touching the glass rooftop when her descent stopped. She hung there motionless, half a foot away from the atrium's roof. She tugged on the hose, trying to signal to Russell to continue letting out the hose, but there was no response.

"Russell! Russell!" she yelled up louder than she wanted to.

There was no answer from the open window above.

"Russell?" Melissa called out again.

Nothing.

The fear that Melissa tried to keep at bay ran rampant. Her body froze as the hose started to be pulled back up toward the window.

"Russell!" she screamed, not caring now who heard her.

The hose moved quickly up the side of the building as if it were tied to a mechanical winch. Melissa tried to gather her bearings and think about her predicament. *I'm fucked.*

She looked up at the storage room window. Within seconds she would be back, and she did not want to know what was waiting for her there.

The monster stuck his head out of the window and looked down at Melissa as he pulled her closer toward him. Melissa's scream echoed off the glass roof of the atrium and bounced back up at her. The monster started to smile an ugly smile; the thrill of the chase started to come back to him. He hadn't experienced that in a long, long time and the blood in his thick veins started to boil with the anticipation of the catch he was reeling in.

Melissa frantically tried to untie the hose around her waist. She knew that falling to her death was an easier way out than what was in store for her. Her fingers pulled and yanked at the knot. *Damn Russell for making it so tight!* she thought.

The monster pulled her up faster. She was two stories away from his sickly smile.

Melissa's fingernails dug deep in the hose's material and ripped at the old strands. She looked up to see the monster's head highlighted by the moon. It hung out from the building, hard and stonelike, grinning like a hungry gargoyle carved into the side of a Gothic cathedral.

Her hands gripped and pulled with strength she never thought she had, a strength that had never needed to be summoned before this very moment. The hose started to give way a little.

The monster pulled her up closer to him, closer to his wide, crooked smile, closer to his large, all-consuming eyes.

The hose was loosening; in seconds Melissa would fall to her death and be torn to shreds by the glass roof of the atrium. It was a fate she welcomed, as she could feel the first wave of the monster's hot, fetid breath beating down on her.

The monster gave one last hard pull on the hose and yanked her up toward the window.

The monster reached out to bring Melissa in. Fresh blood covered his hand and his thick fingers slid off her sweaty flesh. She arched her back as her feet pushed against the window frame and tried to wiggle out of his grasp.

The hose loosened and started to slip down her waist but the knot quickly tightened around her knees, causing her to lose her balance and start to fall again. For a few seconds, she felt like she was soaring. Her fall was abruptly stopped as the hose fell down past her knees and snapped tightly around her ankles. Her head hit the building with a sharp crack and she found herself dangling upside down. Every thought was wiped clean from her mind the moment the back of her skull collided with the hard bricks. She was momentarily unaware of what was happening to her.

The hose started once again to move, but this time it was moving toward the atrium roof and not toward the window. She could feel the blood rushing to her head and filling her skull. Her hands reached out and her fingertips touched the glass surface of the roof. Melissa's hands grabbed onto a crack in the thick glass and tried to pull herself down to the rooftop.

"Please, God. Please, God," she prayed over and over again to someone who was definitely not listening.

Suddenly, her body was yanked up. Her fingers were sliced on the cracked glass she was holding. Her body was being dragged up the side of the hotel, and her flesh was starting to be rubbed raw by the bricks. Once again, she stopped and was dangling, suspended in the summer night. She looked down to the roof of the atrium. She saw the cracked panels and the courtyard beneath. If she could have gotten there, she would have been safe.

Melissa held her breath and waited to be pulled back into the window and into the arms of the thing that waited for her. Instead of moving upward, the hose gave way and she plummeted back toward the ground, toward the glass roof of the atrium. She put her arms over her head to protect her face as her body smashed through the glass ceiling. The sharp shards of glass tore her arms, neck, and back, and the open wounds bled profusely. She saw the hard concrete floor of the court-yard and waited for the life-ending smash as her head burst open like a ripe melon on the ground.

She had put her hands out in front of her face. The incredible force of her fall caused the bones in her wrists to snap and sent them ripping through her flesh when her hands hit the ground. Her body didn't fall onto the hard concrete, and her life didn't end with a bone-shattering splatter. It stopped two feet before impact when the last inch of the hose was stretched to its fullest. She hung there like a fresh side of meat in a slaughterhouse—bleeding and open, blinded by tears mixed with blood. The hose was wrapped around her ankles, and the tendons and muscles in her feet were strained from the fall. An incomprehensible pain was savaging Melissa's body, from the bottom of her toes to the tips of her fingers.

The monster looked down and saw that Melissa was no longer moving. She was no longer fighting. *Good*, he thought. She would bleed out now and save him the trouble of having to siphon the last drops of blood from her body. He would retrieve her when he was done with the others.

He looked over at Russell, who was lying at his feet. The boy's head was crushed from the viselike pressure the monster had applied to his head. The monster heard the bones crack like an eggshell as Russell's body went rigid in death. The monster rolled Russell onto his back and saw that the boy's eyes were wide and white with fear. The monster tapped gently at Russell's eyes. They did not flinch or move. He pressed down and felt the jellylike resistance of the eyes and pushed his sharp nails deep into the corner of the eye socket and past the eye. With his nail sharpened like a scalpel, the monster severed the tendons that held the eye in place and pulled the dead orb out. A wet pop sounded as it was ejected from the socket. He did the same to the other eye and looked at both of them in his hand. He had to put these with the others before something happened to them. He carefully cupped his other hand over the eyes in his palm and hurried out of the storage room and back to his lair.

10

MICHAEL WANDERED AROUND THE TENTH FLOOR FOR a while, swinging his pipe and smashing light fixtures, sconces, and anything else his mind seemed bent on destroying. He thought about Kira every time he swung the pipe. He wanted nothing but the chance to get Kira alone, without anyone around to protect her this time. He remembered how he'd had his chance when he saw her in the tub. She had been alone and vulnerable. He should have struck then while he had the chance. *Why didn't I, though?* That bugged him.

If only Kira had kept her mouth shut when she had gotten caught, then Michael wouldn't have to be in this situation. He wouldn't be forced to have to take his revenge on her. It wasn't Michael's fault that something bad was going to happen to her. It was Kira's own fault. She forced his hand in all this. What did she expect him to do? If it ever got out on the streets that he'd never gotten his retribution on the bitch that sent him up, how would he look? His image and reputation would be damaged. Damn Kira for making him do this to her. It's not that he wanted to; he *had* to. Deep down Michael had feelings for Kira. Even when she'd told him that she didn't feel the same way toward him, he still felt something toward her. When she was selling his drugs, he worried about her safety. When she was pulling tricks for him, he felt jealous of the johns whose money he counted up at the end of the night. He'd felt bad when he had to slap her around for stepping out of line. He didn't want to punch her or burn her, but she had to be put in her place. She had to know that she belonged to him. What type of trouble would she have gotten into if she hooked up with some of the other characters on the streets? Kira didn't see that Michael was doing things for her own good. She always ate and had a place to crash with him at the end of the night. He was the only one who made sure that if some guy went a little too far, he got stomped on real bad for doing it. Michael fumed as he thought about all of this. He swung the pipe around like a majorette's baton and smashed his way down the hallway, back to Zoë and her stolen cell phone.

He stopped at one of the stairwells in the corner of the floor and noticed that the door was barricaded with old machines and seemed to be bolted shut. He clanged the pipe off some of the old machinery and thought, *Who the hell would bring this stuff up here in the first place?* He tried to move a motor block that was leaning against the pile of old rusty metal pieces but could hardly budge it. *Fuck! Who the fuck dragged this thing up here?* The object seemed immovable. *Somebody went to a lot of trouble to make sure that no one got through this door.*

As soon as the notion came into his head, it quickly left when he turned away and went to search out Zoë. He wanted to see if he could get anything out of her before the night was over.

Melissa awoke from a painful daze, suspended by her ankles as she dangled from the fire hose. All of her blood had rushed to her head, and her thoughts swam against a tide of dull aches that were slowly becoming sharper with every second that passed. Her eyes cleared as she felt her bones sticking out of her wrist. Fear took control as she started to scream. She didn't yell out for Russell. She didn't call out for Williams or Hannah. She simply bellowed in deep agony, pleading to anyone who could hear her. She assessed her surroundings, but everything was wrong and askew. Right side up was now wrong side down, and the entire atrium seemed as if it were nailed to the floor and hanging from a ceiling. Gravity seemed to be playing against her vision as she tried to see if there was someone else around in this upside-down world.

She heard something moving in the shadows and turned her whole body to see a figure coming toward her. It was the dog. The same pitiful creature that she had shown mercy to that afternoon came closer to her.

"Good boy, good boy," Melissa said as her eyes bulged from the pressure that was being exerted behind them. *What the hell could the dog do for me?* she thought. *He isn't fucking Lassie, and Timmy didn't fall down a well. This dog sure is not going to run for help,* she reminded herself.

The dog approached Melissa with caution. It sniffed. It was still weary from the first trick that she had played on him. The dog remembered reaching out for food that Melissa offered, only to be frightened away by the soda can that exploded inches from its face. The dog had a sense that Melissa brought trouble. He sniffed again and walked closer to the dangling girl.

The dog noticed the bone sticking out of Melissa's wrist. The scent of her marrow was strong. He smelled the fresh blood that flowed from the many open wounds on her body. Its salty aroma intensified as the red puddle of blood started to grow beneath her head. The dog sniffed again and started to growl as the hairs on his mangy hide stood up slowly on his bony spine.

Uneasiness helped fight back some of the pain as Melissa tried to sway herself away from the mongrel that started to circle her. The dog moved in quickly. He was a blur of dirty, matted fur. The dog's teeth bit down hard on the bones protruding out of Melissa's wrist. His jaws clamped down and he turned his head with a sharp jolt, snapping the bone in the process.

Melissa screamed. Her voice traveled up and burst through the broken atrium ceiling, past the twenty-one floors of the hotel, and spread across the night sky covering the city, dissipating somewhere in the heavens above. The pain was on incomprehensible levels as the dog chomped at her bone.

The starving animal chewed hungrily on the bone and in seconds his powerful mouth had cracked it into splinters and had sucked the marrow out of it. The sounds of Melissa's screams and the dogs hearty munching brought other visitors to the atrium. Unwelcome guests that Melissa had wished she had never seen from her upside-down view. Coming out of the shadows from a hole in the wall were several pairs of yellow eyes that seemed to glow in the darkness of the night. They were cold and feral eyes that twinkled with a hungry curiosity. Melissa could see that the pack of dogs sneaking in from the outside world was made up of a ragtag bunch of starving mongrels. They were a scavenging crew with tightly drawn flesh pulled over their skeletal bodies. Their mouths hung open like salivating traps eager to snap shut.

Melissa didn't have time to think. She didn't have to yell out for help. The dogs lunged at her one at a time, each animal finding a piece of exposed and torn flesh and ripping it off in long bloody strands. Melissa couldn't even scream anymore because blood had already filled the back of her throat and poured down her face, covering her eyes. The dogs went wild as they licked the warm, sticky fluid. Their licks turned to nibbles. They continued nibbling until they could not hold back anymore. Several sharp pairs of teeth ravaged her face. Other dogs jumped up and tried to burrow into her belly. The smell of her bowels filled their nostrils and they danced in a blood-splattered frenzy as her intestines started to spill out and hang down like tempting sausage links. The pack howled with delight and devoured the girl's body. She felt every excruciating moment as she dramatically fell from the top of the food chain.

Michael walked along the tenth-floor hallway with his

lead pipe tucked under his arm. He came upon a stair-well that wasn't barricaded or blocked. Zoë was still behind him, still talking on the cell phone, and he wondered how anyone could talk so long about absolutely nothing. He had been listening to Zoë's end of the conversation and had heard nothing of sub-stance come out of the girl's mouth during the entire time she wasted with idle chatter. Then he thought of Kira and how different the two girls were from each other, how different they were from other girls. Michael used to like to hear Kira talk. For a girl that wasn't even fifteen when they first met, she seemed to know a lot about things. She wasn't pretentious like many of the girls Michael knew in school. She didn't come off as being overly worldly, either. Kira just spoke from an honest place in her heart. Kira used to like to talk to Michael and he used to like to listen. *What hap-pened?* he wondered as he opened up the door to the stairwell. *What the fuck happened to her? What happened to me? To us?*

The stairs going up to the next two floors were gone. They had been completely destroyed. Nothing was left of them except a few broken pieces of con-crete and bent bars. It seemed that someone had taken great measures to make sure that no one could make it up past the tenth floor and toward the penthouse. There were lights on in the stairwell, not more than a few dim bulbs that stuck out of the walls at the landing of each floor. A thought started to form in Michael's mind. *How the fuck did the power come to light these bulbs? Who the hell wanted to be able to see this old stairwell anyway?* The thoughts were knocked out of his mind when Zoë walked into him because she wasn't paying attention to where she was going. He turned to give her a dirty look, but she gave no indication that she was even aware that she had bumped into him. Michael just shook his head.

"Fuck," Michael said under his breath as he looked up into the darkness. "Let's head down."

Michael knew he wasn't going to get any action from Zoë, and he didn't want to waste the rest of his pot on her. He didn't feel like waiting around for Russell and Melissa either. He figured they could find their own way back down. He didn't want to see Russell's smug face and have to deal with the fact that Russell had scored and he hadn't. Besides, it was getting late and Michael wanted to get back downstairs to find Kira. He had smoked too much, and that had started to ease some of his anger toward her. He didn't want to think about their past together. He needed to keep his edge, so he decided to call it a night and head back down. If Zoë wanted to follow, that was fine with him. If she wanted to stay up on the tenth floor and drone on and on about nothing to one of her equally vapid friends, that was fine with Michael as well.

Zoë followed Michael, and as he started to walk down the stairwell, she never questioned him. When the door closed behind them, a strange feeling came over Michael. Even though Zoë was with him, he felt alone—totally alone—in the stairwell. The few mysterious bulbs that shined down the stairwell did not help Michael's frame of mind. For some reason, they made him feel worse. It felt like someone wanted Michael to travel down this stairwell—like they were *urging* him to. He felt an irrational prompting to go down because someone or something waited for him at the bottom.

Zoë started to lose reception and told whomever she was talking to that they should call her back. She slid the phone in her back pocket and for the first time realized that she was walking down the dimly lit stairwell.

"Where the fuck are we going?" Zoë asked.

Michael wished she had stayed on the phone. He didn't feel like answering her stupid questions. He could feel his skin crawl as they passed the ninth floor and kept going down. He wanted to stop. He wanted to get out of the stairwell, but he found himself continuing his descent. With each step down, he felt another wave of fear start to swell in his stomach. He didn't know why, but going down this stairwell seemed like a bad idea now. Another uneasy feeling was building up inside his brain. Something worse than fear started to come over him: dread. At least with fear, you knew what you were afraid of. Many people were afraid of fire, heights, flying, things Michael could understand. They were tangible fears. But Michael had no idea why he was dreading walking down those dark stairs. With each step, they traveled closer to an unknown that he felt was not going to be pleasant once it revealed itself to them.

Zoë was talking, but Michael had no idea what she was saying. Her voice seemed to be muffled by the murkiness that they found themselves in. He was halfway between the eighth and ninth floors when he looked over the railing and stared down. He saw that the lightbulbs seemed to twinkle and sputter. The faint halo they cast shined just enough light to say, *I dare you to take another step closer.* Michael didn't want to retreat back to where they'd just come from. He didn't want the hassle of trying to come up with an excuse that would be believable enough for Zoë, but he didn't want to go down any farther. He felt trapped. For the first time that evening, he could feel the humidity. It felt heavier than most hot summer nights. Being in the dark stairwell made him feel as if he were in an oven that was slowly getting hotter and hotter. The air was thick, and he could taste the staleness of neglect and rot that came off the walls and stairs.

Zoë nudged him in the ribs, wanting to know why he'd stopped. He almost jumped out of his skin when she touched him. He wanted to punch her teeth out. He wanted to scream, but all he did was grip the railing.

"Come on. What the hell is the holdup?" she complained.

Her whining cut through Michael's worried thoughts. He looked at her and didn't say anything. He started to walk again but stopped at the eighth-floor landing. Here the darkness that waited for him below seemed to tease him. *What's a matter, tough guy, afraid to come down a few more steps? Afraid of the dark? Afraid to realize what you really are? A coward. A scared little pussy that wants to be a big man by beating up girls. I dare you to take another step into me. Come on down and see what you are made of.*

Michael didn't heed the challenge: a warning went off in his mind. It was the same survival mechanism that had been triggered when he'd wanted to attack

Williams for hitting him earlier that afternoon. He'd known that tangling with the one-armed cop would have been a bad idea. Now he knew that taking another step down into the darkness of the stairwell would have been worse. He feared Williams—he didn't want to admit it, but he did—but he dreaded what may be waiting at the bottom of the stairwell even more.

"Let's check this out," he said over his shoulder to Zoë as he pushed on the door that led to the eighth floor. He didn't know why he'd said it. It was just something to say so he could hear his own voice. He prayed that the door would open, and when it did without a problem, he felt a rush of relief come over him. He didn't know that less than an hour ago Tye had tried to open the same door and it wouldn't budge. Michael had no idea that someone had unlocked it just for him. If he had, he would have run straight back up to the tenth floor, leaving Zoë on her own.

He walked onto the eighth-floor landing and into a seriously fire-damaged hallway. Since he was more at ease at being out of the stairwell, no thought of the hazards that might lie in the burned-out hallway in front of him entered his mind.

Zoë pushed past him and walked down the hall, not knowing or caring that the entire place was coated in a black patina of soot.

"What a fucking dump this place is," she commented.

Everything she said grated on Michael's ears, but at least when she spoke, he could concentrate on her aggravating voice and not the unnerving silence that seemed to follow them out of the stairwell.

"So you and Kira gonna get back together?" Zoë asked, knowing full well that Michael's intentions concerning Kira were anything but reconciliatory. He knew she was trying to bust his balls. He knew that she had made sure that he would be tipped off to Kira's participation in Project: Renewal. He knew a lot of things, but for the moment he didn't care. She thought he was nothing but a thug, someone who would wind up dead on the streets or on death row, but he didn't give two shits how she felt about him. All he wanted was to be away from her.

They kept walking down the hallway, past burned-out rooms and fire-ravaged walls, moving farther and farther away from the stairwell. Michael had the strongest urge to look over his shoulder, but something told him not to. He didn't want to think that something was following them up from the stairwell. He knew nothing was behind them, but he wouldn't look anyway. He realized that his lead pipe was still tucked under his arm, almost like a security blanket. He took it out and starting banging it against his thigh as he walked. With each step, he swatted himself a little harder to keep his mind focused on finding another way out.

Zoë noticed the force behind Michael's blows. She thought that he was priming himself for Kira. She felt a slight twinge, but she couldn't recognize her guilt for what it was. She saw Michael's eyes filled with determination. She assumed that the strength behind the pipe's blows mirrored the anger that was ready to blow him apart. She didn't realize that it was his way of fighting back a fear that was knotting up inside of him.

Michael and Zoë turned the corner and walked for about ten yards when a hallway appeared to them. The perpendicular corridor was hard to see if you weren't right on top of it. The damage the fire had caused helped to add to the mazelike effect that was part of the hotel's floor plan. At the end of the new hallway, they discovered a large foyer and a bank of elevators.

Michael was glad to see the scorched metal doors of the elevator. The foyer was large. Once Michael and Zoë reached the elevator, they realized that they were in the main section of the eighth floor.

"Do you think it works?" Zoë asked him.

"We'll find out," he said, jamming the down button.

He looked up to see that the number above the door indicated that the elevator was on the ninth floor.

"Do you think they're on the ninth floor?" she asked. Michael knew she was referring to Russell and Melissa, but he didn't answer.

The elevator started to descend toward them. Suddenly, Michael started to laugh to himself.

"What's so funny?" Zoë asked, not liking the sound of his laughter.

Michael knew why he was afraid, why he'd been scared once he'd gotten into the stairwell. He realized why the unnameable fear was poking at him. *It's the pot*, he thought happily. It had been so long since Michael had gotten stoned that he forgot how paranoid smoking weed had made him. He hadn't smoked since he'd been locked up. He'd needed to be sharp all the time there. Here, with his guard down and getting baked, he just felt all fucked up in the head. He felt a great sense of relief as the elevator dinged to a stop in front of them. There was nothing to fear. There was no uncertainty waiting for him. It was all in his head. He felt a sense of renewed confidence as the doors to the elevator opened.

His relief was still strong when flies started to swarm out from the elevator.

"Wow! Where the hell are they coming from?" Zoë said in disgust as she started to wave them away from her face. They buzzed loudly as they darted past Michael. The renewed sense of confidence he had soaked up thirty seconds ago had all but drained from his body. Something about the flies made him sick. Something about the flies made him nervous. The flying black parasites made him realize that his entire life until then had been one big fucking mistake.

The buzzing flies seemed to say *Look this way or you'll miss the show*. Michael would never know that the flies beckoned to him in the same way that Langley Blackwell had beckoned Valentina as he lifted up the woman's face to watch her daughter's defilement that was caused by his hand.

Zoë hesitated before she started to walk into the elevator, her hand waving back and forth in front of her face. Michael stared past her, into the darkness where the flies wanted him to look.

Suddenly he saw a flash of metal striking out from the shadows behind Zoë. The faint elevator light bounced off the sharp blade of the axe that slashed out toward her. This was the same exact image Officer Frank Williams had seen four years ago, before his arm had been severed off. If the cop had still been alive and if Michael survived the night, the two could have exchanged identical horror stories over a beer.

Michael's body reacted before his mind knew what was happening. In one smooth move that he would never have thought about or attempted if he'd had time to think, Michael grabbed Zoë by the collar and pulled her toward him with one hand. With his other hand, he swung the pipe up in a hard underhanded arc. The pipe landed square in the groin of the massive figure that was being pulled out of the shadows by the swing of the axe. The axe missed Zoë's face by a fraction of an inch. A strand of her hair had been sliced off as the blade flew by and smashed into the wall in front of the elevator, sending marble flying everywhere.

The monster grunted. He could fight against the pain to his head and his body. He was always ready for that. Both mind and body had been prepared for combat, but he never could tolerate being hurt in his dangling bits. That had always been a weak spot for the monster—it was where the badness grew in him. That was where he had been punished with the hot water. The voice in his mind told him that it was that part of him that would get him into trouble. And now that spot ached in pain as the monster's dangling bits started to swell up.

Michael never saw the face of the thing that had almost decapitated Zoë. She had started screaming and running. Any chance of getting away undetected while their assailant was recovering from a testicle-crushing blow was obliterated while Zoë went screeching loudly down the hallway.

Michael quickly followed suit and got the hell away

from the elevator. The huge fucking thing with the axe came after him.

What the fuck? What the fuck? was all that Michael's mind could come up with while he caught up and overtook Zoë. That frantic three-word expletive was universally the second-to-last thing that went through the brains of people who encountered the monster. The last thing entering it usually was an axe blade.

The monster winced and pulled the axe blade out of the wall that it was embedded in. His dangling bits were burning, and a sickness was pushing up to his stomach. He knew pain and how to fight it. When the man with one arm made his head hurt, he'd fought it. When the shaman cut the pain out, he also fought. This ache was nothing compared to the suffering the monster had endured his entire life. It was not pain, just an annoyance. The monster would see real pain as soon as he squeezed the eyes out of the intruder with the pipe. He staggered and gave chase to the two who had just barely escaped his blade's prowess.

Michael's arms moved like pistons and the wind flew through his pipe, sounding as if it were a train whistle. He passed Zoë and left the girl in his wake. Hearing her desperate cries, he slowed down and waited until she caught up with him. He held out his pipe as if it were a relay baton and she grabbed it. He pulled her close, held her hand, and started running faster again. His momentum pulled her along. He turned the hallway and met with more darkness.

Goddamn it! roared inside his head. He could hear

the mighty footfall of the thing rumbling after them. He opened a door and jumped into a guest room, pulling Zoë with him. Michael closed and locked the door. A sinister laugh sounded in his mind. *Like locking that door is going to stop us from getting chopped to death.*

Zoë started to blubber but Michael slapped her hard across the face and that one sharp jolt cleared her mind. He didn't have time for explanations or theories on who or what was out there. It came down to a big fucking dude with a bad attitude and sharp axe blade. He needed Zoë to be coherent and aware that any fucking slip-up meant a painful end for both of them.

Michael opened a closet. His eyes darted quickly around the small area. He saw that part of the back of the closet was open. He moved aside a row of wooden coat hangers and pushed the wall in with his shoulder. The back of the closet gave way. A narrow little niche was behind the wall. Michael grabbed Zoë and wedged her in. It was a tight fit and only she could get in there, but it would do. He looked at her, and the expression in his eyes said all there was to say. Michael pulled back the wall of the closet and sealed it enough so that if someone were to look, they wouldn't be able to notice her right away. He quickly moved the coat hangers in the middle of the rack and made sure they weren't moving or swaying so they wouldn't give any indication that someone had recently been in the closet.

Now that Zoë was out of the way, he thought about taking off again, trying to make a run for it. He knew he could run faster without Zoë holding him back. He went to listen at the door and heard the monster's footsteps coming closer. The choice of running was now gone. He needed a place to hide or to escape from. He opted for the latter and ran into the bathroom looking for an escape. The window over the bathtub was too small, but as he smashed the glass out with the pipe, an idea sparked in his head.

He spun around the room to see if there was anything he could use as a weapon. There was nothing. He started to tap the pipe against his head and chanted, *Think, think, think*. Then he saw the two doors under the sink and opened them. There was a thin shelf that ran between them and the pipes from the sink didn't take up too much room. Michael grabbed the shelf and it broke off easily from decay and the force of his fear.

Without even measuring it, Michael drove his shoulders and head into the back of the space under the sink. Luckily he met damp sheetrock instead of hard concrete and his head burst through it. He pulled his upper torso in and grabbed on to the pipes that ran behind the wall and pulled the rest of his body in. His muscular frame seemed to bend like a contortionist's body. He seemed to get stuck halfway in but abject terror made his body stronger than he thought possible. He squeezed into the space behind the wall and once he was in there, he thought that there was more room than he expected. He got himself secured and put his arm out to close the two doors, but he couldn't reach. He tried to extend his arm but his head was jammed against the back of the wall. He held his breath and thought. Remembering the pipe he had laid near the open doors under the sink, he reached down and felt for it. His fingers came upon the metal and he grasped it tightly. He lifted up the pipe and caught the edge of one of the doors and closed it tightly, and repeated the process with the other door. He found himself trapped behind the wall in blackness, waiting and hoping that whatever was after them was not going to find him.

11

THE MONSTER TRUDGED DOWN THE HALLWAY. HE knew every inch of his domain. It didn't matter if the walls were blackened and unrecognizable or that the fire had damaged much of this floor. He was king here, and a good king knows his kingdom well. His hand felt between his legs, and he could feel the swelling of his dangling bits. They were three sizes bigger than the last time he'd felt them, and they ached.

He would watch the boy die slowly, painfully. He wanted to hear the sound of his skull crushing as he caved in the intruder's head between his two massive hands. He wanted them all to be dead. Dead and gone. He wanted to be alone in his home again and to have these trespassers vanquished and destroyed, once and for all.

He had killed some already. He couldn't count now—numbers wouldn't stay still in his head—but he thought about the ones he had killed in the last few hours and knew that their numbers were getting smaller. He went down the hallway, and his eyes started to roll up in his head. Instinct guided him as he sniffed with a bloodhound's skill.

He stopped in front of a door and tested the handle. The door was locked. He pulled back his hand and punched the brass door handle. The handle shot back into the room as the locking mechanism was knocked out by the monster's power. He opened the door and entered. He sniffed. He could smell their fear. It made his appetite grow and his stomach growl. The monster smiled as he walked toward the closet. He opened the door with his axe and looked in. Disappointment spread over his face as he stared into the empty space. He put his head in and looked around. He moved the coat hangers back with his axe and sniffed once more. He wondered where they could have gone. They had not traveled far from their fear because he could smell their scent. He looked around the room, tossed over the bed, yet found still nothing. The monster started to get nervous. He looked to see that the bathroom door was open and went in. *There would be no escape for them in there*, he thought. He saw that the bathroom was empty. He stopped when he thought he saw a shadow behind the shower curtain. The monster smiled and swung the axe toward the curtain. A massive tear ripped across the curtain, and the blade smashed into the walls and crushed the fixtures, but there was no one there. Confusion was starting to set in as the monster wondered why their scent was here and they were not.

He looked at the window and noticed the glass had recently been knocked out. The monster stood on the side of the tub and tried to look out, but his head couldn't fit through the small frame. *Did they escape through the small window?* he wondered. If so, they would have fallen to their deaths. He could retrieve their bodies later if they were lying dead in the court-yard below. *But what if they aren't down there? What if they got away?*

He left the bathroom and looked around the room again, but they were gone. He had been tricked. The monster's anger started to boil, and he went out to search the rest of the floor for the two intruders.

He had stepped out of the room when he heard a sound. He didn't know what it was. It was a ringing. At first he thought it was the ringing that sometimes echoed in his ears and caused him to lose days of sleep, but it was different. It was a foreign-sounding ring, one that he had never heard before. He walked back into the room and followed the strange, shrill sound to the closet. He opened the door again and looked into the emptiness he had just left. The ring-ing continued in short, loud intervals. Suddenly, the monster knew where the sharp sounds were coming from—behind the closet wall. A smile that was both anxious and angry spread across his wide, skull-like face as his thick fingers grabbed an edge of the closet's back wall. He pulled it with a mighty burst of energy and the thin plywood wall flew off in his hand.

Shaking before him was the female intruder. She was alone. The monster wished that the boy had been with her, but she would do for now. The girl began to whimper, and the monster reached in and pulled her out. He held her up and sniffed. He could smell that the girl was soiling herself from the odor that she emitted. He listened as the ringing continued and wondered what was making those horrible little sounds.

His hand reached around her and felt something foreign in the girl's back pocket. He pulled it out and stared at the funny object that was chiming loudly in his hand. The monster fumbled with the thin metal object as the display screen lit up repeatedly. The buttons with groups of letters and numbers meant nothing to him. He heard a voice that seemed to be coming from the device. He stared at the thin ringing object with fascination for a moment before he put it up to his ear to listen to the sounds of strange voices coming from somewhere within its small frame. He sniffed and heard a female voice giggle and squeal something from within the object. He wondered what type of sorcery these intruders had brought into his castle. He closed the lid of the metal object and shut off the voices that came from somewhere else.

The girl was trying to say something, but it was lost under her blubbering. The monster knew that she had somehow signaled to a rear guard with the metal object that had been emitting the strange noises.

This one is a treacherous one, he thought. *Just like all of the other treacherous ones. All of the soft ones, all the females of their species.*

He pressed the metal object to her lips. She tried to close her mouth but he pressed harder. The device that everyone in the civilized world knew as a cell phone was pushed into her mouth. The monster rammed the phone into the back of her throat and he could feel the soft part of her flesh start to give way. His filthy fingers jammed into her mouth and his thick, sharp nails ripped open her gums. He forced the phone farther down her throat until it got stuck and he couldn't push it anymore. The girl's body shook wildly and her eyes spun around in frantic circles. The monster looked over his shoulder to where the girl was looking but nothing was there. Whoever she hoped would be there was gone.

Something of a scream passed over the phone lodged in her throat, but it came out as a gurgle as her face turned blue. She kicked and punched, but the monster held her at arm's length to examine and enjoy her struggle. He waited and watched until the girl finally stopped kicking and punching, and all the waste poured out of her body. He dropped her into the puddle of her own filth. The monster grabbed her by the hair and dragged her out of the room. With his axe over his shoulder, he looked like a demonic woodsman done with his workday. He went to search for the others.

Kira looked around the monster's lair and tried to calm her fears. The place reeked of a stench that was beyond foul. She had to keep herself from vomiting, so she took shallow breaths and tried not to breathe in too deeply the repugnant air that hung heavily over the room like a thick, smelly blanket.

Her body burned with pain. The wound on Kira's back was so tender and sore that she couldn't find a comfortable position to sit or lie in without pain traveling throughout her body. She was huddled in the corner of the cage, closer to the dead woman's rotting corpse than she wanted to be, but she wanted to be as far away from the prison's edge and her jailer's grasp as she could. The insides of her fingers and palms were lacerated to the bone from the razor-sharp barbs on the bars.

The cage was locked and the keys sat on a filth-covered workbench against the wall. She didn't know what to think or how to feel. She tried to think about a plan of escape, but her mind kept snapping her back to the reality that there was no way out. She thought that perhaps she was already dead and she was in hell. The big, bald lunatic that was keeping her locked up must be Satan himself. She figured that Michael must have killed her when she had been in the tub and everything else was just the last fleeting image of her life before her brain functions ceased forever.

This has to be hell. No other place on earth could ever be like this. The thought of spending eternity in this horrid place made her puke. She threw up on the corpse that was next to her and did not stop until her stomach was empty and aching. Kira wiped away the spit from her lips with the back of her hand, buried her head between her knees, and prayed.

She heard a rumbling in the corner of the room. When she looked up, she was expecting to see Satan standing there, but was still shocked to see Richie's dead body. Kira was so numb that she almost had no reaction to the rat that scurried about. She saw that Richie's face was smeared with blood and tears. Hanging from his hollow eye sockets were tendons and ligaments that brushed against his crimson-caked cheeks. Kira knew that Richie's life was over. She, on the other hand, was still alive and wanted to stay that way, eyes intact.

"Richie. Richie," she cried out softly.

The monster walked into the room, dragging Zoë behind him. Her neck was bulging from the phone that was rammed down her throat. Her eyes were open with a look of incomprehensible horror still glowing deeply within them. The monster stopped in front of Richie's lifeless body. He felt around and touched the long chain that dangled down from his wide torso. Kira wanted to scream but could not find her voice. The monster reached down, grabbed Richie by the head, and lifted the boy straight up. The monster started to squeeze the boy's head as if it were a pimple. The sounds of his skull cracking made Kira cover her ears. The monster pressed his hands closer together, and the bones in Richie's skull started to pierce his brain. The monster jerked sharply and snapped Richie's neck so that it sounded like a dry branch being broken off a dying tree. He dropped the boy's body on top of Hannah's, and the two corpses lay as if they were romantically intertwined. He tossed Zoë's body into the room, and it landed with a dull thud next to Kira.

The monster knelt down next to the cage and studied Kira. She didn't want to look into his eyes but she couldn't help herself. She was drawn to them. The big, dark pupils sucked all of the spirit out of her like a black hole devouring and destroying all that it trapped into its gravitational pull. She tried to find a glimmer of humanity in his large glistening eyes, a sense of deep forgotten mercy that she prayed she could once again stir and restore to the cold face that looked at her with undetermined malevolence burning in its gaze. There was none left. Whatever quality of mercy or forgiveness this thing may have been born with had dried up and blown away many, many years ago, like dead weeds in a desert. There was nothing within this creature but a barren wasteland of inhumane emotion that led to depravity and death.

The monster thought about the best way to use the girl's powers against the others. He would use the ornate symbols on her back. The big one, the cross. The monster knew what the cross was. It meant pain and suffering. He would make the others suffer for their transgressions against his house. They would feel pain for bringing the vile outside world into his home. They brought disease and corruption. They brought sin. And the monster would eradicate the sin that now lived and roamed within the hallways of his kingdom like a deadly virus pulsating through the arteries and veins that were the hallways and floors of the old hotel.

The monster walked past the giant neon "T" that took up a large portion of the corner of the room to a row of knives that hung next to it. He examined the sharpness of the different blades. He let the blades run against his fingers. He had found the knives in the kitchen when he'd first found refuge in the hotel. Since then, they had served him well. He honed and sharpened them with such care and precision that even after years of flaying, cutting, and boning, they still could slice the top layers of skin off an intruder several times before drawing blood. He found the right blade; it was just sharp enough to cut into the girl's flesh and slice the holy image off her back without killing her. The monster did not want the girl to die quickly. He had other plans for her after the siege of his kingdom had been put down.

He looked over at the girl in the cage and started toward the workbench. He had to prepare his altar so that she would be tied down on her belly and wouldn't be able to move around when he began to skin her alive. He had to hurry. The others were still out there, spreading the pestilence of their world in the sanctity of his home.

Christine and Tye realized that they were going in a dark circle. They were lost, and they didn't know what to do. The last three hallways they had gone down led them almost back to where they had started. Christine was afraid that they would come across Williams's body again and she didn't want that.

"How fucking big *is* this place?" Tye asked. He rested against the wall and banged his head back on the burnt wallpaper.

Christine remembered the puzzle books she used to play with when she was a little girl. They had simple crossword puzzles and word searches where you would find certain words hidden within blocks of seemingly random letters in a neat square. She used to love to find where the words were hidden and she used to love to solve the little mazes in the back of the book. She remembered that the mazes usually had something in the middle of them, a cartoon of a piece of cheese or a slice of pie. On the outside of the maze was the drawing of a little mouse or a boy who would venture into the maze to find the cheese or pie. She thought now how ironic it was that they were stuck in the middle of a maze and they couldn't find their way out. *Maybe we're the prizes. What happens if that thing is chasing us like we are his slice of pie? What will he do to me if he finds me?* She didn't want to imagine what would happen to her if the killer that was stalking them caught her. Without even thinking about it, Christine made a mental note to make sure she saved the last bullet in Williams's revolver for herself.

"This place is like a nightmare," Tye complained, and Christine agreed. They started walking again and came to another locked stairwell. Christine was certain that if they didn't get to Kira soon, her friend would be killed. She thought about going back to where Williams's body was lying to try to climb up through the hole in the ceiling that he had fallen from. It would lead them to the next floor, but it would also probably lead them to the killer as well. She squeezed the gun and pressed it against her face and tried to decide what to do next.

"Let me hold the gun," Tye requested.

"What?"

"I want to hold the gun. Let me carry it. I know how to use that thing," he declared, wanting the gun for his own protection.

"Fuck you!" she replied. It was Christine who had had to pull the gun from the dead cop's fingers, not Tye. He had been too busy trying to run away. She had earned the right to have the gun. She pulled out the stun gun that Williams had given her and gave it to Tye.

"Here, use this," she told him.

Tye looked at the stun gun and turned it on. An electric crackle buzzed.

"Big deal," he said, discouraged.

"You don't like it, find something else," was her answer as she kept walking.

She stopped. Tye stopped behind her. They heard something coming down the hallway toward them. Footsteps. They were loud and heavy. Tye was backing up when Christine looked over to see if he would stay and fight. She got her answer; he started to run. Christine gripped the gun tightly as the footsteps got closer to her. She held the gun up and waited for whatever was coming out of the darkness to show its horrid face. The footsteps were almost upon her when her courage broke and she fled. She turned and chased after Tye, who had run back to the stairwell door that they just came through and was frantically trying to push it open. Christine ran up to him and slammed her shoulder into the door and they both started pushing. The door would not budge.

"Shit!" Tye seethed. The footsteps were rounding the corner and would be on them any second.

Christine had no choice now. She aimed the gun at the corner of the hallway and pressed her finger on the trigger of the gun. Tye held the stun gun in his hand and hoped whatever currents flowed through it would be enough to immobilize the beast that wanted to kill them. He knew it wouldn't be enough to kill it.

"We're going to fucking die," Tye moaned, and Christine thought how right he was.

The figure came around the corner, and the obscuring

shadows that ran alongside of it fell away as it came into the dimly moonlit hallway. Christine pulled the trigger.

The bullet went wide, and the figure dove for cover and rolled. He came up screaming.

"What the fuck?" Michael exploded as he jumped up and looked at Christine. She was still pointing the gun at him.

Christine and Tye sighed as Michael walked toward them angrily, waving his pipe menacingly.

"Jesus Christ, bitch. You almost blew my head off!" he said, looking at her in shock.

Tye started to laugh and Christine smiled nervously. Michael did not want to say it, but he was happy as hell to see Christine and Tye. The thoughts of retribution were erased from his mind the moment he'd seen the monster's axe blade almost slice off Zoë's head. Christine stood in front of Michael, still training her gun at him. He knew that she was calling the shots as well as firing them.

"Where the hell did you come from?" Tye asked as he walked past Christine and toward Michael.

"Man, you ain't going to believe it," Michael said as he realized that the fact that Christine was holding a gun was a pretty good indication that they had had their own close encounters with the creature.

"Let me guess. Big fucker? Bald head? Bad breath? Bunch of flies swarming all around him?" Tye speculated.

Michael nodded slowly.

"What the fuck is it?" Michael asked.

"Don't know," Christine answered as she lowered the gun. "Whoever it is, Williams knew him. He said the guy was some type of nightmare, and I believe him."

"Where's Williams now?" Michael asked.

"Dead. Real dead," Tye said.

Michael felt his stomach start to churn. He felt a profound sadness, not for Williams but for himself. He knew that if Williams were alive, the cop would find a way out of this. Michael hated to admit that Williams was one tough son of a bitch and that he had felt secure knowing that Williams would come to his rescue. Now the cop was dead and whatever slim chances Michael had had of getting out of the hotel alive were getting slimmer.

"Goddamn," Michael cursed.

"What about the others? Russell and Melissa and Zoë?" Christine asked him.

"Zoë's dead too," Michael said, not wanting to relive the sounds of her death as he'd hid under the bathroom sink.

"What about Russell and Melissa?" she asked again.

"Don't know. We split up. They may be all right. I don't know. I hope to hell they are." Michael had a genuine compassion in his voice that surprised Christine and Tye.

"I think Hannah's dead. Maybe Richie too. He took Kira," she told him.

"What?" Michael blurted out. His feelings of vengeance toward Kira were gone, as if they had never existed in his heart or mind. The once passionate emotions he'd had for her were burning strongly again. Whatever Michael wanted to do to Kira was nothing compared to what was already happening to her. No one deserved that, not even those who betrayed him. Everything that led up to this point seemed trivial and unimportant. The idea of hurting Kira now seemed to be a foreign concept to him, one that he couldn't wrap his head around. She was someone that he once loved and despised. Anyone who could evoke those emotions in him meant something to him.

"We have to find her," Christine said to Michael.

And Michael knew she was right. If Kira was still alive, they would have to find her. No one else would. He hoped that Russell and Melissa were okay, hiding somewhere in the hotel or getting it on and not knowing what terror the others were going through. He didn't want to run anymore. He wanted to stay, to fight, to find Kira. All plans for revenge instantaneously turned to plans of rescue. He didn't know where this foolish sense of courage was coming from. Realistically, it would probably get him killed; passionately, it was the only thing to do.

"We have to get up to the top floors. That's where I think he is keeping her," Christine said.

"Good guess. Most of the stairwells are blocked. I found one that goes up to the tenth floor, but we can't go any higher than that. Stairs above that are gone. If we make it back to the tenth, maybe we can find a way up that isn't blocked."

"Whoa! Hold on. Hold on. You still think that she's alive? You think Richie's alive? That crazy fucker has probably already killed them. He's gonna do the same to us, and you want to find where this asshole lives? Are you *insane*? They're dead!" Tye cried out.

Michael and Christine thought about what he'd just said. They both knew there was a ninety-nine percent chance that Kira and Richie were dead, but as long as there was margin left over, the odds were still worth betting on.

"No, Williams said that he would keep Kira alive for a few hours. I think that he may've been right," Christine countered. She almost believed that her determination would will it to be true. Michael didn't know what she was talking about, but he liked the bravado in her voice. It made him feel better about the situation.

"You have to have a screw loose, girl," Tye said. "I know you two are tight, but Williams was probably only saying that shit to keep you from freakin' out. Ain't no way anyone is alive. Not Richie, not Kira, not that Anders broad. I bet Russell and Melissa are dead too. And all you want to do is fucking join them. Well, not me. I ain't running straight into that big-ass motherfucker and gettin' myself killed for no one." There was genuine fear in Tye's voice.

"Fine. Stay here. I'm going up. You coming with me?" she asked Michael.

Michael didn't hesitate with his agreement. The quickness of his reply surprised even him. He would go up and he would find Kira. He didn't want Kira to suffer a fate similar to, or worse than, Zoë's. Michael felt a strong sense of protectiveness over Kira, one he hadn't felt in years.

"Let's find them," Michael said.

Michael and Christine started to walk away from Tye, leaving him against the immovable stairwell door. Tye knew going with them would be crazy. He'd known it when Williams had originally decided to search for Kira, and look what had happened to the cop since then. It was insane, and they were nuts for trying to think they could find her and save her. *Let them go get killed*, he thought. *Ain't my problem. Fuck 'em.* He watched them as they turned the corner. When he realized he was all alone, it suddenly became his problem.

"Wait up!" he yelled up, and he ran up to them.

He didn't have to say that he was afraid to be alone—they knew it and they felt the same way. If Christine and Michael were determined to find Kira, then it looked like Tye would be shanghaied into their rescue mission. Christine nodded, and the three of them traveled down another hallway looking for a way out and up.

Christine didn't see the thin wire that stretched across the hallway until she was almost tripping over it.

"What the hell?" she yelled as she started to stumble over it. Michael grabbed her. The three of them bent down to examine the wire that was six inches above the ground.

"What is this?" Michael asked as his fingers ran across the wire.

"Don't know. If it was a trap it would have been sprung by now," she said, touching the wire and studying it. It ran from one little hole on one side of the wall to another on the opposite wall. Her fingers strummed it. It was as taut as a piano wire, and a sick thought hit her.

"I think we just told that fucker where we are," she told the others.

"Shit! It's like a signal," Tye said.

"I can't think of anyone else that would put this here, can you?" she replied.

"He knows where we are now," Tye said.

"Where we were. Let's get the fuck out of here."

They all agreed and hurried away from the trip wire.

The monster had prepared his workspace. He cleared away all of the old blood and flesh from the top of the workbench and started to tighten the restraining straps he would use on the girl. He tossed the bigger pieces of flesh into the darkness of another room, and the sounds of rats converging on the tasty morsels squeaked out.

The monster looked down at the girl in the cage. Her eyes were red from crying, but soon they would be gone, so it didn't matter. He didn't want to harm her yet. He needed her whole because he still needed to understand the powers that she possessed. He wanted to know why the boy with the pipe and the other girl with the long black hair both wanted to possess this one. *Why would they quarrel over her?* he thought. She must have some mystical powers that were invaluable to the outsiders. Now those powers were in the monster's grasp. All he had to do now was figure out what they were and how to use them.

The others who were still alive were crafty. He would need all of his skills to get the rest of them. He had made a good game of blocking off certain stairwells and leaving others open. He wanted to sow confusion.

The monster knew that once they were mystified with the mazelike structure of the hotel, frustration would set in and they would make a mistake. He enjoyed the bizarre labyrinth that the hotel turned into once the upper floors were reached. On his first night in the hotel, years ago, he had wandered around the weird layout of the Blackwell, but he'd never gotten lost. From his first footstep in the hotel, he'd known where he was going. He found it odd that he should come to such a strange place and know it so well. It was like some unseen hand had guided him along. Something inside of him knew where every secret of the hotel lay. He did not know where this knowledge came from, but it had always been inside of him. At first, he'd found this troubling, but soon he began to accept the fact that the hotel wanted him; it needed him. The building shared its secrets with him and he shared his with the hotel. The Blackwell was built for dark and sinister purposes. For years it had sat dormant, with only the distant memories of debauchery and brutality echoing throughout its empty hallways and vacant rooms.

Now the hotel was alive once again, breathing in the foul air and pulsating with the flow of blood from a new crop of victims. Langley Blackwell was born to do evil, and he'd embraced his calling with an unquenchable relish. The monster was born to do the work of God, which was what he believed he was doing. He went about his tasks with a cold workmanlike efficiency. The ones the monster punished were bad. They had sin on them. He knew sin was bad. He had been told that. They wouldn't come to this place if they weren't attracted to the sin that had once lived there. The monster thought of no better place to live than a place that was once crawling with evil. But ever since he'd made the hotel his home, he'd cast out the sin, banished it to the streets.

The monster knew deep inside that this place had once been a shrine to sin. He found it everywhere he looked, and he tried to wash it out with the blood of the defilers that tried to sneak into his home.

Once, as he rummaged through the hidden rooms of the building, he came across many rolls of black plastic with images on them. It took time, but he figured out how to spool them through the machine that hummed and cast light. He watched all the scenes play out on the blank walls. He remembered watching the men and women on top of each other, doing all sorts of things to one another that he knew were bad. He tried to touch the women that were projected as faded specters in various poses opening themselves up in all the ways that the monster knew were evil. He wanted to feel their bodies when they quivered and wiggled with sin but his fingers only felt the coarseness of the wall the moving images played on. God had left those metal cans with the sin captured in them for the monster to find. God wanted him to know what sin looked like firsthand. Even when the monster was tempted by watching the men and women sin with each other, he fought back the urges.

He knew that the only way to fight sin, once it tried to creep up his body and down to his dangling bits, was to bring back the pain. The pain had made the sin go away when he was younger. Although the monster could never remember a time when he wasn't who—*what*—he was now, his earliest recollections were always of the young boy in the cage. The monster never knew who the young boy was, but he always felt a bond to the child in the filthy prison. When the young boy sinned, he remembered the boiling water that was poured on his dangling bits. It made the monster mad to remember the young boy being punished. The monster wished that he could remember what the cruel figure looked like, the one who was lurking in his head. He didn't know who it was who preached about sin, poured the waters of redemption on the boy's young flesh until it blistered red and raw, and sang hymns after the boy had finished crying. Why couldn't the monster see the person's face?

The monster knew the image of that figure was somewhere inside his head, walking among the sounds and noises that played constantly in his mind. These questions plagued the monster, but because of this unknown savior he knew what to do when sin tempted him to go off the path. He punished himself until the sin left his body. The pain would push the sin out and make him pure again. The more pain he could endure, the purer he would become. Fire had always been the great purifier, so when the monster felt the tingling touch of sin starting to tickle him, he would burn himself with fire until the skin on his body boiled and blackened. No sin could survive the flame of repentance. Every burn made him stronger and closer to God.

Now, as the monster looked down at the girl with the holy images etched into her soft skin, the urges of sin started to take hold, but he would fight them, hold them back from clouding what he had to do. He would not listen to her cries, because lies lived within her pleas for mercy. He would ignore her when she begged, because he knew her kind to be insincere. No matter how much she thrashed and screamed, he would do his work. He would slice off the sacrilegious images that decorated her young body, and he would wear them into the final battle.

He stood over the cage and looked at the girl, the knife in his hand scraping across his callused palm. The keys to the cage dangled in his other hand. The time of deliverance was here.

The sound of the bells made him stop. Someone was closing in. He looked up at the bells on the wall and saw that the ones with the number eight printed above them were jingling loudly. He knew what that meant. They were coming close to the elevator on the eighth floor. He knew the area well. He had let them run as far as they could on the floor where the fire had raged. Some had eluded him; others were not so lucky.

He didn't want them getting on the elevator. He knew the elevator would not go down to the bottom of the hotel unless he allowed it to do so, but he couldn't take the chance of them getting to the elevator and working some of their powers on it so that the elevator took them farther away from his reach. He didn't want to go after the others without a pelt made of the girl's skin wrapped around him, but he was afraid that the others would find a way to get out, that they would have a chance to flee before he could spill their impure blood and wash the walls with it until their sin had vanished from his home.

The monster made up his mind. He would have to get the others now and take care of the girl afterward. He would take his time with the girl when he returned. He dropped the keys on the floor and stormed out to finish the intruders once and for all.

• • •

Christine, Michael, and Tye came upon a service elevator at the end of the last hallway. Its cold metal doors held none of the aesthetic value that the main elevator in the lobby held.

"What are the chances that this thing still works?" Tye said, tapping the doors with the stun gun.

"Pretty fucking good, I'd say." Michael was looking up at the elevator's indicator lights to see that it was descending.

"Oh, shit! Do you think it's him?" Christine asked, nervousness clenching her voice.

"I don't see who else it could be." Michael's tone was condescending and he gripped his pipe tightly.

"Let's make a run for it," Tye suggested, hoping that his idea would be seconded.

"No. I'm sick of running. Let's kill this fucker right now," Christine suggested.

"Goddamn straight. Blow his freakin' head off the second those doors open." Michael admired the young girl the way Williams had, as a comrade and fellow warrior.

Christine stood in front of the elevator, the gun pointed out and up to compensate for the monster's height. Michael had his pipe cocked back, and Tye had the stun gun on and ready to jam in the monster's eye.

"Just keep aiming at his face," Michael told them.

The service elevator shuddered as it moved down the shaft. Sweat trickled down Christine's face, starting to sting her eyes. Her finger rested on the trigger of the gun. She waited impatiently to apply the pressure that would drop the hammer and hopefully drop the big killer that was after them. Michael thought about smashing away at the thing's head until it was nothing but a bloody mess. Tye wished he were anyplace but here.

"No mercy," she whispered. And it was understood that none would be given from either camp.

The service elevator stopped in front of them. It remained still for a second that felt like an hour. A slight ding indicated that the elevator had reached its destination.

The doors started to open slowly.

"All right, motherfu—" Christine stopped herself in mid battle cry as the doors opened to reveal that the elevator was empty.

"What the . . ."

Michael was interrupted as the wall behind them ripped open with a ferocious burst. Smashing his way through the brittle, fire-damaged drywall was the beast they'd each already encountered, his axe cutting its way toward the kids. The monster had fooled them by sneaking down a back stairwell and hiding while he sent the service elevator down by a crude timer. Finally, the last three were standing in front of him and he would make quick work of them so he could get back to the girl.

Christine turned and fired her weapon. She missed in all the confusion. The monster's axe was heading toward her when Michael swung his pipe and hit their opponent on the side of his head, denting his rusty plate. The axe went wide, and Christine fell under the blade as it sliced by. Tye jabbed the stun gun and struck the monster's neck, but was battered away for his effort.

Christine got to her knees and fired again. Two more shots missed their mark. The monster backhanded Christine and sent her sliding down the hallway. The gun slipped from her hand and left her defenseless. Michael tried to use the pipe to strike the beast's skull again, but the creature held up his axe and stopped the blow. He pushed the axe handle into Michael's chest and sent him sailing into a soot-covered mirror on the wall. The glass shattered and rained over Michael's head as the boy slumped down. His head split, and blood started to pour down his face. He tried to get up, but he fell back down, despite his forced effort. Christine crawled toward the open service elevator. Tye held the stun gun out as if he could intimidate the monster with it. The monster smiled at the attempt.

"Run!" Tye took off, racing away from the monster.

In response, the ogre raised his axe and followed the boy. He stepped on Michael's pipe and slipped. He stumbled to his knee and braced the axe out in front of himself to break his fall.

Tye jumped into the elevator just as the doors shut. He smashed the buttons for the lower floors, but the elevator started to rise. The doors caved in as the monster smashed his body into the elevator to stop it. Like an elephant charging a hunter's jeep, the beast slammed his shoulder harder and harder into the metal doors, bending them in. Sparks burst out from the control panel as the elevator stopped moving.

"He fucking broke it." Christine's disbelief was evident as she kept jabbing the down buttons.

The axe blade sliced into the door. The monster had swung it with a mighty blow.

"Fuck me!" Tye bellowed. The tip of the axe was yanked out. The bastard was getting ready to swing again.

"We gotta go up!" Tye told Christine as he looked at the emergency escape panel in the ceiling of the elevator. Tye jumped up and punched out the panel just as the axe burst through the doors a second time. They both knew that it would probably take less than five swings for the monster to break open the doors. If they didn't do something quickly, they would be chopped to bits.

The panel fell down and Tye shoved the stun gun in his pocket. He jumped up again and grabbed on to the edge of the opening. He pulled himself up and onto the top of the elevator. The axe was busy chewing its way through the metal door. Christine could see the monster's crazed eyes through the rips in the door now.

Tye bent back down into the elevator.

"Grab my hand!" he yelled as he extended his arm down to her.

She gripped his hand tightly as the elevator doors gave way. The monster rushed in, swinging his axe. Christine curled her body as Tye pulled her up with all of his strength. Seconds later, the axe sliced through the air Christine had occupied.

Tye pulled her to the top of the elevator and they pressed their backs against the walls of the shaft.

The beast stuck his head through the panel opening and saw Tye and Christine cowering in the shadows. A dark, hungry smile lit up the monster's face; they were making it easy for him. He tried to climb onto the top of the elevator, but his enormous bulk made it impossible for him to fit through the small opening.

Tye took out the stun gun and jammed it onto the monster's hand. Sparks crackled as the ogre fell back into the elevator, howling. In frustration, he started to slash at the emergency escape exit with his axe. He ran around in a crazed circle in the elevator, then took off down the hallway in a frenzy.

"Do you think he's really gone?" Tye asked Christine.

"Are you fucking high?" she asked sarcastically.

Christine saw the service ladder bolted to the wall. She tested the rungs and thought that they felt strong and secure. She headed up.

"Wait, where are you going?" Tye yelled up after her.

She ignored him and kept climbing up. Up to the top floors of the Blackwell, to Kira, to put an end to the nightmare.

The elevator started to buckle under Tye's weight. Having no other option, he jumped onto the ladder and followed Christine up.

12

THE MONSTER WAS FUMING. HE RACED BACK TO THE stairwell that he had used when he'd snuck down to trap the intruders. His plan had failed miserably. He had only killed one of them and didn't have time to collect his prize. The other two were getting away. They were heading up to his home, to his most private of places. He could not let them infect his domain with their sin. They had fought better than he expected. He didn't know why they chose to stand to fight when all others before them had tried to flee. He had to kill them before they made it to the top, to the girl, and more important, to his collection.

Kira had already been given a reprieve twice by the warning bells that rang in the monster's lair. She was smart enough to know there would not be a third time. She knew the next time the big killer entered the hellhole he called home, she would die. And she knew she wouldn't go peacefully. She saw how he'd looked at her when he was testing the blades of his knives on his hand. She thought about what was in store for her, and no matter how many scenarios she played in her mind, they all ended badly.

She saw the keys to the cage lying on the floor, but they were too far out of her reach, next to Richie's and Hannah's lifeless bodies. She didn't want to end up dying like they had.

She thought about running her wrists across the sharp barbs of the cage until her veins were shredded and she would bleed out and die. She knew she would have to cut much deeper than she ever had in the past. This time it wouldn't be a desperate cry for help on her part. She would rip and tear at her wrist until she got to the bone. She didn't care about the pain now. It would be nothing compared to the agony that awaited her when the barbarian came back. She braced herself and let her fingers find the sharpest and longest barbs on the bars. She found one that was strong and razor sharp. It would take some time to slash her veins open enough to let enough blood out quickly, but she would have to work as fast as possible.

She took a deep breath and lifted her wrist toward the sharp piece of metal. She looked around and took in the sick inventory that the monster valued the most. Pieces of skin tacked and spread out like maps, chains and sharp implements covered in crusty browned blood hanging from the wall, the large neon "T" that lay propped up in the corner like a crucifix waiting for another victim.

And the eyes. Kira was fascinated and repelled by

the rows of tall glass beakers that housed countless pairs of dead orbs that floated lifelessly in a sick yellow liquid. She wondered how many people had given up their sight to this horrific menagerie of the macabre. Kira didn't want to think that Richie's eyes were floating in there among all the others looking out at her. She didn't want to think about Hannah's eyes floating there. She didn't want to picture her own eyes encased forever in that inescapable prison.

Christine had climbed up the service ladder in the elevator so quickly that she didn't even realize that she was almost to the top floors. Tye was right beneath her. He kept looking up at her shapely ass and couldn't help thinking how fine it was. He laughed to himself and thought, *Even when I'm about to get my ass fucking killed, I'm still thinking about getting pussy.*

Christine couldn't go any higher because the ceiling of the service elevator shaft was above her head, and she saw that they'd reached the top floor. Pulleys and cables were bolted to the top of the ceiling. When she looked down, she couldn't distinguish anything in the darkness. The only thing that was visible was the small sliver of light that came from the emergency panel opening of the elevator that they had escaped from.

"Where to now?" Tye asked, stopping an inch away from her behind.

"We go in here," she said, trying to pry open the elevator doors to the top floor.

They wouldn't budge. She tried to wriggle her fingers in between the seam of closed doors and hoped that if she used enough pressure, they would open. Tye climbed up and wrapped his body behind hers. He reached around and stuck his hand in between the door to help her. Both teens pushed and shoved their hands farther between the service elevator doors and finally opened the entryway.

Christine crawled onto the floor, and Tye followed closely. The smell was what hit Christine first. The place was fairly well lit. A simple setup of old electrical cords and sockets with weak bulbs that stretched along the top of the walls gave enough light to guide the way. Unfortunately, it also gave enough light to see the horror that was littered across the floor.

When Christine stopped abruptly, Tye bumped into her. As she started to gag, he looked over her shoulder to see what had stopped her from moving on. Spread out across the floor was a sea of bones and body parts that had been there for years. The place looked like the aftermath of a great battle or a crude Civil War hospital where limbs were hacked off and tossed aside to make room for the next unlucky patient. Tye held Christine by the shoulders for support—not just hers, but his as well. Neither one had ever imagined anything like this before.

There were at least three bodies that could be considered nearly whole propped up against a far wall. They seemed to be the fresher ones of the group. Hungry flies swarmed over their eyeless faces and resembled pulsating black masks. The corpses were naked and bloated, and their limbs were twisted, bent, and broken.

Scattered across the floor were bones that were

brown with rot. Hunks of flesh still clung to the remains, and rats and roaches dined in quiet, nibbling and gnawing the putrid flesh. Several bare skulls lay among the human debris. Teeth marks larger than an animal's pocked the bone, indicating that a different form of life had devoured these bodies. Not a higher life-form but a different one, one that had not evolved in humanity since the first man crawled out of a cave.

Christine could feel her body start to tremble. In response to her shaking, Tye held her a bit more tightly. She shook her head as if she could shake the insanity of her surroundings away. The overpowering odor was making her retch. She bent down and puked in front of Tye. In response, Tye held her consolingly as he looked around at the bones and body parts, trying to figure out how many people lay in ruin before them.

"We're screwed," Tye whispered.

Christine regained her composure. She straightened up and stood tall.

"Not yet," she said as she started walking down the hallway. She moved gingerly around the bones, not wanting to step on a limb or a live rodent. The rats looked up at the girl who had interrupted their midnight snack with annoyance in their black pellet eyes. They did not give her a second thought and went back to their feasting. Tye tried to follow her path. They continued down the long hallway, holding their breath. They came to another corridor that had only a few small bones littered about. The hallway opened into what had once been the luxurious penthouse of the Blackwell Hotel—the suite that was now a madman's charnel house.

Christine knew they had entered the monster's home.

"Kira!" Christine yelled out desperately.

"Goddamn, bitch! Why don't you tell him we're here!" Tye seethed.

"He knows we're here. Kira!" she yelled again.

They both heard a low voice. It seemed distant and muted, but they knew it was Kira's. Christine ran down the hall, screaming out Kira's name. Tye trailed her closely, looking over his shoulder for their host to return. Christine stopped at the main door. She banged on it, and she could hear Kira's screams from within. Unable to open the locked door, she smashed it with frustration. Tye gently moved her aside and bent down with his bent hairpin in his hand. He'd started to pick the lock when they heard the main elevator starting to come up at the end of another hallway.

"Tye . . ." Christine warned quietly.

"I know. I hear it."

Tye's fingers moved expertly, and the lock clicked open. Christine pushed the door open and they ran in. The first room of the suite was large. Sitting in the corner was a safe. The door to it was open and Tye saw that it was empty. Tye knew it was *the* safe, the one that he had hoped to find, and now it was here in front of him.

Christine called out to Kira again so that they could gauge where she was being held. They heard Kira's cries from a room somewhere at the back of the big suite. Christine chased after her friend's voice. Tye moved toward the safe and ran his hands across the old steel. He tried to slam the door shut, but it was so heavy it wouldn't swing easily. He spat in disgust and froze as he saw the wall that his spit had landed on. He walked up to the wall and looked in amazement at what covered it. Money. Lots of it. Thousands of bills were plastered all over the walls. Twenties, fifties, and hundreds. All spread out and coated with a dull pink coating of dried blood that kept them glued to the wall. Tye tried to peel off one of the bills and it crumbled in his hand. He tried to pull off another. It tore off into pieces. He scratched at the bloodstained currency, but only shreds fell. He saw that each eye of the face on every bill was neatly cut out, leaving a faded green curtain of blind presidents mockingly staring back at him.

"Fuck," he muttered, knowing that anyone that would do this to money was definitely not right in the head. Christine ran back into the room and grabbed Tye.

"Worthless . . . it's all worthless," he sighed.

"Come on and help me find her," she said, pulling him out of the money-covered room.

Christine hauled Tye down a dark hallway that connected the sitting room to the main living room. They ran into an outer foyer that led to the main bedroom and stopped. Christine looked around and tried to figure out what was lining the bookshelves that covered the walls. She walked up to the glass bottles, beakers, and containers that filled the shelves and reared back into Tye when she realized that they were filled with eyes. Hundreds of eyes floating in silent repose, staring out at nothing. Her mind had been hit with so much depravity and craziness in such a short span of time that she didn't pause to let the horror of the monster's collection register with her.

She yelled for Kira again. They found their way to

where Kira was calling from, the heart of the monster's home, decorated by the mind of madness.

Christine stopped at a door that was partially opened. She leaned against it and called softly.

"Kira? You alone?" she whispered into the room.

"Hurry!" Kira answered at the top of her lungs.

Christine and Tye went in and descended into the last level of hell. Christine made her way toward Kira in the cage that was in the corner of the room. She knew Hannah and Richie were dead, but she couldn't respond to their dead bodies now. She ignored Zoë, slumped in the corner. All of Christine's focus was on the living, on saving Kira.

"Jesus Christ. Jesus Christ. Get me out of here. Hurry," Kira pleaded.

Tye covered his mouth when he saw Richie's lifeless body. Tears started to swell in his eyes as he looked around and took in all the horror that surrounded them.

Christine knelt in front of the cage and pulled on the padlock. Kira shoved her arms out from behind the barbed bars, her flesh ripping. She grabbed her friend's hand.

"Get me out of here," Kira begged as blood started flowing from the cuts on her arm.

"How?" Christine was worried that time was running out.

"The keys. The keys are on the floor over next to Richie and Hannah," Kira told her.

Christine quickly crawled over the blood-soaked floor and grabbed the keys. She fumbled through the mess of keys, trying to find the right one. Tye stood and just watched her as if he were watching a movie and not part of the whole scene that was unfolding before him. Christine jammed a key into the lock. It didn't turn. She tried another one.

"Hurry up!" Kira barked as she started to shake the door of the cage.

Christine tried another key. Nothing. She tried another. The padlock stayed in place.

"Shit!" Christine mumbled under her breath as her fingers rifled through the large set of keys.

Somewhere in the outer rooms of the suite a door slammed.

Christine and Tye looked at each other. The monster was home. Heavy footsteps thumped their way down the hallway toward them.

Christine clenched Kira's fingers through the bar.

"We'll come back for you," Christine promised.

"What? Are you crazy? Don't leave me. Please, Christine. Don't leave me," Kira begged.

The heavy footsteps grew louder.

"Please, God, Christine, don't leave me with him," Kira whimpered as tears poured down her face, turning it wet and crimson.

Tye pulled Christine away from the cage. He couldn't look at Kira. He knew that the sight of her face as they left her behind would torment him the rest of his life.

The footsteps were right outside the door.

Tye and Christine slipped through a back door that led to the private kitchen and dining room. Christine's heart broke at leaving Kira alone when they had been so close to saving her.

The monster entered his lair and looked at Kira

330

kneeling by the door of the cage, crying uncontrollably.

A sense of pity came over the monster when he saw that Kira was about to fly into hysterics. He didn't want to feel this way. He never liked to show mercy to the sinners. It was the same feeling he used to get when he remembered the young boy that lived in his memories.

The girl suffered. She suffered because she had sin on her. The monster knew that it was her own fault, but something seemed to touch him inside. He would kill the girl quicker than he wanted to, once the others were dead. He stared down at her and heard her choking sobs. When she looked up at him, the look she gave him told him that she was ready to accept her fate.

"I wish you'd just kill me," Kira begged softly.

The monster reached down and stroked her hair through the bars. It was soft to the touch. A strange feeling started to smolder deep within him. He looked at the girl, and the feelings started to burn and the monster felt tingling warmth spreading through him.

Thoughts of the other intruders seemed to be pushed back into the monster's brain. Voices echoed out again in his mind. They all spoke the same language now. *Take the girl. Possess her body. Slice her flesh. Ravage her and push the sin from her.* The monster looked into Kira's eyes, and she knew that terror awaited her. He picked up the keys that had been left on the top of the cage and never once wondered how they had gotten there.

Returning to the room with the safe, Christine and Tye looked around for something that could be used as a weapon. There was nothing.

"We have to get him out of there," Christine said softly.

"Say what?"

"We have to draw him out. You have to make noise so I can sneak her out," she told him.

"I have to do *what*? Are you out of your fucking mind?" Tye looked at her as if she had two heads.

Christine gripped his hand. She squeezed. He felt for the first time in his life what the touch of true friendship was like.

"This is our only chance. Please. You need to make some noise," she said, tightening her grip on him. Tye had reevaluated his entire life in about half a second. He decided that if he was going to cash it in that night, then he might as well go down fighting. If Christine needed a diversion, Tye would give her one. For some unknown reason he felt he owed it to her. He needed to do this for her and Kira. He had a lot to make up for in his short eighteen years, and he thought he'd start now. He nodded in agreement. He let Christine's hand fall away from his slowly as a final good-bye.

13

THE MONSTER FOUND THE KEY THAT WOULD DISEN-
gage the padlock. The burning sensations inside him
were spreading like wildfire. Thoughts of sin, immoral
and impure, started to sear and brand themselves in his
mind. A bloodlust rose up in him, and a primal desire
to tear, rip, grab, grope, and ravage overtook him. He
couldn't fight the power of sin anymore. Its pull was
too strong, and its allure was too enticing. He knew he
was defiling himself with a bestial craving, but he didn't
care. He wanted the girl and all that she was. He
hungered for her scent. Her taste. Her touch. He
wanted to feel her softness. Wantonness controlled
him. It was a wantonness not of his own making but of
someone else's, someone who the monster never knew
but always felt.

The spirit of the hotel came to life. The true
essence of the desolate and deserted building emerged
from a dark slumber. The soul of Langley Blackwell
had awakened once again and controlled his body and

brain. The deviant and evil mind of the hotel's original owner guided him and led the mindless behemoth that he had created to do his bidding once again.

"No! No! No!" Kira pleaded.

The monster slipped the key into the lock.

A loud crash came from the front room, and the monster turned and ran to investigate. In anger, he kicked Richie's corpse off Hannah's, and the dead boy's body fell against the wall. The monster, still lusting after Kira, hurried out of the room toward what he hoped were the intruders.

As soon as the monster left the room, Christine snuck in and knelt down next to the cage. She looked around for the keys. She searched the top of the cage, she felt around the floor. They were not to be found.

"The keys? Where are they?" she asked Kira.

Kira looked up. Barely fighting back tears, she had surrendered to defeat.

"He took them," she whispered.

The monster rushed into the room where he kept his main collection of eyes. He looked down to see that one of his glass containers was lying broken on the ground. The eyes were spilling out in a rancid puddle of liquid. He started to fume. Quickly, he bent down to retrieve the eyes. He looked at each one, seeing if any damage had been done. The monster could not afford for harm to come to these eyes. Parts of his soul still existed deep within their gaze. If they were destroyed or ruined, he would be lost. It would be only a matter of time before his soul was picked apart, piece by piece, until there was nothing left of him. The monster scooped up all the eyes, placed them into other containers, and went to find the one who dared to cast away his soul so he could punish them.

Tye made his way to the first room and tried to open the door to get out. It was locked again. The monster must have locked it once he'd entered the penthouse. He heard the monster hurrying toward him. There was nowhere to run. The footsteps were a few feet away. Tye jumped behind the safe and crouched down. He heard heavy footsteps as the monster entered the room.

The monster looked for the boy but didn't see him. He went to the door and checked to see if it was still locked. Whoever had disturbed his peace was still somewhere in the large suite, somewhere to be found. The monster turned and hurried out, stomping his large feet as he fled.

Tye waited. He held his breath and hoped that Christine had gotten Kira out in time. He couldn't wait around to find out, not unless he had a weapon. He had nothing but the stun gun, and that did little to slow down the monster's charge. He counted to twenty, slowly and steadily, until he heard only silence from the hallway that led to the main room and bedrooms. He stood up slowly and looked over the top of the safe and into the eyes of evil.

The monster stared at Tye from across the safe and

smiled. Tye tried to run, but the monster blocked his path with the safe, moving the massive steel object as if it were made of feathers. Tye put his shoulder to the steel and tried to push the safe back. The monster applied only as much force as he needed. He played with Tye, letting the boy expend all his strength in a feeble attempt at escape. Tye was pushed against the wall. He grabbed the stun gun and flicked it on. Bright blue currents crackled as he readied to jam the stun gun into the monster's face.

The monster gave a mighty push. The safe crashed into Tye's chest. His arm was pinned between his body and the safe. The stun gun that he had just activated was pressed against his own neck and started to spark. Tye's body shook with convulsions as the stun gun burned his skin. The monster smashed his shoulder into the safe again, and blood spurted out of Tye's mouth and covered the monster's face. Tye's ribs broke. His organs began to rupture as the safe ground deeper and deeper into his torso. A raspy death rattle wheezed out of his mouth. He stopped moving. His body was embedded into the wall, among the thousands of dollars of useless currency. Tye's head rolled forward. He died with Jackson, Grant, and Franklin to keep him company.

Christine took one of the monster's knives off the wall and tried to pry open the door of the cage. She worked the blade between the metal doorframe.

"Come on. Come on," Kira encouraged her.

Kira heard the faint creaking of a door opening

behind her. She saw a shadow start to stretch into the room. Christine saw it too. The knife fell from her hand, and she didn't have time to toss it into the cage to Kira. She scurried across the floor and hid behind Richie's body, which was lying in the darkness of the corner. Christine rolled the body on its side to block the monster's view. Richie's empty sockets were inches from her eyes. Christine fought back tears and pushed down the vomit she felt coming up. She buried her head into Richie's chest and waited for the monster to come in.

Kira reached through the sharp cage to grab the knife that Christine had dropped. It was too far for her to grasp. The door opened, and Kira looked up to see a figure coming out of the shadows of the hallway. Her mind reeled. A sense of jubilation came over her as Margaret walked into the room. The woman was holding Williams's gun in her shaky hand.

"Margaret! Thank God," Kira cried softly.

Margaret spun around at the sound of Kira's voice and nearly fired. She became flustered and looked at the captive girl.

"What are you doing here?" Margaret demanded.

Kira sighed with relief. She was too tired to speak.

From under Richie's corpse, Christine heard Margaret's voice. She peered over his body and began to stand up when she saw the massive figure of the monster coming out of the darkness behind Margaret. Christine slid back behind Richie and prayed Margaret would turn around and fire off a shot before it was too late.

Kira saw the monster looming over Margaret.

"He's right behind you!" Kira screamed.

Margaret stopped. She calmly turned around and faced the beast. She looked him squarely in the eyes, which was not so easy to do, given the difference in their heights.

"I'd like you to tell me something. Why is this whore still alive?" Margaret asked the monster in a demanding voice.

He stared down at Margaret. He began to chew on his lower lip. Uncertainty crossed his face as he shrugged his wide shoulders.

Kira sat baffled in the cage, her mouth agape. Lying in the darkness, Christine watched what was happening in terror.

"I asked you a question, mister. Why is she still alive?" Margaret challenged. Margaret made an angry move toward the monster. He flinched and stepped back.

"No . . . No . . . You can't know him," said Kira, confused.

"Know him? I ought to know him. He's caused me nothing but misery since the day he was born. Trouble and heartache. That's all he ever was to me. Yes, I should know my own son," Margaret declared.

Kira started to shake in disbelief.

"B . . . b . . . but you brought us here to help you. You wanted us here. Why?" Kira asked. A slightly whiny quality had entered her voice.

"It wasn't you I wanted. It wasn't any of you filthy little urchins. You are nothing but thieves and sneaks and whores. It was the cop. Williams was the one. He was the one I wanted for all these years. He was the one that hurt my boy. Put a bullet in his head and drove him out of our house," Margaret said. She looked at the monster with disappointment.

Christine couldn't believe what she was hearing. This was all part of the insane nightmare she was having, and when she awoke, it would all be over. It had to be.

Margaret looked deep into her son's eyes, deep past his stony gaze and deep back into time. She remembered a time when she was a young girl and the night meant excitement and fun. She recalled the hot summer evenings she'd spent down below on the dance floor of the hotel's nightclub. She remembered the men. The music. The merriment. Life had been good then.

It had been good until the night she had seen the man sitting at the table all alone. The one who called her over and tempted her with free drinks. She was impressed how the waitress jumped when he spoke, how the maître d' clung to every word he said. She could feel the power and wealth emanate from his body. She liked the way the champagne tasted, its sweet bitterness stinging her lips. She remembered drinking just a few sips and the room growing fuzzier.

She remembered being carried out and brought to a room. The sounds. The brightness, the lights that hurt her eyes when she tried to open them. She remembered the look of the man who was on top of her, inside her. She heard the sounds of the movie camera recording everything, the glare of the lights capturing every petrified emotion. But most of all, she remembered the eyes of the man who had taken her over and over again. His cold black eyes were the same as the ones her son now possessed. The soulless glare of his eyes came from the smear of evil on his soul. The evil man was alive and well, festering in the heart and mind of the massive creature he'd conceived. His murderous progeny carried on the unspeakable acts he had started years before.

"Yes," Margaret said, coming back from her troubled past. "I should know my own flesh and blood. And now it has come full circle, Jacob." She stroked the beast's huge face.

Jacob? That thing has a name? Kira never thought that the killer in front of her was anything but a brute.

Margaret looked at her son, and sad fondness came over her. She tried to remember the time after her attack when her world started to slip away from her. She didn't want to relive the shame of carrying that foul man's seed. The degradation of being sent away by her family. The trauma of trying to abort the unholy offspring of their union and the shock at realizing that months later the fetus still lived within her womb, scarred and damaged but still alive. It was then that she had realized that his father's spirit was too powerful to destroy. Her body had been chosen as a vessel to carry on his seed and soul for another generation of wickedness and cruelty.

Margaret Lucy Gayne had had other plans for her son, her bastard child. Although her baby was conceived and born out of evil, he would do the Lord's work. He would use the sins against the sinners. She

340

would groom the child to eradicate the sin that caused her to lose her purity. The child had been taught that sin was evil. And the only way to stop sin was by pain. The pain of fire, the pain of boiling water. Every drop of scalding water she poured on her son's body, she poured over the soul of his sire. Every scream Jacob had ever produced was a cry of mercy from his vile father, and she turned a deaf ear to both of them. Her desire for vengeance had grown; her fury became unstoppable. If she couldn't have her rapist in front of her to torment, then she had something just as evil, just as vile: his son. The boy's bones, blood, flesh, and soul all reeked of his father. Half of Jacob's genes were from him, and she wanted to destroy the other half of the boy until there was nothing left of his father in him that she could see except his cold, brutal eyes.

And after the boy was nothing but an empty husk of a human, damaged physiologically beyond repair and spiritually devastated, she went to work rebuilding him. She molded him in the image of the Avenger. He would be the one who would wipe away the filth and scum that reminded her of the sin that lingered deep inside of her body. The seed of Cain that grew in her womb would blossom into the fruit of righteousness. And as Jacob grew in size, he withered in reason. The larger his body grew and the stronger it became, the more his soul shriveled until it died, replaced by the insane vendetta of his mother's wrath. He was nothing but a mindless, hollow giant filled with a heavenly fervor on a satanic quest. And now Margaret would reclaim her name again, the name she hid in shame, and the accomplishment of years of abuse, torture, and tyrannical love came home to roost in the monstrous visage of Jacob Gayne.

Kira understood everything as she watched Margaret's eyes touching the ogre's face. The woman was fucking crazy.

"Now we are almost done. We must finish this one and find her vile partner. The one she sinned with, the one she fornicated with, the one she plotted and conspired with. We shall rid the world of two more harlots and thieves. Now, finish this one," Margaret demanded of the monster she had created.

He stood in his spot and didn't move. Margaret grabbed his hand and led him to the cage. She pointed at Kira.

"Judge her!" Margaret ordered. "Judge her like you judged the others. The way I taught you to."

Kira looked up at the object of Margaret's ire. For the first time, she didn't see a monster, she saw Jacob. She saw a human being who had endured the torments of hell by a lunatic's hand throughout his entire wretched existence. She couldn't help but feel pity for the man, who was nothing more than a lifeless beast controlled by a militant.

Jacob looked into Kira's eyes and saw what she felt. He had never sensed any type of human understanding or compassion, but he saw that Kira was sinless from the tired look of her eyes. She was a victim, as he was and had always been. Her pain matched his, and he looked down at the girl and felt the unfamiliar feeling of mercy starting to grow in him.

"Go on. It's getting late. Finish this whore!" Margaret urged.

Jacob stood motionless. Slowly, his head moved back and forth in an arc of defiance, as he shook his head. Margaret was appalled. It had been years since her son had refused to do her bidding. The last time was when he had brought the girl home. A waif he found on the streets and felt pity for. Margaret was outraged that her son would dare bring such a thing into their home. The filthy, disease-carrying whore would taint the sanctity of Margaret's house. She had taught the boy a lesson that day, one he never forgot even though he tried to drown the memory within a sea of troubled dreams. She had tied the girl down to the bed, tearing off her dark tattered dress and exposing her white skin. Her skin had been adorned with tattoos of angels and crosses, the same imagery that was etched upon Kira's flesh. Margaret made the bloated boy with the sallow skin and sad eyes watch her as she tortured the girl, who screamed into the gag in her mouth in vain. She'd made the girl's white skin turn black and blue as she beat the girl with a coat hanger. Red welts and blisters covered her stomach and breasts as Jacob watched in horror and excitement as his mother punished the harlot who had tried to seduce her only son.

After the frenzied attack had left Margaret out of breath and the girl on the verge of death, she pulled her son over to the battered body. She made Jacob look into the girl's eyes that floated in agonized stupor and forced him to see what sin looked like. And she had told him what the prophecy said: "Every time a sinner looks at you, they eat away a part of your soul." She made the boy repeat her edict over and over until those words were the only thing he understood.

He looked into the girl's eyes and saw for himself that his mother was right. For the girl he had pitied, the girl who had sparked a prepubescent curiosity inside of him, was a sinner. He had seen his own reflection trapped within the girl's delirious gaze and knew his mother had been right. The girl was eating away at his soul. He could feel the tingling sensation all over his body, down to his dangling bits, and he knew that she had to be punished.

Margaret demanded that the boy watch her as she reclaimed what the tied-up girl had taken from Jacob. Margaret kneeled over the girl's body, dug her finger deep into the girl's eye, and plucked out the offending orb as her captive thrashed about. She shoved the still trembling bloody eye into her son's face to make him see what had to be done to all who tried to steal away his soul. The soul that she had created from an empty pit within his body. That day, as Jacob's fragile mind started its descent into madness, he learned what his true legacy was.

Now he stood as hesitantly as he had on that day. Margaret fumed at the thought that her son would not do what was required of him. What God *demanded* of him.

"You dare defy me?" Margaret spat out and watched Jacob nervously rubbing his hands over his folded arms.

Margaret aimed Williams's gun at Kira. The girl quickly moved to the back of the cage and used the homeless woman's corpse as a shield. Margaret bent down and picked up the knife Christine had been using to open the cage. She felt the weight of the knife in her hand and was satisfied with its strength. She placed the gun on top of the cage and walked around to the corner where Kira was cowering.

"Watch me, you ingrate, as I slice the flesh off the whore who tempts you," Margaret goaded. "Don't you see the sin?"

She jammed the knife through the bars at Kira. The blade swung inches away from Kira's face. The rotted corpse that Kira was using for protection folded in on itself. The woman's mouth sagged open, and roaches spewed out and scattered around the cage. Kira crawled away to the other end. Margaret stalked her. Jacob was silently immobile. Christine peeked over Richie's body and saw the gun sitting on the cage. She prayed she'd have an opening to run for it before Kira was killed.

Margaret jabbed the knife into the cage again. The blade made its way past the sharp barbs and sliced Kira's arms. She screamed in agony. Christine held her ears as if she could block the sound of her friend's screeches. Jacob watched as his mother stabbed again at the helpless girl. The knife sliced Kira's back.

"You fucking bitch!" Kira screamed at her assailant.

Jacob saw Margaret attack Kira again. He saw his mother hunting the trapped girl. He saw what he hadn't seen in years. The vision had been locked away somewhere deep in his mind, lost among the screams and voices that were now raging in his skull again. Jacob looked into the cage and didn't see Kira anymore. The girl had vanished before his eyes and in her place, the young boy had returned, huddled, naked, and shivering with terror.

Margaret slashed the blade into the cage again, and

Jacob saw the young boy's flesh open. He felt the burning sear of his own skin as the blade's tip cut into the boy. Margaret tried to slash away at the young boy, but the blade fell short, only pricking his skin with the razor-sharp point. Jacob shuddered every time the boy's body was pierced. He experienced every painful prick and slice. He looked to see that the unseen figure from his past was stabbing the boy, the fuzzy image of his long-lost tormentor had returned. With each stab and jab of the blade, the image became clearer, more focused inside his warped mind until Margaret's image crystallized distinctly in his head.

He thought back to the freezing showers he had endured from Margaret with a cruel look on her face. He saw Margaret daintily carrying the steaming teapot and gently and accurately pouring it over his genitals. He saw the beatings, the whippings, and the fire, and he felt the pain. He relived the hate and betrayal at the hands of the tormenter he knew as his mother.

She was going to kill the young boy. He could see that the murderous look in her face, the look that had haunted him for years and that he had tried to bury was now resurfacing. It was the look of unimaginable hatred. The boy whimpered. She had him trapped. She had the knife in the cage, and the boy was too tired to run anymore. Soon she would cut his throat and the boy would be dead. The only distant strand that connected Jacob to this world, and the monster to his past, would be gone.

"Don't you see the evil in her eyes?" Margaret demanded again.

"I . . . see . . . it," Jacob answered meekly.

He reached out and grabbed Margaret's head. His long, thick fingers wrapped around the back of her skull as he lifted her up. With one mighty shove, he drove her body into the large neon "T" sign that was in the corner of the room. Margaret flew through the air, not knowing what was happening. She saw the sharp, bent spikes sticking out, piercingly brutal. Her face slammed into the spikes with such impact that the bent metal punctured her eye and ran straight through her brain.

Reflexively, her leg kicked once and stopped moving. A noise escaped from her body, but was lost in the gurgle of her terminal breath. Her body slumped, but she was suspended by the spikes that covered the sign. She was dead, having died much more mercifully than she deserved.

Kira watched with awe and horror as Jacob threw his mother to her death. Christine saw Margaret's demise and wondered what he would do next. Jacob stared at Margaret's body hanging limply in front of him. The voices in his head rose loudly in one defiant scream. The last link in the chain that bound the man-monster to either of his worlds had been snapped. His brain spun and his memories started to burn away, each one trying to grab on and hold a part of his mind tightly. Like a cleansing fire, each moment and image that haunted Jacob's past blackened and crumbled away until he was left with nothing in his mind except the young boy running away from the flames. The fire caught up to the boy and engulfed him; his charred body fell and disintegrated into cinders. The winds softly blew the ashes away. The faint glimmer that had once been Jacob "Goodnight" had been snuffed out. The man stood empty.

The voices in his head hollered, and Jacob snapped his head back and let out a wail that made the room vibrate. He reached down and ripped the cage door off with his hand, ignoring the sharp barbs that sliced his flesh. He reached in and grabbed Kira by her leg and pulled her out of her prison. He gripped his axe and squeezed the handle until the wood started to crack from the force he was using. He dragged Kira out of the room, screaming, down the dark hallway.

Christine quickly crawled to the cage and ran for the gun that was still on top of it. After retrieving it, she crept quietly down the hallway that led to a large presidential suite. She pressed her ear against the door and listened. Christine heard strange music coming from inside. She opened the door gently with the barrel of the gun and looked in. The room was dim, with only a few lights scattered about, but the place was awash in a golden hue that tapered off into the brownish shadows that lined the walls. The music was foreign to her, a queer melody that sounded distant and strained. Voices were mixed throughout the piece, sounding as if they were calling across the universe from a dream. Inside the room was an old tape recorder, weakly playing a worn cassette. Old batteries surrounded the recorder, and cheap cassettes of religious music were piled up next to it. The batteries in the tape recorder died down, and the last piece of music to come out sounded like a low, drawn-out moan.

The recorder had stopped playing, but Christine heard the strained music continue. When she looked toward the canopy bed, she could not see through the curtains.

Christine steadied herself and marched toward the bed. The canopy was closed. She hoped Kira wouldn't be in the way when she went to shoot him. She wanted to press the barrel right against Jacob's face when she fired. She wanted the gun to be jammed in his eye so the bullet would tear into his brain. She held her breath and pulled back the curtain. She saw Jacob humming the devotional tune and rocking Kira to the melody.

The bed was empty. A strange feeling of relief and confusion set in. She still heard Jacob's thick humming. She turned to look at the far wall and froze as she saw him staring at her with his axe in one hand. Kira was clenched in his other arm. Jacob continued to rock back and forth at a slow pace, humming to himself.

"He's fucking out of it," Kira whispered.

Christine snuck up quietly toward them.

"The guy's catatonic," Kira informed her.

Christine stood in front of Jacob, but he made no sign that he noticed her. She aimed the gun.

"Can you move?" Christine mouthed.

Kira tried to shift her body. It was pinned against Jacob's torso with his thick arm. He stopped rocking.

Kira stiffened. No one moved. Slowly, Jacob started rocking back and forth again. Christine made a gesture with the gun, indicating she was going to shoot his head. Kira's face lit up in approval.

Christine got closer to Jacob's face. She didn't want to miss, and she didn't want the bullet to deflect off the plate in his head. The floor began to creak as she moved closer. She lined the shot up with Jacob's left eye. When he rocked back toward her, it would be a perfect shot.

Flies started to appear around Jacob's head. They began to crawl over his plate and take up guard on the crusty scar between his skull and the rusted metal. His thick voice continued to hum the old tune. He rocked back into Christine's aim. Suddenly, he stopped humming and sat still. The flies buzzed angrily.

"Now!" Kira screamed.

Christine pulled the trigger. *Click*. Her heart sank. She pulled it again. *Click*. *Click*. Jacob awoke from his daze, his eyes narrowed into two glowing pinpricks that bored into Christine with a murderous look. She pulled the trigger again, but the gun still didn't fire. Kira began to scream.

Jacob stood up and grabbed Christine by the throat, the axe falling from his lap. He lifted her up and squeezed. He wrapped his other hand around Kira's neck as she scratched at his eyes. He hoisted both girls up and watched them as they kicked and clawed at him.

Sinners! Whores! Treacherous sluts! The words echoed through Jacob's mind in one loud chorus.

Kira began to turn blue as her throat started to close. Jacob stared into Christine's bulging eyes. He wanted to tear the lying eyes out of her head. He dropped Kira on the floor. She coughed and choked, trying to get air back in her lungs. Jacob slammed Christine against the wall. Her back and head burst with snapping pain. As his sharpened fingernail started to scrape under Christine's eye, his rancid breath washed over her face. Kira tried to get up and attack him, but she collapsed and almost blacked out.

Jacob's lips stretched into a devilish grin and he started to press his finger into Christine's eye. She waited for the excruciating pain and the unwashable blackness to come over her. She heard the bang that sounded like a blacksmith's hammer smashing against an anvil. No pain yet. She looked past Jacob's shoulder but couldn't make out the figure that was clubbing away at his head with a pipe, each hit resonating with a metallic thud. When her eyes finally focused, she saw Michael swinging away at Jacob's skull.

Jacob dropped Christine and turned to face his attacker. Michael got off a devastatingly accurate shot and dented the metal plate fastened to the giant's skull. Screws flew out as the plate shifted.

The massive man swung wildly at Michael, sending him reeling back. Michael dropped his pipe as Jacob ascended on him. Michael grabbed the axe that was lying next to him and held it tightly.

Kira scrambled over to Christine and helped her up. The girls ran out of the room, holding each other for support.

Jacob was livid. He couldn't see straight as he lunged at Michael, bent on destruction. Michael sat up and swung the axe with more force than he had ever exerted in his life, more force than he knew he had. The blade ripped into Jacob's knee. With a tremendous splat, tendons and cartilage were severed as the blade almost completely cleaved the thick bones in two. Jacob bellowed in pain and fell like a giant tree. He hit the ground and the impact shook the floor. The axe was lodged in his leg, and blood shot out in thick spurts. Michael was up and beating the maimed creature with the pipe before Jacob could recover.

Michael brought the pipe down repeatedly on Jacob's skull, each blow harder than the previous one. The loosened plate in Jacob's head caved in from the many blows Michael rained down with an unleashed fury. Like a manic machine taking batting practice, Michael's swings were wild but precise. Jacob's eyes rolled back into his large sockets. The plate shifted, and Michael saw his chance. Flies seemed to be swarming all around him. He jammed the end of the pipe into the opening between the metal plate and the rotted bone. Michael pressed down hard. The plate snapped up, one lone screw keeping it from falling off.

Michael stopped and stepped back, looking at the damage he had done. He'd had no idea that someone with such injury could still be alive.

Jacob moaned and leaned forward. Michael got a better view of the things that crawled within his head. Even in the weak light, he could make out the maggots that teemed on Jacob's brain. Hundreds of small white larvae burrowed deep and feasted on the perforated gray matter inside his skull. The flies tightly circled his open wound in defense of their hive.

Jacob heard a million voices screech out in pain when the metal lifted up. The world could now peer in and see the dark secrets he had been hiding for years. Jacob started to rise.

Michael stumbled back, the pipe still in his hand.

Jacob stood and looked at the boy. His thick hand pressed against the plate, and he bent it back down over the hole in his head, over the passage into his world, sealing off from the outside the secrets he cherished most.

Michael ran out of the room. Jacob yanked the axe out of his leg. There was no pain anymore, no suffering. All feelings and emotions were gone, and only one thought remained: kill.

Kira dragged Christine down the hallway and tried to find a way out. Every room in the suite was locked. They came to another door at a dead end, and Kira tried the door. Thankfully, it opened.

Christine tried to stop her from going in.

"It's a dead end," Christine rasped through damaged vocal cords.

"It doesn't matter now," Kira said as she pulled her in and locked the door behind them.

Michael sprinted down the hallway, trying to figure out which way the girls had gone. He ran down and checked the same doors Kira had just tried. With each locked door Michael got more desperate.

"Shit!" Michael cursed.

Kira heard his voice from behind the locked door. She knew the sound of his anger and his frustration. She knew the sound of his determination. She opened the door.

"Michael, over here," Kira whispered.

Michael ran to the door and Kira let him in. He locked it behind him and braced himself against it. He looked at Kira and saw that she was holding Christine up and thought, *What an ironic way to go.*

Down the hallway they could hear Jacob coming,

checking each room until he found them. The kids looked around the room frantically. There was no way out, no escape.

"What are we going to do?" Kira asked.

Michael clenched his teeth and squeezed the pipe. He saw a wooden chair against a table. An idea sparked in his head, a desperate one, but the only hope they had.

"Kira, grab the bedsheet," he ordered.

Kira pulled the covers off the bed and ripped off the sheet without asking for his reasoning.

"Tie the sheet to the table leg," he said as he pointed to the table. Kira climbed under the table and quickly knotted the sheet around the leg. Michael lifted up the chair.

"We gotta get him near the window. It's our only chance," he told the girls. In silent understanding, they each knew what was expected of them.

"Hide in the bathroom," Michael told the girls as he handed them his pipe. He hoisted the chair over his head. When they ran to the bathroom, Christine ripped off the shower rod and slipped the curtain off. She jabbed the rod in the air like a lance. Kira returned Michael's pipe. Opting to use the heavy marble toilet top for protection, she held it against her chest. Michael stood near the window with the chair over his head, waiting for Jacob to get closer, hoping he would be hungry with blind rage and take the bait.

Jacob knew that these intruders were crafty, their guile unsurpassed. They had looked deep within his mind and saw what no one had ever seen: his secrets. They knew where the voices were hiding. They understood where the screams echoed. Now the world would know. Now his weaknesses would be revealed and others would come with their curious eyes and treacherous looks. Soon they would eat away at Jacob's soul as the voices devoured his memory and mind. Nothing of what he had become would remain.

He tried each door along the hallway with the same results as the teens had had. He splintered the doors to slivers with his axe and looked inside for the intruders that he would kill slowly.

He heard the crash that sounded like glass being shattered. The intruders were trying to escape out a window and rappel down the walls of his castle to safety. He would not allow that. He *could* not allow that. Jacob limped to the door behind which he thought that crash had come. Blood gushed from his leg as he wobbled to the last room in the hallway.

Jacob smashed open the door and the thin wood fell away. Dust plumes rose, and he stood in the doorway as a silhouette of evil, epic in proportion. He saw the broken window and the sheet tied around the table leg and hanging out of the window. He would not let them get away. He staggered toward the window, massive amounts of blood marking his trail. Jacob looked out, expecting to see the desperate intruders dangling from the sheet. There was no one clinging to it outside. The only thing he saw was the atrium's roof, with a heavy chair smashed into its glass frame.

He had been tricked. He heard their battle cry as they sprung their ambush. Jacob's instinctive forces were starting to slow as he hemorrhaged profusely from his wound. He never would have been caught in such a simple trap if his blood wasn't ebbing out in massive amounts and his mind was clear.

Michael, Christine, and Kira charged him with one goal in mind—knocking him out of the fucking window. They came out screaming and attacked him as one well-oiled unit. Christine rammed the shower rod into Jacob's neck. He bent forward, and Kira slammed the marble toilet top over his head with such power that it broke in two. Michael smashed him across the face with the pipe and crushed his eye.

Jacob's axe fell from his hand, and he punched Kira in the chest, sending her flying across the room and crashing onto the table. Michael swung the pipe again and cracked it across Jacob's mouth, causing brown teeth to fly from it.

Jacob staggered near the broken window. He put his hand out on the ledge to steady himself as Michael kept beating him. Christine shoved the curtain rod into his torso, but the hollow metal bent as it pressed into his thick chest. Jacob was now deflecting some of Michael's blows with his forearm. He thought that if he was to get squarely on his feet, the tide of battle would change. Christine ran to the table where Kira lay and grabbed a heavy chair. She swung the chair around and charged at Jacob like a furious bull that was about to gore a wounded matador. Michael sidestepped, and Christine smashed the chair into Jacob's body, sending him back. He tumbled toward the broken window, and his back ripped on the broken glass. He tried to grab on to something—anything—that would stop his fall. He reached desperately for the sharp shards that stuck out of the windowsill and sliced his fingers to the bone for his trouble. Unable to hold on, he fell.

Christine slumped to her knees, her emotions barely under control. Kira climbed off the table to hug her. Michael leaned against the wall in disbelief.

"We did it. We did it!" Kira said, sobbing.

Christine looked at Michael, and a battered smile appeared on her face. Michael gave her a nod of respect. Slowly the jubilation of victory drained away, and Christine frowned with realization.

"There was no crash," she said.

"What?" Kira asked.

"We never heard him hit the ground," Christine explained as she ran toward the window.

She looked down to see the man/monster dangling from the building. A large rusted pigeon spike just below the window was impaled into his wrist.

Christine stared down at the helpless man. He looked up at her and their eyes met, and they knew hunter and hunted had changed places. In one last final burst of crazed energy, Jacob reached up and grabbed Christine's hand. She screamed as he pulled her toward him and out of the building. Kira held Christine by the hips and tried to pull her back.

"You can't have her!" Kira yelled down at him.

Michael slammed the pipe against Jacob's hand, trying to break his grip on Christine. Jacob squeezed Christine's forearm, and her bones felt like they were snapping. He yanked his wrist from the rusty spike and used Christine's body to hold on. He reached up and grabbed the window ledge. He released Christine and she fell back as Kira pulled her in. Jacob was starting to pull himself back in despite Michael's blows. His blood poured down his face, and his large skull was coated crimson. He was weak, but still dangerous.

Christine roared and jumped up. She pulled the pipe out of Michael's hand and leaned out the window to face the oversized man. She swung the pipe down sharply at his face.

"Fuck you!" she yelled.

Jacob saw his own reflection in her eyes. His own demented image was mirrored in the girl's pupils. He knew that death was at hand.

Christine drove the pipe's jagged edge into Jacob's left eyesocket. The eye exploded and blood squirted out. He let go of the edge and fell.

Christine watched as he plummeted toward the ground. When his head crashed into a ledge several stories below, the pipe ripped through his brain and out through the back of his skull. The plate flew off, and maggots and chunks of brain scattered every which way. His body hit the top of the atrium and almost caved in the entire structure. Broken glass showered down as he fell on the ground among the shards.

The few dogs that were still gnawing on Melissa's corpse scattered and ran back into the night with frightened barks. Jacob lay on the cement ground. A large circle of blood had poured out of his head, resembling a scarlet halo. He quivered; the last electrical currents surged through the massive turbine that was his body. The uncontrollable engine that was his soul sputtered out and seized up and lived no more.

• • •

Michael, Christine, and Kira looked down. They couldn't see from that great a distance, but they knew that Jacob was gone for good. Kira spat and walked away.

The kids made their way back to the main room in the suite. No one wanted to look at Richie, Hannah, or Zoë. Michael walked up to Margaret, who still hung from the neon "T" with her face embedded in the steel rods. As he felt around the dead woman's body, he felt queasy and laughed at himself for being so sensitive after facing the horrors he had just endured.

Margaret's body twitched with postmortem spasms. The girls screamed and Michael jumped back. Kira shoved Margaret's body deeper onto the spikes. It stopped moving.

Michael caught his breath and continued to search the dead woman. He found the keys to the hotel's front door and Williams's cell phone. He walked out of the hellhole, and the girls followed.

They found that the main elevator now took them directly to the lobby; they assumed that Margaret must have tampered with the elevator so she could get to Jacob's living quarters when she needed to.

"How did you find us?" Christine asked Michael.

"When I came to, I realized I wasn't dead. I started to look for a way out, then I thought about . . ." His voice began to taper off. ". . . anyway, I heard you and Tye going up the ladder in the elevator shaft. By the time I made it to the roof of the elevator, you guys had gone in. I just followed."

The elevator doors dinged open and they found

themselves in the lonely lobby. The silence of the night permeated the hotel.

As the kids walked down the large marble staircase, Kira's legs gave out. Christine and Michael both grabbed her. They steadied her and helped her walk down slowly.

Michael unlocked the chain around the hotel's front door.

"Michael?" Kira questioned.

He looked up. She saw the boy he'd been years ago, the terrible weight of vengeance lifted from his shoulders.

"You didn't have to come back for us," she said.

"Yeah, well . . . I didn't want to walk out of here alone." He shrugged.

They walked out into the summer night. Christine hugged Kira, and they walked across the street and sat on the curb to look at the Blackwell. Michael stood protectively behind them as they waited for the sun that was starting to sneak over the horizon that was the city.

His territory already marked, the dog came out of the shadows to see who had disturbed his domain. Sniffing the acrid air, he noticed the flies that were hovering about. Recognizing the form on the ground as Jacob's body, he investigated further. Twisted on the courtyard floor, the corpse lay with its lifeblood oozing out. The dog creeped over, lifted a slender leg, and relieved the pressure in his bladder. Satisfied that the man would not be moving, he sauntered off.